Atteans

Lon G. Taylor

In loving memory of my mother.

Who dreamed of being a writer in her youth. And whose constant support and critiquing of my books was deeply appreciated and now missed.

This was her favorite story, and she was reading the chapters as I finished them. Sadly, she passed away while reading chapter 23 and never got to see the ending.

Contents

Chapter - 1

I became aware of a bright light shining on my face and opened my eyes. My vision was a little blurry, but I could make out four bright lights above me now. Then I got the feeling of space, like I was in an enormous room now. Looking around, I couldn't see the roof or the walls as everything beyond the ring of the lights was dark. And it was so quiet that I could hear my heart beating in my chest, and each beat produced a wave of pain in my aching head. Looking down at my chest, I could see I was lying on a stainless-steel table now, like you would find in an operating room. I could feel that my clothes had been removed, and I was naked now except for the clean white sheet covering my body.

As my vision began to clear, I lifted my head up slightly and could make out the smooth grey stones covering the floor and the metal stand supporting the lights by my feet. To my right were two more stainless steel tables with the same style lights shining down on them. And I concluded I was in some sort of hospital recovery room now. But why was it dark? And where were all the beeping equipment, trays, tubes, and other medical paraphernalia? Hell, where were the doctors and nurses?

Turning left, I breathed a sigh of relief upon seeing my fiancé Amy laying on the table next to me now. Her beautiful face exposed and the same white sheet covering her body. Amy's eyes were closed, but the rhythmic rise and fall of her sheet now assured me that she was alive, just unconscious still. A strand of Amy's unruly red hair clung to her face, and she looked like a sleeping angel now.

Which made me start thinking about where we were? I remember leaving Sao Miguel in the Azores for the Strait of Gibraltar when the hurricane came out of the south. And I remember raising the storm jib and running before the storm. Then hitting the submerged reef and taking on water before our boat capsized. These things were starting to come back to me. And I wondered now, did we drown? Is this the morgue, not the recovery room?

All these questions raced through my mind as I strained my eyes looking around the room trying to penetrate the darkness around me. And I thought I could make out the walls of the room now, but they seemed to be made of the same large grey stones as the floor. And the stones seemed to glisten, like they were damp. Then I tried to sit up and discovered I was strapped to the table now. Metal restraints holding my arms and legs down firmly, and a wide restraint across my chest. The sudden exertion made my head spin, and I lay back and closed my eyes now until the dizziness passed.

Suddenly, I sensed someone on my right. And opening my eyes again, nothing could have prepared me for what I saw now. The figure standing over me was humanoid in shape, but his entire skin was pale grey, and in a pattern that almost resembled a frog. Even the eyes were grey, no whites showing. And its pupils were black like a sharks as it was stared down intently at my face now. I closed my eyes, hoping that this was just a dream and when I opened my eyes again the nightmare would be gone. And counting to ten, I opened my eyes again. To my dismay, the same grey face stared back at me now, but this time a smile spread across its face, exposing normal looking human teeth beneath its grey cover. Panicking now, I struggled desperately to free myself from the restraints. Only stopping when I started to black out, and reason telling me I didn't want to pass out with that thing here.

The creature raised its grey arm now and put its webbed fingered hand on my chest, then it started to speak. At first, I couldn't understand a word it was saying. It seemed to be repeating the same thing over and over again, but in a different language each time. Finally, I recognized one of the languages, and overcoming my terror, I managed to utter, "French."

This caused the creature to pause and smile again, and it was a little less threatening this time. And it repeated the last sentence again. The creature could tell from my expression that I still didn't understand what it was saying. Finally, after a short pause the creature spoke again, and this time in proper English, saying "Do you understand me now?"

Still petrified by the creature's appearance, I managed to reply, "Yes."

And smiling again, the creature removed its hand from my chest now and said, "Good, I like English, it's a difficult language, but one I know fairly well."

Feeling a little less scared now, I asked, "Where are we? And uh, who, or what are you?"

Covering his mouth, the creature cleared his throat first before replying, "Ah, let me introduce myself. My name is Nestor, and I am the senior physician here amongst my people."

"And where exactly is here?" I asked.

Ignoring my question, Nestor replied, "And what is your name, if I may ask?"

My head was still a little fuzzy, so it took me a moment to remember, but I managed to say, "Andrew, Andrew Tallfer."

"Well Andrew, I know you have a lot of questions. And I will be happy to answer them in a few minutes. But you have a large bump and cut on the left side of your head, and you appear to be in some pain now. So, let's deal with that first, okay?"

And I said, "Oh, there's something else you should know, Doc."

And Nestor calmly asked, "What is that, Andrew?"

"There's something wrong with my vision too," I replied, and pausing to second to choose my words now, I added, "You appear to be totally grey to me now from head to toe, and your hands are blurry. Making your fingers look webbed?"

To which Nestor smiled again and replied, "Hmmm?" Then he took a few seconds now before calmly adding, "Well, there is nothing wrong with your vision. I am grey from head to toe. And my fingers and toes are webbed." Too stunned to speak now, I just lay there. My mind racing in a million directions all at once while I tried to absorb that information.

Then Nestor raised his webbed hands and touched my head slowly turning it to the right. And I felt him gently pulling the hair out of my cut. Then he spent a moment inspecting the wound before turning and speaking into the darkness now, said, "Sandra, would you bring me my bag please?"

In a few seconds, another creature appeared. Topless, this one was definitely a woman. She had long blonde hair, solid green eyes, and red lips. Her pale, olive-green skin sparkled in the light. And all she had on now was a short blue sarong tied around her slender waist.

In her hands she carried a large white leather satchel with a shoulder strap, and stopping by the table she held it out to Nestor now. And taking the satchel from her webbed fingers, Nestor slipped the strap over his head in a smooth, well-practiced motion before flipping the flap on the satchel open. Pausing, the woman Sandra looked down and caught me checking her out now from her head down to her shapely waist and back up again. And grinning wryly, Sandra said, "Oh, this one going to live alright," before turning and walking back into the darkness out of sight again.

Removing a small green vial from inside the bag, Nestor noticed me staring in the direction that the girl had gone now, and said, "My daughter is lovely, isn't she?" Slightly embarrassed now, I turned back to Nestor and nodded in agreement. As Nestor removed a gob of what looked like green tomato paste from the small glass vial, then gently smeared it over the cut on the side of my head. And as soon as the salve touched my head the pain was gone, as the whole area went numb now. Then Nestor said, "I bet that feels better," and not waiting for me to answer, Nestor continued, saying, "Now, back to your questions, Andrew. Where are you? Well, we are roughly three kilometers, um. . . yes, kilometers is the right word, below the ocean's surface now." And spending a moment looking at the cut on my head now, Nestor seemed satisfied and closed the vial again before putting it back in the medical bag at his waist.

Then taking a step back now, Nestor continued, saying, "I am an Attean, or that is to say, we are called Attean's." Then he added, "How did you get here? Before his death, our great seer Telemus foretold of this storm, and the exact location of your ship's sinking. And Telemus said it was imperative that we rescue you and your mate and bring you back here, as the fate of all Attea depended on it. Though oddly, he declined to tell us why at the time. But no one, not even the Queen herself would ignore one of Telemus's visions, or his instructions either. So, Captain Theron and his glide-sub were sitting submerged by the reef all day waiting for your arrival. And had it not been for them, you and your mate would have both drowned when your ship hit the reef. As it was, two of Captain Theron's men were injured during the rescue. Luckily, their injuries were minor."

Just then we heard a small moan come from Amy, and Nestor stepped back into the darkness now, before saying "Andrew, it will be a less traumatic for her if she sees you first and gets oriented before she sees me."

Nodding in agreement with Nestor, I changed the subject now, asking, "Nestor, why am I tied to this table?"

And stepping back into the light again, Nestor replied, "Once you have seen Attea you can never leave, I am sorry to say. And you must both become Atteans now. You are not the first outworlder's we have brought down here. And some have resisted, that is why you are tied to the table. If you refuse, I am required by Attean law to inject you with sea snake venom and stop your heart."

Raising my eyebrows and frowning at Nestor now, I replied, "Well, that makes it an easy decision."

"If it's of any help? No outworlder who has ever seen the Kingdom of Attea has ever wished to leave again. Though, it has been a hundred years since the last outworlder came here," Nestor replied apologetically.

I wanted to ask Nestor more about that, but just then Amy yawned and opened her eyes. And Nestor stepped back into the shadows as I looked over at Amy now. Amy lay still for a moment, taking in her surroundings. Then she tried to sit up and realized she was tied to the table. Struggling against her restraints for a minute, Amy lay back on the table and called out, "Andy, where are you?"

Answering her now, I replied, "I am right here, my love," And turning to look at me, Amy let out a small sigh of relief now as she recognized my face. Then Amy rattled off three questions back-to-back without a pause, asking, "What happened? Where are we? And why am I tied to a table naked?

Smiling at Amy now, I tried to reassure her before replying, "I'm going to tell you. But you're never going to believe me." So, I quickly told Amy everything I had been able to learn so far from my brief conversation with Nestor. And I could tell by her expression on her face, that Amy didn't believe a word I said. And the combination of being tied to a table naked and my preposterous explanation, was only making her angrier now.

Just as Amy was about to say something un-lady-like, Nestor stepped out of the shadows and back into the light. And for a second, I thought Amy was going to scream, as her mouth was moving but no sound was coming out. Then I watched the color drain out of Amy's face as she fainted. Amy's sheet started to slide off as she collapsed back onto the table. But Sandra stepped out of the shadows now quickly catching it. And pulling the sheet back over Amy's body now, Sandra tucked the edges under Amy though Sandra was completely topless herself. This accomplished, Sandra stepped back into the shadows disappearing again.

Stepping around my table, Nestor moved over next to Amy. And flashing that gentle smile of his, Nestor removed a small vial from the pouch at his waist. Then opening it, he passed it back and forth under Amy's nose. Amy opened her eyes again and started to scream but froze as she looked up and saw Nestor standing over her now.

Recovering quickly, Amy blurted out, "What are you?"

And smiling again, Nestor calmly replied, "I am an Attean, my dear young lady. My name is Nestor, and I am the senior physician amongst my people here." Fear still on her face, Amy looked up at Nestor then over at me for help. Of course, we were both strapped to the tables. So, there wasn't anything I could do but look at Amy now and say, "It's okay Amy, I don't think they mean us any harm." And thinking about it a second, I added, "In fact, they the risked their lives to rescue us!"

Nestor stepped back from Amy's before facing us both and saying, "I want to show you something that will alleviate your fears now." And stepping into the darkness for a moment, Nestor reappeared holding a small silver box with several small colored circles on top of it. Then touching the box to his chest, Nestor hit the red circle now. And we heard what sounded like a dozen people in the darkness gasp suddenly in surprise. And Sandra stepped back into the light again, her hands on her terrified face now as she gasped, "No father!" But it was too late, the silver box began sucking all the grey off Nestor's body exposing to our amazement now, a normal looking man underneath. Nestor had grey hair and looked to be in his mid-50's.

Smiling at his daughter, Nestor waved her back saying, "Don't worry Sandra, it'll be okay."

Tears on her face now, Sandra pleaded, "But father, there is no way to knowing what germs these outsiders are carrying." An older Attean female appeared now wearing a white tunic and sash over her green and grey bio-suit. And putting her arm around Sandra now, tried to comfort her as she led Sandra back into the darkness.

Turned his attention back to Amy and me again, Nestor said, "As you can see, we are what you call 'humans' too." Then Nestor pressed the green circle on top of the small silver box, and the clear, jelly-like substance poured out of the box and quickly spread over his body. And once it had completely covered him again, it slowly changed color back to the exact same pale grey frog-like pattern that Nestor had before. And continuing now, Nestor said, "What you are looking at is a biological suit that was developed long ago making it possible for us to live this far below the ocean's surface. The bio-suit have many uses. It allows us to breath underwater, while keeping the pressure down here from crushing our bodies. And it cleans our skin and protects us from any germs we might encounter. It also seals any wounds and speeds up the healing process. The bio-suits are actually quite amazing."

Moving over to the right side of my table now, Nestor depressed a small silver circles on the corner of the table that I hadn't noticed before. And I heard what sounded like a seal breaking as a drawer on the left side of the table slowly slid out now. Then Nestor removed a silver box identical to the one he had just held to his chest from inside the drawer. And holding the box in both hands now, Nestor asked in a loud voice, "Do you, Andrew Tallfer, choose to become an Attean now?"

And knowing that I didn't have a choice, I answered in an equally loud voice now, saying, "I do."

Then placing the silver box down on the table next to me, Nestor removed a small vial from inside the open drawer. And leaning over me, Nestor lifted my eyelids up one at a time as he put one drop in each of my eyes now and let go. The drops neither stinging nor seeming to bother my eyes in any way. And picking up the silver box again, Nestor folded my sheet down halfway before placing the silver box in the middle of my chest. Then without waiting, Nestor hit the green circle on the top of the box and the clear jelly like mass poured out from multiple openings which suddenly appeared in the sides of the box. And leaning forward now, Nestor whispered, "When the bio-suit reaches your throat, you're going to feel like you're drowning or choking. That's normal, just try to relax. It only lasts a few seconds."

The suit quickly spread across my body as it had done on Nestor. And I closed my mouth and eyes as the cool jelly-like substance reached my neck and started up my face. But it didn't make any difference to the transparent liquid as it shot up my nose and down my throat now. And Nestor was right, it felt just like you were drowning. Suddenly, I felt normal again, in fact I felt better than normal. I felt relaxed now, like a large weight had been lifted off my chest.

Then I heard Nestor and Sandra suddenly gasp and catch their breath in surprise. And fearing something was wrong, I opened my eyes again. And I could hear excited mumbling coming from the people out in the darkness now. But when I looked up at Nestor, he was standing over me grinning from ear to ear. So was Sandra now, having stepped forward out of the shadows again. Unable to bear the suspense any longer I asked, "Okay, what is it? What's wrong?"

But Nestor didn't answer, he just stood there now with a big grin on his face not speaking. Suddenly a dozen people walked forward into the light. Each with a slightly different colored bio-suit, though they were all basically either grey, green, or brown. And each one coming forward to smile and stare at me for a second, before turning to shake Nestor's hand enthusiastically. And a couple of the older looking ones patted Nestor on the back now.

Confused now, I turned to Amy and asked, "What is it?"

Amy froze for a second, just staring at me before replying, "Well, the colors and the pattern of your bio-suit are quite striking Andrew. And different from all the other bio-suits here, but in a good way!" And looking down, I could see bright blue and mahogany brown on my chest and something gold on my left breast. But I was getting a kink in my neck from looking down now. And finally laying back on the table, I asked Amy, "Describe it to me Amy?" Just as Nestor pulled the sheet off me exposing the rest of my body now. And Amy said, "Well, your split into two colors from under your right arm down to your left waist. The top half is a beautiful shade of aqua blue, with a faint, shimmering gold, fish-scale pattern to it. And your lower half is a mahogany brown. But that's not the interesting part, on your left breast is an elaborate gold cross. And there's a gold band around your head with points sticking up every few inches, well. . . like a crown."

Still grinning, Nestor cut in now saying, "And that's exactly what it is." We waited for Nestor to explain or elaborate, and I got the feeling he wanted to say something now but decided against it. And stepping forward, Nestor said, "You're an Attean now, so there's no need for you to remain tied to the table." Then Nestor pressed something under the table, and my restraints suddenly retracted and disappeared into the table. Now, I was able to sit up and swing my feet over the side of the table. I was still feeling a little shaky, so I slid off the table and slowly put my feet down on the floor. And after testing my balance, I stood up. When I did, every Attean in the room put their hands over their hearts and suddenly bowed. Which was weird and made me feel uneasy. Looking down I could see my aqua blue webbed hands, and my mahogany brown webbed feet. And I could sense the stone floor beneath my feet, but it was neither cold, nor did I feel barefooted. The bio-suit having formed padding under my feet now. There was an awkward silence for a moment, before Nestor broke it, saying, "Now for the Lady Amy."

Removing a second silver box from the drawer now, Nestor hit the button closing the drawer. Then holding the silver box with both hands, Nestor moved around the table and over to Amy's side. And stopping beside Amy, Nestor looked down at her now before saying, "Oh, I am sorry." Then letting out a small sigh, Nestor said, "It seems in all the excitement, we forgot proper introductions. Please forgive my poor manners." Then Nestor bowed to Amy and said, "As you know, my name is Nestor. What is your name, my lady?"

Startled now, Amy replied, "Amy Ryan," after a few seconds.

And straightening back up, Nestor smiled and said, "It's our great honor to meet you, Amy Ryan."

Then very formally, Nestor asked, "Do you, Amy Ryan, wish to become an Attean now?" And Amy shot me a glance as I emphatically nodded my head "yes" to her now! And looking back up at Nestor, Amy hesitantly replied now, "I do."

Setting the box down on the table now, Nestor folded the white sheet down revealing the metal restraint covering Amy's breasts and exposing her flawless stomach. Then using the same small vile he had used on me, Nestor gently lifting each of Amy's eyelids, and applied one drop to each eye now. Then Nestor picked up the silver box and placed it in the middle of Amy's chest before hitting the green button on the top and taking a step back now. This time the other Atteans in the room moved into the circle of light intently watching as the bio-suit spread across Amy's body. And we all watched as Amy struggled against her restraints when the bio-suit reached the top of her neck now and started over her face. But I knew it was a futile effort.

And we watched in anticipation as Amy's bio-suit started to change color. From beneath Amy's breasts up, the suit turned the same light olive-green color as Sandra's. But from there down it turned a dark forest green with a gold feather-like pattern that glistened in the light. It was stunning and really added contrast to Amy's flowing red hair and her bright blue eyes. And I heard all the Atteans suck in air now as a slender, golden line appeared on Amy's forehead and lower neck just above her shoulders and continuing around her forming a ring in both places. Then a wide gold band appeared on Amy's left arm, and it slowly spread around her arm until it completely encircled it. Whatever it meant, it must be epic. Because the Atteans suddenly broke their silence and began cheering loudly.

And just as suddenly, they all stopped cheering and bowed to Amy before turning to each other shaking hands now and patting each other on their backs. Amy and I just looked at each other with our mouths ajar and dumbfounded. And I began to wonder now if these bio-suits actually worked as well as Nestor claimed?

Bowing to Amy again, Nestor moved forward and released Amy from her restraints. And moving to Amy's side, I helped her up off the table now. Then I stood there holding her until she was steady on her feet. Holding each other steadying us both now. Though the bizarre spectacle of the last few minutes was completely beyond either Amy's or my comprehension now.

Then Nestor signaled for the others to be silent, and holding his left arm out now, Nestor said, "If you will follow me now, please." And the lights in the room suddenly came on and we could see the large grey stones making up the walls, ceiling, and floor of the enormous room now. A half a dozen large, silver, cylindrical tubes with windows covered the right wall, two of which stood open now and appeared to have beds inside of them. While there were medical benches, cabinets, and carts taking up the left wall. Beyond those in the direction Nestor was gesturing now, was a set of steel-framed glass doors.

Reaching the righthand door, Nestor rotated the first of three gold seahorses on the right side below two lights on the wall. And we heard a hissing sound now as the door began to open, and we felt a small gust of air pelt us now as the door opened. Then Nestor gestured for us to enter, and Amy and I entered the narrow hallway now which must be an airlock, followed by Nestor and Sandra. And moving to the panels in the center, Nestor turned the second seahorse on the righthand panel, and the door behind us slowly shut as Amy, Sandra, and I stood in the center of the narrow chamber. Then Nestor turned the first seahorse on the left panel ninety degrees, and we heard the inner door's seal and lock now as the outer door hissed and slowly swung outwards.

Following Nestor out of the airlock, I was surprised to find ourselves in a long hallway. The walls comprised of the same large grey stones as the room we had just left, but the floor and ceiling here were made of wood planks and beams now. Pale light shone from some sort of flameless torches mounted on both sides of the hallway every ten feet or so. And the wood planks at our feet were smooth and polished. Large round silver shields with red seahorses on the front and sets of crossed spears hung on the walls now between the colorful tapestries. The hallway to the right ended fifteen ahead at a large wood door with black banded hinges, while the hallway to the left ran thirty feet before passing through an archway and opening into a large room.

Stepping to the front, Nestor led us down the hallway to left now into what appeared to be the great hall of a keep, with Sandra bringing up the rear. There was an elevated table and chairs at the head of the room on the left. And two long rows of wood tables and benches running the length of the hall on either side now. At the far end of the hall, there were three large stone archways. And beyond those an enormous set of wood doors with heavy black ornate steel hinges. Where two intense looking guards stood stationed now on either side of the doors. Their round shields, leather armor, crested helmets and long butt-spiked spears looking similar to those of the ancient Greeks.

Nestor turned right and led us along the right side of the tables to an opening in the center of the room. Which contained a stone staircase leading up to the second floor now. And reaching the top of the stairs, we turned right again and walked to the center of the hall above the elevated table below. Before Nestor turned left into another stone hallway that went back sixty feet before ending at large wooden door. Where four more fierce looking soldiers stood guard now, two on each side of the door. All four holding those eight-foot-long steel-tipped spears and large, round shields with red seahorses on them.

Passing three sets of wood doors on either side of the hallway, Nestor led us directly to the guards on the end. And snapping to attention, they smacked their fists to their chests and nodded their heads now as we drew near. Then the guard on the left stepped forward and opened the door for us before resuming his position with the others again.

Amy and I had been holding hands the entire time and were too overwhelmed to say anything. But after seeing the four guards stationed here we hesitated for a second looking at each other, both a little apprehensive now. Stepping to the side, Nestor held his arm out again gesturing for us to enter the room. And I hesitated for a second unsure what to expect on the other side. But keeping hold on Amy's hand now, we entered the room together.

To our surprise, the room turned out to be a large suite-sized bedroom. With enormous tapestries covering the walls and a large bed on the left with wardrobes on both sides. And a directly across from us was a table and chairs now set inside a small alcove with stained-glass windows. Following us into the room, Nestor shut the door behind us before gesturing to the table and chairs in the alcove now. Crossing the room to the table, I started to reach for the heavy chair on the end for Amy, but Nestor bowed to me and took hold of the chair seating Amy. And feeling like the odd man out now, I turned and pulled the chair out on the other end for Sandra. Who hesitated for a moment, before bowing to me and taking a seat in the chair.

Amy and I were apparently getting the same weird feeling now, as we both scanned the room for the nearest escape route. And I think Nestor sensed this too now as he reached for the elaborate pitcher in the center of the table and asked Amy, "I imagine your thirsty, would like to try our wine, or would you prefer water?"

Still a little overwhelmed, Amy replied, "Actually, what I really need now is a large Scotch!"

And pointing to a small cabinet in the corner, Nestor said, "Sandra, would you mind?" Rising from the table now, Sandra crossed the room and opened the small cabinet before taking an ancient looking bottle out from within. And quickly dusting it off, Sandra returned to the table with the ancient bottle. Then pulling the cork out, Sandra poured a generous amount of liquid into what looked like a gold cup on the table. And nodding to Amy, Sandra handed her the cup now.

Amy glanced at me before accepting the cup from Sandra and taking a sip now. Judging by Amy's shudder and following sigh of relief, it must be really good whiskey. And pulling her feet up onto chair, Amy leaned back now affectionately cradling the cup in her hands with a smug little smile on her lovely face.

I watched Nestor looking over at Amy in bewilderment for a second, then picking up the nearest cup, I held it out to Nestor now, saying, "I think I'll try the wine Nestor, thank you." And Nestor turned back to me and smiled now as he filled my cup from the pitcher, then proceeded to fill a cup for Sandra and himself.

After taking a sip of his wine, Nestor began by saying, "I know you both have a lot of questions. So, let me begin with the symbols on your bio-suits first and our reaction to seeing them." And turning to face me now, Nestor continued saying, "That gold symbol on your chest only appears on those of Attean royal blood. And the crown on your head means that you are the true and lawful King of Attea." It was at this point that Amy and I both snorted our drinks out of our noses!

After recovering and wiping my face, I managed to blurt out, "How is that even possible? I was born in Portsmouth, Maine, so were my parents and my grandparents."

Nodding his head, Nestor continued now saying, "Here's what I believe. Your great-great-grandfather, King Adrastos, had two children. A daughter named Helena, and then later a son named Heros. Princess Helena was a beautiful, fearless, and an adventurous woman who disliked being tied down to palace life. On one of her many unsanctioned forays into the outlands, her small glide-sub was severely damaged in a storm. And though injured, Helena managed to escape. She was later found floating adrift by a young ship's captain, who nursed her back to health. Eventually the two fell in love and married. Shortly after Helena's disappearance King Adrastos fell ill. And he ordered his men not to rest day or night until they discovered what had become of his daughter Helena. They eventually found Helena and brought her back home, but not before King Adrastos had died. By then, Helena was pregnant with the ship's captain's child. So, no one opposed her decision to abdicate the thrown to her younger brother Heros. But Heros was not a good King, and eventually went insane, nearly destroying Attean before dying. Luckily, Heros had one child, our current Queen Hera. And Hera is the greatest Queen to ever sit on the throne of Attea. But her life is at an end now, and she is beyond even my skills. Queen Hera had two sons, Hermes and Helios. Hermes died fifteen years ago under suspicious circumstances. The only witness to this death being his younger brother Helios. And when Queen Hera and the Consul of Elders attempted to question Helios about his brother's death, he went into a fit of rage and stormed out of the palace. Swearing to come back after his mother's death and destroy the Consul of Elders. And it is rumored now that Prince Helios is the mysterious leader of the Wild Ones. The Wild ones are a gang of banished criminals, who dwell in the dark recesses of the kingdom, only coming out to loot and murder. And we believe Helios is behind the recent increase in their attacks." And pausing to let Amy and me absorb that information, Nestor said in conclusion, "Which brings us to you, your majesty. I have no doubt now that you are the great-grandson of Princess Helena and the ship's captain. And our rightful King."

Then turning to Amy, Nestor said, "The gold rings and band on your arm means you are, or will be, Attean royalty. Not by blood, but since you are Andrew's chosen mate. The bio-suit recognizes this and reacted accordingly, your majesty." Then Nestor and Sandra both smiled at us, but we weren't smiling back.

But before we could ask anything, there was a knock on the door. And the door opened now as three extremely nervous young ladies in short blue tunics entered the room, each carrying a tray of steaming food. They were so nervous and bowing so frequently upon entering the room that they nearly spilled the food. But I noticed they weren't too nervous to gawk with their mouths open now at the crown on top of my head or the Insignia on my chest.

After the girls set the food on the table and the left again, I turned to Nestor and said, "You know this bowing thing is really starting to get on my nerves!" And Amy nodded in agreement with me now as we turned to look at Nestor and Sandra. But they just looked at each other and then burst into laughter. Which was highly contagious, and Amy and I ended up chuckling too in spite of the situation.

Then Nestor said, "This food is for you, your majesties. Sandra and I have already eaten." I was hungry, so I didn't stand on etiquette or argue with Nestor now. I just grabbed one of the oval-shaped, silver plates and handed it to Amy.

There was enough food here for six people. Some things, like the crab and shrimp were familiar, but other items I had no idea what they were and steered clear of those now. As soon as Amy and I had our plates loaded and began to eat. Nestor stood up and stepped back from the table. Then bowed to us and said, "If you will excuse me now, your majesties. I need to speak with Captain Ajax, the commander here." After which, Nestor turned to Sandra now and asked, "Sandra, will you stay here with their majesties in case they need of anything else?" Looking up at her father, Sandra gave him a quick nod. And backing up five steps now, Nestor turned and went out the door softly closing it behind him.

Finished eating, I turned to Sandra and asked, "Where exactly is here? And where is this palace that your father mentioned?"

Straightening up in her chair, Sandra replied, "This is the Fort Ares, located beyond the city of Medina at the far end of the South Cavern of Attea. There used to be a four caverns, but the North Cavern was lost to us due to a failed experiment a hundred years ago that breached the cavern wall letting the sea pour in. We have tried to reclaim the North Cavern several times over the years. But an enormous species of squid called "Kraken" live in the cavern now, making it impossible for us to repair the breach. The capitol city of Attea and the royal palace are in the East Cavern. Which is ten days march from here. The West Cavern, like the South Cavern here, is mostly farms and small villages except for the city of Actium and Fort Apollo on the hillside above. The three caverns are tied together in the center by the Caves of Hephaestus, which take a full day to pass through. It is also where the wild ones are the boldest. Attacking our merchant wagons and on rare occasions our soldiers too." I was still trying to absorb Sandra's information when Nestor returned. And entering the room again, Nestor stopped to bow. Then moving to the table, Nestor bowed again before taking his seat.

Then Nestor began with, "If you and her majesty Amy feel well enough to travel, we should leave for the palace first thing in the morning, your majesty?" And after receiving a nod from Amy and me, Nestor continued, adding, "News of your existence will travel fast, and the sooner you two are safely inside the palace the better it will be for your majesties."

Amy and I both simultaneously exclaimed, "Safe?"

And nodding his head, Nestor dryly replied, "Yes, I believe that once Prince Helios learns of your existence, he will stop at nothing to have you both assassinated. And Helios has agents and followers everywhere, your majesties.".

Raising her eyebrows now, Amy asked, "Both?"

Frowning now, Nestor answered Amy saying, "Yes, Prince Helios won't take the chance that you might be carrying his majesty's heir. It's easier for him to have you both to killed now, just to be sure."

A little tipsy from the whiskey now, Amy leaned forward and suddenly slapped me across the shoulder, saying, "See, mother was right all along! She said you were nothing but trouble, Andrew!" Then Amy laughed, and caught in the moment, Sandra let a small giggle slip out now. Which made Nestor and me both chuckle at Amy's timing and Sandra's little slip.

After the humor had past, Nestor spoke to Sandra now, saying, "I think a white medic's robe for her majesty, Sandra. Will you see to that?" And Sandra quickly nodded that she would. Then, crossing his arms and putting a hand on his chin, Nestor studied me for a moment now. And finally speaking, Nestor said, "Your majesty is too big to pass off as a priest or medical student, I think one of the Archer's robes would suit your majesty best. Are you any good with a bow, your majesty?"

Surprised now, I replied, "Okay I guess, I have used one before."

And nodding his head to my reply, Nestor said, "Now that's settled, we will bid you goodnight. Since we have a long day ahead of us tomorrow, and we should all get some rest." Then rising from the table, they both bowed to us, and Nestor said, "Goodnight, your Majesties." Then they both backed away from the table before turning and exiting the room. Leaving Amy and I alone for the first time since our arrival here in Attea.

Chapter - 2

Alone with Amy finally, we had a lot to discuss. The first thing I did was apologize to Amy for getting her into this mess. Of course, there was no way I could have known, or even imagined in my wildest dreams that anything like this could happen. And if it weren't for my great-grandmother being an Attean Princess, we would both probably be fish food on the bottom of the ocean right now.

So, we agreed to be content if not thrilled that we were still alive now. And to try to make the best of our situation here as the new King and Queen of Attea. And chuckling in retrospect now, it could have been a lot worse.

And we both felt a little worn out now. Not physically, but mentally from the complete overload since awakening here in Attea. It was a lot to take in, and we were both ready for bed.

Pulling the covers back on the bed now, we stretched out together and tried to relax. I still had a ton of questions, like, what it's like sleeping in a bio-suit. And after lying there for a minute admiring Amy's amazing figure in her new green bodypaint like bio-suit, I wondered how you made love in these things now. Amy was fairly well-lubed and relaxed after two glasses of whiskey, which had helped calm her in this bizarre situation. And looking over at the bulge in my bio-suit now, Amy chuckled and said, "I was wondering about that too?" As she indicated my current aroused state.

Well, I wasn't going to apologize for something that happened every time I saw Amy undressed, and replying frankly now, I said, "Happens every time I see you undressed my love, bio-suit or no bio-suit." Smiling, Amy leaned over and kissed me now. It was our first kiss in our new bio-suits, and to our surprise it felt completely normal. Like the bio-suits reacted in anticipation of our kiss thinning out. And we were both curious now, so I pulled Amy to me and tried a much longer kiss and found that felt normal too. Then we lay back in the bed together, relieved now as at least that part of our relationship was still intact and unchanged.

Feeling my manhood pressing against her, Amy said, "I'll ask Sandra about that tomorrow when we're alone. Women are always lightyears ahead of you men when it comes to the practical matters of life."

And Amy suddenly laughed, and I asked her, "What's so funny?"

Grinning now, she replied, "I just got a mental picture of Nestor's face as you asked him the proper technic for making love in the bio-suits. Then Nestor trying to demonstrate it for you!" Then Amy laughed again, apparently replaying the image over in her mind and getting an alternate ending this time.

To which I replied, "Well, I can live with you being amused at my expense, my love. As long as it keeps a smile on your beautiful face!" And we kissed again before snuggling up and drifting off to sleep.

It didn't seem like that long before I heard a light knocking on the door. And reaching over, I gently shook Amy's shoulder waking her up. I could tell by the first sound out of Amy's mouth that she was hangover now from the whiskey last night. Throwing the covers back, we both sat up on the edge of the bed for a moment, and after getting a nod from Amy, I said, "Come in, we're awake."

The door swung open, and Nestor and Sandra entered the room now followed by the three serving girls in blue tunics. Two of which were holding trays of steaming food. And all five stopping just inside the room to bow in unison now. Then the first serving girl quickly moved forward clearing and wiping the table, before the other two girls stepped forward setting their trays of food down on the table. And each sneaking a sideways glances at us before excitedly whispering amongst themselves. The three serving girls lining up to bow to us again before backing up and exiting the room.

Nestor and Sandra were both wearing full-length white hooded robes now over plain white tunics with a grey tint. Nestor's tunic being knee length now, while Sanra's tunic went all the way down to her ankles. And both had those white medical satchels hanging down at their waists now. Hoods back, they stood by the door now watching until the serving girls had set the table and left again. And Sandra had a matching white robe and tunic over her right arm now, while Nestor carried a hard leather cuirass in his right hand now, and a brown hooded robe and white tunic over his left arm.

Frowning, Nestor nodded his head before saying, "I'm sorry, your majesty. But your presence here at the fort is too momentous to be contained. Especially for these simple serving girls who might live whole life here in the South Cavern without ever seeing royalty."

Walking around the bed, I offered Amy my hands. And taking my hands now, Amy rose, and I helped her to the table. My attention on Amy now, I replied over my shoulder, saying, "That's fine, Nestor. And good morning to you too, Sandra."

Realizing the situation, Nestor quickly dropped the cuirass and robe into the nearest chair, before moving forward to pull out a chair on the end table for Amy. While Sandra moved to the table and quickly filled one of the silver cups there with water before bowing to Amy and setting the cup down in front of her.

Amy on the other hand, was in no mood for more of their royal etiquette this morning, flat out told them both now, "That's it! No more bowing when we're alone. And you can consider that a royal order, decree, or whatever you want to call it." Then looking at Sandra, Amy said, "What I really need now is a friend. And I am hoping that you Sandra, would be willing to fill that role?" And looking at Sandra, I watched as her cheeks inside her bio-suit started to turn from green to brown. And for a moment it looked like Sandra was going to cry, as her eyes began to get watery now.

Sandra started to bow again, but then caught herself before replying, "Gladly, your majesty!" And sounding a little overwhelmed as she answered now.

Grinning feebly, Amy asked, "Good, that's settled. But right now, my head is pounding from that wonderful whiskey last night, Sandra. What's the Attean cure for a hangover?"

Opening his hand now, Nestor revealed the small vial of reddish liquid in his hand. And removing the stopper from the vial, Nestor handed it to Amy now before picking up the cup of water and holding it out to her, saying, "This will fix your headache, your majesty. But it's not the most pleasant tasting medicine, so I recommend you wash it down quickly with water."

And taking the vial from Nestor's hand, Amy downed its contents in one shot, then making a yuk face, she grabbed the water from Nestor's hand and proceeded to empty the entire cup. Then sitting back in her chair, I could see the medicine really worked fast, as small creases on Amy's forehead relaxed and vanished within seconds. And smiling up at Nestor now, Amy nodded her head and exclaimed, "Wow! Thank you, Nestor."

Returning Amy's nod, Nestor smiled and put his hand on Sandra's shoulder now in a gesture of pride, saying, "Looks like your leaving medical school and moving up to Queens Companion, daughter."

Her hangover gone now, Amy cut saying, "No, Sandra must complete her schooling first. Queen's Companion can wait until Sandra completes her medical training, however long it takes? I will not cut Sandra's education short, that has priority!"

And Nestor turned to look at Amy in surprise, and I think a little impressed now too, as he answered, "Sandra has less than a year left on her physicians training before she graduates, your majesty."

Smiling now, Amy replied, "Good, Queen's Companion can wait until then. I'm happy just to know I have a friend here in Attea." And rising from her chair, Amy moved over to Sandra and gave her a hug now to her amazement. I could see that Nestor and Sandra were stunned by Amy's actions, and just stood there frozen now, unsure of what to say or do?

Speaking up now, I explained saying, "Sorry, this is the way friends greet each other in our world. We have no idea how it's done down here, or what's proper greeting is here in Attea?"

Relaxing now, Nestor replied, "My apologies your majesties, you just caught us off guard. And to answer your question, that kind of greeting is only exchanged between family members here in Attea."

To our surprise, a big smile spread across Amy's face now as she said, "Good, that is what I want our friendship to be like, Sandra. Like sisters!" And Amy kept hold of Sandra's arm now with both hands. And that was that.

Dropping into the nearest chair, I motioned for Sandra and Nestor to sit now, so we could discuss what to expect today while I examined what the Attean's ate for breakfast. And they both sat down at the table now. The breakfast looked simple enough, toasted bread, white cheese, green olives, some sort of cooked sausage, a pot of something hot that smelled like tea, and a large bowl of what looked like cream of wheat. There was enough food on the table for six people, and I asked Nestor, "I suppose you two have eaten already?"

Nodding his head, Nestor replied, "Yes, but I will take another cup of tsai, your majesty."

And echoing Nestor now, I asked, "Tsai?"

Nestor looked up for a moment while he searched for the right word, then looking down again, he replied, "I believe it's called 'Tea' in English, your majesty."

"Oh good!" I replied, and indicating the teapot now, I added, "Please help yourselves." As I began loading a little bit of everything onto my plate now except for cream of wheat. Which I planned to try, but not until after I had finished the items on my plate. Amy began loading her plate too, as Sandra grabbed the teapot and filled all four of the silver cups with tsai. The flat bread tasted like bread, the green olives were normal olives, and the cheese was a traditional salty white goat cheese. I didn't care for the sausage though, as it had a strong overpowering taste to it. The tea or "tsai" was good though, and unlike any I had tasted before, so I couldn't quite put a flavor to it. The cream of wheat looking porridge was little courser and blander than what we were used to. And picking up a small pitcher off the tray now, Nestor said, "You need to put 'Meli' on top of that your majesty, otherwise it's a little bland. I believe the English word is 'Honey,' your majesty." Then Nestor handed me the little creamer cup, and I poured the golden liquid over top of the porridge. And judging by its color and viscosity, it was honey. Then stirring it up, I tried the porridge again and found it pleasantly improved. Amy was quite at home with this kind of breakfast, though she didn't eat much this morning due to last night's indulgence.

After finishing our breakfast, I could see Nestor was eager to get going. And rising from the table, Nestor retrieved the white tunic from the chair now and held it out to me first. And after slipping that on, Nestor handed me the hard leather cuirass next, before opening the brown hooded robe up now for my inspection, and saying, "One standard Archer's leather cuirass and hooded robe. Make sure you both keep your hoods up and pulled down low once we leave this room, your majesties. And don't lower your hoods again until I tell you it safe your majesties, okay?" And we could hear the seriousness in Nestor's voice now. Nestor helped me get the leather cuirass on and buckled up. Then Nestor handed me the leather belt and scabbard for my waist, before putting the brown Archer's robe up over my shoulders. And stepping around to the front now, Nestor attached the robe's small clasps to the metal loops on front of my cuirass. And pulling the hood up over my head, I turned around to face the others. Sandra had done the same for Amy, getting her into the tunic and wrapping a white sash around her waist before helping her into the white robe of a medic and raising her hood now. Then Nestor and Sandra stepped back to inspect our outfits before smiling and nodding their heads that we were ready to go now.

Nestor led the way out of the bedroom now, the four guards outside snapping to attention as soon as they heard the door opening. And we followed Nestor out of the room now single file with Sandra in the rear. Nestor leading us down the stone hallway to the balcony above the great hall again. Before turning right and taking us back down the same stairs that we had come up yesterday and into the great hall again. Reaching the ground floor, Nestor turned right now leading us around the banquet tables and through the stone archways into the foyer in front of large keep doors. The two Spearmen standing guard on either side doors snapping to attention as soon as we rounded the end of the table and passed through the archway. And pausing in front of the doors now, Nestor made another quick check of Amy's and my disguises again to make sure they fully covered our bio-suits. Then Nestor stood there silently, apparently waiting for someone or something now.

A minute later, I heard footsteps approaching from behind. And Nestor grinned now as he turned to greet the person. I couldn't see who it was because of the hood, and I was afraid to swing my head around now to get a better look. Then a large serious looking man with chiseled features stepped into my view smacking his fist firmly against his cuirass and bowing his head. He was stout at 5 foot 10 inches tall and built like a lineman for a professional football team. You know, one of those guys who has to turn sideways to fit through a door. He was a couple of inches shorter than my 6 foot 1 but looked like he easily weighed half again as much as my 220 lbs. now. Clean shaven, he looked to be in his early thirties. Locks of dark brown hair showing around the edges of his helmet. And his sky-blue eyes almost matching the blue plum on his helmet now. All of which were offset now by the dozens of scars visible on the exposed parts of his jade-green and brown bio-suit.

Bowing his head, Nestor made the introductions now, saying, "This is Captain Ajax, commander of Fort Ares, your majesty. He and two hundred of his best men will be protecting your majesties on our journey to the palace in Attea. Captain Ajax speaks English. And by the way, is your cousin, your majesty."

Amy reached out giving my arm a squeeze now, knowing how much it meant to me to find out I still had relatives, and wasn't alone in the world anymore. His head still bowed, Captain Ajax slapped the sword on his left side now proclaiming, "With my life, your majesty."

Delighted to find out I had relatives left, I spoke warmly to Captain Ajax now, saying, "Please rise Captain, so I can get a proper look at you, cousin." Ajax did as was asked, a smile spreading across his face at my warm greeting and acknowledgement of our kinship. One look in Ajax's eyes and I knew instantly we were going to be friends. And noticed that Ajax was holding a four-foot-long worn looking recurve bow and a leather quiver full of black and white fletched wood arrows in hand now. So, I asked him, "I take it those are to complete my disguise, cousin?"

Grinning now, Ajax nodded his head and replied, "Yes, your majesty. This is my old bow and quiver, which have served me faithfully without fail. And they will complete your disguise as one of the personal archers that I keep close to me for running orders and messages, your majesty." Then holding the quiver up by the strap, Ajax asked, "May I, your majesty?" And nodding my head, Ajax took a step forward now and I lifted my left arm slightly so Ajax could slide the quiver into place on my back. Once the quiver was on, Ajax took a step back and fondly handed me his bow. Raising the long, thin bow up now, I felt its weight and ran my finger down the bowstring until I felt the nock point in the center. A small, knowing grin crossing Ajax's face now, though I don't think the others noticed.

About then, one of the older women whom we had seen yesterday walked through the archway now carrying a white leather satchel like the ones Nestor and Sandra were wearing. And bowing first, she handed the satchel to Sandra before turning and disappearing back through the archway.

Sandra started to speak, but I cut her off now, saying, "You three need to stop bowing and start calling us by our names if you expect these disguises to fool anyone. My name is Andrew." And pointing to Amy now, I added, "And her name is Amy from now on, okay?"

All three nodded in agreement, then Sandra spoke, saying, "Amy, this is your medical bag, may I put it on you now?" Amy nodded her head, and Sandra carefully lifted the strap up over Amy's head and set the bag in place on Amy's left side.

Turning to Ajax now, I asked, "Ajax, was that salute you gave me when you entered what I need to do from now on whenever you give me an order?"

Ajax started to say your majesty, but I caught himself now replying, "Yes, that is correct response and acknowledgement of any order you receive. Andrew is not an Attean name, but it's close to Andreus. Will Andreas work?" Grinning at Ajax, I slapped my right fist to my chest now and nodded my head in acknowledgement. Then Ajax added, "Then sling that bow over your left shoulder, and follow three feet behind me wherever I go from now on Andreas, okay?" And snapping my fist to my chest, I nodded my head to Ajax again. Then turning to Nestor, who was still trying to recover from us throwing the royal etiquette out the window, I nodded my head to him to let him know we were ready now.

Turning, Ajax waved his arm at the two guards standing by the keep doors, and they quickly moved forward swinging the doors inward now. Then Ajax led the way out through the open doors, followed by Nestor, me, and Sandra. Who had latched onto Amy's arm now and led her out through the open doors into the brightly lit courtyard outside.

Once our eyes adjusted, I could see we were inside an enormous stone fortress. And two hundred Attean soldiers stood before us now in four perfectly formed squads with their squad leaders. Taking up most of the cobblestone courtyard here as they waited for Ajax.

There were two squads of Archers on the left with bows, quivers, and long knives on their leather belts. And two squads of Spearmen on the right with those long steel-tipped wood spears. Their large shields were slung over their backs now, and the hilts of their short swords were visible in the leather scabbards on the left side of their chests. They all snapped to attention now as Ajax stepped out of the keep doors. And I could see at least twenty more soldiers either patrolling the walls or standing guard in the flanking towers of the fortress. Blue banners with gold seahorses on them flopping back and forth lazily above their heads in the faint breeze. And a half dozen Spearmen stood guard by the front gates now below a thick wood portcullis.

And seeing Ajax step outside, the four squad leaders left their positions in the center of the formation and came running forward. Stopping at the base of the stairs now to snap their hands to their chests and bow their heads waiting for Ajax's orders.

Standing at the top of the stairs, Ajax stood there for a moment looking out over the men. I could tell now the longer he stood there the more nervous it was making them. And I thought I heard a faint sigh of relief from the squads when Ajax turned to face the officer approaching now, judging by his silver cuirass and brightly plumed helmet. The officer stopped to salute Ajax before handing him a sealed scroll, which Ajax broke open and quickly read. It was about then, I noticed the four squad leaders at the base of the stairs giving me an odd look. Obviously, something wasn't right with my outfit, because they glanced at me, then at each other, then back at me again.

Ajax noticed this too but didn't let it show. And turning to look at now, leaned over and whispered something into the other officer's ear. After which, the officer looked at me before wheeling around and disappearing back in though the keep doors. Only to return a few moments later carrying a long dagger in his right hand. Then the officer grabbed me forcefully by the collar of my cuirass and drug me off to the side now. And shaking me back and forth a couple of times now, he pulled me in close before whispering, "I am truly sorry, your majesty. But these were Captain Ajax's specific orders." Then the officer thrust the dagger into the sheath at my waist hard before shoving me back towards Ajax and raising his foot like he was going to give me a kick in the rear now but missed. And there was some chuckling out amongst the ranks now, and Ajax and the squad leaders whipped their heads around trying to catch the guilty party.

Then the other officer casually walked back to Ajax's side. And the two men whispered back and forth before chuckling loudly. After which, the two men clasped each other's arms firmly now as they looked at each other in an obvious show of respect and friendship. After which, they each took two steps back and snapped their hands to their chests before nodding their heads to each other. Which actually made sense to me, as these men were soldiers, and knew this could easily be the last time they ever saw each other. Then raising his hand in farewell to the officer, Ajax turned and started down the steps to his squad leaders waiting at the bottom.

Ajax paused at the bottom of the stairs and issued his orders. And we watched as the four squad leaders all snapped their hands to their chests and nodded to Ajax. Ajax returned their salutes, and they all ran back to their squads and began barking out orders.

Then we watched as all four squads did an about-face, and the first squad of Spearmen on the right began filing out the gates. Followed immediately by the first squad of Archers on the left. And we followed Ajax as he walked across the courtyard and fell in behind the first squad of Archers as they marched out through the gates.

Once we cleared the gates, Amy and I got our first look at the South Cavern. The hillside here gradually sloping downward a hundred yards to the valley floor below. The upper portion of the hillsides here covered in orchards, while the lower portion of the hill was covered by row after row of grapes and some sort of berries. Out on the valley floor, we could see a variety of crops growing now, though from here, the majority of it appeared to be wheat.

And it looked like it was a good mile across to the rock wall on the other side now. With the same hundred yards of sloped hillside before the massive rock walls rose straight up and disappeared into the humidity at the top of the cavern. Looking to the right, we could make out the sheer rock wall that must be the southern end of the cavern. But to the north, in the direction we were travelling, the other end of the cavern was lost in the haze, too far off for us to see yet.

But the oddest thing by far though, was the blindingly bright light coming from the center of the cavern. It was so bright that it even shone through the humidity at the top of the cavern. And like the sun, it was too bright for me to see what was creating the light. Fascinated, I had to avoid staring up at the light and drawing attention to myself. Also, I had to worry about my hood sliding back and someone seeing my bio-suit now. So, I decided to wait and ask Nestor about it later, not wanting to miss anything else here in the South Cavern.

Four long, squat, tarp-covered carts waited for us outside the gates, each with its own driver and man riding shotgun. And they fell in behind us now as we passed through the gates. Each cart pulled by a team of four braying donkeys, who complained loudly about their loads until the crack of the driver's whips split the air above their heads and their braying abruptly ceased. Turning to look back at fortress, I saw the other squad of Archers and Spearmen pouring out the gates and taking up position behind the carts now.

Despite the enormous rock walls looming up on both sides, the cavern itself was actually quite serene and beautiful. The dirt road quickly descending down from the fortress onto the valley floor, then wound its way north along the base of the orchard covered west slope. There was row after row of grapes here on the lower part of the hillside, basically separating the hillside from the valley floor. The farmers piled the rocks they plowed up along the east side of the road, forming a low wall here over the years. I assumed they stacked the rocks here for future road work, but there was no way to confirm that.

Unlike the Romans, apparently the Attean's had never discovered the wonders of concrete and therefore the road here was little more than a rutted wagon trail now. And making it necessary for Archer's to break ranks and assist the carts over the rough and wet spots. I asked Ajax about this later, and he said the Spearmen in the front and the rear take the brunt of all attacks, so the Archers in the center were tasked with assisting and protecting the food train. It was fair trade, and each group respecting the other one's role while they were on the move. I saw on one instance where in a particularly difficult spot, the Spearmen broke formation and fanned out protecting the Archers as they were fully involved in getting the four struggling carts through a muddy spot. Only after the wagons were through and the Archers reformed, did the Spearmen leave their flanking positions and return to their own formation.

We passed several farmhouses and a small village as we marched north. The young children and female residents smiling now as they rushed out to greet the soldiers with buckets of water and ladles. And Ajax calling a short halt at all of these locations, I assumed not just to get water for his men, but also to promote good will among the farmers and villagers of the cavern since they were expected to contribute a portion of their crops or income to feed the garrison at Outpost Ares. At one farm, the farmer's cart was stuck up to its axle out in the muddy field. And Captain Ajax ordered a dozen Archers to stay behind now and help the farmer free his wagon. Their mission accomplished, it wasn't long before the Archers came running back and rejoined their squads.

Amy was taking it all in too, and I could hear occasional bits of her conversation with Sandra as they walked along behind us arm in arm like a couple of old friends or classmates. And Amy asked Sandra a variety of questions about the city of Attea, the palace, and Sandra's life in general. Ajax and Nestor both intentionally avoided speaking to me now, so they won't draw any attention to me.

We stopped at midday alongside the road, and Ajax stationed flankers around us while our troop took a shorty break and had a bite to eat. Our troop making use of the low wall on the east side to sit and eat. Ajax sat beside Nestor, while Sandra and Amy sat on the other side of Nestor. After they were seated, Nestor rose and went to the nearest cart. And after exchanging words and nods with one of the men riding shotgun, Nestor returned with what looked like a stack of sandwiches wrapped up in a white cloth and leather bota bag.

The crude sandwiches were just a piece of folded flatbread with a slab of dried meat inside. And we found out now that the men riding shotgun in the carts were actually the camp cooks. After the women had both had a drink from the bota bag, Nestor took a quick drink before passing the bota bag to me. I was expecting it to be filled with water, but to my surprise, found it filled with a light wine instead. With no one nearby except the ladies and Ajax, I took this opportunity to lean over now and quietly ask Nestor what the source of the light was at the top of the cavern. And Nestor quietly told me this was the legend of the "Six Staves of Attea," and that story would have to wait until we had more time, as the soldiers were beginning rise and reform now to move out again. Fully formed up and ready to go, Ajax gave the order to move out and we were on the way again.

The donkeys brayed loudly in protests for a moment until the drivers cracked their whips over the top of their heads again. And the road continued to wind along the west edge of the valley floor as we traveled north for the rest of the afternoon. The road seemed to improve the further north we got. And the Archers were spending less and less time now assisting the carts, so we were making better time.

After traveling for several hours, I noticed that the light at the top of the cavern had begun to dim. Shortly thereafter, a large black rock appeared on the east side of road in the distance ahead. The black rock was odd and unnatural looking like it was man-made. And as we got closer, I guessed the enormous square rock to be about six feet high, though the four corners of the rock stuck up twice as high as the rest of the rock now, like towers. I came to believe that this was our destination for tonight, and I was right.

The large black rock turned out to be a small fort or compound. And the Spearmen in the front broke ranks and ran forward now opening the wood gates as our whole formation filed directly into the grounds of the compound. There wasn't much inside the compound, just a couple of dozen firepits on the north side, stacks of firewood against the north wall, and a rickety old corral in the southwest corner. The four raised corners of the compound were indeed lookout towers, and it was only a matter of minutes after we arrived that I noticed a pairs of Archers manning each of the towers now. As well as a half dozen Spearmen standing guard by the gates.

The light at the top of the cavern had continued to dim and resembled dusk now. And it wasn't long before the soldiers had several fires going in the firepits. It turned out now that the fourth cart contained two large tents. Which the soldiers quickly removed and erected on the east side of the compound. The first tent being for Ajax and his squad leaders, and the other tent being for Nestor and the ladies. Apparently, Nestor's status as the Queen's Physician afforded him VIP treatment whenever he traveled.

With Nestor and the ladies inside their tent, and the troops settled in for the night, the Staff of Attea finally went dark. And I watched as the soldiers all reach up now and raise their hoods. Then suddenly it started to rain. It wasn't much rain, more like a heavy drizzle, and it only lasted for about five minutes before stopping again. Just enough rain to wet the ground slightly before disappearing. I guess that after the Staff of Attea went dark each night. The moisture at the top of the cavern cooled and released its water.

After which, Captain Ajax summoned his squad leaders to him and issued his orders for the night. Then turning his attention to me now, and Ajax grabbed my shoulder pulling me in close to him so no one else could hear and whispered, "Go stand guard inside Nestor's tent, Andreas." Then Ajax made an open display now of releasing me and pointing towards Nestor's tent. And taking two steps back, I slapped my hand to my chest and nodded my head acknowledging Ajax's orders. Ajax returned my salute now with a small, wry grin on his face before turning and striding off to ensure that his orders were being carried out in a timely manner.

Wheeling around, I strode directly up to Nestor's tent. Then standing outside the tent, I checked to make sure no one was close by before clearing my throat. And Nestor responded, "εἰσβαίνω" or "enter" now in Attean from inside the tent. And lifting the flap, I quickly stepped inside the tent and let the flap drop again.

The inside of the tent was lit by a battered looking lantern sitting atop the small wood table now in the center with three chairs. And there were three canvas cots inside the tent now, one per wall, with a large bedrolls laying on top of each cot. And I noticed there was a fourth smaller bedroll, like the ones the soldiers were carrying leaning up against the front corner of the tent. Nestor, Amy, and Sandra were standing by the table quietly talking now as I entered.

I started to reach for my hood, but Nestor raised his hand stopping me. About then, we heard a voice outside speaking in Attean, and Nestor responded in kind. And stepping to the left, I stood at attention by the door as two men entered. It was two of the cooks who had been riding shotgun in the carts today, white aprons around their waists now. The first cook was carrying a tray laden with food, while the second cook carried a tray with three plates, three silver cups, and a copper pitcher on it now.

Turning my head slightly, I quickly glanced at the trays they were carrying as they passed me before looking straight ahead again. The two cooks bowed to Nestor before setting their trays down on the table. And Nestor gave them a nod in return. After which, the two cooks turned and quickly left again. Apparently my presence here by the door now with the hood covering my face making them nervous.

Once the cooks had left and the tent flap was down again, Nestor and Sandra both gave us a quick nod, before Nestor gestured for me to join them at the table. Nestor grabbing the corner of center cot and sliding it forward once Amy and I sat down. And Sandra reluctantly took the third chair, after offering her father the other chair and volunteering to take the cot. But Nestor waved her off now and sat down on the cot.

Once we were all seated, Nestor and Sandra annoyingly waited for Amy and me to grab what we wanted from the trays before taking anything themselves. And Nestor was the first to speak, and he started to say, "Your majesties." But he stopped and corrected himself, before saying, "Andreas, Amy, be warned. The cooks will return again in an hour to pick up these trays, so make sure you both have your hoods are up, or the whole camp will be in utter chaos. A happy joyous chaos I admit, but still chaos. And we don't want to make Ajax's job any harder than it already is."

Nodding my head, I replied, "I agree, Nestor. Let's not make Ajax's job any harder than it has to be." And taking hold of Amy's hand now, I asked, "And how are you doing, my love?"

Amy smiled and replied, "Fine so far, Sandra and I have been talking all day about things here in Attea. And she told me about her life here. And I told her of my life in the outworld. How we met, and how my parents weren't particularly thrilled about you, Andreas!" Then Amy and Sandra both laughed, and Amy added, "And I got the answer to that question of yours. Though I don't see us doing anything about it anytime soon!" Causing Sandra to let another small giggle slip out, and I had to admit, Amy was right about that part now.

The copper pitcher turned out to be full of that same light wine from earlier. And Amy and I shared her plate and wine glass now as we ate our dinner. It wasn't long after we had finished our meal that we heard one of the cooks outside the tent announce himself again. And Nester spoke briefly to the cook in Attean now stalling for a few seconds to give Amy and me time to get our hoods back up, and the cot slid back into position again. Rising, I took my bow and quickly moved back by the tent flap again. Nestor waited until I was back in position before giving the cooks permission to enter. This time there was only one cook, and he moved inside quickly bowing to Nestor and the ladies before proceeding to stack everything onto the food tray. He left the wine pitcher and cups on the table and picked up the food tray now, then bowed to Nestor again before making a hasty retreat back out of the tent.

Alone again, we all returned to our previous positions. And it was at this point I asked Nestor about the light at the top of the cavern and the legend of the "Six Staves of Attean," again.

Nodding his head now, Nestor began telling us the story, saying, "Long ago, before Attea sank beneath the waves. A meteor fell from the sky landing in a humble farmer's field. The small meteor split into six pieces upon impact. Finding the meteor in his field the next day, the farmer wrapped the six crystal up and took them home with him. Later that night, he discovered that the crystals glowed in the dark. And thinking he could sell them now and get rich. The farmer took the six crystals to the market in Attea the next day. Luckily, one of the king's advisors happened to be in the market at the time. And upon hearing the farmer's tale and seeing the crystals. The king's advisor claimed the crystals in the name of the king and had the farmer and the crystals taken before King Atlas in the palace. Fearing for his life now, the farmer offered the crystals to the king as a gift. But King Atlas simply asked the farmer how much he was hoping to get for the six crystals. And the farmer meekly blurted out fifty pieces of gold. So, King Atlas ordered that the farmer to be paid one hundred pieces of gold for the crystals and sent the farmer on his way. Then taking the largest crystal for himself, King Atlas gave one crystal to each of his five advisors now for them to study. And as they began experimenting with the crystals, they found that the crystals had amazing powers and a multitude of uses. So, Atlas had five staves made for his advisors and had their crystals set into each of the staves. And the king had his crystal set into his symbol of power, the golden trident. And thus became the 'Six Staves of Attea.' And with these amazing staves, our science and culture began to advance rapidly. But the King's General and military advisor, armed with his staff, soon became greedy, and decided to overthrow Atlas and claim the thrown for himself. The ensuing battle of the crystal staves was horrific and beyond imagination. The General and his followers were finally defeated, but not before the city of Attea was nearly destroyed and sank beneath the waves. King Atlas and his four loyal advisors, in a desperate effort, used the combined power of their staves to hold the sea at bay, while enclosing the surrounding rock around the city. Thus, saving Attea and its remaining citizens, but sealing the kingdom of Attea beneath the waves forever. Then those same staves were used to create the bio-suits which we are still using today and the three caverns. Later, King Atlas and his advisors decided that the crystals were just too powerful and too dangerous for any one man to possess. So, they set one staff into the roof of each cavern to provide the necessary light to grow our food. And forever putting the staves out of the reach of all Attea. And since the King Atlas was old and nearing the end of his time. It was agreed that his trident and its crystal, would be entombed with him upon his death." In conclusion, Nestor said, "And now you know the story of the 'Six Staves of Attea.' And how the kingdom of Attea you see before you was created, your majesties." I could tell he regretted his slip, but he quickly recovering now adding, "I mean Andreas and Amy!"

Amy, Sandra, and I all smiled trying to hold it in, but we couldn't, and we finally all burst into laughter at Nestor's little slip and speedy recovery. And realizing the humor of his mistake, Nestor joined us now in having a quick laugh. Then after another glass of wine and some small talk, we were ready for bed.

Both Nestor and Sandra insisted that I sleep in their cots, and that they would be fine on the floor. But I reminded them now, if someone were to enter the tent during the night. It would look odd for the guard to be sleeping on a cot while the Senior Physician or his daughter slept on the floor. After pointing out the logic to them, I told them that this wouldn't be my first time sleeping on the ground. And Amy backed me up now, quickly explaining our outworld camping trips. Nestor and Sandra finally accepted it, as I untied my bedroll and spread it out on the ground now between Amy's cot and the tent flap. And giving Amy a quick kiss goodnight, we all climbed into beds. The combination of the long march today and the second cup of wine after dinner doing the trick, and we were all out cold within minutes.

Chapter - 3

It was Ajax's voice outside our tent that woke us the next morning. As he proclaimed plainly and not too quietly that it was time to get up. And Nestor sat up and answered him, as we all rose now and rolled our bedrolls back up. Tying them shut with the small leather straps sewn onto the ends of the outer cover. Done with our bedrolls, Amy, and I both dawned our robes and pulled our hoods up now. And shouldering my bow, I moved back by the tent flap again to stand guard. While Sandra and Nestor dawned their white robes too but left their hoods down now showing their faces to the cook who arrived outside just a few moments later with our breakfast.

After requesting permission to enter and receiving it, the cook brought in a platter of food and a steaming pot of tsai. Nestor stopped the cook now after he had set the food down and picked up the wine pitcher and cups. Then Nestor spoke with the cook for a moment in Attean. After which, the cook glanced at me, then nodded his head to Nestor before leaving with the wine tray. And the cook returning in a few minutes later with the fourth plate and tsai cup. Entering the tent, the cook set them both down on the table before turning to leave again and sneaking another sideways glance at my hooded form by the tent flap. Amy noticing the cook's nervousness, and moving over next to me, Amy slapped me across the shoulder now before saying, "Stop that Andreas, you're going give the poor man a heart attack!"

Shrugging my shoulders, I replied, "I'm not doing anything other than standing guard here like I was ordered." Then turning to Nestor, I asked, "What did you say to the cook?"

Grinning smugly now, Nestor replied, "I just told him very bluntly and sarcastically, that if Captain Ajax insists this man guard me day and night! To bring another mug and plate, as you might as well eat with us too!" And we chuckled now at Nestor's comment.

Moving to the table, we all sat down and had a quick breakfast now. Knowing, the soldiers were waiting outside for us to exit the tent so they could break it down and get it loaded back into the cart again.

And I was right, there were half a dozen soldiers milling around outside now trying to look busy while they waited for us to exit the tent. As soon as we stepped out, one of them pulled the flap back, and checked to make sure the tent was empty now before signaling for others to start breaking down the tent. I could see the soldiers had already taken down Captain Ajax's tent and loaded it back into the cart. Once we were clear of the tent, Nestor, and the rest of us moved over beside Ajax. Who was standing in the middle of the compound, pointing at whatever he wasn't happy about and loudly barking out orders. Ten minutes later, we were formed up and headed north on the narrow road again.

The Staff of Attean on the cavern roof growing brighter now making more of the cavern ahead visible. Which unfortunately, looked the same as the valley behind us now. And the entire day went by without anything of interest happening. Amy and Sandra continued their conversations and occasional giggles as they walked along arm in arm now, seeming to have no end of topics or questions for each other. But Nestor was silent most of the day and Ajax was busy with his duties. As the morning past, the only noise now was the occasional bray from the donkeys and the steady thud of the soldier's feet on the dry roadway. We stopped three times, twice at small farming villages for water, and once for a crude lunch. And the Staff of Attean had begun to dim again before we rounded a small finger ridge, and the next compound came into view.

It wasn't until we were all fully inside the compound and the tents erected that Ajax turned to me, and winking first, made a public display of pointing at Nestor's tent again. And slapping my hand to my chest, I bowed my head in acknowledgement of his order. And with Nestor's tent completed, I followed Nestor and the ladies inside now. Ten minutes after the Staff of Attea went dark again, I heard fain sound of rain falling on the tent's roof. So, apparently it did rain here every night after the Staff of Attea went dark and the moisture at the top of the cavern cooled.

This time the cooks brought four plates and four cups with our food. Though they didn't bring a fourth cot, so I would still be sleeping on the ground like the rest of the soldiers. Not that I minded being perfectly comfortable on the ground with the thick bed roll, and I made sure to mention that to Nestor and Sandra when the opportunity arose, so we wouldn't have a repeat of last night's offers. I even joked if that if I was too uncomfortable, I would just squeeze in with Amy, before dislodging either of them.

The next morning, we were up, and on our way again at first light. Captain Ajax stopped by and made sure to tell Nestor that he could expect to sleep in a real bed tonight as we would reach Medina today. Though I suspect the information was more for Amy and my sake, as Nestor and Sandra knew this. It was right after lunch that we got our first look at the city of Medina, looming up in the distance ahead.

As the afternoon wore on and we drew closer to the city, I could make out rows of three-story buildings in the center of Medina, with a large two-story fortress or building at the east end of the rows sitting up slightly on the east slope of the cavern. And there were over a dozen two-story buildings mixed in with the numerous large barns and silos inside the city. All of which were encircled by a low tan wall with a gatehouse over the archway of the south gates. And we could see the occasional reflection off the shields of the guards manning the south gates.

Later that afternoon, Captain Ajax sent a pair of Archers ahead carrying a sealed scroll, which Ajax must have written last night. And two hours later we saw the Archers returning, and they reported directly to Captain Ajax now, still breathing hard from their exertion. Slapped their hands to their chest and bowing their heads as they handed a scroll to the Ajax. Receiving the scroll, Ajax returned the Archer's salutes, and they turned quickly rejoining their squads. Stopping, Ajax broke the wax seal on the scroll and read it, before signaling for his squad leaders to join him. And saluting Ajax now, Ajax discussed something with his squad leaders for a minute before they all saluted Ajax again and ran back to their positions at the head of their squads.

As we drew near the gates, I could see two officers with elaborate red plumes on their helmets standing outside the gates now along with what looked like a full squad of Spearmen in red cloaks formed up just inside the gates. Another half a dozen guards stood at attention now outside gates. And Ajax called a halt now forty yards out from the gates. Then smiling, he strode forward to meet the two officers who were walking out to meet him now. The three men smiling as they saluted each other, and Ajax exchanged the two-handed clasp of friendship with the older of the two officers. And they talked for a couple of minutes, obviously telling a joke or something humorous now, as they all laughed afterwards. Then saluting each other again before turning back to their respective troops.

Passing through the gates, we heard the older officer barking out orders now as the city guards turned and led the way in through the city. Returning to the center of our formation, Ajax barked out the order now to proceed into the city. Then turning to Nestor and the rest of us, Ajax whispered, "Stay close to me." And we filed through the gates now following the squad of red-caped city guards. As we marched into the city, I could see pairs of city guards stationed in the opening of each of the side streets. And up ahead, I could see the city guards clearing the streets now as we moved forward.

There was no sign of resistance. All the citizens were smiling and welcomed Ajax's men like heroes on parade. Women hung out of the windows above, waving scarves. And the men rose from their café tables to wave to friends or relatives among the soldiers. Children crowded forward between the guards now and looked up in fascination as the squads marched past.

Reaching the center of the city, we turned right onto a wide street containing the city's market and headed uphill now towards the large building on the east end. I don't think anyone else noticed now that Ajax's hand never left the hilt of his sword. And I was fairly certain that wasn't due to etiquette, either.

As we passed through the streets, a second squad of city guards gradually formed behind us now as they were released their posts. A few minutes later, we left the market and marched through the gates into the courtyard of the city's main structure. Our two squads of Spearmen moved to the left while our two squads of Archers moved to the right and the four squad leaders into the middle. And the two squads of city guards stopping outside the gates now.

The Administration building was just an old fortress with its stone walls plastered over and a small fountain and garden added here on the east end of the courtyard to make it look a little less formidable. And I noticed that once we were all inside the courtyard, Ajax finally released his grip on his sword.

From out of the keep doors now strolled the largest, or should I say portliest Attean we'd seen so far here. Smartly dressed in brightly colored clothes, he was obviously the mayor or chief magistrate of Medina. And he was followed by the smallest Attean we'd seen so far, wearing a plain, dark grey tunic. The latter I assumed was some sort of secretary or scribe, as he was holding a clipboard and had an ink quill in his hand now as he tried to keep up with the mayor's longer strides.

Walking down the steps and through the center of the garden, the mayor smiled and held up his huge mitt now as he warmly said, "Welcome back my old friend, and hello to you too, Captain Ajax! I hope all is well?" Lowering his hood, Nestor stepped forward now extending his hand out to meet the mayor's enormous mitt. Ajax just grinned and saluted the mayor now nodding his head. At the same time the two squads of city guards began moving in through the gates now taking up position behind Ajax's squads. But turning to face the open gates now before coming to a stop.

Taking the mayor's hand in open friendship, Nestor kept hold of it now while he leaned in and whispered into the mayor's ear for nearly a minute. The smile disappearing from the mayor's face now as Nestor let loose his hand. The mayor immediately raised his hand signaling for the two officers of the city guard to come forward now and join him. The older, senior officer was the same one who had exchanged handshakes with Ajax outside the city gates and had been watching for the mayor's signal. The two officers quickly moving forward now joining the group. And after the officers saluted the mayor, Nestor, and Captain Ajax again, The mayor put his large hand on the senior officer's shoulder and whispered something into his ear. And nodding to the mayor first, the senior officer turned to his subordinate and whispered something to him in Attean. After which, the junior officer immediately slapped hand to his chest and nodded his head, then wheeled and strode towards Ajax's squad leaders.

Then the senior officer turned to face Amy and Sandra now, and bowing to them first, said in English, "Ladies, I am Captain Erastus, Commander of the Medina city guard. I am sure that you are both probably tired and hungry now. If you would follow me, please?" And holding his arm out now, Captain Erastus gestured for the ladies to enter the keep. Then turning to me, he added, "Archer Andreas, you are to come with us too."

Slapped my hand to my chest, I nodded to Captain Erastus before following the three of them up the stairs and through the large open doors into the main hall of the keep. The main hall was well lit, and Captain Erastus led the way around the left side of the open banquet area to a wide set of stone stairs leading up to the second floor. Then turning left, Erastus led us north down the hallway towards a large carved wood door with guards posted in front of it. And seeing Captain Erastus approaching, the guard on the left stepped forward now and opened the door for us as we drew near.

And the four of us entered what was a surprisingly large room with a large elaborate wood desk on the left side of the room in front of two tall stained-glass windows on the north side behind it. There were two padded chairs in front of what must be the mayor's desk, and a large comfortable couch and coffee table on the far side of the mayor's desk. And there were two smaller plain desks against the south wall now. Large colorful tapestries hung down covering the east wall separated in the middle by the standard crossed spears and seahorse shield of Attea in the middle of the wall. This was the mayor's office, judging by the large desk and fancy furnishings here.

And stopping just inside the entrance, I assumed a guarding position by the door now while Captain Erastus and the ladies continued into the office. Then turning around, Captain Erastus said in English, "Ladies, Mayor Agafya asked that you please make yourselves comfortable until he arrives." And lowering her hood now, Sandra answered him in English, saying, "Thank you Captain. I am sure we will be fine here until my father, and the mayor join us." I saw Captain Erastus's eyebrows shoot up now as he realized he was speaking to Nestor's daughter. Also, I could tell Erastus was a little suspicious now that neither Amy nor I had lowered our hoods when Sandra did. Sensing this too, Sandra spoke up now adding, "Captain Erastus, you will have to speak with my father or Captain Ajax as to the nature of our mission. We are not permitted to speak of it." And understanding, Captain Erastus gave Sandra a salute and quick nod, before turning and starting for the door. But he gave Amy's and my hooded faces another quick glance before exiting the room.

Amy started to reach for her hood, but Sandra stopped her mid-swing now, saying, "It's safer to wait for my father before showing your faces, your majesties. I know that father and Mayor Agafya are old friends, but I don't know or trust anyone else here yet. We'll have wait for Captain Ajax, he knows them all." And Amy and I both nodded in agreement as Sandra led Amy over to the couch and sat down now. I was content to stand here by the door and keep up my pretense of guarding them.

We didn't have to wait long. Five minutes later the door opened again. And in walked Mayor Agafya, followed by Nestor, Ajax, Captain Erastus, Agafya's scribe, and four women carrying platters of food and drinks now. The little scribe set his clipboard down on the first desk now before instructing the serving women to set their trays down on the other desk. Then, he ushered the serving women back out of the room and closed the door behind them.

Nestor turned to me now and bowed before saying, "You can remove your hood now your majesty, you are amongst friends." Reaching up now, I slid my hood back from my face and watched as Mayor Agafya's, Captain Erastus's, and the little scribe's faces all went blank now and their mouths dropped open. And Sandra bowed to me now while Ajax just smiled snapping me a salute.

Mayor Agafya, Captain Erastus, and the scribe just stood there now with mouths agape, too stunned to move or speak. After a few seconds, Agafya and the scribe each dropped to one knee in a formal bow, while Captain Erastus, who was smiling now, slapped his hand to his chest and bowed his head.

Then Nestor turned to Amy and bowing again, said, "Your majesty?" And Amy stood up now and slid her hood back revealing her face. And I think the air pressure actually dropped in the room as all the three men turned and gasped at Amy now before bowing and saluting again.

After a several seconds the three men failed to move. And I turned to Nestor now and said, "Nestor, you know how Amy and I feel about the bowing thing. Could you please ask your friends to rise?" And Nestor turned to face Agafya, but all three men understood English and rose now without Nestor having to translate. Walking forward now, I held out my hand to Mayor Agafya first. And the enormous man hesitating for a second before taking my hand in greeting, then bowed again after I released his hand. Then I moved to Captain Erastus and held out my hand to him. And he took it without hesitation, a large smile still on his face now, as he said, "It's a great honor to meet you, your majesty!" And after releasing his hand, I saluted Captain Erastus, and he returned my salute.

Then turning to the small elderly scribe now, I held my hand out to him. And I thought for a moment the poor little man was going to pass out, but he took my hand gingerly now, and I asked him, "We have not been introduced yet. What is your name?"

Again, the little man looked like he was going to pass out or expire, but he managed to reply, "Zoe, your majesty," in surprisingly good English. And smiling at this shy little wisp of a man now, I could tell immediately I was going to like Zoe.

Hoping to break the awkward silence now and snap everyone from out of their awestruck dazes, I turned to the Amy and boldly said, "I don't know about you my love, but I am hungry!"

And it was Agafya who snapped out of his trance first, bowing again and saying, "Forgive us our rudeness, your majesties. But seeing your majesties now is like a sudden blinding ray of light after spending months in the bottom of a dark pit. Zoe, please make sure that their majesties have whatever they wish to eat and drink." Then turning to face the Captain Erastus, Agafya said, "Double the guard on my door, and make sure no one enters this room without my permission? Then return when this is accomplished, Captain." Nodding first, Erastus saluted Mayor Agafya acknowledging the order now. Then turning right, Erastus saluted Amy salute before turning and saluting me again. And after I had returned his salute, Erastus turned and strode back out of the door.

Walking over to Zoe's desk, I grabbed a couple of silver plates from off the desk and moving to the couch handed a plate to Amy now and pausing to give Amy a peck on the cheek as I did it. Everyone watching us in fascination now, but it had been days since Amy and I had been able to be together, so let them stare. Zoe brought me another plate, and Sandra got up now and gestured for me to sit down next to Amy. Then Zoe kept busy, bringing each of the trays over and holding it for us to make our choices. Then he brought wine glasses over and asked if we preferred water or wine. Amy and I both choose wine now. After which, Zoe went back to his desk and sat down on the edge of the chair, watching us eat and waiting for any other requests.

Agafya was all smiles, and bowing to Amy and me again, he said, "Please excuse us for a moment, your Majesties." Then turning to Nestor, Agafya indicated the chairs in front of his desk, before saying, "Please sit Nestor, you too Captain Ajax. And tell me please dear friend, how in the name of Attean did you ever manage to find the King, and how that is even possible?" Nestor and Ajax did as they were bid and sat down in the chairs. Then Nestor turned to look at Amy and me again, like he needed our permission. And grinning, I waved my hand at Nestor now for him to go ahead, my mouth full of the delicious food they had brought.

Nodding his head, Nestor turned to Agafya again who was sitting on the edge of his fancy desk now, his chair apparently too far away for this story. And Nestor began in English, whether out of politeness or added secrecy, I don't which? Of Telemus's urgent message to Queen requesting she meet with him in secret as soon as possible. The urgency being no surprise. Since Nestor was the Telemus's physician and had been keeping the Queen Hera updated on Telemus's failing health. So, they had gone to visit Telemus with Queen Hera and Captain Pylos disguised in the white robes of physicians. However, Telemus insisted on speaking to Queen Hera alone and in private. Upon their return to the palace, the Queen Hera told Nestor of

Telemus's odd instructions, and of his refusal to tell her why, other than to say that the fate of all Attean was at stake.

Because of the nature of the task. Queen Hera assigned Nestor this task, wanting her best physician and someone she trusted there during the rescue. Then Nestor related how everything had happened exactly as Telemus foretold, and of Captain Theron's rescue of Amy and me. And their utter astonishment when the bio-suit produced their true King, and Queen. And that Nestor believes now that I am the great-grandson of Princess Helena and the sea captain.

Agafya sat quiet for a minute absorbing all this, then suddenly he stood up with a huge smile on his face as he turned to Amy and me now and bowed again before saying, "Welcome to Attea, your majesties. It is our great honor and joy to meet your majesties!"

Nodding to Agafya, I replied, "Okay. And it is our honor to meet you as well. But first, you need to stop bowing to Amy and me. or you will give away our disguises. And that goes for you too Zoe, understand?" Suddenly, I felt Amy's elbow me in the ribs, and saw Sandra turn her face away now so the others wouldn't see her stifling a chuckle. Oh, I had this down pat, and there was no way for them to argue the need for secrecy now, and I knew it. And I thought I caught a faint hint of a smile on Nestor's and Ajax's faces now too.

Between the full day's march and the wonderful food and wine Agafya had served us, Amy was pretty much done for the day. And we all took note of her eyes fluttering shut and her head slowly rolling back onto the couch now. Amy snapped back awake and righting herself once her head touched the couch. Then Amy smiled shyly, slightly embarrassed. But it wasn't long before her eyes started to droop, and her head started its journey back to the couch again. This time a loud knock on the door snapped Amy awake again, and we heard a voice say, "Captain Erastus sir!"

And Mayor Agfya spoke up now, replying, "Enter."

Stepping into the room, Captain Erastus had his helmet under his left arm as he turned around making sure the door was closed. Then turning to face Amy and me now, Erastus saluted us before moving forward to stand at Mayor Agafya's side. And it was Nestor who spoke up now, saying, "I think Sandra and I should make a big show of taking the guestroom tonight. But their majesties should stay here in the vault tonight. What do you think, my friend?"

Smiling at Nestor, Agafya nodded his head now replying, "That's a very good idea, my friend. I agree." And Agafya walked past Amy and me on the couch to the weapons display between the two tapestries on the east wall now. Then Agafya suddenly pressed one of the stones to the left of the shield, and there was a faint audible click followed by a low grating noise. And lifting the tapestry on the left now, Agafya revealed a section of the stone wall had opened. And pushing on the section of wall now, Agafya slid the door to the secret room open fully, before turning back to us and asking, "If you would follow me now please, your majesties." Amy and I both rose from the couch now and followed Agafya into his secret room.

Agafya quickly moved around the room turning the torch shaped lights mounted on the walls on. And once all the lights were lit, I could see the room clearly. There were two small beds against the east wall, bookshelves covering the north wall, a round table with five chairs in the center, and a padded chaise against the south wall. Nestor and Sandra following us into Agafya's "Vault" now. And Zoe began transferring a portion of the food and wine from the platters in Agafya's office into the vault now, setting them down on the round table before returning for another load. The lights all lit now, Agafya turned around and bowed to us again before saying, "I am sorry this room isn't nicer. We use it for playing the occasional game of 'Heads and Tails,' and storage mostly, your majesties."

Chuckling now, Nestor added, "And hiding from Basilia when she's angry!"

Hanging his head in defeat now, Agafya replied, "And yes, hiding from my lovely wife Basilia when necessary." And a small giggle escaping from Amy and Sandra now after Agfya's confession.

Turning to Agafya now, I said, "I've been sleeping on the ground, and Amy has been sleeping in a cot for the last two nights. So don't worry about us Agafya, we'll be fine in here."

Agafya nodded again, then said, "If I may, let show your majesty how to re-open the door." And he gestured to a matching set of Attean spears and shield mounted on the west wall inside the vault. Agafya moved over next to them, and I watched now as he pressed the stone directly to the left of the shield's center. And it slid in about two inches before stopping, then there was the same mechanical clicking noise as the secret door unlocked again. Resting my hand lightly on the mayor's shoulder now, I said, "Okay, got it."

Zoe was a cunning old man, and I noticed he piled the food into two bowls now, leaving the rest of the bowls, platters, and cups outside on the table so the servants wouldn't notice the missing items and become curious. They all backed up to the secret door stone and bowed once more before Agafya said, "Goodnight your majesties, and again let me say again how delighted we are to have meet you both!"

Then Zoe, Sandra, and Agafya turned and stepped back outside, and only Nestor remained behind. And bowing again, Nestor asked, "Is everything okay, your majesty?" And I nodded that it was, and Nestor smiled at us before turning and pulled the heavy stone door shut behind him now.

And turning to look at Amy now, she had already moved to the bed on the left and was turning the covers to check the bed out. I worried for a moment that this room might be airtight, but then I saw there was a large steel grate at the top of the bookshelves on the north wall. And looking down, I saw another large grate in the floor at the base of the bookshelves, so obviously they taken care of that issue. Then I wondered how far our voices would travel through those grates now, but I guessed they had probably thought of that too.

The bed must have been satisfactory, because Amy had taken a pillow off the bed on the right, then laid her medical pouch and robe down on the bed before scooting over on the left side of the bed now making room for me. Taking off my quiver, robe, and belt now, I laid them on the bed next to Amy's robe and pouch along with my bow. My Archer's cuirass was a little more difficult to remove and it took a few moments, but I finally got that off and climbed into the bed with Amy. It was a little cramped, but that's what we had been missing for the last two days. I was about to ask Amy if she learned how to make love in these bio-suits from Sandra. But when I looked down, Amy was already sound asleep. Not that I blamed her, it had been a long day, topped off with Agafya's wonderful food, wine, and a chance to sleep in a real bed now. I was tired too, and it wasn't long before I joined Amy in sleeping.

Suddenly, I awoke several hours later. It was quiet, but I sensed something wasn't quite right. Amy was sleeping comfortably on my chest, the room was still lit now and looked exactly as I remembered it before I nodded off. So, I lay there for a moment listening and watching the room. Then I heard it, someone was outside in Agafya's office trying to force the stone door open now.

Gently waking Amy up, I held a finger up to my lips as she opened her eyes. Amy instantly alerted now by the look on my face. Then pointing to the door, I slid out of bed and got up. And picking up the cuirass, I quickly slid it back on before putting the quiver of arrows up over my shoulder. Then I slid the long dagger out of its sheath and flipped it over, I handed it to Amy hilt first now as she slid over and got out of bed. And pointing to the area behind the stone door now, Amy nodded her head she understood and quietly crossed the room to the wall behind where the secret door opened. And picking up my bow now, I pulled one of the long steel-tipped arrows out of the quiver. Then kneeling down between the two beds facing the door, I notched the arrow now. Amy and I could clearly hear the person, or people on the other side throwing their weight against the door now But the stone door didn't budge. They must have been afraid of alerting the whole fortress to use any tools on the stone door now. And after what seemed like fifteen minutes of throwing their weight against the vault door. They either gave up or were busy trying to figure out some other way to open the door now.

Lowering my bow, I moved the stone door and began inspecting it. And I was relieved to find the secret door still flush with the wall now. So, all their efforts have been futile so far. And whispering to Amy now, I said, "The door is holding. There's nothing we can do but wait, so you might as well go back to bed and try and get some sleep now. But keep the dagger with you. I'll stand guard until Nestor and Ajax arrive."

Smiling at me, Amy moved over and gave me a kiss now before replying, "I don't think I can go back to sleep. But I am tired Andrew, and I will go lay down again." And climbing back into bed, Amy looked at the dagger for a second before sliding under her pillow and laying down facing me now. And taking one of the chairs from the table, I moved it between the two beds. Then sitting down, I set the bow on the other bed within easy reach.

Twenty minutes later, I heard Amy's rhythmic breathing as she had fallen asleep again. Getting up, I poured myself a cup of water and grabbed a large bunch of grapes from off the table. I could have really used a pot of tsai and some caffeine right now but settled for the sugar in the grapes. There was no way to gauge the passing of time here in the vault. But I guessed it was around two hours later when I heard the first alarm horn sound, then quickly echo throughout the fortress. Then, I heard the faint shouting of men and the commotion outside as the entire fortress woke up now.

I was a little groggy when I heard the door unlock and the grating noise, but I managed to grab my bow and get into position before the door opened. And I recognized Nestor's worried voice now, as he asked, "Your majesties, are you okay?" Then there was a short pause before he added, "May we come in?" Amy was awake and standing next to me with the formidable dagger in her hand now.

Rubbing her eyes with her free hand, Amy nodded to me that she was ready. So, I answered Nestor now, saying, "Come in Nestor, we're awake." I saw the shocked look on their faces as they entered the room and saw Amy's and my defensive stance between the beds on the east wall now. And once I was sure it was just Nestor, Sandra, and Zoe, I lowered my bow. Nestor and Sandra were shocked and stood there unable to speak. But I spoke to Zoe now, asking, "Zoe, would you please go find Captain Ajax now and tell him I would like to speak to him at his earliest convenance?"

The old man bowed before replying, "Yes, immediately, your majesty!" Then Zoe disappeared back out the door. And Sandra moved around Nestor's still frozen form over to Amy's side now almost like it was instinctive. And sensing the danger was over, Amy shoved the dagger back into its sheath at my waist now before turning to accept Sandra's embrace.

After Sandra reached Amy, Nestor snapped out of his trance, and said, "The guards were at their post outside Agafya's office, and we assumed everything was going as it should. I am extremely sorry your majesties and wish to apologize formally to you both now for mine, and our blatant failure." Then Nestor bowed formerly and remained that way now waiting for me to speak.

With a slight edge in my voice now, I replied, "Stand up and quit acting silly Nestor, it's annoying!" And he stood back up looking at me in surprise now as I added, "I don't hold you responsible in any way. But there are two things we know for certain now. One is that the news of Amy's and my existence has reached Helios. And two, it's obvious that we have a spy or spies, either here among Agafya's staff or among Ajax's troops!" Nestor seemed to relax for a second then he tensed back up as my words sank in. I could hear Zoe's heavy breathing before he even reached the vault door, and he paused outside, before asking, "It's Zoe your majesty, may I enter?"

Answering him now, I said, "Come in, Zoe."

The old man entered the room now and bowed before saying, "I have notified Captain Ajax of your request, your majesty. And he will be here directly." Then pausing to catch his breath, Zoe added, "And I spoke with the guards at the door, and they said the night guards were gone when they arrived this morning. They thought it was odd and reported it, though they just figured the night guards were lazy and left their post a little early. And they are searching for the guards now, your majesty."

Then we heard the outer door open and heavy footsteps approaching, which must be Ajax. And I heard the all too familiar sound of a hand slapping a cuirass, as Ajax's said, "It's Captain Ajax your majesty, may I enter?"

And I was tempted to say cousin, but thought better of it since Zoe was here, and replied, "Yes of course captain, enter."

Ajax strode into the room now, helmet in hand, and saluted us again before saying, "Good morning your majesties. I am sorry for what happened, and I am ashamed of my failure now to properly protect your majesties. I won't make that mistake again, your majesty." I could see Ajax was completely in earnest and looked really pissed about what had happened. And had to grin now thinking oh man, I wouldn't want to be on the receiving end of that anger!

Seeing the look of confusion come across my cousin's face as he saw me grinning at him now. I replied, "You both need to relax. Your decision to put us here in the vault last night was completely correct. If we had been in the guestroom with Nestor and Sandra last night, we probably wouldn't be having this conversation right now! I don't know how many men there were outside the door last night, but they tried for quite some time to open it and couldn't. I think they were too worried about making noise to use any tools on the door, so they finally gave up."

Suddenly, we heard loud voices in the outer room now, the angriest of which was Mayor Agafya's. It was at this moment that Zoe bowed, and said, "If I may, your majesties. You should both put your robes on and your hoods up now. As the servants will be arriving soon with breakfast." And Zoe remained bowed now waiting for my answer.

Turning to look at Zoe now, I replied, "Thank you, Zoe. You right to warn us now." Amy released Sandra's arms and reached for her robe and medical pouch now, while I took my quiver off, and dawned my Archers robe again.

Nestor spoke up now, saying, "If your majesties are ready, I suggest we move out into the office and close the vault before the servants get here too." I nodded to Nestor, and then we all filed back out into the mayor's Agafya's office now in no particular order. Bringing up the rear, Zoe paused to make sure the vault door was closed, the tapestry was back in place, and all smoothed out again.

Bright light flooded into Agafya's office now through the stained-glass windows behind his desk. And Captain Erastus was standing in front of Agafya, his head bowed holding a salute, his face looking like he had just been on the receiving end of an unpleasant butt chewing from the mayor now. And both men turned to look at Army and me now as we entered the room before turning to bow. Agafya's looked like he was getting ready to start apologizing, but I raised my hand up stopping him now before he could speak, and said, "Don't apologize Mayor Agafya, or you either Captain Erastus. There was no way you could have known. And your decision to put us in the vault last night saved our lives, and possibly those of the Senior Physician and his daughter."

A small wave of relief passed across Agafya's face now, as he replied, "Thank you your majesty, though I am disappointed in our security here now."

Captain Erastus spoke up next, saying, "We found the four guards dead a storage room. Apparently, they were poisoned, your majesty."

Nodding in acknowledging to both announcements, I turned to Captain Erastus now and said, "I am sorry about your men, Captain." And he saluted and nodded again in acknowledgement now.

Then there was a knock on the door, and we all moved now to our various locations for appearance's sake. I picked up my bow and moved over by the door, as Amy and Sandra sat down on the couch, and Zoe moved back to his desk. Ajax and Nestor dropped into the two chairs in front of Agafya's desk. And Captain Erastus bent over Agafya's desk now like they were busy discussing something. After taking a quick look around the room, Agafya proclaimed, "Enter." And the door opened as four serving women entered followed by two city guards now. The servants seemed nervous, whether from the news of the four murdered guards last night or the unusual security now, I couldn't say. But they came in, bowed to Agafya and Nestor, then set the trays of food down on Zoe's desks before bowing again and quickly leaving the room followed by the guards.

Zoe stood up and bowed now, asking, "What would your majesties like first?" Amy and I both replied, "tsai," at the same time, then chuckled. Zoe poured a cup of tsia then started towards me, but I winked at him and tilted my head indicating he should serve Amy first. Zoe grinned and nodded his head now as he changed direction without spilling a drop of the hot tsai.

The façade over now, Ajax rose and saluted me before saying, "I suggest we get moving again as soon as you finish breakfast, your majesty. I would feel better a whole lot about your safety out in the open where I can see which direction the danger is coming from!" I was expecting Captain Erastus and Mayor Agafya to react, but they both nodded in agreement with Ajax's suggestion. And I looked at Amy to see if she was ready to move. She saw me looking at her now and nodded her head over her cup of tsia. So, I answered, "Okay, whenever you're ready, Ajax."

Saluting again as he responded, Ajax said, "Thank you, your majesty. I will make all the necessary preparations while you finish your breakfast. Then I will return to escort you personally, your majesties." Then turning to Captain Erastus, Ajax said, "Can you have your Store Master stand by to fill any last-minute requests from our cooks, my friend." Erastus nodded to Ajax now and they both turned to salute Amy and me again before striding out of the room.

Moving away from the door, I walked over and sat down on top of Zoe's desk and grabbed a plate before putting some flatbread, olives, and white cheese on it now. We needed to be ready to go when Ajax returned. Zoe started to object to me serving myself, but I whispered, "See to ladies, Zoe. I can feed myself and it won't appear odd if someone walks in, okay?" Zoe gave me a dry little smile now before nodding his head and taking the first tray of food over to Amy and Sandra on the couch.

And as I ate my breakfast, Agafya and Nestor conversed back and forth over tsai. And I caught bits of their conversation in between mouthfuls. As they quickly discussed Queen Hera's health, the problems Agafya had here in Medina, and the increasing number of Wild One raids on the surrounding villages. I guess Nestor would be expected to give a full report to the Consul of Elders when we reached the palace in Attea. Twenty minutes later we heard a knock on the door, and Ajax requesting permission to enter. Rising now, Agafya gave me time to resume my post by the door before giving Ajax permission to enter. Ajax entered now with one of his squad leaders. I stood by the door as they walked past me and Ajax saluted Nestor and Agafya before informing Nestor that we was ready to move out now.

Chapter - 4

Nestor stood up and said, "It's time for us to go, old friend."

And moving to the right of the mayor's desk now, Nestor and Agafya exchanged the two-handed clasp of friendship, and Agafya said, "Goodbye my friend." Then stepping back, the two men nodded to each other, and Nestor turned for the door. Ajax saluted and nodded to Agafya before turning and moving into the lead now. Sandra and Amy were next in line. And after they exchanged nods, I gave Agafya a quick salute and nodded before turning to follow the ladies. Ajax's squad leader must have been instructed to bring up the rear, because he waited for me to leave before saluting Agafya and falling in behind me.

Slinging my bow over my shoulder, I followed the ladies down the hallway to the top of the stairs. And looking down into the main hall now, I was surprised to see a variety of activities going on down below. There were clerks set up in various locations around the room, and dozens of what must be farmers, merchants, and shop owners standing in line talking or conversing with the clerks. It was quite a colorful scene, as there were a variety of different colored bio-suits and attire here in the great hall now. Rather than just the standard green and brown bio-suits of the soldiers. We went down the stairs and skirted the scroll laden tables before passing out the keep doors.

It was bright outside, and Ajax paused for a moment in the shade of the entrance here to let his eyes adjust before continuing down the steps into the courtyard. Ajax's four squads were lined up facing us now. And behind them was Captain Erastus and his two squads of red cloaked city guards. It seemed a bit conspicuous to me, but maybe not so much after the murder of the four guards last night. Ajax's other three squad leaders and Captain Erastus's lieutenant, whose name I never got, were waiting for Ajax at the bottom of the stairs now.

The six men exchanged salutes, then Ajax spent a minute doing a quick inspection his men before giving the order to move out. And the lieutenant wheeled around and took off at a fast jog for Captain Erastus now. And I watched as the lieutenant saluted Erastus and reported that Ajax was ready to move out now. Erastus moved to the front of the first squad of city guards before ordering them to face right and march out the gates. The four of us followed Ajax now as he walked through the small garden and into the space of the between his four squads of soldiers. As Erastus's lieutenant and the second squad of city guards marched out the gates. Then the first squad of Ajax's Spearmen on the left, did an about-face and marched out, followed by the first squad of Archers on the right. And Ajax lead the us through the gates now with the third and fourth squads following behind.

Once we were outside the gates, Ajax paused for a moment to let our supply carts move up behind us. Then Ajax began walking down the slope into the center of the city again. I could see Erastus's men up ahead clearing the path for us. Reaching the end of market street, we turned right now heading for the North Gates. Captain Erastus's two squads parting to the left and right as we reached the gates. Though I could see Erastus and his lieutenant standing outside the gates now waiting for Ajax.

Ajax stepping out of the line as we cleared the gates to speak with Erastus as we marched past. I noticed the squad leaders had saluted Erastus as they passed him, so following suit now, slapping my hand to my chest and giving Erastus a quick nod as I passed him. Erastus's face was blank but there was a genuine smile in his eyes now as he returned my salute. I didn't need to look back to know what was transpiring behind me as the two men bid each other farewell. And a few moments later Ajax came jogging back up and resumed his usual place beside Nestor.

As the day wore on, it seemed to be getting warmer than I remember on the south side of Medina. And though the road was well-worn here, it was slightly wider and in better condition. That, and there were wood and stone bridges over the gullies and the wet spots now. Which the archers had previously had to help our supply carts through on the south side of Medina. I started to notice a change in what the farmers were growing here too. There were more citrus and olive trees here than apple and pear trees. And there were fewer green vegetables out in the fields now and more wheat. I asked Nestor about this during lunch break, and he confirmed that it was indeed warmer, and would continue to get warmer the closer we got to the Caves of Hephaestus.

After lunch, a caravan of twelve wagons passed us. The soldiers quickly formed a single file on either side of the road letting the wagons pass through and doing it with the speed of practice. The soldiers and wagon drivers teasing each other as they passed. Nestor told me later that the soldiers were telling the drivers they were going the wrong way. And the drivers teased the soldiers right back. Saying they may be going the wrong way, but at least we're not walking!

The light at the top of the cavern had started to dim before tonight's camp appeared ahead. And we reached the camp about 30 minutes later. And after everyone was inside and the tents pitched, Ajax ordered me to wait for him inside his tent now rather than following Nestor and the ladies to their tent. Saluting Ajax, I did as was ordered and took up a guarding position inside Ajax's tent while I waited. A few minutes later, I heard Ajax outside giving instructions to his squad leaders. Then the tent flap opened, and Ajax walked in and dropped his helmet on the table before turning around to face me.

And giving the tent flap another quick check, Ajax quietly said, "Captain Erastus used to be in the palace guard. And since you two are about the same size, he had something he thought you should have, and I agreed with him." And reaching under the table now, Ajax pulled out a large canvas bag with drawstring and opened it. Then he removed a black metal cuirass with a four-inch gold seahorse on the chest. The new cuirass was the body-hugging type. And had a fine fish scale pattern over the top of the entire surface. Then Ajax added, "This metal is much stronger and lighter than your outworld metals, and unlike that leather cuirass you're wearing, this cuirass will stop all arrows, spears, and swords."

And I replied, "It's wonderful, but won't it draw attention to me?" As I accepted the black cuirass from Ajax's hand now and realized that this new cuirass actually weighed less than the leather cuirass I was wearing now.

Smiling now, Ajax replied, "Yes. And my squad leaders have reported that there is a lot of gossip and speculation amongst the men as to why you are constantly with Nestor and the ladies, and that no one has actually seen your face yet." Then pausing for a second, Ajax continued adding, "This will dispel all the gossip. Once someone sees that gold seahorse and black cuirass, they'll conclude that Queen Hera assigned you to protect the Senior Physician. And that's why you are always guarding Nestor and the ladies." And grinning wickedly now, Ajax added, "Maybe you could leave your robe open enough so that the cooks get a good look at your armor when they bring supper tonight?" And a big smile spread across Ajax's face after he said it.

Grinning at Ajax, I quickly removed my quiver, robe and belt now to make the swap. And Ajax moved to the tent flap to make sure no one entered while I was changing. Pulling the leather cuirass off, I slid the black metal cuirass over my head, then Ajax stepped forward to help me get straps buckled. And once I had the new cuirass buckled on and secured, I donned my Archer's robe and raised the hood again, as Ajax circled me now making sure everything looked correct again.

Finished now, Ajax stuffed the leather cuirass into the canvas bag and tied it shut again. Then standing up, Ajax pointed towards Nestor's tent and loudly said in Attean, "Andreus, return to guarding Nestor!" And slapping my hand to my chest, I nodded my head and wheeled around leaving the tent.

Once I was outside, I turned right and walked directly over to Nestor's tent. There were two guards stationed outside Nestor's tent now. And nodding head to the guards, I announced myself now, saying, "Ἀνδρέας, Κύριε." Or "Andreus sir," in Attean.

And Nestor responded, "εἰσέρχομαι." Or "enter," in Attean The guard on the left lifted the tent flap now and I stepped into the tent. Nestor, Sandra, and Amy were seated at the table having some wine when I entered. And I could tell they were all curious why Ajax had ordered me into his tent after our arrival. So, I opened the front of my robe now and showed them my new cuirass. Nestor and Sandra both immediately smiled upon seeing the black cuirass and golden seahorse of the palace guard. Amy just looked confused until Sandra leaned over and whispered into her ear, then Amy smiled too. And speaking quietly now, I said, "A gift from Captain Erastus."

Nodding his head now, Nestor replied, "Very clever, and almost impenetrable too. I think Captain Erastus's has also shown you where his loyalty lies too, Andreus." About then we heard one of the cooks clear his throat outside. And one of the guards outside spoke briefly, saying that the cooks were here with our supper now.

Leaving my robe open sufficiently now, Nestor gave me a couple of seconds to get into position by the door again before giving the cooks permission to enter. This time after the cooks set the food down on the table and turned to leave. They both got a good look at the gold seahorse and the black cuirass of the palace guard. And I saw them freeze for an instant their mouths agape as they recognized my cuirass and almost fell over each other now trying to get out of the tent. After the cooks had gone, Nestor poured me a cup of wine as I sat down next to Amy to eat dinner now. And Amy leaned over and whispered, "You're s-o-o bad!" Chuckling, I picked up Amy's hand now and kissed it, which made Amy smile. While Nestor and Sandra seemed embarrassed now and both quickly looked down at their plates pretending to be busy with their food.

Dinner was a disappointment after the delicious food Agafya had served us, but considering the circumstances it could have been worse. I hadn't seen what the soldiers were eating, but I am guessing it wasn't as nice as what Nestor and Captain Ajax were served. I noticed my bedroll was by the door again. And it wasn't long before we agreed it was time for bed.

It was Ajax's voice again the next morning that woke us, with his usual greeting and Ajax asking Nestor if everything was satisfactory. After breakfast, we went outside, and I noticed the soldier's attitude towards me had changed completely. Now instead of sneaking sideways glances at me, they all looked directly at me and nodded their heads. Of course, I had to acknowledge and return their nods. And by the time we formed up and got underway again, I knew what a bobblehead on a car dash felt like now.

When we stopped for lunch, Nestor told me that one of Ajax's squad leaders had asked Ajax why he hadn't just told them I was a royal guard in disguise assigned to protect the Senior Physician. And Ajax chewed the man out. Saying because when he received his orders from Queen Hera, she hadn't mentioned his name! I bet that squad leader felt like a complete fool. Nestor and I both had a chuckle now imagining the squad leader's face during that ass chewing.

The rest of the day passed without incident, as the road continued to wind along the base of the western slope. We had citrus trees on both sides of us now, as the orchards didn't go as high on the hillside here, and there were half a dozen rows of trees growing on the valley floor to our right now. The farmers growing wheat mostly here at the north end of the cavern. Ajax had several pairs of Archers out in the Orchards now flanking us as we continued north.

When we reached the camp that evening, I could tell everyone in camp had heard the news now. As the whispering around the campfires had ceased. And even though they were speaking in Attean, I could tell the conversations had moved back to normal topics now. Even the cooks seemed more relaxed. After setting dinner on the table, both cooks gave me a quick nod on their way out of the tent.

The next morning after we started out, I noticed Ajax had changed our formation. Now there were two rows of Spearmen in front of us and two behind us here in the center. Nestor said Ajax was worried about an ambush now from the hillside or possibly from out in the orchard on our right. Apparently, there had been someone up in the rocks watching us this morning, and whoever they were, they were following our progress now. The twenty Spearmen had been repositioned to shield us in the event of an attack. Ajax also doubled the number of flankers out around us now. Shortly after lunch, we got back on the move again and there was a rockslide on the hill above us. And Ajax called a halt for several minutes before resuming our march again.

We reached camp just before dark, but things were different tonight. There was less talk around the campfires. The soldiers were busy now either checking their gear or gathering around at one of the large stones in the compound sharpening their spears, swords, and arrow tips. These were the Ajax's best men, each one a battle tested veteran, and they sensed something was coming now.

Ajax stopped by our tent after supper to tell us what he expected would happen tomorrow. Saying the Wild Ones would probably try a few random ambushes from the hillside tomorrow. But they wouldn't try an open-field attack or storming the encampment, as they knew they would get slaughtered. But Ajax feared that the runners he had sent out before we left Outpost Ares had all been killed now. Since they should have returned last night or early this morning at the latest. Each set of runners carrying a sealed scroll requesting support from the palace in Attea, and from Outpost Apollo in the West Cavern, minus the specifics. But telling them both to meet Ajax's men at the encampment outside the Caves of Hephaestus in the South Cavern, which we would reach tomorrow. Ajax was planning to stay there a second night if necessary, to give support time to reach us in case his runners had managed to get through. But on the third day, with or without support, we would be going through the Caves of Hephaestus.

And Ajax was right, the next morning after we rounded a small finger ridge, we were met with a shower of arrows raining down from the hillside above. The Spearmen instantly forming a defensive square or phalanx around us, like a Roman "Testudo" or "turtle" until the arrows stopped falling.

Unfortunately for our attackers, they hadn't planned their escape well. As there was only two routes off the hillside, north, or south. And Ajax's Archers were waiting in both locations when they broke and fled. None of which escaped alive, and the Archer's dragged one of the bodies back for Ajax's examination. The Wild One looked like a normal man in his mid-forties with furs across his chest, and a crude leather and bone helmet on his head. There was no bio-suit on the body. But Nestor told me later that once a person dies, his bio-suit leaves and makes its own way back to the vault in Attea where the empty containers are stored. And that the Wild One's bio-suits are normally dark gray except for the two thick white stripes across their chest and forehead, which accounted for the helmet and furs now.

After the attack was over, we took a short break while Nestor, Sandra, and Amy made the rounds attending to the soldiers who had taken arrows during the ambush. The bio-suits stopped you from bleeding out externally, but not internally. Luckily, all the wounds were flesh wounds on the exposed areas, so none of them were serious. Nestor and Sandra quickly patched up the wounded and had them either loaded into the carts or back in formation in a few minutes. And we were on our way again.

Ajax's flankers spotted the next ambush before we reached it. But one of the Archers took an arrow to the back when he stood up to shoot the shrieking alarm arrow. Ajax's men immediately formed three rectangular phalanxes, the two large one's front and rear, and our smaller one in the center. Nestor wanted to go out to the wounded soldier, but Ajax ordered him to remain here. As the soldiers quickly carried the wounded Archer to our smaller phalanx in the center.

Nestor quickly cut the protruding tip off the arrow with a tool from his medical bag. Then he coated the protruding shaft with two different medicines before taking hold of the thick wood shaft and yanked the arrow out while the other soldiers held the man. Amy and I watched in amazement now as the bio-suit immediately sealed both sides of the wound and stopped the bleeding.

Then, with the wounded man supported between two soldiers, and the cart drivers and cooks driving from the sheltered side of their carts, we slowly moved forward. With our phalanxes fully formed now, the Wild One's ambush looked like a gesture in futility, failing to injure even a single soldier as we moved past the ambush and out of their range again. And Ajax sent a two dozen archers up the hillside now to ambush any Wild Ones that attempted to follow us.

That was the last attack before we stopped for lunch. I left Amy with Sandra and dutifully followed Nestor now as he made his rounds of the injured. Nestor said the soldiers with leg wounds only needed to stay off their feet for 24 hours and by then the wound would have healed sufficiently for them to return to duty. The arm and flesh wounds only took half as long. Lunch finished, we reformed our ranks and started out again. And we could make out the rock wall at the north end of cavern now, visible through the shimmering heat waves ahead. The east and west slopes were steeper and closer together here at the north end of the cavern. As the whole cavern began tapering down to the Caves of Hephaestus. And the whole rock wall was stained a dark now, which must be due to the volcanic activity that Sandra had mentioned earlier.

While we were stopped for lunch, Ajax told us there was only one good ambush spot left between here and the encampment now. And we formed our phalanx's just before reaching the spot. Sure enough, another shower of arrows rained down on us from the hillside as we reached the spot. But once again it proved futile against our phalanxes. Ajax didn't bother sending out his Archers this time, as there was no way for the Wild Ones to follow us on the steep slope.

With the danger of ambushes behind us now, we spread back out and continued our march to the encampment. And it took just over an hour for us to make through the gates and into the camp.

I immediately noticed several differences in the compound here. First, this camp was slightly larger than the others we stayed in. And the black stone walls here were eight feet high, instead of six. The guard towers here were also higher and better protected. And the wood gates had steel reinforcements. Plus, there was a four-foot allure running around the inside of the walls for the soldiers to defend from. In the northeast corner, there was a small shack made of heavy wooden planks. And the roof was covered with the same black stone as the camps walls. I wondered now what the shack was for as I watched the soldiers pitching the tents.

I could sense the mood in camp was more serious tonight than it had been in the other camps. The men speaking briefly around the campfires. And I noted they all double-checked their equipment to make sure it was within easy reach before bedding down. Many of which I noted were sleeping with their swords in their hands now.

Ajax on the other hand, was just the opposite, he seemed more relaxed tonight than usual. Maybe because all the camp's preparations were completed quickly and correctly tonight, without Ajax having to scold or remind anyone.

It was an hour after dark, and we had just finished our dinner, when we heard Ajax announcing himself outside our tent. And getting a reply from Nestor, Ajax lifted the flap and stepped into our tent. Once the tent flap was closed, Ajax made a curt bow to Amy and me, then quietly said, "Grab your bed rolls and follow me, please." Surprised, I started to ask why, but Ajax held up his finger silencing me. And knowing Ajax had a good reason we all did as he asked now.

Once we had all our bedrolls in hand, Ajax turned the lantern off and held the tent flap open for us to make our way outside. This time the guards outside the tent didn't snap to attention when Ajax opened the flap. So, we knew something was up. And once we were all outside, Ajax led us over to the little shack in the northeast corner. Then stopping outside open door, Ajax gestured for us to enter. And then waiting until we were all inside, Ajax stepped in behind us and closed the door. It was pitch black in the room, and I heard Ajax fumbling with something on the table before he lit the lantern.

The room was about twelve-foot square, with bunk beds on the north and walls. And a table and chairs against the south wall. With heavy black curtains hanging across the inside of the doorway. Nodding again now, Ajax said, "Sorry for the secrecy. But we needed to move you in here quietly after dark. You can bet that the camp is being watched. I wouldn't be surprised if both our tents got showered with arrows later tonight. But you'll be safe here." Ajax pointed to the bunks as he said the latter part and nodded his head again.

Returning Ajax's nod, I smiled and said, "Thank you, cousin." And smiling back at me, Ajax moved to the curtains by the door drawing them closed now. And I asked, "And what about you cousin, are you sleeping in here too?"

Smiling, he shook his head and said, "No. I will be out with my men tonight." Then he added, "I am pretty sure the Wild Ones will concentrate their fire on the tents. So, I'll be safe with the men." Finding no fault with Ajax's logic, I moved to the nearest bunk and dropped my bedroll on top of it now. Then Nestor and the ladies followed suit, dropping their bedrolls on the other bunks now.

Suddenly there was a knock on the door, and since Amy and I still had our hood up now, Ajax responded, "Enter." The curtains parted and one of the Ajax's squad leaders entered the room now carrying a tray with our glasses and the copper wine pitcher on it. Nodding to Nestor and Ajax, the squad leader he quickly set the tray down on the table before moving back to the door and slapping his hand to his chest as he nodded his head. Ajax returned his nod, and the man wheeled and went back out though the curtains again.

I could see Ajax was ready to go, as he parted the curtain now, and turning back to face us, slapped his hand to his chest and nodding his head, before saying, "Looks like your set for the night. I know it isn't very fancy in here, but it's the safest place in the camp." And pausing for a second, Ajax added, "There's are no guards posted outside this door, so put the bar on the door after I leave, Andreas. And if you don't need anything else? I will bid you all goodnight." We returned Ajax's nod, then he turned and disappeared back through the curtain and closed the door behind him.

Moving to the door, I parted the curtain and found the drawbar standing in the corner, so I set the drawbar in place across the door now. Then stepping back into the room again, I removed my robe, and Amy followed suit. We were all tired from the day's excitement and it was a little stuffy here inside the shack. Within minutes we had all shed our robes and hung them on the pegs embedded in the west wall. And sitting down at the table now, we had just enough energy left for a little conversation and another cup of wine before agreeing it was time for bed. I was tempted to remove my cuirass now, but it was time-consuming and took too long to get back on should the need arise. Plus, Nestor, Samantha, and Amy were all adamant that I keep it on now until we reached the safety of the palace. Since I was the primary target of all these Wild One attacks.

We only got a couple of hours' sleep before the alarm horn sounded loudly from the guard tower above the shack. And I could hear Ajax's shouting orders now above the clank of armor and shields. Almost as soon as it started, it was over. And a few minutes later there was a knock on the door. Nestor sat up now and answered, "ναί!" Or "yes" in Attean.

Rising, I quickly dawned my robe and raised my hood, while Amy pulled her blanket up over her head. And moving to the door, I removed to the drawbar and opened the door now. I recognized one of Ajax's squad leaders as he stepped inside now and snapped Nestor a salute. Rising from his bed, Nestor spoke with the squad leader in Attean for a minute. Then Nestor nodded to the man and moved forward turning the lantern on the table back on again. The squad leader snapping Nestor another salute before wheeling and striding back out the door shutting it behind him. And Nestor translated now as he grabbed his medical pouch and robe off the wall, saying, "The squad leader said Captain Ajax asked for him. As they have a couple of wounded men, and Ajax wondered if I could treat them. I said yes. And told him to let Ajax know I would be out presently."

Turning to Amy, I said, "Stay here. I am going with Nestor to protect him since I have this fancy new amor now and he doesn't!"

Hearing my request, Nestor turned to Sandra now and said, "I can handle this Sandra. Stay here with Amy please?"

I could tell the women weren't happy with our requests, but they didn't argue either. Both up now, Sandra and Amy replied, "Okay." And rising now, Sandra moved over and sat down with Amy on her bunk as Nestor and I turned for the door. And I held the curtain back now or Nestor and myself. Once we were on the other side, Nestor started to reach for the door, but I stopped him saying, "Let me go first, Nestor, I have the amor and it might look odd if you were to step out first." Nodding his head now, Nestor let me go first.

And stepping out the door, I could see the camp was lit by several torches. Most of the Archers were up on ramparts south and east ramparts now with their arrows notched but not drawn. And there were about twenty Spearmen huddled together by the gate in a small phalanx. The rest Ajax's men having formed a large phalanx in the center of the camp now around their wounded comrades, I presume.

Bow in hand, I notched an arrow now before leading Nestor over to the large phalanx in the center of the camp. Several heads popped up as we approached, one of those being Ajax's. And I got the distinct feeling from the expression on his face that he wasn't too happy to see me outside right now but remained silent. The phalanx parted as we approached to let Nestor and me inside. Once we were inside the phalanx, there were several lamps in here providing light. And I could see one soldier had an arrow sticking clear through his left thigh now, while the other had a nasty looking gash in his right arm, though their bio-suits had stopped the bleeding.

Nestor knelt down next to the soldier with the arrow sticking through his leg now and removed the cutting tool from his medical bag. And Nestor quickly cut the front part of the arrow off before asking his comrades to hold the man. Then in one quick motion, Nestor pulled the arrow out of the man's leg. And I watched in amazement as his bio-suit quickly closed sealing the wound. After which, Nestor applied some of that thick red liquid to both sides of the soldier's leg. This done, his comrades quickly helped the man back up on his feet again. While Nestor went to work on the soldier with large gash on his arm. Taking the cloth from off the soldier's arm, Nestor examined the gash from the top of the man's right bicep down to his forearm. Then Nestor spoke to the soldier in Attean, and the man nodded in return. And reaching into his medical bag, Nestor removed a tiny leather pouch from inside. Then he opened the flap and withdrew a black curved needle with two feet of thread dangling from it. And I watched as the bio-suit withdrew slightly at the needles touch, then quickly closed again as Nestor completed each stitch. Nestor put nine stitches in the man's arm now before proclaiming he was done. Obviously, this wasn't the soldier's first time. As he didn't even flinch as Nestor stitched his arm back up. And producing a small pair of scissors from his bag, Nestor quickly cut the excess thread off. Then Nestor gently smeared that same red liquid over the wound before putting everything back into his satchel and standing up.

The soldier got up and nodded to Nestor now thanking him. Then all the free soldiers, not part of the phalanx's shell saluted and nodded to Nestor. Nestor nodded to the left and the right, and it was clear how much these men respected and appreciated the senior physician.

Ajax said something I didn't understand, and the phalanx suddenly shifted. And Nestor and I found ourselves inside a smaller phalanx now with Ajax. Then turning, Ajax walked back to the little shack now with our smaller phalanx moving along with us. And stopping outside our door, Ajax turned and saluted Nestor before stepping forward and opening the door. I saluted Ajax now, and he returned my salute, before following Nestor inside and Ajax shut the door behind us. Pausing by the door, I replaced the drawbar on the door now, knowing that Ajax was waiting outside to hear that sound before moving back to the larger phalanx.

Once we were inside, I could see ladies were still sitting on Amy's bed with their robes and medical bags next to them now. And Sandra looked up at her father as he entered the room, and Nestor smiled at her saying, "Minor, it's handled."

Relaxing a bit, Sandra rose from the bed and hung both hers and Amy's robes and medical bags back up on the wall again. And Nestor and I followed suit. Then pausing by the table for a minute, Nestor gave each of us a quick look before turning the lamp off again and crawling into his bunk. The rest of the night passed by quietly.

We awoke the next morning to the cook's voice announcing, "Breakfast sir," in Attean. And sitting up, Nestor replied, "One moment please." And we all rose now and dawned our robes again, Amy and me raising our hoods. And grabbing my bow, I opened the curtain and removed the drawbar from the door. And Ready now, Nestor gave the cooks permission to enter. Her hood up, Amy pretended to be busy in her medical bag as the two cooks entered the room carrying trays of steaming food. And bowing to Nestor, they deposited the food on the table then turned and went back out again. And as I closed the door, I noticed there were guards posted outside the entrance now. Replacing the drawbar on the door, we all hung up our robes up again and sat down at the table to have breakfast.

Once we were all seated at the table, I turned to Nestor and asked, "I hope Ajax doesn't expect us to stay couped up inside here all day?"

Nodding in agreement, Nestor stated, "Yes, we can all go out after breakfast, when I go to check the wounded soldiers." And we took our time over breakfast this morning, knowing that we weren't going anywhere today. The cooks anticipated this and brought a second pot of tsia when they came to get the breakfast dishes. But we didn't take too much time over the tsia, as it was quickly getting uncomfortable warm here inside the shack.

This time when the cooks returned for tsia tray, Captain Ajax came with them. And after the cooks had left, Ajax suggested we move to his tent for the rest of the day as it was cooler. And we all agreed, and getting up, we followed Ajax over to his tent and noted that it had a couple dozen arrow holes in it now.

Chapter - 5

Around mid-afternoon, we suddenly heard the alarm horn sound, followed by shouts from the guard towers. And the gates were opened now to allow a small caravan of merchant wagons to enter the camp. The five wagons were covered in Wild-one's arrows and there were several dead men laying in back the wagons.

Nestor and Sandra both grabbed their medical pouches and quickly moved to the wagons, as Amy and I followed behind. The lead driver, who had an arrow protruding from his shoulder spoke first, asking, "Who is Captain Ajax?"

Having reached the wagons already, Ajax answered, "I am!"

And turning to face Ajax, the driver took a sealed scroll from out of his shirt now, before saying, "We picked up a couple of travelers just outside the east entrance to the caves. And when the Wild Ones attacked, they identified themselves as soldiers, and one of them gave me this dispatch and made me promise to deliver it to you personally."

And receiving the scroll from driver's hand now, Ajax looked at the sealed scroll for a second before looking back up at the driver and asking, "And my men?"

The driver looked down at Ajax and said in a low voice now, "They stayed behind with of our two best men to delay the Wild Ones long enough for us to escape." Then leaning back, the driver said in a loud voice, "If it wasn't for your comrade's sacrifice, none of us would have made it out of the caves alive!"

I could see doubtful look on Ajax's now, as quietly ask the driver, "Do you think they could have escaped or made it out alive?"

Frowning now, the driver replied, "No. There was over a hundred Wild Ones in the group that attacked us. Your men knew this but stayed behind to save us. I am sorry, Captain."

Ajax nodded to driver, then issued orders to the squad leaders before turning and slowly walking back to his tent. Amy and I stayed with Nestor and Sandra while they tended to the wounded drivers and their men. The soldiers carefully removing the dead men from the wagons now. And after removing the arrows from their bodies, bound them up tightly in the pieces of the canvas cut from the wagon covers. Then they carried the dead men respectfully pole-bearer fashion back to the wagons, gently placing their bodies in the back of the wagons.

It was nearly an hour before Nestor and Sandra finished with the wounded and we rejoined Ajax in his tent. Rising now, Ajax saluted us, which I returned now. Then Ajax indicated the chairs across from him for Nestor and the ladies to sit. I resumed my post by the tent flap and only sat down after Ajax signaled for me to join them too at the table. Still holding the scroll in his hand, Ajax poured each of us a glass of wine before sitting back down again.

We could see Ajax was upset, and Nestor put his hand on Ajax's arm now and asked, "What news, my young friend?"

Looking across at Nestor now, Ajax frowned as he replied, "The good news is that General Aetolus received our message about your majesty's existence and has sent support from the palace. The bad news is, in our absence our beloved Queen Hera has passed away." And letting that sink in for a moment, Ajax continued adding, "A fact that the Elders have wisely chosen to keep hidden from everyone except the Aetolus and the royal guard up to this point. Fearing that once the news reaches Helios, he will come to the front gates of Attea and demand the throne. Three days ago, four squads left Attea enroute to us. General Aetolus couldn't risk sending more, as large groups of Wild Ones have been spotted gathering on the hillsides above the city. And General Aetolus feared that sending more might raise suspicions and attract undue attention."

Nestor absorbed all this information, before replying, "Queen Hera! May she rest in peace. She will be sorely missed. And I agree with the Elders, keeping her death a secret now is the best thing to do under the circumstances. But from a military standpoint Ajax, do you think the General Aetolus was right only sending us four squads?"

Ajax responded quickly now, saying, "Yes, he didn't have any choice really. If Prince Helios finds out his mother is dead, he can come to the front gates and demand the throne. And without any knowledge of your majesty's existence, Helios could gain the allegiance of the city and palace guard before we even reach Attea.

And we don't have enough men to lay siege to the city while fending off Wild-one attacks on our rear. General Aetolus had no choice, he must hold the city and the palace at all costs until their majesties arrive." Nestor didn't say anything now, he just nodded his head in agreement with Ajax's assessment of the situation.

After a minute of silence, Ajax added, "We will be going into the caves in the morning. And we still haven't heard from back from the runners to Fort Apollo and Captain Crios yet. But with Queen Hera's passing now, we dare not wait any longer." Nestor nodded again and Ajax got up now and returned Nestor's nod before excusing himself to go check on his men and make preparations for tomorrow.

Rising now, I resumed my position by the tent flap, while Amy, Nestor, and Sandra passed the time discussing the implications of Queen Hera's passing and tomorrow's impending march through the Caves of Hephaestus. And when the Staff of Attea started to dim, we moved back to the crude little shack for dinner and the rest of the night. And even the cooks seemed unusually quiet tonight. Everyone was on edge now in anticipation of the Wild-one's attacks tomorrow once we entered the Caves of Hephaestus.

There were three separate Wild One attacks during the night. As a result, we didn't get much sleep. But I could tell by the faces on Ajax's men the next morning that they had had enough. And they were ready to kill something now.

The five merchant wagons pulled out at first light, headed for Medina. And I saw dozens of torches being removed from the third cart and being passed out amongst the troops now. And several of the Spearmen lit their torches in the campfires before putting the fires out. There was no horseplay or small talk amongst the soldiers this morning. Their jaws were set, and they looked pissed now, which made me glad they were on our side.

Our squads formed up, and Ajax's gave the command to move out, and we marched out the gates now towards the entrance to the Caves of Hephaestus. The dirt road at our feet disappearing into a gaping black hole in the rock wall ahead. Reaching the entrance, Ajax called a halt, as the soldiers with lit torches moved through the ranks now lighting their comrades' torches. And Ajax stationed pairs of Archers on all four corners of our formation now. One carrying a torch and the other with a shrieking arrow notched and ready. And our Spearmen holding their shields in their hands now. And when all the torches lit, Ajax gave the order to move into the caves.

It was an eerie feeling leaving the light of the South Cavern behind and entering the total darkness of the Caves of Mephisto. The only light coming from the soldiers' torches and the reflections off their spears and shields. The black floor of the cave was wide enough for our formation, but not wide enough for two carts to run side by side. And the only sound now was the lapping of the torches, clank of armor, and the low grating noise of our cart's wheels on the tunnel floor. A small feeling of dread passed through me now as the tunnel turned slightly and the light from the entrance faded out of sight.

We marched forward through the darkness for close to an hour. Passing several passageways and side tunnels before the first indications of trouble began. At first, it was just the rattle of rocks and the faint sense of movement back in the side tunnels. Then the sudden volley of arrows from out of the darkness. At the first sign of trouble, the front and rear Spearmen had formed into their phalanxes or "tortoise" formations. Which slowed our progress as we continued to move forward through the darkness. Next, the Wild Ones tried rolling rocks down on top of the front formation from elevated openings on either side. But there was no way to do that silently. So, the phalanx's had a few seconds warning, allowing them to either shift or split in time to avoid being crushed by the falling rocks. And the grating sound of the rocks above drew a shower of arrows from our Archers. Some of which shot flaming arrows now, lighting up the ledge and the Wild Ones on it. Several of which were killed for their efforts and fell to the tunnel floor where the nearest Spearmen finished them off.

This went on for an hour before the Wild Ones tried their first full-scale attack from a large side tunnels. The attack only lasted about ten minutes, the Wild Ones being completely crushed by the front phalanx without sustaining a single injury on our side. The second attack came about thirty minutes later.

This time the Wild Ones waited until the first two squads passed before attacking the center of our formation. Our Spearmen quickly surrounded us and held the Wild Ones at bay now while slowly giving ground and backing away from the attack. Our Archers shifted left while continuing to mercilessly pick off the Wild Ones on the edges. And the back half of the front phalanx, and the front half of the rear phalanx split off now forming their own phalanx's before plowing into the Wild Ones from both sides. Surrounded on three sides, the Wild Ones were easily defeated and soon fled back into the darkness of the tunnel. Any Wild Ones who hadn't fled lay dead on the ground.

Our position secure, we stayed here long enough for Nestor and Sandra to treat a couple of injured soldiers before moving on again. And we marched for two hours without another major assault. Though the Wild Ones continued to shower us with arrows from out of the darkness and tried to roll boulders down onto our phalanxes to no avail. Apparently having learned their lesson now, the Wild Ones were either busy trying to come up with a better plan or waiting for re-enforcements before trying another full-on attack.

It was near midday when we reached a section of the tunnel without any side passages. And Ajax called a halt now for lunch and a short break. The Spearmen and Archers split in half now. The outer groups remained in place while the inner groups moved to the carts to receive their lunches, get a drink, and take a short break. Then after twenty minutes or so, the two groups switched places. The fresher inner soldiers replacing the outer soldiers now in the front and rear for lunch. And switching places for the next leg of the journey.

Ajax briefly speaking to his squad leader before moving in amongst his men, putting his hand on their shoulders, and either complementing them or speaking words of encouragement to them now. After which, he approached us and sat down for a moment next to Nestor and me. And speaking in a low voice now, Ajax said, "We're close to the crossroads now. And that is where they'll try another full-on attack, as they will be able to hit us from four directions at once with a much large number of men, so be ready." And we both nodded our heads now, having nothing to say in response to Ajax's warning.

While the second group was eating their lunch and having a break. I saw the drivers and the Archers open the back of the two center carts and begin transferring the items from center carts to the outer carts on the front and rear. Clearing the back of the two center carts now. And seeing my gaze, Nestor answered my question before I could ask it, saying, "It's for the wounded. We have to keep moving, so the wounded will be piled into these center carts as they fall."

To which, I replied, "Aah!"

This time when we moved out, Ajax let the front two carts go first and we hung back in the middle of the four carts now. The men knew what was coming and had formed their phalanx's before we even started to move. And Ajax was right, I wouldn't even have known we reached the junction of Crossroads if it weren't for the sudden flare of torches and the shouts of hundreds of Wild Ones as they poured out from all directions now. The Crossroads was just a large cavern in the center of the Caves of Hephaestus about sixty yards in diameter where the four tunnels came together.

The Wild-ones were prepared this time and had small catapults that hurled basketball-size rocks and oil-soaked flaming balls at the front phalanx now. And it took some time before we were even able to move forward enough to see the opening of the Crossroads ahead. Ajax was in the front, and I could see him dropping a Wild One with every stroke of his sword. The noise inside the tunnel was deafening now, between the sound of weapons clashing, battle cries, and the screams of the wounded as they went down. The front phalanx seeming to have completely stalled now, whether by the sheer number of Wild Ones, or the pile of dead bodies at their feet. And I could hear the rear phalanx was under attack now too.

I watched Archers, their quivers empty, pulling arrows out of the dead now to keep firing. Or slinging their bows and helping the wounded up into the second carts. Where Nestor and Sandra were working non-stop treating the wounded. Still other Archers, their quivers empty, were picking up the spears and shields of their fallen comrades now to join the fight in the front. Amy and I stood by the back of the second cart now helping the wounded up into the cart. Where they were quickly treated by Nestor and Sandra before being moved back to the third cart.

This went on for good twenty minutes, before Ajax called for half the rear phalanx to come forward and join the front phalanx. And splinting in half, Spearmen ran past us now on both sides. It looked hopeless from here, even though Ajax's men were killing Wild Ones at a rate of five to one. There was just too many Wild Ones for the phalanx to move forward. And all the dead bodies and blood was making it difficult for Ajax's men to get any footing and drive the Wild Ones back now.

With the front phalanx stalled now, the Wild Ones started bringing in logs to use as battering rams as they tried to bust open the front phalanx. At the same time another group of Wild Ones appeared behind us and attacked the rear phalanx again. The battering rams proved to be relatively effective now, punching holes in Ajax's phalanx, which the Wild Ones immediately filled with arrows. And though they wounded as many of their own as they did ours, Ajax's men were still being wounded in the process. And front phalanx was slowly being driven back into the south tunnel again.

Then Wild One arrows started flying back into the center of the formation now where we were. And suddenly one of the arrows struck Amy in the left shoulder just as she reached up to pass Sandra her medical bag. The arrow knocked Amy over backwards, causing her hood to fly back now as she hit the ground. Exposing her olive-green bio-suit and the gold rings around her forehead and neck now. And I heard one of the wounded soldiers in the back of the cart suddenly gasp and exclaim, "ἡ Βασίλισσα!" Or "The Queen" in Attean. As Nestor, Sandra, and I all moved to Army's aide. Then I heard, "ἡ Βασίλισσα," passing through the ranks now like a chain lightning. Nestor snipped off the end of the arrow protruding from Amy's back with his cutting tool before nodding to Amy and putting his hand on her shoulder now. Then Nestor took hold of the arrow's shaft and yanked it free from Amy's shoulder. And Sandra, who was standing by, quickly applied the red healing paste to the front and back of Amy's shoulder before bending over Amy now and shielding Amy with her body.

Angry now, I stood up and grabbed the nearest short sword and shield, then I pushed my hood back exposed my aqua-blue bio-suit and the gold crown around my head. And there was another series of gasps, as I heard, "ὁ βασιλεύς!" Or "The King" in Attean sweep through the soldiers now.

And I watched in amazement now as the wounded, arrows sticking out of their bodies began scrambling out of the carts. And taking the time to bow to Amy and me now, picked up their weapons and began dragging themselves back to the front phalanx again.

Suddenly the momentum changed, and the front phalanx started to move forward now. But it I could tell it still wasn't enough, as Ajax's men were just too badly outnumbered. And soon the forward momentum of the phalanx stalled again, and the front phalanx slowly began to be driven back into the tunnel again. Suddenly Ajax appeared at our side, and taking a quick glance at Amy first, he turned to me and saluted now before dejectedly saying, "I am sorry your majesty. There are more Wild Ones here than we even knew existed."

And just as I was about to put my hand on Ajax's shoulder and say, "I know!" We suddenly heard a horn sound and echo through the tunnels. And a cheer rose up from Ajax's men now. Unsure of exactly what the horn meant, I turned to look at Ajax. And he had a smile on his face now as he shouted, "It's either Captain Crios's or General Aetolus's men arriving now, your majesty!"

Feeling hopeful, I asked, "Will that be enough?"

Still smiling from ear to ear, Ajax replied, "I don't know your majesty? But it will take the load of us and definitely make the Wild Ones nervous!" Then he added, "Excuse me your majesty, I have to get back to the front!" Sword in hand now, Ajax saluted me, and bowed to Amy, before wheeling and disappearing back to the front.

And Ajax was right. Suddenly our phalanx started to move forward again. Probably our men with their hopes renewed, were re-doubling their efforts, eager to join up with Captain Crios's or General Aetolus's men now. And the Wild Ones were hesitating too now, realizing they no longer had the advantage, and would soon be fighting on two fronts. Looking back, I could see Nestor and Sandra had moved Amy back to the third cart, and Sandra was leaning over

Amy, shielding Amy with her body. And Nestor was moving back to the second cart now to resume work on the wounded.

Climbing up into the third cart now, I turned to Sandra and said, "I'll take over, Sandra. Go help your father with the wounded."

Seeing I had a shield to cover Amy's front now, and my amor to protect her back. Sandra bowed and replied, "Yes, your majesty." Then climbing down out of the cart, Sandra moved back to the second car and up beside Nestor's now. And I saw Nestor touch Sandra's arm, then lean over and speak to Sandra before pointing to the back of the cart. And Sandra nodded and moved to the rear of the cart just as the four Archers arrived with two more wounded soldiers.

Sitting down behind Amy now, I swung the shield up over the top of her head and brought it down in front of Amy. And with my arms around her now, I asked, "How are you doing, my love?"

Leaning back against me, Amy dryly replied, "Bah! All that fuss over such a small injury." Then shaking her head now, Amy added, "And Sandra laying over me protecting me with her body!"

Letting out a small chuckle slip out as I replied, "I think your Irish is showing, my love!" And I immediately felt Amy's good elbow smack my cuirass, confirming that Amy was indeed okay now.

Almost hidden from sight in this position, I watched the soldiers running back and forth past the rear of the cart as the fighting continued. And looking over Amy's shoulder, I could see two of the donkeys on the forth cart behind us had taken arrows and were down now. And a couple of the wounded Archers were busy cutting them loose with their long knives so the cart could move now.

Just as our cart started to move forward, we heard another loud horn sound from out of the west side tunnel, and it was immediately followed by a loud, "Hurrah!" And the sound of the fighting ahead suddenly started to diminish, as the Wild Ones broke for cover now and fled. But soldiers were blocking all three exits now, and we could still hear shouts and fighting coming from the Crossroads.

Just as suddenly as it started, it was over. And we rolled out of the south tunnel now into the cavern of the Crossroads. Ajax had the rear phalanx block the south tunnel while the front phalanx spread out forming a defensive square around the carts now And we stopped here by the entrance waiting for the re-enforcements to reach us.

The soldiers from the Attea appeared first, their phalanx coming out of the east tunnel on the right and quickly moved towards us. Our perimeter parted to let their captain, along with the two squads of Archers and their carts into our defensive square now. While the two squads of Attean Spearmen spread out completely encircling our Spearmen. The Attean Archers splitting and forming a second inner line of defense behind our Spearmen now.

Our soldiers, exhausted and nearly every one of them either wounded or having an arrow sticking out of them now, dropped to the ground once the new perimeter was complete and they were relieved. Our Spearmen with minor injuries moving across the square to relieve their more seriously wounded comrades in the south tunnel now. And the second squad of Attean Archers, their bows slung now, moved to the aid of wounded brothers.

At the same time, our uninjured Archers refilled their quivers from the back of the first cart now before moving outside the perimeter. And I watched in surprise as the Archers split into pairs and started going around the cavern, mercilessly finishing off any wounded Wild One's who were still alive. And we heard their muffled cries, as our Archers took revenge now for their fallen comrades. It wasn't pretty, but I can't say I felt any pity for the Wild Ones. And I could see grins of satisfaction on the faces of the wounded as they lay on the ground listening to their comrades avenging them now.

While this was going on, Captain Crios's phalanx entered the Crossroads from the west tunnel. His Spearmen, carts, and first squad of Archers turning and moving directly towards us. But Captain Crios's second squad of Archers broke ranks now and spread out assisting our Archers in finishing off all the wounded Wild Ones. And I realized this was necessary. No sense taking a chance on having to fight the same Wild Ones again later.

I watched as the west perimeter split and Caption Crois and his carts moved into our circle now, his Spearmen smoothly filed around the Attean Spearmen forming a second row of Spearmen now. And the Attean wounded being helped out of the carts and set on the ground with the others inside our perimeter. And each group's physician quickly nodded to Nestor before setting to work. And now there were four physicians working on the wounded.

Ajax had just finished exchanging the two two-handed clasp of friendship with Attean Captain, when Captain Crios entered the square. And both men moved to greet him now. Saluting each other and exchanging the two-handed the clasps of friendship now as they greeted each other. After which, Ajax turned to look for me now. And as our eyes met, Ajax nodded his head and discreetly signaled for me to join them in the center.

Giving Amy a quick peck on the cheek now, I said, "Protocol, my love. Looks like Ajax wants me to make an appearance. Just stay here and rest, okay?" Turning and nodding her head now, I could tell Amy had no intention of moving anywhere at the moment. And rising now, I scanned the square for Sandra. At the same time all the soldiers inside the perimeter slapped their hands to their chest and nodded their heads now, even some of the wounded ones on the ground. Which was annoying, but made it easier to locate Sandra, who was bowing now by the rear of our cart, apparently having anticipated the situation.

Smiling at her foresight, I said, "Sandra, could you stay with Amy until I return?"

Her head still bowed, Sandra replied, "Certainly, your majesty."

And moving to the rear of the cart, I bent down and offered Sandra a hand now to help her up into the cart. Sandra hesitated for a moment looking around at all the bowed heads before accepting my hand and climbed up into the back of the cart. And before stepping down off the cart, I slapped my hand to my chest now and nodded to the left, and then right. And it worked, as everyone stood and went back about their business now.

Moving around the cart, I started walking towards Ajax and the Captains. When suddenly one of the Archers behind the captains, turned and fired an arrow straight at my chest now. There wasn't any time to react or even move now, all I could do was hope this new cuirass stopped the arrow, and it did. The arrow ricocheted off my cuirass and stuck in the ground at my feet. I had my robe closed, so there was no way the assassin could have known I was wearing the black cuirass of the royal guard underneath, otherwise he might have tried a headshot.

The Archers on either side immediately grabbed for the man now. But not before one of the wounded soldier laying at the assassin's feet drove his short sword up under the assassin's cuirass to the hilt. Then giving it a violent twist, yanked his sword back out from man's abdomen. The traitor was dead before he hit the ground. And the soldiers on either side of their wounded man enthusiastically clapped him on the back now praising his quick action.

Nestor and the captains were at my side in an instant. And I just stood there for a moment stunned, feeling my chest with both hands, and expecting to find an arrow sticking out of it now. And I heard the Attean Captain suddenly bark an order suddenly, and a dozen spearmen came running to our sides before doing an about-face and forming a circle around us now. Standing there still checking the chest, I finally looked down and saw the arrow sticking in the ground between my feet. And noticing the Spearmen encircling us now had on black shin guards made of the same material as my cuirass. So, these weren't regular just regular Spearmen but palace guards in disguise.

It was Nestor who spoke first, and panic in his voice now as he excitedly asked, "Are you okay, your majesty?"

Turning to look at him, I replied, "No, my friend. But luckily this armor saved me." And pulling my robe back now, I exposed the golden seahorse of my black cuirass. And I heard all four of them breathe a small sigh of relief now as they saw that my armor was undamaged. Then three captains saluted me, and Captain Crios's with his head bowed now as he said something in Attean which I didn't understand. And Ajax quickly translated, saying, "Caption Crios wishes to sincerely apologizes for what happened. And begs your forgiveness, your majesty?"

The other two captains stared at me now as I smiled and put my hand on Ajax's shoulder and replied, "Assure Captain Crios there is nothing to forgive. And tell Captain Crios that I am relieved we found the traitor now without injury! Rather than later, cousin."

Smiling, Ajax quickly turned and translated my words to Captain Crios now, who bowed his head again and snapped me another salute. Then Ajax said, "Let me introduce Captain Pylos of the Royal Guard, your majesty." Then smiling, Ajax leaned in and whispered, "Who is also our cousin, and speaks better English than I do, your majesty." Nodding my head in thanks to Ajax, I smiled and turned to greet Captain Pylos now.

Pylos saluted me again, and bowing his head now said in perfect English, "It is my great honor to meet you. . . and to learn of your existence, your majesty." And smiling now, Pylos added, "And when I say that. I speak for the Consul of Elders, General Aetolus, and all Attea now, your majesty!"

Happy to learn I had another relative, I returned Pylos's nod and smile now, as I replied, "Wow, that's a lot. But thank you, cousin." Which drew a smile from both Pylos and Ajax now. Then pointing to the cart to my right, I asked, "Pylos, could you send a few of your men over to that cart to guard my betrothed, Amy? Who was injured earlier and is resting in the back of that cart now with Nestor's daughter, Sandra."

Snapping another salute, Pylos answered, "Immediately, your majesty!" Then Pylos barked out an order in Attean, and four guards stepped out of formation, and ran over to Amy's cart taking up positions on the four corners now. Follow by the guards around us shifting inwards now and closing up our little circle again. And I watched as Pylos barked another order, and the royal guards let their long Spearmen robes drop to the ground now revealing their black cuirasses and short blue capes underneath. And I heard a murmur among the soldiers, as those who didn't already know what was going on were being educated now.

Then snapping me another salute, Pylos asked, "If you will excuse me for a moment, your majesty? I have a reward bestow."

Confused, I turned to look at Ajax, who smiled and nodded his head now knowing what Pylos was referring to. So, I nodded my head to Pylos and replied, "Of course Pylos, feel free."

Captain Pylos gave me a quick nod before replying, "Thank you, your majesty." Then Pylos turned around and walked directly over to the wounded soldier on the ground who had killed the traitor. And the two men spoke briefly, then Captain Pylos produced what looked like a large gold coin from a pouch at his waist, and kneeling down, presented the gold coin to the wounded soldier now. After which, Pylos stood up and he saluted the man before wheeling around and walking back into our little circle with a sly grin on his face. And I watched the soldiers around the wounded man move in patting him on the back again and congratulating him now before leaning in to get a better look at the gold coin in his hand.

Leaning towards Ajax now, I asked him, "What did Captain Pylos just give that soldier?"

Chuckling now, Ajax replied, "It's the gold coin of the palace guard, your majesty. His quick thinking and actions today have earned him a place in the royal guard. It is the greatest of honors."

And still grinning, Pylos entered our circle and saluted me again. It was at this point, Ajax spoke up, saying, "If it's okay with you, your majesty? I suggest we get moving now and get out of these caves before the Wild Ones have time to regroup and try another attack."

Then turning to Nestor, Ajax asked, "Can we move the wounded now?"

Nodding his head, Nestor took a quick look around the inside of our defensive square before answering, saying, "Yes, just give us a few minutes more, Ajax."

After which, Ajax turned to look at me, and I said, "You heard the physician, start making your preparations to move out, cousin." And Ajax turned to Crios now and translated my orders. Then all four men bowed and stepped out of the circle, leaving me alone now and staring at the blue-caped backs of the eight royal guards.

Oh well, I wanted to go back to the cart and check on Amy anyway. So, speaking up now, I asked, "Do any of you speak English?"

One of the guards saluted now and answered, saying, "Yes, your majesty."

And pointing to four guards by Amy's cart, I said, "Okay, I am going check on my betrothed in that cart now."

And the guard saluted and nodded, before replying, "Yes, your majesty," then he quickly translated my words to the other guards. And they parted on the left exposing Amy's cart and lined up on either side of me now as they escorted me back to the cart with Amy in it. It was a little annoying but tolerable, as long as they didn't block my path or start bowing.

Reaching the back of Amy's cart, I climbed up inside. And the royal guards spread out around the cart now before snapping back to attention. Shaking my head, I moved over to where Sandra and Amy were seated. Sandra immediately rising to bow, and I put my hand on Sandra's arm now whispering, "Not you too, please."

Sandra smiled briefly before replying, "Your majesty."

Smiling back, I continued saying, "I'll take over Sandra, we have plenty of protection now. You'd best go see if your father needs any help now so we can get out of these caves."

Bowing to me and Amy again, Sandra smiled and replied, "Yes, your majesty." Then she turned to leave, and one of the royal guards stepped forward and held his hand out to Sandra now to help her down from the cart before resuming his position again.

I slid in behind Amy and sat down again so she could lay back against me. And as soon as I was seated, Amy asked, "Are you okay? I didn't see what happened, but Sandra said someone attacked you."

Smiling at her, I replied, "I'm fine, the armor saved me. Luckily, I still had my robe on, or the traitor might have tried a head shot."

And trying to get my goat, Amy chuckled and replied, "Well, no danger there!" And I chuckled in response, knowing Amy was just getting even with me for my "Irish showing" crack earlier. I was glad to see that Amy was feeling well enough now to tease me back.

Then Nestor walking up to our cart, and bowing first, said, "We are nearly ready to move, your majesties." Then addressing Amy now, he asked, "We have a lot of wounded men, does your majesty feel up to walking?"

Looking down at Amy, she smiled and nodded her head. So, I got up now and offered Amy my hand, which she accepted. And we both moved to the rear of the cart now, as Amy replied, "Absolutely Nestor. The wounded should ride in the carts."

Amy waited at the back of the cart while I climbed down then turned around and put my arms up under her now. Then I gently lifted Amy up off the cart and lowered her to the ground. After which, Nestor nodded again and said, "Thank you, your majesties." Then Amy and I moved around to the left side of the cart out of the way as the royal guards encircled us again. Nestor turned and spoke to the two Archers standing beside him now. And they turned and spoke to the other Archers nearby. Then they all began helping the wounded up into the back of the cart.

Then we watched three Spearmen approach our guards now, the first one carrying a long canvas covered bundle on his shoulder, and the other two carrying large sacks on their backs. And stopping a few feet from our guards now, they set their loads down on the ground. Then the three Spearmen opened their loads, and I saw that the long bundle contained black spears, and the large sacks contained black shields and helmets. And our guards stepped out of line one at a time now. Quickly exchanging their wooden spears and silver shields for black spears and a slightly larger black shield with a blue seahorse on the front of it before stepping back in line. This went on until all twelve of the guards had changed out their spears and shields. And while that was happening, the third Spearmen had walked around the group now and exchanged their tan plumed brass helmets, for a longer, more formidable looking black helmets with a blue plumes. The black helmets having a seahorses imprinted on sides, the tail of which encircled a small starfish with a hole in the center. Which I assumed was put there to allow the guards to hear better.

Done now, the three Spearmen quickly bundled up the discarded armor and disappeared back into the mix again. And it wasn't until the royal guards' outfits were complete that I noticed the small gold seahorse on the hilts of their swords.

The air inside the cavern was suddenly shattered now by the sound of a loud horn on the right, which was answered by an equally loud horn on the left. As our defensive perimeter split up and the soldiers reformed into travel formation. The carts all had torches in front corner now. We watched as soldiers ran up to the carts and lighting their torches before running back to their squads to light their comrades' torches now. And from what I could see, Captain Pylos's and the four squads from Attea were taking the lead now into the east tunnel. While Caption Crios's and squads were bringing up the rear.

Most of Ajax's men were wounded and riding in the carts now. But Ajax formed what was left of his Spearmen into a small squad in front and the Archers into a squad behind us. Our guards parted momentarily as Nestor, Sandra, and the other two physicians joined us in the center now. All four quickly bowed to Amy and me before moving in behind us. Then Sandra moved up on Amy's left, and Nestor stepped up on the right now. Suddenly the palace guards started forward and we were on the move again.

And everyone quickly fell in line on the wagon trail as we crossed the in cavern and entered the east tunnel now. Ten minutes after we entered the east tunnel, Ajax joined us in the center again. Saluting me before nodding to Amy and Nestor. Nestor excused himself now, and stepping back to speak with the two other physicians, vacating the spot beside me for Ajax. Whether relieved or worn out from all the fighting, Ajax seemed relaxed now as he walked along beside me.

Spread out in the tunnel as we were, our train was so long now the that we couldn't see Pylos's carts in the front or Captain Crios's carts in the rear. And we walked along quietly for twenty minutes before hearing Pylos's alarm horn sound in the front. Which was followed by the muffled sound of fighting ahead in the tunnel out of sight. Frowning, Ajax saluted me, and said, "If you will excuse me, your majesty?" And I returned his salute, as Ajax quickly bowed to Amy and disappeared forward. Suddenly, our Spearmen in front stepped to the outside now and stopped. While we continued forward, and once our twelve guards were in the center of the Spearmen, they stepped in around our guards forming a phalanx now. Then half of the Archers behind us ran past us on both sides and reformed between us and the cart in ahead, their arrows notched and ready. This all happened in under a minute, and our guards neither slowed nor changed pace.

We continued forward for about five minutes before we started seeing the bodies of the slain Wild Ones lying on the sides of the tunnel. And a pair of Pylos's Archers standing in the tunnel holding a wounded comrade between them. And somewhere up ahead in the tunnel, I heard Ajax order a halt now as the Archers quickly loaded their wounded comrade into the cart in front of us. And Nestor and two of the physicians bowing to Amy and me before Nestor said, "If you will excuse us, your majesty?" Then turning to Sandra, Nestor said, "Stay with her majesty, Sandra." And Sandra nodded to her father as the three physicians moved forward and climbed up into the back of the cart to tend the wounded soldier. And we were moving again.

Thirty minutes later, we heard Captain Crios's horn sound in the rear sound, and the formation abruptly came to a stop. Apparently, they wanted to keep the formation together without any breaks. So, we all stopped to let Crios's men handle the attack on the rear. Ten minutes passed and three Archers approached from the rear now. One carry a torch and the other two carrying a wounded man between them. And they quickly loaded the wounded man into the back of the cart with the physicians. And having delivered their comrade, the three Archers turned and disappeared to the rear. Then we heard Crios's horn sound, and we were on the move again.

Apparently the goal was to keep moving at all costs and clear the Caves of Mephisto before nightfall. And I remembered Ajax saying the Wild Ones were not match for his men in the open-field combat and they would get slaughtered if they tried it.

Finally, after about three hours of marching, and several small attacks on the front and rear. I saw a faint light ahead in the tunnel. To my surprise, when we reached the entrance to the East Cavern, Pylos's men had stopped and formed a defensive square now like the one Ajax had formed in the Crossroads. And as we cleared the tunnel and moved out into the open, I could see why now. There were hundreds of Wild Ones blocking the road ahead and more spread out on the slope to our left now. All brandishing their weapons now and shouting taunts at our men.

Filing out of the tunnel, the Spearmen moved forward reinforcing Captain Pylos's perimeter now, while half of the Archers filed in behind the Spearmen. And the rest of the Archers set to work now unhitching the donkeys and forming a large square in the center with the twelve carts. Before helping the wounded out of the carts and underneath them now. Once the wounded were unloaded and under the carts. The larger portion of the Archers, climbing up into the carts and taking up firing positions overlooking the Spearmen now. While a dozen Archers quickly began lashing the carts together with rope. Leaving the cart in center out but positioned so it could easily quickly be rolled forward now and close the gap.

And we watched Captain Crios's squads march around our defensive square forming up round Pylos's Spearmen. Then Ajax and Pylos stepped into view now and began walking towards our little circle in the center of the carts.

Saluting now, Ajax said, "I'll leaving you here with cousin Pylos's now, your majesties. And if you watch, you will see why the Wild Ones should never challenge our men in the open-field combat!" And Ajax gave me a wink before turning to quickly exchanging the two-handed clasp of friendship with Pylos now. Then they each took a step back and saluted each other. And Ajax chuckling as he told Pylos, "See you soon, cousin." Then turning to Amy and me, Ajax nodded again before wheeling and striding straight out through the opening in the carts now.

Pylos stood there watching Ajax go. Then Pylos turned and saluting us again before holding out his arm now indicating the cart in front corner now, and saying, "Your majesties will have a better view of the battle from the corner there, if you wish?" Which was a polite way of telling us that we needed to take cover under the cart in the corner now.

Chapter - 6

Taking Amy's right hand now, I led her over to the cart in the corner as Pylos and the royal guard followed behind. And reaching the side of the cart, I knelt down and helped Amy under the cart before climbing in next to her. Pylos and the guards kneeling behind us and lowering their spears slightly now. I assume to reduce the attention those black shafts would draw.

And taking Ajax's advice, I rolled over onto my elbows and looked out through the wheels of the cart now as the battle unfolded. Amy followed suit, leaning up against me, and I lifted my arm up and put it around her now.

Our defensives ready, the Spearmen formed a large phalanx out in the front. While the Archers spread out in a line now four rows deep and forty feet wide behind them. And I could see half a dozen more Archers standing behind the formation with their bows slung now and their arms full of arrows.

Wasting no time now, the large phalanx moved forward at a steady pace right at the Wild Ones blocking the road. The Archers following behind now at a slower pace letting the distance between the two groups increase slightly. And I see Captain Crios out amongst the Archers, which meant Ajax was inside the phalanx now leading the attack on the Wild Ones.

Suddenly the Wild Ones on the slope to our left rolled several small catapults forward and immediately began launching flaming balls down onto the phalanx. But Ajax's phalanx was tight, and the oil-soaked flaming balls didn't have sufficient weight to punch through the phalanx and simply bounced or skidded off the top of their interlocked shields. At the same time, the Wild-one archers on the hillside began raining arrows down onto the phalanx too. Their arrows have no more effect on the phalanx now than the flaming balls did. In response though, Captain Crios had his squads of Archers turn left and begin taking long shots at the Wild ones up on the hillside. And they slowly began to pick off the Wild-ones Archers and the catapult crews.

Seeing this, the horde of Wild Ones blocking the road howled and jeered but didn't move. And after several volleys, the Wild-one's catapults crews either gave up or ran out of flaming balls to shoot. As soon as the catapults ceased firing, I saw torches flare up down on the hillside. As a dozen Wild-ones lit up oil-soaked logs with chains on the ends now and ran down the hill at Ajax's phalanx. It was right out of the scene from Spartacus with Kirk Douglas, except these logs weren't as big now as the ones in the movie.

I watched as the flaming logs got closer, and the whole phalanx suddenly shifted left. As the high side of the phalanx knelt down and the soldiers on the left overlapped their shields forming what could only be described as a ramp now. It was extremely effective, as the Wild Ones caught off guard simply ran right up over the top of the phalanx now. Falling off the other side and losing their grip on the flaming logs as they landed sprawled out on the ground. Crois's Archers having anticipated this, were standing ready now. And as soon as the Wild Ones hit the ground, they were greeted by a shower of arrows from Crios's Archers, quickly finishing off the flaming log teams.

Enraged, the horde of Wild Ones shouted madly and charged the Ajax's phalanx now. And having resumed its normal shape, the phalanx advanced on the Wild Ones. At the same time, Crois's Archers leaned back and fired a huge barrage of arrows over the top of the phalanx now at the Wild Ones. Their first volley released, the Archers ran forward now quickly reforming Ajax's Phalanx again while continuing to fire volleys of arrows over the phalanx at the Wild Ones. The Archers were dropping Wild Ones left and right, but it wasn't nearly enough to break the massive charge of the Wild Ones.

When the Wild-ones had closed two-thirds the distance to phalanx, the front of the Wild Ones line opened revealing a half dozen sets of men in the center now carrying battering rams. And when the Wild Ones were thirty feet from the phalanx, the phalanx suddenly split down in the middle, rapidly moving outwards to the left and right. Catching the Wild Ones completely by surprise. And exposing the battering ram crews to Captain Crois's Archers, who were standing ready. The battering ram crews, their target gone and the path ahead suddenly clear, hesitated now trying to slow down and turn. That's when Captain Crois's Archers released their arrows. The first row of Archers fired their arrows then dropped to one knee, as the second row fired and dropped, followed by third row, and the fourth row finally. Caught in open now with their hand full and no shields, the battering ram crews were quickly cut to ribbons.

The rest of Wild Ones crashed into the front of the two phalanxes, but without any way to bust the phalanxes open now. The Wild One's charge came to an abrupt halt, before slowly being driven into the middle between the phalanxes now and right into the arrows of Crios's Archers. The Wild Ones in the open between the phalanxes immediately being hit by Crios's Archers and going down.

Realizing they were losing ground, a group of the Wild Ones decided to charge the down the middle at Crois's Archers. And they got about thirty feet before the two phalanxes changed direction and moved inward now closing the formation. And realizing the danger, the Wild Ones tried to retreat, but only half of them made it out alive. Once two phalanxes had joined up, they changed direction again and advancing on the remaining Wild Ones. About then, I noticed a flash up at the top of the north slope one ridge over. Which looked to me now like it had come off a soldier's shield or helmets.

The Wild Ones, with half their number lying dead or wounded on the ground now. Decided it was time to make a run for it, or risk being wiped out. So, they all turned and began running for the safety of the north slope. And Ajax's phalanx split down the middle now, moving to the east and west to give Crios's Archers a clear field of fire at the fleeing Wild Ones. The Archers shooting then dropping to one knee, as the next row stepped forward and fired trying to pick off as many Wild-ones as possible as they fled up the hillside. In full flight now, the Wild Ones quickly scrambled up the rocky slope. Some even dropping their weapons in a desperate attempt to escape the arrows of Crios's Archers now.

They got about halfway up the slope before two squads of Archers with red capes came marching over the top of the hill and stopped. These new Archers quickly fanning out and opening fire on the Wild Ones scrambling up the slope at them. The new group of Archers taking a terrible toll on the fleeing Wild Ones. Dropping a third of the Wild Ones in their first few volleys.

Panicking now, the survivors turned back downhill again into Captain Crios's Archers. The hundred or so remaining Wild Ones, turned east now, running down across the road headed for the valley floor. Disappearing over the hill for a moment before reappearing out in the fields on the cavern floor. Presumably headed for the safety of the south slope now.

Ajax's Phalanx's spread out now. The west phalanx moving back towards us, while the east phalanx broke ranks and either began helping the wounded back to the carts or going around assisting the Archers in finishing off any wounded Wild Ones. The Archers on the hill had spread out now too and were working their way down the hillside finishing off the wounded Wild Ones they found.

Thinking of Amy now, I said, "Best not to watch this part, my love."

Amy turned away her face away now, replying, "Yeah!"

Then I indicated to Amy that it was time to get up, and crawling back out from underneath the cart now, I offered Amy my hands to help her get up. On our feet again, I saw soldiers carrying the wounded into our defensive square as Nestor, Sandra and the other two physicians quickly moved forward to treat the wounded now.

This time however, considering how badly Ajax and his men had been outnumbered, there were surprisingly few wounded soldiers coming in. And I smiled now remembering Ajax's stating the Wild-ones should never try an open-field attack on his men.

The west phalanx smoothly split left and right now with practiced precision as it reached the carts and formed the protective perimeter around us again. A few seconds later, Ajax came walking in through the opening in the carts, and Pylos moved to greet him. The two men saluting each other, and Pylos thumped his fist on Ajax's shoulder three times now congratulating Ajax on his crushing victory over the Wild Ones. Then my cousins turned and walked back into our little circle of palace guards. Both saluting and nodding as they stepped into our circle, and Ajax spoke first, saying, "We should be able to reach Attea now without any further attacks, your majesties."

Returning their salutes, I grinned at Ajax now and said, "Congratulations! Now I know why the Wild Ones should never attack your men in the open field!"

Returning my grin now, Ajax nodded again and replied, "Thank you, your majesty. But don't forget Captain Crios's Archers, they actually killed more Wild Ones than my Spearmen did!"

And answering Ajax, I said, "I know, Amy and I watched the entire battle."

Then Pylos, who still smiling, cut in saying, "And that your majesty, is why I won't play 'Kings and Soldiers' with Ajax anymore!" Then looking upward for a second, Pylos added, "Sorry, I believe it's called 'Chess' in English, your majesty."

Laughing now, I said, "Thanks for the warning Pylos, I'll remember that!" And all three of us chuckled now. Then I asked Ajax, "Whose Archers were those up on the hill?"

Pylos answered now, saying, "Those are the city guards' Archers, and it looked like Captain Hyllus is leading them, your majesty." Then glancing up at the hillside, Pylos added, "But we will know in a minute, as their almost here now, your majesty."

Ajax spoke next, saying, "If you will excuse me, your majesties? I need to see to my men and prepare to move out so we can reach the encampment before it gets dark."

Nodding to Ajax, I replied, "Of course, Ajax." And Ajax saluted me again before turning and walking out into the throng of Archers moving back and forth. Busy now separating the carts, hitching up the donkeys, and helping the wounded into the back of the carts.

I could see Nestor and the physicians moving about, and it looked like they were just about finished treating the wounded now. And Sandra entered our circle now, bowing to Amy and me before moving to Amy's side. And they began chatting as Sandra stepped forward now to take another quick look at Amy's shoulder.

Then an unusually tall, fancy, red-crested helmet appeared outside the carts now catching my eye. The owner of which was easily six inches taller than everyone else. Though the man was a little on the chubby side, and thick black curly hair hung down from his shiny silver helmet. His brightly colored bio-suit and shiny cuirass reminded me of Mayor Agatha now. I suppose you needed to be part politician to be in charge of the capitol's city guard.

After stepping through the opening between the carts the man took off his helmet now, revealing his thick, black, unruly hair, long nose, and thick eyebrows. Which were offset by his deep green eyes. And pausing for a moment to look around, he spotted our royal guards and strode over to our little circle now. And taking a quick glance at Amy's and my bio-suits now, he saluted and bowed his head. And remained bowed, as he said, "It is my great honor to meet you, your majesties."

And Pylos spoke up now, saying, "Your majesties, may I introduce my friend Captain Hyllus, commander of the Attea city guard." I looked at Pylos now, as he added, "Captain Hyllus speaks English, not as well as me, but he can understand what you say, your majesty."

Grinning at Pylos for the assist, I turned to Hyllus and said, "Rise, Captain Hyllus. Amy and I are choking on all this protocol."

And raising his head, Captain Hyllus gave me a puzzled look now before replying, "Thank you, your majesty." Then turning to Plyos, he saluted him, and smiling now, saying, "Thank you my friend."

Returning his smile, Pylos replied, "Your timing was perfect, Hyllus. I assume General Aetolus has taken over the city guard now in your absence?"

Nodding his head again, Hyllus replied, "Yes, he didn't have much choice once the Consul of Elders found out the Wild Ones were massing here outside the entrance to the caves. That, and the news of Queen Hera's death leaking out somehow. They just ordered him to do something, and to do it now! So, he came up with this plan. Though, I think the three of you would have crushed the Wild Ones without our aid."

Grinning, Pylos replied, "Yes, I think so too. But thanks to you now, Helios can neither attack his majesty or lay siege to the city."

And Captain Hyllus nodded in agreement with Pylos's assessment of the situation. Then Ajax walked back into our circle, saluting and bowing to Amy and me again, said, "We'll be ready to move out in a few minutes, your majesties." Then turning to Hyllus now, the two men exchanged salutes before moving forward to exchange the two-handled clasp of friendship now as Ajax said, "Thank you, Hyllus. Your timing was perfect!"

And Hyllus smiled now, flashing his perfect teeth and replying, "It was little if nothing, Ajax. Congratulations on your victory. You had them fleeing for the hills before we even topped the ridge. Smartly done, my friend." Then frowning, Hyllus added, "I only wish that my men were half as well trained as yours! All my men seem to do is sit around getting fatter and lazier with each passing year." And all three men chuckled now.

Then Nestor walked into our circle, and quickly nodding to Amy and me first, turned to Ajax now and said, "The wounded are ready to move out now. So, anytime you're ready Ajax?"

And nodding now, Ajax said, "Well, let's get out of this place, it's starting to smell of died Wild Ones!" Then turning to Amy and me now, Ajax said, "Your majesties." Then he saluted us and the other two captains, before striding out of our little circle now.

Caption Hyllus nodded to Amy and me again, before saying, "If you will excuse me now, your majesties?" And I nodded to Hyllus, who dawned his fancy helmet again before following Ajax out of our circle. And we watched as the Spearmen on the perimeter broke up now and began forming into squads again. Then the first two squads of Spearmen led off followed by two squads of Archers and six carts behind them now.

And we moved out again, with our half squad of Spearmen in front and our half squad of Archers behind us, following Pylos's squads and the carts now. With Captain Crios's two squads of Archers and Spearmen bringing up the rear. It was a long formation. And I saw Captain Hyllus Archers had split taking up flanking positions on both our high and low sides now. And I caught a glimpse of Captain Hyllus' fancy crested helmet leading the archers on the high side.

We walked for an hour before rounding a small spur ridge and tonight's encampment appeared ahead. But we still couldn't see the capitol yet through the haze in the cavern. And this time when we poured into the grounds of the encampment, it was cramped. After our tents were pitched, there were palace guards posted on all four corners of our tent, and two more at the door. I assumed the other six guards were sleeping now, so they could relieve their comrades later tonight.

The three Captains each had tents, Ajax and Crios sharing theirs with Hyllus and the physicians. While I suspected but couldn't confirm that the missing royal guards were sleeping inside Pylos's tent now. Amy and I insisted that Nestor and Sandra stay in our tent, and Nestor finally agreed. Reluctant to let us out of his sight until he safely delivered us to the palace and fulfilled the last task given to him by Queen Hera. And this time there were four cots and four chairs waiting for us inside the tent.

Though having two guards follow you around while you took care of your toiletries was a bit awkward, especially for Amy. But after Sandra and Amy returned, we discussed it, and Amy said that the guards were actually quite helpful in maintaining their privacy.

And after receiving permission to enter, the cooks smiled and bowed to Amy and me before depositing the trays of food on the table. Then the older cook put his hand on his chest like a salute and bowed before saying something in Attean. And he remained bowed as the second cook bowed now and said something in Attean. And raising our eyebrows, Amy and I turned to Nestor for help now.

Nestor quickly translated, saying, "The senior cook stated that he has personally tested all your food. And the assistant cook stated that he witnessed the Senior cook testing all your food, your majesties."

And Amy and I looked at each other with our mouths' agape now, dumbfounded and speechless. Then we turned to look to Nestor again. And realizing our dismay, Nestor quickly spoke to the cooks now, thanking them and dismissing them. After which both cooks rose and gave Nestor a quick nod before leaving the tent.

And Sandra spoke up now, saying, "Don't misunderstand, your majesties. True, it's the cook's duty to test all your majesties food. But they're not doing it out of duty alone, they're doing it out of respect and gratitude. Prince Helios is feared and hated amongst the people. And your majesties existence and arrival has saved them from years of uncertainty and misery! And like father and I, ninety-nine percent of all Attea will be besides themselves with joy when they learn of your existence, your majesties."

And Nestor replied, "True, daughter, true!" Then he added, "I already know from the few days that we have spent together, your majesty. That you are a far greater king than Prince Helios could ever hope to be!" And Amy mouthed "wow," now before giving me a slap on the shoulder and chuckling. And seeing Amy's reaction to Nestor's words, Sandra joined Amy in letting a small chuckle now.

Nodding to Nestor, I frowned now and said, "Thank you, my friend. But if you keep talking like that, this crown on my head will soon be too tight to fit!" Not understanding my sarcasm now, Nestor just sat there with a blank look on his face now. Which made Amy break out in a fit laughter. And Sandra and I both joined her now as we looked at the blank expression on Nestor's face.

Nestor turning to look at his daughter now, and Sandra told him, "His majesty said, if you keep talking like that. You're going make his head too big for his crown!" And finally understanding, Nestor joined us now in having a laugh. Then we all sat down and ate our dinner like friends. Sitting back after dinner over a second glass of wine. We discussed the battle, Ajax's victory, and the condition of the wounded. Then we discussed what the palace and Attea looked like, and what to expect once we reached Attea.

The next morning it took a little longer to get going. I suspect the number of wounded being the cause, even though there were fewer soldiers in the carts this morning than yesterday. Plus, Ajax had the road ahead scouted and waited for his scouts to return before giving the order to move out. Anyway, we finally formed up and got under way again. With a full squad of Captain Hyllus's Archers flanking us above and the other one flaking us below again.

Amy and I took note when we stopped for lunch, that it was cooler now further away from the Caves of Hephaestus. And Amy and I had to endure another declaration from the cooks as they bowed and handed our sandwiches to Nestor and Sandra. Too timid to hand the sandwiches to us directly. Also, I noticed that no merchant caravans had passed us yet on what should be the busiest road in the entire kingdom, and I said as much to Nestor. Nestor informed me that Captain Hyllus had sent runners out to all the merchants and farmers as soon as his scouts spotted the Wild One's gathering at the entrance to the Caves of Mephisto. Our lunches finished and the men fed now, we formed up again and continued our journey east.

The rest of the day passed without incident. It wasn't until we had spotted tonight's camp ahead that we got our first glimpse of the capitol city of Attea off in the distance through the haze. The massive tan walls surrounding the city were at least four-stories high and had a pinkish hue to them as they spread out from the northern slope halfway across the valley floor now. The enormous gates on the west side were so big that we could make them out clearly from here. And the pale grey walls and towers of the palace with their bright yellow roofs standing out clearly now on the hillside above the city.

Once we were settled in camp with our tents pitched and campfires lit, the Staff of Attea went dark. And shortly after dinner and the table had been cleared, we heard Captain Ajax outside asking for permission to enter. And I bid him enter, and all four captains entered together followed now by four soldiers, each carrying one of the crude folding wood chairs. The captains immediately saluted and nodded to Amy and me. While the four soldiers quickly deposited the chairs before saluting and leaving again. I could tell by the captain's faces now that something was bothering them.

Rising from my chair, I returned their salutes now before gesturing for them to take a seat and saying, "Sit my friends. And please don't let 'protocol' prevent you from speaking your minds now." Smiling, Ajax nodded at me then leaned over and quickly translated my words to Captain Crios before flopping down in the nearest chair. And the other captains followed suit now, but in a more restrained manner. But before we could begin speaking, we heard one of the cooks outside request permission to enter, And receiving it from Nestor now in Attean, the cook entered the tent and quickly bowed before setting a tray of wine cups and second pitcher of wine down on the table. Then bowing again, the cook quickly left the tent.

Hoping to break the ice now, I grabbed the pitcher of wine off the tray and proceeded to fill the four captains' cups. Caught by surprise, the other three captains just sat there with their mouths open. While Ajax on the other hand, had a large grin on his face. And a chuckle escaped from Amy and Sandra now as they looked at the stunned faces of the captains. Even Nestor had to turn and hide his face now.

And it was Ajax who spoke first, saying, "Sorry to bother your majesties, but we are split on how to enter the city tomorrow." And pausing for a second to let that sink in, Ajax continued adding, "Captain Crios and I think we should conceal your majesties inside one of the carts until we are safely inside the palace walls. While Captain Hyllus and Pylos think you should walk proudly through the streets of the Attea and let the people see you. And let all of Attea celebrate now, their hopes restored. But Captain Crios and I believe that Prince Helios won't give up so easily, and this an unnecessary risk, your majesties." Then turning to Nestor, Ajax asked, "What do you think, Nestor?"

Nestor thought about it for a moment, then said, "I don't know. Hiding your majesties in a cart would get you into the palace safely. But marching though the city would let the people see your majesties and not only raise the people's morale. But put an end to any claim Helios's has on the throne now. But it is worth the risk?" And Nestor hesitated for a second, before adding, "I think in the end, it's your majesties decision?" And continuing, Nestor added, "Your majesties will have to make a public appearance at some point and show themselves to the people. It might be better to do it now while we have all these soldiers surrounding you, who expect an assignation attempt and are prepared for it!"

To which Ajax replied, "I know, it's not an easy decision, which is why we are split on the issue."

Speaking up now, I said, "The first assassin tried to shoot me in the chest, not knowing I was wearing the cuirass of the palace guard. I assume he took that information to the grave with him without passing it on. How about I march through the city, wearing my robe over my armor with only my head and crown exposed, letting the people see me. While her majesty Amy is concealed inside a cart, would that work?" Ajax translated my words to Captain Crios, and the four captains spoke amongst themselves for a moment, before turning back at me. Glancing at Amy now, I could see that she wasn't happy with my idea at all. But she was waiting for the captains to finish before voicing her complaint.

The captains nodded in agreement, and it was Ajax who answered now, saying, "We agree, that with your armor concealed beneath your robe and the royal guard around you, the risk is greatly reduced. And ending Prince Helios's claim to the throne, while restoring the hope of all of Attea, would be a great achievement, your majesty."

Her Irish temper flaring now, Amy blurted out, "If you men think I that am going to hide in a cart while Andrew makes himself a walking target, you have a lot to learn!"

And Amy was about to add something unpleasant when Pylos spoke up, suggesting, "Would it be acceptable to her majesty, if I sent runners ahead to the palace tonight, informing General Aetolus and the Elders of the situation. And your majesties decision. Then request that Queen Hera's armor be sent out to us directly. My men should be able to return before we reach the city gates tomorrow, then her majesty could walk along safely with his majesty. And only requiring her majesty to hide in a cart, if my men should fail to return in time?"

Turning to face Amy, I could see her cooling off now as Pylos's suggestion met with her approval. And smiling graciously at Pylos now, Amy replied, "Yes, thank you Plyos." Surprisingly, it was Ajax who let out a sigh now and clapped Pylos on the shoulder for his quick thinking. And ignoring us now, Sandra and Amy went back to their previous conversation.

Rising from his chair now, Pylos saluted me and bowed to Amy, before saying, "I will see to it immediately, your majesty." Amy and I both smiled and nodded to Pylos now as he turned and exited the tent.

Then Captain Hyllus rose, saluting us before saying, "With your permission, I will return to the city tonight with Pylos as well, your majesties? To personally make sure everything is in order and ready for your arrival." Then he added, "I will leave one squad of Archers behind now with Captain Ajax for flankers and take the other with me." Then Hyllus looked at Ajax, who nodded in agreement now.

And I replied, "Thank you, Captain Hyllus. We will see you at the gates tomorrow." And returning his salute, Hyllus turned and ducked out of the tent.

Ajax and Crios quickly downed the rest of their wine now before rising together. And saluting and nodding again, Ajax said, "Everything appears to be settled, your majesties. Please excuse us now, while we make the necessary preparations for tomorrow?"

Smiling at Ajax, I returned their salutes and nods. And knowing that Crios didn't speak English, I added, "Don't forget to get some sleep tonight, cousin. We'll need you at your sharpest tomorrow!"

Grinning now, Ajax gave Amy and me a quick wink before saying, "Thank you, your majesties," then turning, he and Captain Crios left the tent together.

Turning to Nestor and Sandra now, I asked, "What do you think, Nestor? Sandra?"

It was Nestor who replied first, saying, "I think your majesties made the right choice. And I think General Aetolus will agree with your majesty. But I fear the Consul of Elders will not, claiming the risk to is too great. Preferring that your majesties reach the safety of the palace safely first. But since your majesty made this decision himself, there isn't anything they can do about it now." Then all three of us turned to look at Sandra.

Who was sitting quietly holding Amy's hand, and Sandra replied, "I think it's the logical choice, your majesty. And I agree with her majesty's objection to hiding in a cart. I'm just glad Captain Pylos's quick thinking resulted in an acceptable solution, your majesties."

Smiling now, I nodded and said, "Thank you both." Then turning to Amy, I softly asked, "And what do you think, my love?"

Pretending to be drunk now, Amy faked a burp before answering, "Andrew, if you go and get yourself killed tomorrow and leave me here all alone. I swear to God, I'll kill you myself!" And we all chuckled now at Amy's attempt to make light of the situation.

Then Nestor and Sandra spent the next thirty minutes describing the city and palace to us again, trying to prepare us for tomorrow. Though none of us was really sure what to expect tomorrow. And after giving Amy a kiss on the cheek. We decided to call it a night and climbed into our cots. Though we all tossed and turned a little tonight, each a little anxious about the big day tomorrow.

Chapter - 7

Morning came sooner than expected, and it was the cooks outside our tent asking for permission to enter that woke us. Rolling out of our cots, we were all still half-asleep when Nestor bid them enter. And Amy and I had to endure another declaration from the cooks after they had deposited our breakfast and stood there heads bowed waiting. After Nestor dismissed the cooks and they left, we all rose and moved to the table to eat breakfast.

Breakfast actually tasted good to me this morning, though I couldn't but help think to myself, "the condemned man's last meal," the whole time we were eating. But I kept that to myself. After breakfast, Amy and I dawned our robes again before stepping outside. And as usual, there were half a dozen soldiers milling around outside, trying to look busy while they waited for us to vacate the tent. The soldiers pausing to salute and nodding to us now before continuing about their duties. And Amy and I felt like a couple of bobbleheads on a dashboard before camp got broken down and we had formed up for the march into the capital.

Once our entire formation was stretched out on the road, it suddenly came to an abrupt halt. And we saw Ajax working his way back from the front, stopping to briefly speak to each of the squads separately now as he did. After he had spoken to the Spearmen, they smacked their spears hard on the ground three times before saluting Ajax in unison. And returning their salutes, Ajax moved back to the Archers. And after speaking to them for a minute, we heard what sounded like a low growl coming from the Archers now as they saluted Ajax in unison. After returning their salutes, Ajax moved to the half squad of Spearmen in front of us. And I watched as he spoke to these Spearmen a little longer than the others. And he wasn't barking orders, but speaking to them in a low tone, as if personally speaking to each soldier now. I couldn't understand what he was saying, because it was in Attean. But afterwards, he received the same response from the Spearmen, and Ajax returned their salutes. And before moving past the us in the center now, Ajax paused to nod to

Amy and me before moving back to the squad of Archers behind us. And after receiving the same loud growl and salute from them, Ajax moved on to the squad of Spearmen bringing up the rear. Finished in the rear, Ajax walked back passed us now stepping in between our royal guards and his half squad of Spearmen in front before barking out the order to move out again. The squad leaders quickly repeated the order to move out as we began marching towards the city again.

The road here was wide, well maintained, and almost flat except for the ruts made by the wagon wheels. And there were wood and stone bridges here over all the small gullies and wet spots now. After about three miles, the road left the hillside and moved out onto the flat on the north edge of the valley floor. Still miles away, Attea loomed up large in front of us now, filling our vision and blocking out the east end of the cavern. The road was straight and less dusty here on the valley floor than up on the hillside.

And we walked another mile before we noticed a group of soldiers approaching us ahead in the distance. When they had closed half the distance between us, I could make out their black armor and blue crested helmets. These were royal guards returning and after a while I could make out the slightly taller crest of Pylos's helmet out in front now leading the group. And turning to Amy and Sandra, I saw the smiles on their faces, and I smiled at them, sure that one or more of these men was carrying Queen Hera's armor now.

Just before the royal guards reached our column, Ajax called a halt. And to my surprise, the Spearmen in the front and rear smacked their spears three times on the ground in unison and then Archers, front and rear, let out that low growl now saluting the royal guards as they passed them and came to a stop by their comrades surrounding us. Pylos and the six guards breathing hard and sweating heavily now from their run. But they all stopped to salute and nod as the reached us. And returning their nods, Pylos barked out an order and two of the royal guards stepped forward before turning around revealing the canvas bags strapped to their backs. And the other guards quickly stepped forward to help remove the two canvas bags from their comrades' backs before handing them to Pylos and bowing to Amy and me again before saluting Pylos. And returning their salutes, Pylos barked an order and the guards quickly moved forward forming a tight circle around us now before doing an about-face in unison and raising their shield up forming a privacy screen around us.

Privacy screen formed, Pylos nodded to Amy before opening the first of the two canvas bags exposing the elaborate black cuirass inside. And lifting the cuirass free of the back now, it had gold seahorses on the shoulders and a jeweled seahorse on its chest. And Pylos held it to Sandra now, who stepped forward, putting a grateful hand on Pylos's arm before accepting the cuirass from his hands. Amy removed her robe now, and I stepped forward taking it from her hands. Sandra, with a few helpful words from Pylos, lifted the cuirass up over Amy's head and brought it down over Amy's chest. And with a few words of instruction from Pylos, Sandra buckled the straps on the sides securing it place. Luckily, Queen Hera and Amy were close enough in size that the cuirass fit well. The Queens armor also came with shin, thigh, and forearm guards, which were in the second bag. And opening the second bag now, Pylos began handing them to Sandra one at time, as Sandra set them in place and secured them on Amy. Her armor complete, I smiled at my sexy battle queen now and handed Amy back her robe. And Sandra helped Amy get her robe on and closed over the armor. Then Sandra walked around Amy making sure nothing showed before bowing to Amy. And Pylos made the same check of Amy's outfit before bowing to Amy again. And smiling, Amy graciously nodded now and said, "Thank you Pylos, and thank your men for me too, please. This is greatly appreciated."

Nodding to Amy again, Pylos barked out a command and the privacy shield opened up now as the guards moved back into their travel positions. Then I heard Ajax bark an order, which was repeated by the squad leaders and our train started forward again.

I had Nestor on my left, and Pylos on my right now, while Amy and Sandra linked arms behind us again and began discussing Queen Hera's armor now. We continued across the valley floor until we got within a hundred yards of the city's main gates.

We could see hundreds of people crowding the top of walls now above the blue and gold banners hanging from the battlements. And two dozen city guards in red capes were lined up outside the city gates now, along with Captain Hyllus and one of his lieutenants. Even without his elaborately crested helmet, Hyllus was easy to spot, being a six inches taller than everyone else there. And the people on the ramparts waited until we came to a stop, before raising an enormous cheer from the top of the wall. Followed by a shower of white flowers and confetti floating down from above.

Ajax and Crios stepped out of our formation now, I assumed to go greet Hyllus and his lieutenant. But instead of moving to greet Hyllus, Ajax suddenly barked an order, and the front and rear Spearmen formed into phalanxes now. And the half squad of Spearmen between in front of us and the carts suddenly did an about-face and marching back around our royal guards formed a smaller phalanx around us here in the center. And in battle formation now, we prepared to enter the city. Just as suddenly, the cheering and flowers from the top of the walls stopped as the crowd reacted, stunned into silence now by what they were seeing.

Quickly checking the formations, Ajax wheeled and walked forward to greet Captain Hyllus with one of his squad leaders as protocol demanded. Captain Crios never moved, he just stood there with his hand on his sword, scanning the valley and watching the men. Suddenly I was sure where Crios's loyalty lay now.

Ajax didn't waste time, as he saluted Hyllus and his lieutenant, then the two captains stepped forward exchanging the traditional two-handed clasp of friendship. And they spoke for a minute before stepping back and saluted each other again. Then Ajax and his squad leader turned and strode back to our formation. While Hyllus and his lieutenant turned and walked back in through the city gates. And we watched two squads of the city guard's Spearmen in bright red capes marched out from the sides and came to a stop in the middle of street.

We could see the thongs of people lining both sides of the streets ahead, as the city guards moved forward spreading out and pushing the crowds back now with the shafts of their spears. Forcing the people back off the street as they crowded forward hoping to see their new king and queen. And being forced back now by the Spearmen, which wasn't being taken that well by the crowd judging by their reactions and the surprised looks on their faces.

Then Ajax gave the order, and we began moving toward the massive wooden gates of the city. Ajax's squad leader stepping into the front of the phalanx as it passed, while Ajax waited until our small phalanx reached him before joining our phalanx. The soldiers smoothly parting to let Ajax in now before closing back in around him. And stepping into our inner circle, Ajax replaced Pylos on my right, as Pylos stepped back beside Amy and Sandra. And turning now, Ajax quickly nodded to Amy, Nestor, and me. Then Nestor stepped back and nodded to Amy now, indicating that she should step forward now and take her rightful place at my side. And Amy moved up on my left as we passed through the archway of the west gates into the city now. The enormous battlement overhead at least thirty feet thick.

Passing into the city, the cheering of the crowd resumed again. And every window in the buildings above us on both sides crammed full of cheering Atteans now, most of which were waving small blue and gold banners down at us. And Nestor whispered from behind, "You should wave back, your majesties."

I nodded, and we began waving back, the whole situation having a surreal feeling to it, and leaving Amy and me a slightly dazed. And in a low, urgent voice now Ajax blurted out, "Don't raise your elbows so high, your majesties!"

And we nodded in acknowledgement as we continued to wave but kept our elbow below our shoulders now. I understood Ajax's concern, as raising our elbows created an opening under our arms in our armor. And I heard Pylos repeat Ajax's warning to Amy now to make sure she had heard it over the roar of the crowd. Looking up at people waving in the windows above, I noticed the red capes of Hyllus's Archers standing on the corner of every rooftop above now watching us with arrows notched and ready. Hyllus wasn't kidding when he said he would have the city guards ready for our arrival. The people were all looking down unaware of the archers standing above them on the rooftops now.

We continued forward for three blocks, before a half dozen arrows suddenly burst forth from curtained windows on either side. It happened so fast and so unexpectedly that our phalanx didn't have time to react. But the royal guards, whose reflexes were slightly quicker, managed to block all the arrows directed at me, and all but one of the arrows directed at Amy. Pylos didn't think, he just reacted, and grabbing Amy he shielded her with his body now taking the arrow in his back. I watched in horror now as Pylos's face contorted in pain and he released Amy before slumping to the ground. Our formations slammed to a halt and there was a chaotic explosion of shouts and cries around us. Followed by the sound of heavy footsteps, as our soldiers ran forward busting open doors, following shouts and cries coming from the startled people inside the buildings now.

Nestor and Sandra were already kneeling beside Pylos working on him. And pulling the shaft from his back, Nestor handed it to Sandra, who passed the arrow to me now, saying, "Careful your majesty, that arrow is poisoned." And receiving the poison arrow from Sandra, I noticed it was tipped with the same material as our armor. And there was two inches of Pylos's blood covering the grooved tip now, the grooves put there to hold the poison.

Ajax was outside our phalanx now, pointing with his sword and barking out orders. And the archers moved in around us now forming a perimeter facing outwards, their arrows notched and drawn. Quickly pushing the panic-stricken crowd back twenty feet as the front and rear phalanxes moved in around us now tripling the size of our phalanx and effectively blocking off the streets all directions.

Looking down at Pylos again, I saw Nestor and Sandra were still working on our cousin. While Amy had dropped to the ground beside Pylos now, tears pouring down her lovely face and falling onto the rough stones beneath her feet. And realizing there wasn't anything I could do, I knelt down and took Amy in my arms now trying to comfort her, while we waited for Nestor's verdict.

Suddenly, a commotion above caught my attention. And looking up through a small gap in the shields, I was just in time to see the bloody body of one of the assassins coming fly out of a third story window and land with a dull smack on the street. And to my surprise, it wasn't our soldiers or city guards in the window now, but the citizens themselves. Brandishing kitchen knives or whatever they had managed to grab out the window now, while spitting and hurling insults down at the dead assassin in the street. Which made me grin, in spite of the desperate situation here at my feet with cousin Pylos. Right then, I wished Pylos could have opened his eyes and seen this.

After ten minutes, Sandra smiled at her father and gave him a hug. Then they both turned to look at us, and Nestor nodded now before saying, "Be relieved, your majesties. Captain Pylos is going to recover." I let go of Amy and stood up now while Amy remained on the ground next to Pylos wiping the tears from her face. Overjoyed now, I stepped forward and grabbed Nestor giving him a brief hug, then I grabbed Sandra and gave her a quick hug too now. They were both a little started but recovered quickly and smiled now as they nodded to Amy and me. Having recovered a little, Amy rose and gave Nestor a quick hug now, saying, "Thank you my friend." Then releasing Nestor, Amy wiped her face again before accepting Sandra's open arms.

The shouting and commotion outside the phalanx had died down to a low murmur now. As apparently, all six assassins had paid for the attempt with their lives now. And I heard Ajax and Crios speaking to Hyllus outside our phalanx before the phalanx parted and all three Captains entered our inner circle. Probably to check on Pylos now, as much as on Amy and myself. Saluting and nodding, Captain Hyllus started to apologize, but I held up my hand stopping him. And all three stood there now with hand on their chests and their heads bowed waiting for me to speak. And looking at them, I said, "No need to apologize," and as they looked up, I added, "We were expecting this. Luckily, due to Nestor's and Sandra's skill, our brave cousin Pylos is going to make a full recovery."

I saw Ajax's relax now as he leaning over to translate my words to Crios. Who also relaxed now after hearing the good news about Pylos's condition. But Hyllus did not, and I could see he was taking the injury of his friend seriously and as a personal failure on his part now. Returning the captains salutes, I stepped closer to the three men and quietly asked, "Is it safe to move to the palace now, Captains?" And the three men nodded as Hyllus humbly replied, "Yes, your majesty."

Then Nestor spoke to the nearest royal guards, who immediately turned and made their way out of the phalanx now. Then turning back to us, Nestor said, "I think, and I think her majesty Amy would prefer that Captain Pylos remain here with us until we reach the palace, if that is okay with your majesty?"

Nodding to Nestor, I replied, "I agree."

Nodding again, Nestor added, "I have already sent a guards for a stretcher, your majesty."

Smiling at Nestor's foresight, I replied, "Thank you, my friend."

Then Hyllus saluted and bowed again, before saying, "If you will excuse me now, your majesties? I will lead your way up to the palace now."

Returning his salute now, I answered, "Certainly Captain Hyllus, lead the way." And Hyllus quickly bowed to Amy before turning and leaving the phalanx. A couple of minutes later, the royal guards parted, and two Archers came into our inner circle and saluted Amy and me, before setting a stretcher down next to Pylos now and pausing just long enough to confirm that Captain Pylos's was still alive. Then the two Archers saluted us again before leaving.

Then four of the royal guards stepped out of position now as the other guards closed ranks behind them. And saluting Amy and me first, the four guards quickly slung their shields over their backs before assisting Nestor and Sandra in lifting Pylos up onto the stretcher. And once Pylos was situated on the stretcher, the four royal guards bent down and carefully picked up their fallen commander.

Suddenly there was that loud growl from the archers, followed by spears smacking the ground three times now. And the crowd of people who had been pressing forward now trying to see what had happened suddenly began to back away. Their murmuring silenced now as fear of the soldiers took over. And the crowd remained quiet, and I heard Captain Hyllus out barking out orders in Attean now. The people in front tried to back away, but they were packed in so tightly there wasn't anywhere for them to go. Then I heard the city guards start to move, and Ajax bark out order to move out. Which was picked up and repeated by the squad leaders as the front and rear phalanxes pulled away from our group in the center and reformed now. Once the groups had separated, all six groups came to a halt for a moment before resuming the march forward to the palace.

We moved through the streets in silence now. People still hung out the windows above holding banners and looking down at Amy and me, but their faces were sober now, almost sad. And leaning over to Ajax now, I quietly asked him, "What's going on?"

Ajax leaned back and whispered, "Our cousin is well liked and respected here in Attean. And word of the assignation attempts on your majesties, and of Pylos's injury protecting her majesty has spread like wildfire, your majesty." Then turning to look at me, Ajax continued adding, "Also, they know Pylos is your cousin. So, not knowing your majesty as we do, they're scared that your majesty will his anger out on the city now."

Turning to stare at Ajax now, I said, "That's ridiculous! There is only one person to blame, and that's Helios."

Nodding his head now, Ajax frowned and replied, "Yes, your majesty. We know that, but they don't." Reaching the end of the city, we started up the switch-back cobblestone road to the palace now. And as we climbed, I could see scores of Hyllus's Archers and Spearmen scouring the hillside now looking for any more would-be assassins. The remainder of Hyllus's troops forming up now outside the palace gates as we continued to climb.

Once we reached the top of the switchbacks I could see through the gates. And I saw a dozen royal guards lined up on either side of the gates now. Beyond them, in the large cobblestone courtyard stood two full squads of royal guards at attention. At the far end of the courtyard were two large fountains, between which stood two officers now in the armor of the royal guard. And behind them, at the base of the stairs up to the keep stood four white-haired men in full length robes. Each holding a wood staff and having a colorfully dressed attendant standing by his side now.

As our procession passed through the gates, the Spearmen formed their squads in the empty space on the left now, while the Archers formed up on the right. Our outer shell of Spearmen peeling off now and joining their comrades on the left. When we reached the center of the courtyard we halted and waited as the Archers and Spearmen behind us continued filing in through the gates now and forming their squads on either side of the courtyard. Then when all the soldiers had stopped moving, our circle of royal guards opened up again resuming their normal escort positions on either side of us.

And once our guards exposed Captain Pylos on the stretcher, we heard that same loud growl come from our Archers, followed by the Spearmen loudly smacking their spears on the stone courtyard three times again. Then as we started forward with Pylos, that same low growl and three strikes of the spears on the ground was echoed by the two squads of royal guards here in the courtyard, followed by the city guards outside the gates now. The officers and squad leaders ignored this, as apparently this was the accepted method for the soldiers to vent and show their anger now.

Reaching the two officers, we stopped as they both saluted and nodded their heads to Amy and me. Amy and I returned their nods now as Ajax and Crios saluted them. Then Ajax stepping forward to make the introductions now, saying, "Your majesties, may I introduce General Aetolus, commander of the Attean armies, and Captain Duris of the royal guard."

General Aetolus saluted again and said in English, "It is my great honor to meet your majesties. And I humbly beg your forgiveness for the trouble you had in reaching us here."

I thought about it for a second, before replying, "As long as cousin Pylos recovers, consider yourself forgiven, General. And I thank you for sending us Captain Ajax, without who's his skill and guidance, none of us would have made it out of the Caves of Hephaestus alive."

The General snapped us another salute, and the look of concern on his face as he looked down at the Pylos on the stretcher was plain to see. And now that required protocol was completed, Aetolus moved to Pylos's side and bent down putting his hand on Pylos's arm before looking up at Nestor.

With a sympathetic look on his face, Nestor nodded to Aetolus and said, "Don't worry old friend, he's going to be fine." And Aetolus looked up Nestor's face to get a visual conformation as well as the verbal one now before relaxing.

Suddenly a young, slender, blonde girl came flying out of the keep and ran down the steps pausing briefly bowing to the Consul of Elders before running past fountains and straight up to us now. And giving Amy and me a quick glance, she quickly bowed. Then without waiting for our return bow, threw herself across the top of cousin Pylos clutching him tightly. And seeing he was still alive, she kissed him on the cheek as tears streamed down her pretty face now. Then she looked up at Nestor, and he gave her a reassuring smile before saying, "He's going to be fine Cressida, I promise."

Then rising, the girl quickly wiped the tears from her face with the back of her hands as she tried to regain her composure. And turning to face us, she nodded her head, and said, "I am sorry, your majesties."

And saluting us now, General Aetolus said, "I would like to apologize for my daughter Cressida's actions, your majesties. Captain Pylos is Cressida's betrothed, so please forgive her lack of etiquette."

I returned Aetolus's and Cressida's nods before turning to look at Amy now. Whose eyes were watery too, and getting my message, Amy smiled at Cressida before saying, "There's nothing to forgive, Cressida. Captain Pylos was injured protecting me!" Then Amy held her hands out to Cressida now, who quickly moved forward accepting Amy's outstretched hands. And I heard Amy whisper, "Don't worry about the stupid protocol, Cressida. There's nothing to forgive!"

And not quite believing her ears, Cressida turned to look at Sandra, who nodded her head to Cressida. Then Cressida turned to look at me. And smiling at Cressida, I nodded my head and gave her a wink before saying, "Besides, once you marry cousin Pylos you will be family, Cressida." And Cressida's face lit up as my words sank in.

Relieved, General Aetolus bowed again and said, "Thank you, your majesty."

Nestor spoke next, saying, "Can you and Cressida see to Captain Pylos now, Sandra? I have to report to the Elders, and that will take some time. But I'll drop by afterwards to check on Pylos. With your majesty's permission?" And Amy and I both nodded to Nestor now.

Sandra nodded to her father, then looked at Amy. And receiving a sympathetic nod from Amy now, answered, "Certainly father." And stepping back now Sandra and Cressida bowed to us, followed by

Cressida saying, "With your majesties permission?" And we both smiled at Cressida as we nodded our heads. Then Sandra spoke to the guards, who bent down and picked up Captain Pylos's again. And Sandra held out her hand to Cressida now, who accepted it, and the two women led the way over to a three-story building on the left, which must the barracks with the guards carrying Pylos behind them.

At which point Nestor said, "With your permission, it's time to meet the Consul of Elders, your majesties." And Nestor moved forward past the two fountains to where the four Elders stood now waiting patiently in front of the wide marble steps of the keep. And the four officers followed a few paces behind us. Reaching the steps at the other end of the fountains, we faced the four gray-haired Consul of Elders now. The four Elders were all wearing full length blue and gold robes over their dark grey bio-suits and appeared to be in their late seventies or eighties now, though they varied in appearance.

Once we stopped, the four Elders nodded their heads and the youngest looking of the four spoke now, saying in perfect English, "It is our great honor to finally meet your majesties. And I speak for the entire consul when I say that your majesties presence here, has restored the hope of all of Attea now."

Amy and I returned the Elder's nods, though I couldn't think of anything to say now in response to that declaration, other than to say, "Thank you. I will do my best not to disappoint the people of Attea."

The younger Elder turned and translated my response to the other Elders now. And apparently my response met with their approval. Because they all looked at each other for a second before smiling at Amy and me. Then younger Elder said, "Thank you, your majesty. And we, your Consul of Elders, will do our best to help and advice your majesty."

It was at this point that Nestor stepped forward and nodding again, said, "Let me make the introductions now, your majesties, if I may?" And we nodded to Nestor waiting for him to continue.

Nestor began by indicating the younger looking Elder on the far left saying, "This is Elder Tydeus, in charge of administration and Attea's army. Next to him is Elder Sippas, minister of finance and commerce. Then Elder Thestor, minister of agriculture and farming. And on the right is Elder Kallinos, minister of science and medicine."

Then turning to the Elders now, Nestor continued saying, "Consul of Elders, I am pleased to introduce you to his royal majesty Andrew Tallfer, last descendant of Princess Helena, and his betrothed, her majesty Amy Ryan.

It was Tydeus who spoke next, and bowing again, he gestured to the keep behind him before saying, "I am sure their majesties are tired, hungry, and wanting to get cleaned up after their long journey. And would prefer to speak tomorrow, after they have had time to rest and recover. With your permission, your majesties? Captain Duris, would you escort their majesties to their royal chambers now?" Then Tydeus continued, adding, "The royal stewards and handmaids will see to your every need, your majesties."

I looked at Amy, and she smiled now. I think we both had enough excitement and protocol for one day. And I was sure Amy was ready to shed her armor, have a decent meal and a large scotch now. Followed good night's sleep in by a comfortable bed So, I replied, "That sounds wonderful."

And they all bowed again, then Captain Duris signaled to the royal guards behind us now. And the first eight guards quickly came jogging up on either side of Amy and me. Then saluting Amy and me again, Captain Duris nodded his head and said, "If you will follow me now please, your majesties?" And receiving our nods in return, Duris lead us up the steps into the keep now. The large black doors standing two stories high, with intricate seashells, octopuses, and an enormous gold Seahorse covering the doors. The guards on either side snapping to attention and nodding their heads as we reached the top of the steps and stepped onto the large landing here outside the entrance. Taking Amy's hand in now, we followed Captain Duris through the open doors and into a large foyer and waiting area on the other side. There were two story glass windows lining either side of the room, and enormous tapestries depicting what must be the battle of the "Six Staves of Attea" hanging on the walls between the large white columns. On the other side of the foyer were two curved white marble staircases leading up to the second floor. And below those another smaller set of intricate adorned white doors with guards stationed in front of them.

Reaching the center of the foyer, the two guards by the doors snapped to attention and moved forward opening the doors onto what must be the throne room. As there was a raised blue platform at the far end of the room now with two intricately carved gold chairs with padded blue seats in the center. Continuing ahead, Captain Duris led us through the doors and into the throne room. The wall on the left was covered an enormous mural with a set of white double doors in the center. While the right side of the room was all stained-glass windows ceiling to floor. Rows of white marble columns ran down both sides of the room. And between the columns on both sides were statues or busts sitting on stone pedestals. Which I assumed now were the previous kings or queens who had sat on the throne of Attea.

There were two sets of double doors at the far end of the room, one on either side of the podium. And two royal guards stationed by each set of doors. Captain Duris leading us across the polished floor of the throne room towards the doors on the left now. And passing through the doorway, we followed Duris down a wood paneled hallway for about a hundred feet before the hallway opened up again into a large atrium with glass window. And curved marble white stairs on each side leading back west up to the second floor now.

Two-story clear glass windows covering the entire east wall. On the other side of which was a large perfectly manicured garden. And I could see water squirting from the mouth of a blue crystal seahorse in the circular fountain out in the center of the garden. At the far end of the garden stood another building, with wide stairs leading up to eight white stone columns on the front.

Turning, Captain Duris led us up to the north stairs to the second floor. As we climbed, I could see the hallway contained several doors on the west side now. The largest of these being a set of double doors in the center with gold seahorses on front of the doors and two royal guards stationed in front of them. And I assumed these were the royal chambers. The two guards snapping to attention as we reached the top of the stairs before stepping forward and opening the doors for us.

There was a short entryway, then we passed through a second set of doors into a large room now. The first thing I noticed was the oversized bed on the far wall. Two large seahorses coming together to form the enormous headboard, and their elongated tales curling around the end of the bed forming the foot of the bed. Which, by my estimate, could sleep six comfortably. Then there were two carved wooden doors on either side of the room. To the right of the bed was a dining table with six chairs. And to the left of the bed there was a sitting area with two couches, four padded chairs, and their associated tables. The high vaulted ceiling had a ring of stained-glass around it, and a mural in the center depicting the city of Attean, before the "Battle of the Six Staves" I'd guess. Judging by sun and clouds painted on the mural's sky now.

There were four men standing on the left, and four women standing on the right now. All wearing those below the waist blue tunics with gold seahorses on the front and gold sashes around their waists. And as Amy and I followed Captain Duris into the room all eight servants bowed simultaneously. Our eight-man escort having outside in the hallway and remained there at attention. Then the older man and woman from each group took a step forward now though their heads remained bowed.

Captain Duris walked fifteen feet into the room before stopping and turned around to salute us again. Then pointing to the older man on the left, Duris said, "Your majesty, let me introduce you to your head steward, Agis." Then Duris pointed to the older woman on the right now before looking at Amy and saying, "And this is Petra, the head maid, your majesty." Then nodding again, Duris added, "Both of which speak English. So, with your permission? I shall leave you in their care now, your majesties?" And we both returned Captain Duris's nod. And keeping his hand on his chest and head bowed, Captain Duris backed up five paces before turning and walking back out of the doors closing them behind him.

Agis reminded me a little of Mayor Agatha's little scribe Zoe, except for he was taller. Agis's bio-suit was a blueish grey with a bright blue showing on his shoulder beneath his tunic. And his solid grey hair made him look like he was in his mid-fifties.

Petra was a full-figured attractive blonde, with below the waist hair tied back in a single braid. With a touch of grey showing on her temples and in her braid. Petra looked to be in her late forties to early fifties, still fit but past her prime now. The top half of her bio-suit was a scarlet red with a sparking fish scale pattern to it and her lower half a caramel brown. And she had those same bright blue patches on shoulders like Agis. All and all, I'd bet Petra was something to see in her younger days.

Rising now, Agis spoke first saying, "We are honored to meet your majesties. If your majesties wish, we have hot baths and clean clothes waiting for you." Then bowing again, Agis asked, "And if there is anything particular that your majesties wish to eat, please let me know, and I will have it prepared and waiting for you on your return, your majesties?"

Amy spoke now, saying, "Thank you, Agis. Yes, his majesty and I would prefer to wash before dinner. And simple fish or seafood with steamed vegetables would be wonderful if that is possible please?"

Smiling, Agis bowed to Amy and replied, "Most certainly, your majesty." Then Agis held his hand out now indicating the door to the left before adding, "If his majesty would follow me now, please?" And the other stewards by the wall all turned left now.

At the same time, Petra bowed and asked, "If her majesty will follow me, please?" And Petra gracefully swung her arm out indicating the door on the right now. And Amy turned to look at me giving me a small smile now. And I realized now this was the first time that Amy and I had been apart since arriving in Attea.

And flashing Amy a quick smile in return, I turned and followed Agis through the open doorway into the hall. And passing two sets of closed doors, Agis turned into the third open doorway on the left. Which turned out to be a changing room with a single-step podium in the center. There was a padded light blue couch against the east wall below a tall row of stained-glass windows that ran the entire length of east side and two-thirds the way across the south side now. The right side of the room was completely covered in white closets. And in the southeast corner next to the closets was a collection of ceremonial swords hanging up on the wall. In front of which stood a mannequin with an elaborate set of gold trimmed black armor on it. With the matching helmet, shin guards, and gauntlets hanging on from it. The four stewards stopped to bow, as Agis asked, "Do we have your permission to remove your robe and clothes now, your majesty?"

Nodding to Agis, the three junior stewards stepped forward and removed my robe. And they were a little surprised to discover that I was wearing the black cuirass of the royal guard beneath my robe. Overcoming their surprise, they removed my sword and cuirass now.

Speaking to Agis now, I said, "That was a loan from Captain Erastus in Medina. It saved my life twice, and I would like to make sure it is returned to him with a personal thank you note, Agis."

Shaking his head now, Agis replied, "I can't imagine, your majesty. But I understand. And we will set Captain Erastus's armor here next to your royal armor until you are ready to send it back, your majesty." Stripped down to my bio-suit now, Agis and the stewards took a step to have a look at my bio-suit now. Then smiling and bowed again before holding up a thick blue robe with a gold Seahorse on the back for my approval. And nodding my head, the stewards stepped forward now and slipped the robe up over my shoulders. They all bowed again, as Agis held out his arm and said, "If you would follow me across the hall now, your majesty?" And nodding again, I followed Agis across the hallway into the bathing room.

The bathing room was half the size of the dressing room, with a sunken pool in the center and white marble benches along the walls. There were steps in both the front corners, with gold seahorses running down in the center, their elongated tails forming the handrails. And small gold seahorses lining the walls on both sides, their tails curved outward forming hooks now. After Agis had removed my robe and hung it on the nearest seahorse, he gestured to the pool now. And I slowly worked my way down into the hot water and sat down on one of the benches lining the inside of the pool. Then Agis bowed and left the room now.

A moment later, three attractive young women carrying trays of soap, bottles of shampoo, and towels entered the room. All three had different colored hair and were wearing nothing but a gold sash around their waists now. After they shut the door, they all turned and bowed to me before setting their trays down on the edge of the pool now. Then they calmly removed the gold sashes around their waists and hung them up on the seahorse hooks. And smiling at me now, they walked down into the water with me before taking turns bending over now and blatantly showing me their wares as they grabbed items off the trays. Then indicated for me to lift my arms and set to work softly scrubbing me down from head to toe. Working slowly but steadily now and smiling flirtatiously at me when they reached my nether regions.

Apparently, it was a great honor to have sex with the King. And I was hard pressed not to take advantage of the situation now. And though I'm sure these young ladies had all been chosen now for their beauty and well-toned bodies. None of them was as beautiful, or as sexy as my Amy. So, I tried to think of other things until they finished and led me back out of the pool.. And after drying me, they put the bathrobe back over my shoulders again. Then they picked up their trays and bowed to me in unison before exiting the room.

And a few seconds later, Agis reappeared and led me back across the hall into the changing room again. Where the stewards presented me with several choices of clothing. In the end, I chose a simple long blue tunic, knee-high laced leather sandals, and a plain gold sash. It was the least gaudy of the outfits they showed me. And apparently being appropriately dressed now, Agis led me back out into the main chamber again.

Chapter - 8

I was neither surprised nor disappointed to find the royal chamber empty when I returned and Amy my still in her chambers. Nor was I surprised when one of the handmaids came out of her chambers carrying a tray with an ancient-looking bottle of scotch and a crystal tumbler with a quarter of an inch of scotch left in it now. And seeing me, the handmaid paused to bow before continuing to the table and setting the tray down. Then bowing again, the handmaid turned and quickly went back into lady's private chambers.

Agis, who was standing on my left, patiently taking it all in as I did. The other three stewards were standing by my chamber door now waiting. And Agis spoke up, saying, "I suspect her majesty will be a bit longer yet. Would you care for something to drink now while you wait, your majesty?"

Turning to Agis, I replied, "Yes, thank you Agis. Some wine would be good now."

Smiling proudly now, Agis said, "We have the best wine cellar in the kingdom. Does your majesty have any preference?"

Grinning back at Agis, I said, "We're new here to Attea, Agis. So, I'll trust to your judgement in the selection of a wine."

And nodding again, Agis replied, "Understood your majesty, and thank you." I nodded to Agis, and he raised his hand, and the young steward on the right came running forward and bowed. Then Agis spoke briefly to the young man in Attean. And the steward turned and ran back into my private chambers and disappeared. One of those doors on the left I had seen earlier must be the servant's passage out into the hallway. At which point, Agis asked, "Would your majesty prefer his wine here in the sitting area, or at the table now?"

"Here in sitting area I think. Thank you, Agis," I answered, my eyes still lingering on Amy's door. And Agis held his arm out now gesturing to the sitting area, and I moved over to the large white couch with carved wood adorning both ends and sat down. There was a beautiful woven carpet covering the marble floor here, and Agis stopped now at the edge of the carpet. A few minutes later, the young steward entered the room carrying a tray with two gold cups and a bottle of wine on it now. Bowing first, the slightly winded young steward handed the tray to Agis. And after handing off the tray, the steward bowed and moved back beside the other stewards again.

Agis moved forward now, setting the tray down on the white marble coffee table in front of me before briefly showing me the label on the bottle. Then Agis filled the nearest cup and set the bottle back on the tray before carefully handing me the cup of wine. Then bowing again, Agis resumed his previous position at the edge of the carpet.

I was halfway through my second glass of wine when the door to the lady's chambers opened, and Amy entered the room followed by Petra and the three handmaids. Amy looked amazing now. Dressed in a sheer, shimmering, dark green dress, the bottom of which hung just below her shapely waist. And Amy had a gold sash over her right shoulder down to her left waist now. In the center of which, just below her cleavage, was a large, ruby broach now. Amy's beautiful red hair had been cleaned, combed, and tied into a bun on the back of her head now, showing off her lovely neck. And a fancy ruby-tipped gold comb stuck up behind her head now. Rising from the couch, Petra and the handmaids stopped to bow as Agis and I both bowed now acknowledging Amy's beauty.

Smiling now, Amy lifted her arms up and made a slow circle before asking, "So, what do you think?"

And smiling widely, I replied, "You look amazing, my love. Can we skip dinner and just go straight to the sleeping part?" Amy blushed now comprehending the full meaning of my compliment. And I noticed that the handmaids were blushing as well, while Petra on the other hand smiled. Taking my compliment to Amy now as a reflection on her performance in completing her duties.

Moving to Amy side, I took her hands in mine. And looking into her lovely face, I leaned in kissing her on the cheek now. Which increased the color in Amy's cheeks and made all the servants quickly turn their heads in various directions. And it was Agis who spoke now, asking, "Would you care to dine now, your majesties?" And looking at Agis, we both nodded our heads now.

Agis moved to the table now and proceeded to pull the chair out on the end for Amy, while the first steward on the right quickly stepped forward, bowing and pulling the chair on the other end out for me. At the same time, Petra and the handmaids, followed by the other stewards all moved to the double doors. And opening the doors now, exposed the food-laden carts waiting on the other side. And the handmaids quickly began moving the trays from the carts to the table now. The handmaids bowed before setting the trays down on the table, then removed the covers exposing the steaming food beneath. While the stewards moved forward and bowed before proceeding to set the table now. Petra remaining in the entryway with the two cooks. Their heads bowed now as they gave their declarations that they had personally tested all our food. By the time they finished putting all the food on the table, there was enough food here to feed six people. With three types of fish, lobster, and shrimp. And several plates of steamed vegetables, most of which we recognized, but few we didn't. Agis served me now, while Petra helped Amy load her plate.

Once this was done, Agis leaned in and quietly explained to me the purpose of the two ribbons hanging behind me on the wall. The blue ribbon and bell calling the stewards, while the gold ribbon and bell called the handmaids. After which Petra and Agis both bowed again, then taking the stewards and handmaids with them they left the room. Leaving Amy and me alone to eat our dinner.

We were both hungry, and several minutes before our hunger was under control and we slowed down to talk. Amy talking mostly about her bath now, as apparently Petra had brought both male and female bathers into Amy's bathing room, before asking Amy which she preferred? Completely embarrassed, Amy had chosen the female bathers, though she admitted the young men were all very attractive. And when Amy asked me, I told her I only got female bathers. Leaving out the part where they bent over and showing me their finer attributes or smiling at me as they cleaning my nether regions. I could tell Amy's was becoming suspicions, either by something in my description now, or possibly the vagueness of my description. But Amy was too tired to start a fight and changed the subject now. After we had finished dinner, we sat and talked for a while. Amy had another glass of scotch, while I finished off the wonderful bottle of the wine that Agis had selected.

Rising from the end of the table, I moved over next to Amy, and we each tried a sip from the other's glass. We could see the Staff of Attea had gone dark through the ring of stained-glass above, and we were both ready to try the enormous bed out now.

But we knew that Agis and Petra would want to clear the table before we slept. So, I pulled both ribbons on the wall now, and a few moments later Agis and Petra entered along with the stewards and handmaids. And while stewards cleared the table, the handmaids turned down the bed now. Then Agis and Petra brought out what could only be described as full-length nightgowns. And I informed Agis and Petra now that we preferred to dress ourselves for bed. So, the servants lay the ridiculous nightgowns across the foot of the bed before bowing and leaving the room again.

Amy and I stood on either side of the enormous bed now smiling at each other. Neither of us having the slightest intention of putting those ridiculous nightgowns on. And removing our clothes, we climbed into the enormous bed now. It took a moment to scoot across into the middle of the bed. But once this was accomplished, we snuggled up comfortably together. After spending over a week apart, we were both ready to make love. Amy and I kissed for a while before Amy mentioned that we didn't have any birth control now. Originally, Amy and I had planned to wait a couple of years before having children. But all of Attea was expecting us and counting on us now to give them an heir.

So, we decided to just let nature take its course now. But Amy being raised catholic, made me promise again now to marry her if she got pregnant. And I promised her now, though we were already engaged and planning to get married as soon as we got back from our trip. And we made love for the first time now in our new bio-suits, in this strange new world, and in this enormous bed.

I awoke early the next morning to find that the stained-glass windows above, combined with a couple of well-placed mirrors in the room which I hadn't noticed before, reflected the Staff of Attea's light right into our bed. And I was pretty sure this was no accident either.

Amy was still sleeping in her usual position, cradled up on the left side of my chest with my arm around her now. The early morning light reflecting gloriously off her beautiful red hair now. And I lay there for a while just admiring Amy's beautiful face and thinking how lucky I was that Amy had chosen me.

Then there was a knock on the door to my private chambers. And Amy opened her eyes now smiling shyly up at me. And I answered the knock now, saying, "Yes, give us a minute, please."

And I recognized Agis's voice now as he replied, "Certainly, your majesties." Amy and I both sat up now and scooted back to the edge of the bed. And reaching the side of the bed, we both rose and scooped up our clothes from last night before moving to the foot of the bed. And laying our clothes on the bed, we picked up the hideous nightgowns now and quickly wiggled into them. Then Amy and I looked at each other and burst out laughing. After which, Amy nodded her head letting me know she was ready now.

And turning to the door, I said, "You may enter now, Agis." To my surprise, both my door and Amy's opened at the same time, as Agis and Petra stepped into the room now and bowed. And receiving our nods in return, Agis and Petra stepped to the side now as the stewards and handmaids filed into the room assuming their previous positions before facing us and bowing in unison. Then Agis walked forward stating, "Breakfast is outside waiting your majesties. And so is the Senior physician Nestor, your majesty."

"Thank you, Agis." I returned. Then I looked at Amy for a second and she nodded, and I added, "Can we get changed first please, Agis." Agis bowed, then translated my orders into Attean for the stewards and handmaids. Who turned and proceeded us into our changing rooms now. At the same time, I saw Amy lean over and whisper into Petra's ear. And Petra bowed to Amy before leading Amy into their private chambers now. Agis and the stewards quickly changed me into an outfit similar to last night's one before showing me to my private bathroom. And after relieving myself, Agis and the stewards led me back out into the main chamber again. It was several minutes though before Amy and the handmaids returned. Both of us dressed now, I helped Amy get seated at the table on my left first, before turning to Agis, I said, "I think we are ready for breakfast and the Senior Physician now, Agis."

Agis bowed again, and then said, "Very good, your majesties." And all the servants bowed now before moving to the double doors and opening them. I could see trays of food behind Nestor now as he stood in front of the doors waiting to be admitted. Walking in ten paces, Nestor stopped to bow, then said, "Good morning, your majesties."

Quickly answered Nestor, Amy said, "Good morning, Nestor. You wouldn't have any of that hangover medicine on you, would you?"

Smiling now, Nestor replied "Most certainly, your majesty!"

Then Amy added, "Thank you, Nestor. I'll take it when I return." And Nestor bowed as Amy quickly rose from the table and dashed for her private chambers. Petra holding the door for Amy and bowing now, before Petra and the handmaids followed Amy into her private chambers again and closed the door.

The stewards stepped up now and taking over getting breakfast to the table without instruction. Once this was accomplished and the double-doors closed again, Nestor moved up beside me before bowing again, his smile gone now and quietly saying, "We have a few things we need to discuss this morning, your majesty. The first one, best discussed in private without her majesty." And Nestor frowned now as he raised his eyebrows.

Curious now, I replied, "Okay. We can do that over the tsia." And I indicated the table now. And straightening up, Nestor followed me to the table now.

Agis bowed again, asking, "Is there anything further your majesty requires?"

And glancing at the table, I replied, "No. But thank you, Agis."

Turning to Agis, Nestor said, "His majesty and I require some privacy now Agis, please." And Agis nodded to Nestor, then bowed to me before wheeling around and signaling the other stewards to exit the room now. Then taking hold of the door, Agis nodded to me and Nestor again before shutting the door behind him.

Alone now, Nestor picked up the tsai pot and proceeded to fill my cup and then his before looking at me as he picked up his cup and took a sip of his tsia. And I got the impression that Nestor was hesitating now, unsure of how to begin an obviously delicate matter.

Chuckling now, I said, "Speak freely, my friend. After waking up in this strange new world to your bio-suited face. I doubt there is anything you could say now that would shock or surprise me!"

Relaxing slightly and grinning at me now, Nestor began by saying, "I have spoken with the Consul of Elders at length. Reporting everything that has happened since the rescue, the discovery of your majesty, and our journey here. And the Elders agree with me that your majesty is none other the great grandson of Princess Helena and Captain Tallfer, and the true and rightful King of Attea. And with Ajax's defeat of the Wild Ones at the Cave of Hephaestus. All the major issues facing the kingdom have been put to rest. The only problem the Consul of Elders foresee now, is your heir. And after consulting Attean Law, the Elders have concluded that your heir must have royal blood on both sides to take the throne."

Worried now, I blurted out, "So, what are they saying, that I can't marry Amy?"

Shaking his head, Nestor replied, "No, no, never, your majesty!" Relieved, I leaned back and took a sip of my tsai while I waited for Nestor to explain. And he did, continuing, Nestor added, "This is not the first time that the heir to the throne has fallen in love with a non-royal. And Attean Law clearly provides for such a situation."

Sitting there now, I was curious how Attean Law handled this, so I asked, "And what does Attean Law say we must do to fix this?"

And ducking unconsciously, Nestor replied, "Your majesty must take a second wife of royal blood. And the child from this second marriage will become the next crown prince or princess of Attea."

I understood why Nestor ducked now as I got a mental image of Amy going ballistic when we tried to drop that bomb on her! Shaking my head trying to clear the image, I wanted to ask Nestor a dozen questions that popped into my head now, but asked, "And what becomes of Amy's and my children?"

Relaxing slightly, Nestor replied, "They will still be born princes and princesses, just not the crown princes or princesses. Also, her majesty Amy's and your grandchildren would be eligible to marry the grandchildren of your second wife and ascend the throne."

And I replied, "Okay, that seems reasonable. I mean the part about our children and grandchildren. But Amy to agreeing to me taking a second wife, royal blood or not, I can't see Amy accepting that!"

Nestor hung his head now and replied, "I understand, your majesty. And I am sorry to have to say that her majesty Amy doesn't have a choice in the matter. Attean Law clearly states that any refusal by her majesty would be considered an act of treason against the crown. The penalty for which I am sorry to say, is the same as refusing to become an Attean. . ."

And looking at Nestor in stunned silence now, I replied, "Well then, we best tell Amy as soon as she returns! Better to give her the bad news right away rather than waiting." Then I asked, "I am still be permitted to marry Amy first though, right?"

Nodding, Nestor replied, "Yes, your majesty. The second wedding would be held about forty-five days after your marriage to her majesty Amy. Provided your majesties can agree on the second wife."

Surprised, I looked at Nestor now and asked, "Agree?"

And nodding his head now, Nestor replied, "Yes, her majesty will be present at the selection and has an equal say in which candidate you chose as your second wife. If your majesties cannot agree on the second wife. Then the Consul of Elders will choose whichever candidate is in the best interest of the Kingdom."

Shaking my head, I changed direction now, asking, "Do you know how many women there will be at this inspection? And do you know any of these women?"

Nestor nodded and replied, "Yes, I know most of them, your majesty. But I am not permitted to speak of the candidates, only the ones which have already been excluded from consideration."

Curios now, I repeated, "Excluded?"

And nodding again, Nestor answered, "Yes, excluded for obvious reasons, your majesty. There were fourteen possible candidates for your majesty's second wife. Three of which are too old and already married. And four of which are too young but could be considered later if your majesties fail to agree on the second wife from the remaining candidates. One of the candidates being Cressida, General Aetolus's daughter. But I convinced the Elders to exclude her now from the Inspection. Pointing out that your majesty already has one cousin trying to kill him, best not to make it two. And they agreed."

Interrupting Nestor now, I said, "Thank you, Nestor. Cressida is lovely, but I already think of her as family. And I am sure Amy would never agree to taking the betrothed of the man who nearly dead protecting her." Then I asked, "And the remaining six?"

And Nestor replied, "The rest are here in within the capitol, and all received royal summons from the Consul of Elders this morning. Notifying them that they are candidates for your second wife. And commanding them to present themselves in their best attire at the palace this afternoon. It's a great honor, and no one would refuse such an opportunity."

Looking at Nestor now, I said, "Wow, that's quick. The Consul of Elders aren't giving Amy any time to accept this, let alone get used to the idea of a second wife. I think we may want to dawn our armor before we try dropping that bomb on Amy!"

And Nestor nodded his head now, replied, "I am expecting that same reaction too, your majesty." Just then the door opened, and Amy walked back into the room looking amazing, followed by Petra and the handmaids. Amy and Petra walked directly up to the table while the three handmaids stopped by the door bowing now. Petra following Amy to the table now and seating her. Then bowing again, Petra left again taking the handmaids with her. Nestor rose from his chair when Amy entered the room and remained there head bowed until Amy was seated before taking his seat again.

Smiling at Nestor, Amy said, "Good morning again, Nestor."

And Nestor nodded his head to Amy before replying, "And a good morning to you too, your majesty. I hope you slept a little better last night?" As Nestor calmly set the little vial of reddish hangover medicine down on the table in front of Amy before picking up the tsai pot and filling Amy's cup now. Nodding in thanks, Amy quickly opened the little red vial and downed its contents, then making that "yuk" face again, took a large sip of her tsia. Amy's smile returned to her face a few seconds later, and she said, "Thank you, my friend." Then Amy asked Nestor, "No Sandra this morning?"

Frowning now and nodding, Nestor replied, "I am sorry your majesty. Besides watching over Captain Pylos's recovery for me. Sandra has been diligently trying to finish her remaining studies. While privately being tested by my friend and assistant Timnes, the headmaster of the 'Paideia,' or university in English, among other issues. So, Sandra is a bit overloaded at the moment, your majesty."

Smiling again, Amy replied, "Poor Sandra, I feel exhausted just from listening to all that. And how is Pylos doing, if I may ask?"

Nestor's smiled and answered now, saying, "Much better, your majesties. He was sitting up being fed breakfast by Cressida when I checked on him this morning."

Amy's face lit up now as she said, "Oh, I am so happy for them both. Thank you, my friend!"

Then Nestor looked at me, and I hesitated now before saying, "Amy my love, we have some bad news now that you're not going to like, but there's no way of avoiding it. So, I am going to just tell you straight out and let you vent it all at once." Amy's smile suddenly vanished, but she looked more curious and concerned now than pre-hurricane. But I knew from previous experience that could change in the blink of an eye. And I fully expected Amy to blow her stack and go ballistic once we gave her the bad news.

With a frown on her face now, Amy replied, "Well, don't keep me in suspense, Andrew. Out with it, and let's deal with whatever it is!" I could sense her Irish beginning to rise now, so I dare not dawdle.

Continuing now, I said, "According to Attean Law my heir must have royal blood on both sides, mother's and father's. Which means, that our children won't be able to ascend the throne when I die."

Amy took the news without reaction, then she asked the big question, "So how do the Attean's plan to replace you when you die? And what does the Attean law say we must do to fix this?"

Nestor and I both braced ourselves as I hesitated for a moment before answering Amy, saying, "Attean Law says that I must take a second wife of royal blood." And Amy's face went blank now for a moment, then it started to turn red as Nestor and I both began leaning back from the table bracing for the approaching storm.

Then suddenly the storm clouds vanished, and Amy asked, "But we're still getting married, right Andrew?"

Caught off guard, I muttered, "Yes, of course my love. And we will be married first!"

I could see Amy pausing to think it over now for a moment before asking, "And what of our children, what becomes of them?"

Relieved now, I replied, "They will still be little princes and princesses. Also, our grandchildren if they choose, may marry another royal and ascend the throne."

Then looking from me to Nestor and back again, Amy asked, "And if I should refuse, what are our other options?"

Looking at Amy, I grimaced and replied, "There aren't any other options, my love." And I let that sink in for a moment waiting for Amy's reaction. And I could see her rolling it around in her head now trying to get a grip on it. Nestor and I were both silent now, neither of us daring to speak as we waited to see how Amy was going to react to the ultimatum.

Then suddenly Amy blurted out, "Andrew, when you say there aren't any options, what exactly do you mean?"

Leaning in, I looked Amy in the eyes now before replying, "If you refuse, you will be declared a traitor to the crown. And our poor friend Nestor here will be forced to give you that sea snake venom injection that I mentioned when we first arrived here."

And Nestor spoke up almost in tears now, saying, "Please don't make do that, your majesty. It would break my heart and Sandra's too, your majesty."

Sympathy showing on her face now, Amy answered, "No, my friend. I would never do that to you, nor do I have a death wish either." Then switching the subject on us, Amy asked, "And who picks this second wife? Or do we know who it will be already?"

Looking relieved now, Nestor answered Amy saying, "There were fourteen women who qualified, your majesty. We have eliminated eight now for various reasons. One of those we eliminated was

Cressida. The other six remaining candidates will be here in the palace this afternoon for your inspection."

Surprised now, Amy squeaked out, "My inspection?"

Nodding to Amy again, Nestor answered, "Yes, your majesty. You has an equal say in which candidate his majesty Andrew takes for his second wife." Upon hearing this, Amy burst into a fit of laughter. Though neither of us dared to ask her what was so funny. But I had a fairly good idea and gave Amy a sour look now until she finally quit laughing.

Then Amy frowned and said, "Okay you two, I agree for now, since I don't have any choice in the matter. But only on both your promises now, that Andrew and I will be married first, okay?"

Rising from the table now, Nestor bowed deeply to Amy and replied, "Thank you for understanding this difficult situation, your majesty. I am hopeful that this will turn out better than it appears!" And turning to face me, Nestor nodded again and said, "I have much to report and prepare now. So, if your majesties will excuse me?" We returned Nestor's nod, then he put his hand over his chest and backed up five paces before turning and walking back out of the doors.

Looking over at Amy now, I said, "I am sorry, my love. Nestor only told me few minutes before you came back. And I was just as surprised as you were."

Frowning sarcastically, Amy replied, "Well, don't be surprised when I pick the homeliest looking women there today!"

I wasn't thrilled to hear that, but I understand where Amy was coming from. And all I could do was nod in agreement now, reply, "That's only fair, my love."

The issue seemed to be resolved or at least put on the back burner for the moment. And we took our time eating our lukewarm breakfast now. Chatting about this so called "Inspection," over a second cup of tsia. Both of us trying to imagine what this "Inspection" was going to be like now.

Then I suggested that we ask Petra if they knew anything about the "Inspection," when they came to clear the table. I suspected we would require us to dress for the occasion, and I could just imagine what that was going to look like. Finished with our tsia, I got up and pulled the gold ribbon on the wall for the handmaids now.

And a moment later the door to lady's private chambers opened, as Petra and the three handmaids entered the room and stopped to bow. Nodding to the handmaids now, the handmaids moved forward quickly clearing the table, while Petra moved around the room straightening things up. And after the table was cleared and the handmaids were lined up against the wall again, Amy signaled for Petra, who moved to Amy's side now and bowed her head.

And not wasting any time, Amy asked, "Petra, the Consul of Elders has just informed us that Attean Law requires his majesty take a second wife. Do you know anything about this "Inspection" we are attending this today?"

And Petra answered now, saying, "Yes, your majesty. We were informed there would be an Inspection this afternoon. And I am sorry, your majesty." Then after a second, Petra added, "I believe this is the third time in Attean history that this has happened, your majesty."

Then Amy asked, "So how is this 'Inspection' done?"

Petra, her face blank of expression now, replied, "The candidates will appear before the Consul of Elders for questioning first, then the Elders will make suggestions to improve their appearance or attire if needed. Once that is done, the candidates will be sent out one at a time into the throne room to be accepted or rejected by your majesties. That is all that I know, your majesty."

I answered this time, saying, "Thank you, Petra." And Petra nodded her head to me.

Then Amy asked, "Petra, when does this start?"

Smiling now, Petra replied, "In about two of what you call hours, your majesties." Then she added, "And we should begin dressing you in about an hour, your majesty."

And looking at me again, Amy said, "Not sure if I need a scotch, or more tsia now?"

Chuckling now, I said, "Let's stick to tsia for now." And looking at Petra now, she nodded and raised her hand up. And the first of the handmaids came running forward and bowed, then Petra spoke to the young handmaid now, who turned and vanished back through the door into Amy's chambers. A couple of minutes later, the girl re-entered carrying a tray with two new cups and a fresh pot of tsai. Moving to the table, the girl stopped and bowed to Amy and me before setting the tray down in front of Petra. Then bowing again, young woman turned and moved back to the other handmaids by the lady's chamber door. Petra filled the two cups, then handed one to Amy, and the other to me. Then nodding again, Petra turned and left the room again taking the three handmaids with her.

Shortly after which, Agis and the stewards entered the room from the other side and stopped to bow their heads. It was too early for me to begin dressing, so they must have a message. Returning Agis's nod now, I waved him forward. And moving up to the table now, Agis nodded and said, "You have a visitor, your majesties. Captain Ajax is outside waiting now."

Amy and I both lit up as I replied, "Good, Agis. Please show Ajax in and bring us another cup and some wine too please, just in case."

Agis replied, "Immediately, your majesties," And Agis signaled the nearest stewards forward, who, after receiving his instructions from Agis, wheeled and disappearing into my private chambers. After which, Agis crossed the room to the double doors. And opened the right-hand door now for Ajax, bowed his head as he motioned for Ajax to enter now. Agis closing the door again after Ajax strode into the room then stopped to salute and nod to Amy and me.

Helmet in hand, Ajax looked good. His armor had cleaned and polished, and his unruly brown hair was combed and slicked back on his head now. After we returned Ajax's salute and nod, Ajax moved up to the table stopping to nod again. Amy and I both smiling up at Ajax as we returned his nod whole-heartedly. Then I pushed one of the chairs out with my foot now, and using a mock authoritative tone, said, "Sit, captain."

And Ajax grinned as he saluted me now acknowledging the order, then moved forward taking the chair I had pushed out for him and setting his helmet down on the empty chair next to him. Agis relieved the steward of the tray at my chamber door and approached the table now. And pausing to nod, Agis sat the tray down on the table between Ajax and me now before asking Ajax, "Tsia or wine Captain Ajax?"

Seeing our half full tsia cups now, Ajax replied, "Tsia please." And Agis quickly filled a tsia cup and set it in front of Ajax before nodding again and quietly shooing the stewards out of the room.

Trying to break the ice, I said, "Did you hear the news Ajax? Their forcing me to take a second wife of royal blood?"

Frowning, Ajax nodded to Amy and replied, "Yes. I'm sorry, your majesty. Pylos and I have both spoken to General Aetolus and Nestor on this matter. Complaining that our Attean Laws are antiquated and out of date. And I informed General Aetolus that Captain Pylos, Crios, Erastus, Hyllus, and myself have all pledged our swords and our lives to your majesties. But neither Nestor, nor General Aetolus, were able to change the Elders minds about the Attean Laws."

I could tell Amy was touched by Ajax's confession, and replied, "Thank you, Ajax. And thank Pylos and the other captains for me as well for me when you see them." And Ajax nodded his head to Amy, though there wasn't much more to be said at this point. The "Inspection" was scheduled to take place in a couple of hours.

Ajax spoke now, saying, "Captain Crios and I have to start back in the morning, so I wanted to come by and say goodbye to your majesties." I could tell Amy was as unhappy as I was now to hear of Ajax was leaving. And for a moment, I considered making it a royal command that Ajax remain here in the palace to protect Amy and me. But before I could speak, Ajax added, "Not to worry though, your majesties. My tour in the South Cavern is nearly finished, and Captain Duris and I are due to rotate in thirty days. So, I will be back here in again in time for cousin Pylos's wedding, your majesties."

And I replied, "Good, Amy and I both sleep better knowing you are here guarding us, Ajax."

Nodding his head now, Ajax replied, "Thank you, your majesty." And after a few seconds, Ajax leaned over and whispered, "So do I, your majesty!" And we both had a small chuckle now.

Amy gave us an odd look, and I raised my index finger now, which meant I would tell Amy what we was so funny as soon as we were alone. Ajax downed the rest of his tsia, then got up now and saluted us again before saying, "I have preparations to make before we depart in the morning. So, if your majesties will excuse me now?"

Amy and I both rose now, me to return Ajax's salute and exchange the two-handed clasp of friendship with my cousin. While Amy catching Ajax off guard now, stepped forward and gave him a hug. And I saw Ajax blush before quickly recovering and smiling at Amy now. Then Ajax stepped back and bowed to both of us again, saying, "You do me a great honor, your majesties."

Returning Ajax's nod now, I said, "You will be missed, cousin."

And Amy, tears glistening in her eyes now, added, "Yes, we will miss you, Ajax." And Ajax's looked sad seeing the tears on Amy's face, but hand on his chest, Ajax backed up five paces now before turning and striding back out of the room.

Then Agis and Petra both entered the room now. And bowing first, Agis said, "If your majesties are ready? It's time to dress for the Inspection."

Nodding to Agis, I stepped over to Amy now and took her in my arms before asking, "Are you okay?" And I felt Amy nod her head on my chest, as I added, "You heard him my love, Ajax said he would be back here in the palace in a month for Pylos's wedding."

Recovering a little, Amy looked up at me and said, "I know, but with Sandra busy, and Ajax leaving too now. . ."

I stroked Amy's hair for a moment before leaning down and kissing her pretty tear-streaked face. And out of the corner of my eye, I saw Agis and Petra quickly look away again, embarrassed by our display of affection. And letting go of Amy now, I gave her a smile as I started backing away from her while holding onto her hand until the last second before turning to follow Agis into my chambers now. Briefly glancing back, Amy smiled back at me before turning to follow Petra into her chambers to dress for the Inspection now.

Chapter - 9

Agis led the way into the dressing room now and once we were inside, he asked, "If your majesty would sit, please?" As he indicated the low backed sofa to the left of the podium. Nodding, I moved over the sofa and sat down. Then one of the stewards bowed holding up a hairbrush before stepping forward and proceeding to slowly brush my hair. Then a second steward moved directly in front of me, and bowing first, held up what could only be a toothbrush. And smiling now, he showed me his perfect line of white teeth. Mimicking his action, I smiled, and he stepped forward gently cleaning my teeth. Judging by the feel now he wasn't actually cleaning my teeth, just making sure there wasn't any breakfast stuck in my teeth. Which made me suspect that the bio-suits somehow kept your teeth clean too. And explained the steward's flawless teeth now. At the same time as this was happening, Agis and the other steward began bringing forward different outfits for me to view and choose from.

I was a short sleeved, casual dress kind of guy, and all these fancy outfits just looked gaudy to me. But then Agis showed me an above-the-knee length dark blue tunic with gold trim and a large gold seahorse embroidered on the chest, which I thought wasn't that bad. And I nodded "yes" to Agis now, who bowed and said, "Excellent choice, your majesty." Then speaking to the other stewards in Attean, they quickly finished their grooming then moved to the closets, and removed a couple of items, which I assumed were the appropriate accessories to the blue tunic now. Then nodding, Agis asked, "If your majesty would please stand here?" And indicating the podium in the center of the room, Agis added, "We can finish dressing you, your majesty." Returning his nod, I got up and stepped up onto the podium.

They removed my blue tunic, they replaced it with the dark blue one now. Then they added a gold sash around my waist, and an over the shoulder short sword that hung down on my left side, with a blue jewel in the hilt and three more jewels embedded on sides of the scabbard. Once they had finished dressing me, they stepped back bowed again, as I pulled the fancy sword free of the scabbard now to inspect the blade. The polished silver edges of the sword were sharp, so this wasn't just a ceremonial blade, but a functional one too. Though the oversized jewel on the hilt made it difficult to wield. Carefully sliding the blade back into its scabbard, I looked back at the stewards again. Who had lined up on the right side now waiting patiently with heads bowed.

Turning to them now, I said, "It looks good. Thank you, Agis. And thank you stewards too. I think her majesty will be pleased."

Agis hesitated for a moment like he was a little confused, then he smiled and replied, "Yes, thank you, your majesty" After which Agis indicated the doorway. And turning right, I walked out the door and down the hallway again to the main chamber with Agis and the stewards following behind.

Back in the main chamber, I could see that the table had been cleared, and the bed remade in our absence. And I wasn't surprised that Amy and the handmaids were still inside her private chambers. Then there was a knock on the inner door, and Agis crossed the room opening the door just enough to speak to whomever was on get the other side now. Before opening both doors revealing Captain Duris and Nestor waiting in the entryway. And Agis turned and announced, "Captain Duris and the Senior Physician, your majesty."

Smiling, I waved them forward now. And walking in ten paces they stopped to salute and nod now, and I nodded back to them. Then Nestor spoke first, saying, "Your majesty."

Then Captain Duris saluted again saying, "Your escort is ready whenever you are, your majesty."

I returned Duris salute which I could see surprised him now before saying, "Thank you Captain Duris. Please relax for a minute while we wait on her majesty Amy."

Both men nodding in acknowledgement now as we stood there patiently waiting. Four minutes later, the north door opened and Amy, Petra, and the handmaids all walked into the room now. And as Amy entered Nestor, Captain Duris, and the stewards all bowed to Amy as Petra and the handmaids stopped by the door to bow to me. Amy and I both nodded back without thinking now. And smiling, I chuckled as I noticed my love was wearing a matching dark blue dress that hung down to the middle of her shapely thighs with a gold seahorse in the center and gold sash over her right shoulder down to her left waist now. Amy's red hair had been tied up in a bun behind her head again, but this time, the gold comb sticking up behind her head was taller and had a variety of jewels sparkling from it spiked tips. Amy was dazzling to behold, and still smiling, I held my hands out to her now. And Amy moved to my side accepting my hands as I leaned in and whispered, "You look stunning my love, and take my breath away. I have half a mind to send everyone out and take you to bed now!"

Sliding her hand around my arm now, Amy leaned in and whispered, "Thank you for the offer my love, but do you have any idea how much work it took to get me looking like this?" Amy smiled as she said it, though I noticed some color showing in her cheeks now.

Turning to Nestor and Captain Duris again, I said, "Gentlemen, we are ready." Nestor bowed and stepped to the side, as Captain Duris quickly saluted us again before wheeling around now and leading the way out the doors. Nestor remained bowed until we passed, then he fell in behind us. And I saw Agis, Petra, and the servants all bow again as we left the room. Duris paused briefly outside doors to bark an order before turning to right and heading down hall with the first six guards behind him. And after Amy, Nestor, and I had passed through the doors, the remaining six guards fell in behind us now.

Duris leading us down the south stairs and through the south hallway to the throne room this time. The two guards at the end of the hall opened the door for us now as we entered the throne room and Captain Duris stopped in front of the thrones. Then turning to face us, Duris saluted again, and he stood there head bowed waiting as Amy and I climbed the three steps up onto the podium now. And Nestor following us up onto the platform now before moving to the left of the thrones. As Amy and I stood there hesitating, unsure which chair was whose? Understanding our dilemma, Nestor quickly bowed and whispered, "The one on the left is traditional the kings, your majesty," as he indicating the throne on the left now. Returning his nod, I led Amy to the throne on the right now and seated her. Then I turned around and sat down in the left throne, sliding the sword and sheath forward slightly as I did.

Once we were seated, the guards split into four groups. The first two climbed the steps and nodded to us before taking up position behind the thrones. Followed by four more guards climbing the steps and nodding to us now before splitting and taking up position on the left and right side of the podium. After which, the remaining six guards nodded their heads before splitting and taking up positions on either side of the steps now. Once the royal guards were in position, Captain Duris stood up and nodded again. Then he climbed the steps and took up position on Amy's left now. Then Captain Duris barked out something Attean, and the guards at the far end of the room stepped forward and opened the doors now and stood there holding the doors with heads bowed.

I could see a large crowd of people waiting on the other side now. And in front, was a tall regal looking older man with silver hair. Dressed in blue and gold heraldry and holding long white staff now. And taking five steps into the room, he struck his white staff on the floor three time loudly, before bowing his head and waiting. Returning his nod, the herald took two steps to the side now before turning and gesturing for the first group of courtiers to enter.

The first group of people, whom I had no idea who any of them were, moved into the throne room ten paces before stopping to bow now. Amy and I nodded back to them, then the first group rose and moved forward filing into the space on the right between the white columns and mural on the wall, as the next group of courtiers stepped forward, and the process repeated. This continued until the entire waiting area outside was empty and the guards holding the doors moved forward and shut the doors again. These people had a variety of different colored bio-suits and were all dressed in fancy attire. Some wore large fancy jewels now, and most wearing some sort of brightly colored feathered or plumed hat. The last two people to enter were Captain Hyllus and his lieutenant. But instead of bowing, they both saluted and nodded their heads, and after receiving my nod, they turned and bowed to Amy. And receiving a nod from Amy, they moved to the left taking position by four padded chairs on the left. Which I hadn't noticed up to this point, and which I assumed now were for the Consul of Elders.

With everyone in position now, the regal-looking herald stepped forward and bowed to Amy and me again. And returning his bow, the herald raised his head then struck the ground twice with his staff now before proclaiming in Attean, "With your permission, may I introduce the lady Danae, your majesties?"

Nestor quickly leaning in to translate as a guard on the right stepped forward and opened the righthand door now. And a tall attractive brunette, with long straight hair, and a pleasant face and figure stepped into the room now. Bowing deeply as the guard closed the door behind her. Then the herald stepped up next to the Lady Danae and escorted the girl forward now to the center of the stairs. Then bowing to us again, the herald turned and walked back to the double doors, leaving the girl standing there alone in front of us now.

Then the Lady Danae bowed, and after receiving our return nods, she lifted her head up and raised her arms up now making a slow circle and lowering her arms again, before saying, "It is my great honor to meet your majesties." Amy and I looked at each other, then back at the Lady Danae again as Nestor leaned in now and quietly said, "Your majesties can now ask any questions that you may have for Lady Danae." And nodding to Nestor, I leaned over and passed the message on to Amy now.

And Amy spoke up now, asking, "Lady Danea what is your training or occupation, if I may ask?" Which Nestor translated now.

Lady Danea seemed a little surprised by the question, but nodded replying, "Cooking and pleasing my future husband, your majesty."

Then Amy asked, "Are currently in love, or have you picked out a man that you want yet?"

Again, Lady Danea hesitated for a few seconds, before looking directly at Amy and answering, "Yes, I have, your majesty."

And turning to Nestor now, Amy said, "I have no more questions for the Lady Danea." Then Nestor looked down at me and I nodded.

And Nestor said, "Thank you Lady Danea," in Attean. Then a guard came out of the north hallway and bowed before indicating for Lady Danea to follow him into the north hallway now.

Once lady Danea had gone, the far door opened again and the herald struck the ground twice before bowing, and saying, "With your permission, may I introduce the Lady Gaia, your majesties?" And the process repeated itself.

This time contestant number two was a slender attractive blonde with a wide smile. And Amy asked her the same two questions, number two being an artist, but she too had someone in mind already.

Once number two had left, contestant number three the Lady Helen entered, she was a shorter slightly heavier full-figured brunette with a round jovial face. And I sat back now, content to let Amy ask her questions. Understanding what and why Amy was asking each contestant the same questions. Lady Helen answered cooking, sewing, and pleasing her future husband. And like the previous ladies, she too had someone in mind already.

Contestant number four was the Lady Kassandra. Who was a tall extremely attractive raven-haired woman with a slender face and shy smile. Lady Kassandra answering that she was currently studying science and stated that though she had several men vying for her favor, none had won her heart yet. Amy and I smiled at each other, both impressed by her honesty and by her looks now.

Contestant number five, the Lady Ophelia, was a tall stunning blonde, with soft green eyes which captured and held your gaze when she was looking at you. And I got the impression now that Amy would never choose Lady Ophelia for fear of having to compete for my attention. And Amy asked the Lady Ophelia the same two questions and got back, cooking, and pleasing her future husband. And she admitted that she had several suitors, but looking in Captain Duris's direction now shyly, admitted she favored a certain Captain in the royal guard. Amy and I both turned to look at Captain Duris now, who was standing at attention looking eyes straight ahead, but whose face was more than a little red now. Which caused Amy and me to both let a small chuckle slip out, which was quickly picked up and copied by the entire room now until Amy and I turned and looked over at the courtiers. And Captain Duris's face remained red even after the royal guard had escorted Lady Ophelia out of the room.

Then both Amy's and my jaws dropped now as the doors opened again, and Sandra stepped into the room as the herald rapped his staff twice on the ground and announced the Lady Sandra. Amy and I both turning to glare at Nestor now, whose face was red as he bowed and whispered, "I am sorry, your majesties. But as I stated earlier, I am not permitted to speak of the candidates prior to the inspection or influence your majesties' decision in anyway." Sandra came forward and bowed, then raised her arms, and made a slow circle before lowering her arms again. Then Amy asked Sandra the same two questions out of fairness now, and got back Physician and "no," there wasn't a man she was seeing or who had won her heart on yet. Which, to my surprise, caused Amy to breathe a sigh of relief and smile now.

And standing up now, Amy signaled for Sandra to approach. And climbed the three steps Sandra stopped to bow to Amy and me again. I returned Sandra's bow, but Amy stepped forward and gave Sandra a hug. Which drew a startled reaction from the crowd now, but a positive one, not a negative one. And still holding onto Sandra, Amy turned and looked at me, and smiling at Amy, I nodded my head in agreement now. Then Amy and I turned to look at Nestor now before I asked him, "Do we have your approval to choose the Lady Sandra as my second wife, Nestor?"

And Nestor looked at Sandra, who was smiling and nodding her head now to her father. Then Nestor bowed to me replying, "It would be our great honor for Sandra to be your second wife, your majesty."

I turned and looked at Amy and Sandra now, who were still holding each other, and Amy said, "Then it's settled, I am willing to share Andrew with Sandra. Though I suspect he may eventually begin to feel a little neglected!" And I heard a small chuckle escape from Nestor's and Captain Duris's mouths. Which was fine, considering how this day hard started. And I was thinking, "And once again, peace returns to the valley!"

Then the courtiers gasped in surprise now as Sandra's bio-suit suddenly started to change right before our eyes. As a matching gold ring appeared around Sandra's head and neck, followed a gold spot appearing on Sandra's left arm, then slowly spread around it until it formed a gold band around Sandra's arm. And we all stood there transfixed, a joyful murmur of surprise rising from the crowd as Sandra's bio-suit changed to match Amy's now. And turning to

Nestor now, I said, "Okay, even Sandra's bio-suits agrees with our choice. What's next?"

Nestor bowed and whispered, "Your majesties move to the foot of the stairs and wait for the Consul of Elders to come and confirm your majesties choice. Then after Sandra is approved, the Elders and the entire court will line up to congratulate your majesties." Nodding to Nestor, I stood up and stepped forward smiled at Amy and Sandra as I offered each of them an arm now. Which they both graciously accepted, and I led them down the steps to the bottom of the stairs.

As soon as we reached the floor, the herald rapped his staff twice on the floor and the guards opened the west doors revealing the four Elders waiting on the other side. The Elders and scribes entered now, walking in ten paces before stopping to bow in unison. Receiving our return nods, the Elders moved forward now stopping a directly in front of us before bowing again.

And taking a step forward, Tydeus who spoke now saying, "I approve of the Lady Sandra, your majesties." And turning to bow to Sandra, he added, "Congratulations, your majesty." Then he stepped back into line again with the other three elders.

Next Sippas took a step forward and bowing first, said in Attean, "I approve of the Lady Sandra, your majesties." And turning to face Sandra now, he bowed and said his congratulations to Sandra before stepping back into line. This was followed by Thestor, and then Kallinos, who also both approved of our choice of Sandra. And I could tell by the smile on Kallinos's face that he was especially proud of Sandra now. Then the Elders and their scribes all bowed again, and receiving our return nods, turned and moved to the four chairs on the left and sat down now.

After the Elders sat down, the courtiers came forward next forming into a line on the right now as they drew near. The first of these being an attractive older woman who was the spitting image of Sandra, except for the wrinkles on the corners of her eyes and a touch of grey showing the long blond braid running down her back. And stepping forward now, she bowed deeply waiting.

Sandra and Nestor both smiled, as Nestor stepping forward and nodding now, said, "Your majesties, it is my honor to introduce you to my beautiful wife Sophia, her majesty Sandra's mother."

Amy and I both smiled, quickly returning Sophia's and Nestor's nods. Once they straightened up, Sophia stepped up to Sandra, and bowing first, opened her arms and embraced her daughter. Both the women teary eyed now but smiling. After a minute of this Nestor cleared his throat, and wiping her eyes now Sophia stepped back bowing to Sandra again. Then Sophia moved next to Nestor to receive her congratulations from the courtiers with the rest of us. It was apparent between Nestor and the Lady Sophia they knew every one of the courtiers here and smiled now as they received their compliments and congratulations. When we finally reached the end of the line and the courtiers had all got a chance to congratulate Sandra, Nestor, Sophia, and to meet Amy and me. Nestor leaned over and whispered, "I am sorry to say there's more, your majesties."

Once the courtiers and the Elders had filed back out of the room. Captain Duris and the royal guards moved back into their escort positions, and saluting us now, Duris said, "If you will follow me please, your majesties?"

Wrapping Amy's and Sandra's hands around my arms again, we followed Duris and the guards across the throne room into the empty foyer. Then up the curved stairway on the south side to the second floor balcony. Where there were two guards and our stately looking herald stood waiting by a set of glass doors for the terrace outside.

And we could hear the muffled roar of the crowd outside as we approached the doors. The guards snapped to attention now as our herald bowed his head and waited. And after the three of us returned his nod, the herald signaled to the guards, who stepped forward now and opened the glass doors.

Then our herald turned and walked out through the open doors and across to the balcony's railing now. As a sudden hush fell over the crowd outside. Striking his staff three times on the tiles of the terrace now, the herald loudly announced the three of us in Attean.

Letting loose of the Amy's and Sandra's hands now, I slowly moved forward to the terrace until I could peer through the stone railing into the courtyard below. The entire courtyard packed full of Atteans now with their heads bowed waiting. Overwhelmed, I hesitated now not sure if I was ready to face all of Attea yet.

Then Amy stepped forward and took my right arm, and we looked at each other for a second, before walking out to the railing now and returned the people's nods. An enormous cheer rose up from the crowd as they raised their heads and saw Amy and me on the balcony. All cheering and waving the blue and gold banner of Attea now.

Then after a moment, we both turned to look at Sandra now and I stretched my hand out to her. Nodding her head, Sandra moved forward now and took my left arm. And seeing Sandra, the crowd went wild, as ribbons and streamers burst into the air now, along with showers of white flower petals and confetti. Sandra and Amy both raised their free hands now waving at the thousands of cheering Atteans packed into the palace courtyard below.

After about five minutes of this, Nestor stepped outside and cleared his throat before saying, "You may withdraw now if your wish, your majesties?" Nodding in response to Nestor, I looked over at our herald, who nodded his head, then stepped forward and struck his staff three times loudly on the terrace and a hush fell over the crowd as they all stopped now and bowed their heads.

Then I nodded to the crowd below as Amy and Sandra followed my lead, bowing to the crowd too now. To our surprise, the crowd remained silent with heads bent until I had led Amy and Sandra back in through the glass doors. And once we were inside, an enormous cheer rose up from the crowd outside again. As Captain Duris saluted us, and the royal guards did an about-face now moving into their escort positions. Then Captain Duris led us back down through the throne room and south hallway now before leading us up to south stairs to the royal chambers again. With Amy's and Sandra's hands wrapped around my arms, and Nestor and Sophia walking behind us.

Once Duris and the escort delivered us to our chambers. We entered our room to find Agis, Petra, and the servants standing on either side of the room with heads bowed. And I noticed a tray of wine and half a dozen wine glasses sitting on the table now. So, I lead the ladies across the room to the table. Nestor and Sofia waited as I seated Amy on the right and then Sandra on the left before sitting on the end of the table. Once we were seated, Nestor seated Sophia nodded, then Nestor seated Sophia on the left next to her daughter, before coming around the table and nodding to Amy again, took a seat next to Amy across from his wife now.

Agis and Petra moved forward now, bowing and asking us whether we preferred wine or water. After filling our glasses, Agis and Petra bowed before turning to leave and taking the servants with them.

Sophia who spoke first now, bowing her head and saying, "It is an honor to finally meet your majesties after Nestor has spoken so highly of you. And an even greater honor to know that our Sandra has found favor in your eyes, your majesties."

Amy spoke up now, replying, "Thank you, Sophia. Sandra is and has been our friend since our arrival here in Attean. I was angry this morning after Nestor informed me the Elders were forcing me to share my fiancée with another woman, and I had no choice in the matter!" Then smiling at Sandra, Amy added, "Then Sandra walked out, and I was so relieved, I think I can accept it now."

Sophia nodded, the replied, "We are honored, your majesty. Sandra has told me about your friendship and the journey here. And how envious she was of your majesties obviously love for each other. And how she hoped to someday be as lucky as your majesty."

Smiling, Amy offered her hand to Sophia, who accepted it, as Amy said, "I think Sandra's someday has just started today." And Amy reached out to Sandra now, who accepted Amy's other hand, and the three of them sat there smiling at each other and holding hands.

I could tell Nestor and Sophia had been married a long time, because Nestor just sat back silently now and let Sophia express her feelings without saying anything. And I wondered how all this was going to work. As there was only one bed here in the royal chambers. How did the Attean's handle this situation, and how modern or old-fashioned were Atteans? Or Attean parents for that matter?

Speaking to Nestor now, I asked, "What happens now, my friend?"

And Nestor looked Sophia briefly before replying, "Well, under normal circumstances, her majesty Sandra would be assigned royal quarters here within the palace until the wedding. But since Prince

Helios is still on the loose. And with the recent assassination attempts on your majesties, we fear for her majesty Sandra's safety now. I have spoken privately with General Aetolus and Captain Duris, and they would prefer it if your majesties stayed together, rather than having to protect multiple locations. I also feel that her majesty Sandra would be safer here with your majesty. If your majesties agree?"

I looked over at Amy to see what she was thinking, and she gave Sandra's and Sophia's hands a squeeze, before saying, "I agree. We shared the same tent together for all those nights on the way here. As long as Sophia and Sandra both agree?"

Sophia looked at Sandra for direction, and Sandra nodded her head, and Sofia answered, "It is unusual, but this is an unusual situation. And I agree with my husband, her majesty Sandra's safety come first, your majesties."

So, I spoke up now saying, "Okay, that's settled. How soon can Amy and I be married, Nestor? And how long after Amy and I are married will the second marriage to Sandra take place?"

Nestor thought about if for a moment, then said, "Your majesties marriage can be held in about seven days. The marriage to her majesty Sandra would normally be held thirty to sixty days after that, depending on her majesty Amy's wishes. But I know the Elders would prefer the second marriage to take place sooner rather than later. As the Elders are still worried about the throne and hope your majesties will give Attea an heir as quickly as possible!

About then there was a knock on the door and Agis entered the room now bearing a scroll. And bowing first, Agis said, "The Consul of Elders have sent Nestor a message, your majesty." Nodding, I waved Agis forward now. And reaching Nestor's side, Agis bowed before handing Nestor the sealed tan scroll with a red ribbon around it. Then bowing again, Agis turned and walked back out of the room.

Nestor removed the ribbon and broke the seal on the scroll before quickly reading it. And we sipped on our wine waiting for Nestor to tell us what the Consul of Elders wanted now. Nestor nodded after he read the scroll and looking up now, said, "Apparently Captain Ajax had been watching from the barracks when your majesties stepped out onto the balcony and showed yourselves to the people of Attea. And he was quite upset and went directly to General Aetolus to complain. And Ajax used some very colorful language that I won't repeat, to ask which fool let your majesties step out onto balcony without armor?" And pausing for a second, Nestor continued, adding, "Anyway, General Aetolus was a little embarrassed but agreed with Ajax. And Aetolus went directly to the Consul of Elders. The Consul Elders were also embarrassed. but agreed with Captain Ajax's concern now for your majesty's safety. So, the Consul of Elders have requested that your majesties wear armor from now on, whenever you are outside the royal chambers, until Prince Helios is captured or killed."

I just grinned now, Ajax was right of course. Had there been an assassin out in the courtyard today, we would have been an easy targets for them. And nodding now, I replied, "Ajax is right, Nestor. Let the Elders know that we agree with Ajax's request. Also, Amy and I both have armor, is there armor for her majesty Sandra?"

To which Nestor replied, "I don't know, your majesty."

So, leaning back, I gave a quick tug on the gold ribbon now, and a few seconds later Petra and the handmaids entered the room and stopped to bow. Returning their nods, I waved Petra forward. And Petra moved to the corner of the table between Sandra and me now, before nodding again and asking, "Yes, your majesty."

And I asked her, "Petra, the Consul of Elders have just requested that we all wear armor from now on whenever we step outside these chambers. Is there armor for her majesty Sandra?"

Petra nodded, answering, "Yes, your majesty. It is an older set of armor, but it should fit her majesty Sandra. And since you are taller and thinner than King Heros, your majesty. Work on new set of armor for both you and her majesty Amy has already begun. And now that the Inspection is over, we will order a set of armor for her majesty Sandra now too, your majesty." And pausing to take a breath, Petra added, "But it will take at least fifteen days for our craftsmen to forge three sets of the upgraded armor, your majesty."

Nodding to Petra now, I replied, "Thank you, Petra. That is what we needed to know." And Petra bowed before turning and going back into the lady's chambers now taking the handmaids with her.

Then Agis stepped back into the room again and bowed bowing waiting. Nodding to Agis now, I asked, "Yes, Agis?"

Rising, Agis moved up to the table before bowing again and saying, "It's dinner time. Do you wish to eat now or wait, your majesties?" I was hungry, so I looked at Amy and Sandra. And Sandra nodded, but Amy tilted her head towards Nestor now.

And getting the message, I turned to Sophia and asked, "Sophia, we would be pleased if you and Nestor could join us for dinner?" Sophia glanced over at Nestor, who nodded his head, and smiling now, Sophia replied, "We would be honored, your majesty."

And turning to Agis again, I said, "I am hungry. And we will be five for dinner tonight, Agis. Whenever you are ready, thank you."

Agis nodded and said, "Very good, your majesty. Dinner will be just a few minutes, your majesties." Then bowing, Agis left the room.

Once Agis had left, everyone relaxed again. And Amy resumed her conversation with Sandra and Sophia now, keeping them both busy with questions about Attean wedding ceremonies and Attean wedding dresses of course. Nestor and I just sat back sipping our wine as the three women chatted back and forth non-stop.

Finally, I turned to Nestor and said, "Thank you for staying for dinner, Nestor. And you and Sophia will be family soon, so please speak freely, my friend. I hope that Amy and my choice of Sandra meets with your approval?"

Leaning forward, Nestor put his hand on my arm, and looking me in the eyes now, said, "Yes, your majesty. It is the great honor and relief too, your majesty!" Raising my eyebrows, I waited for Nestor to explain. And smiling now, Nestor continued adding, "We no longer have to worry about Sandra's future. Or worry Sandra would choosing someone that we don't approve of, or we couldn't admire and respect, your majesty."

Nodding to Nestor now, I replied, "Thank you Nestor, you honor me now. Amy and I will do our best to make sure Sandra is happy and never regrets her decision." And Nestor leaned back in his chair again, the women completely absorbed in their wedding preparations now, oblivious to our conversation. Grinning at their distraction, I quietly asked Nestor, "Nestor, so what exactly are my duties as king? Or should I say, what do the Elder and the people expect of me now?"

And grinning wryly, Nestor replied, "Well, after Ajax's crushing defeat of the Wild Ones, the only real issue remaining is Prince Helios, your majesty. Which the Elders have put General Aetolus in charge of. Your majesty's only duty, or what the Elders and people of Attean expect now, is that you give them an heir. And the sooner the better, your majesty."

After today's challenges, and all that has happened to me and Amy since our arrival in Attea. That felt kind of anti-climactic now. So, leaning over to Nestor again, I jokingly whispered, "Tough job!"

Understanding my meaning, Nestor replied, "Your majesties time is mostly his own. If a problem arises, the Elders will request an audience and inform you of the situation. Then give you their recommendations on how best to proceed, then wait for your decision, your majesty." As I absorbed that information, there was a knock on the door as Agis entered again and stopped to bow.

And the women stopped talking now as I nodded to Agis and said, "Yes Agis?"

His head still bowed, Agis replied, "Dinner is ready, your majesties." Smiling, I quickly glanced at Amy and Sandra who both nodded their heads now, and I replied, "Thank you, Agis. You may serve dinner whenever you're ready." Agis nodded in response and both chamber doors opened now as Petra and handmaids poured from the left while the stewards poured out from the right. And crossing the room now they opened the doors. Then the stewards bowed before reaching in to set the table. And the handmaids bowed before setting the food on the table. In less than five minutes, the table was set, loaded with food, and the servants were back at their stations by our chamber doors, heads bowed waiting to be dismissed.

Agis spoke up now, asking, "Is there anything else that your majesties require?" I looked around the table now and got a negative head shake from everybody, before answering, "No, and thank you Agis, Petra." Nodding to each of them as I said their names. Then they turned and all quietly filed out of the room now leaving us alone to enjoy our dinner.

The food was wonderful, as was Agis's choice of wines tonight. The women talked on endlessly about the wedding while Nestor and I sat back and quietly got plastered on the wine while we listened to the women talking. After dinner, we needed more wine. And Amy requested a scotch now, which Sandra and her mother both wished to try. When the drinks arrived, the servants moved in and quickly cleared the table. Amy, Sandra, and Sophia all pausing just long enough to take a sip of their scotches before diving right back into the wedding discussion. I just smiled at Nestor, and he smiled back as I leaned forward and filled our glasses again.

It was midnight before the women's conversation finally began to petter out. And seeing his opportunity now, Nestor spoke up saying, "I'm sorry your majesties, but I need to sleep if I am to accomplish any of the wedding preparations tomorrow, Sophia?"

Sophia got up and steadied herself, then carefully bowed to the three of us saying, "Yes, thank your majesties for the wonderful meal and conversation. We should get some sleep, husband. With your permission, your majesties?" And feeling his wine, Nestor rose from his chair a little too quickly and nearly tipped over. Luckily, I reached out and grabbed his arm in time to steady him before he fell.

Turning to look at me, Nestor smiled and bowed again saying, "Thank you, your majesty," Then giving me a quick wink, added, "And thank Agis for his choice of wines!" Then he bowed to Amy and me again before turning to bow to his daughter Sandra now and saying, "I am overjoyed for you daughter. With your permission, we shall retire now, your majesties?"

Sandra returned his nod before replying, "Thank you father, I am overjoyed too. And you both have my love, and permission to retire." Amy and I returned Nestor and Sophia nods, then the two of them held each other up as they turned and staggered towards the front door now. And I couldn't help but smile as I watched them slowly zigzag across the chamber towards the front door now.

Pulling the blue ribbon now, I summoned Agis. And he stepped into the room before stopping to bow. Waving him forward now, I waited until he reached my side and bowed again before whispering,

"I fear the Senior Physician and the Lady Sophia require some assistance in getting home safely, can you see to that?"

Nodding again, Agis answered, "Immediately, your majesty." And bowing again, Agis turned and hastily moved to catch up with Nestor and Sophia who were just reaching the doors now.

Amy rose and moved around the table to Sandra. And drunk, the two were holding each other now chuckling about what I couldn't guess. Reaching over, I pulled the gold ribbon on the wall now summoning Petra. And a few seconds later the door opened, and Petra and the three handmaids entered and stopped to bow. And waving to Petra, she came forward now while the handmaids remained by the door. And reaching my side, Petra bowed as I told her, "Their majesties are ready for bed I think. And it has been decided now that her majesty Sandra will be staying here with us for her protection."

Nodding her head, Petra answered, "Yes, your majesty. Captain Duris stopped by earlier and informed Agis and me to expect this. Though not the normal Attean custom, he explained their concern for her majesty Sandra's safety." And after pausing for a second, Petra continued adding, "And if I may say so, your majesty? I know Prince Helios, and I share their concern for her majesty's Sandra's safety!"

And I whispered back, "Thank you, Petra. I am glad to hear someone else's opinions on the matter. Her majesty Amy and I are new here, so we appreciate any advice you can give us."

Nodding again, Petra said, "I will have the bed turned down and their majesties clothing prepared immediately, your majesty." Then turning, Petra walked back to the handmaids and quietly began issuing instructions to them. And the handmaids disappeared back into the lady's chambers upon receiving their instructions from Petra.

Agis stepped back through my chamber door and stood there now head bowed waiting. Returning his nod, I signaled for him to approach. And reaching my side, Agis bowed again before saying, "Two stewards and two of the royal guards are seeing the Senior Physician and Lady Sophia home safely now, your majesty."

Smiling at Agis now, I said, "Thank you, Agis." And remembering Nestor's words now, I added, "Oh, and Nestor wanted me to complement you on your choice of wines tonight. Though I suspect it was the reason he required assistance in getting home tonight."

Putting his arm across his waist, Agis lightly chuckled now as he bowed and replied, "It is my honor, your majesty."

Grinning, I told Agis, "It's been a long day, Agis. I need to sleep."

Nodding his head, Agis replied, "Right away, your majesty." And Agis turned and went back into my chambers now. Petra and the handmaids returned with a pair of those antiquated nightgowns for Sandra and Amy now. And Sandra took one look at the nightgowns and burst into laughter as the handmaids laid them across the foot of the bed. Then the handmaids stepped forward and proceeded to remove all the accessories and extras from Amy and Sandra's wardrobes now. Leaving them both with their hair down and only their dresses remaining. I suspect Amy having told Petra now that they preferred to dress themselves for bed.

As Petra and the handmaids exited the room, Agis returned carrying what looked like a set of silk pajamas. And bowing first, he quickly stepped forward and laid the pajamas down across the end of the bed next to the two antiquated nightgowns. Then briefly bowing again, Agis exited the chamber leaving us alone to dress for bed.

Alone now, Amy took Sandra's hand and led her around to the foot of the bed. And removing her dress now, Amy saw my pajamas and picked them up. Then looking at my pajamas for a second, Amy took the tops for herself and handed Sandra the bottoms now. Amy slipped the pajama tops on while Sandra removed her dress and slipped the bottoms on now.

Then taking Sandra's hand again, Amy pulled Sandra back around to her side of the bed again before climbing into the bed pulling Sandra in behind her now. And following Amy's example, I removed my tunic and climbed in on the left. And we all passed out now with Amy sandwiched in the middle.

The next morning, I woke up thirsty with my head pounding from the wine last night. Turning my head to the left, I saw that Amy and Sandra were still holding each other and sound asleep. And they reminded me now of a pair of beautiful children or siblings sleeping together. Getting up, I slipped my tunic on and tied my sash around my waist before moving to the table to get some water.

And wishing Nestor was here now with some of that hangover medicine. To my surprise, there was a white physician's satchel sitting on the table with three little red vials in front of it, one of which had been emptied already. Apparently, Sandra had awoken during the night with a hangover and sent for her medical pouch. Then Sandra left the other two vials on the table for Amy's and me in anticipation of our hangovers. Anyway, I didn't waste any time, pouring myself a cup of water now. I emptied the contents of the little red vial and quickly washed it down with the water. And Nestor was right, it was an unpleasant taste, like vinegar and cold medicine together. But well worth a moment of disgusting taste, as my hangover suddenly vanished. And refilling the glass of water, I set it down next to third red vial now in plain sight for Amy.

Chapter - 10

Later that morning after breakfast with Amy and Sandra, there was a knock on the inner doors. Then the door opened, and Captain Duris stepped into the room now. Duris snapping me a salute before bowing to Amy and Sandra and waiting. Returning his salute, I waved him forward. And Duris moved up to within five feet of the table, before stopping again and slapping his hand to his chest. Obviously, Duris had something urgent to report now that couldn't wait.

Smiling, I tried to make Duris relax a little before saying, "Good morning, Captain Duris, would you join us for a cup of tsai?"

Still holding his hand to his chest now, Duris nodded and replied, "No, but I thank you, your majesty."

Still smiling, I returned his nod and asked, "Okay Captain, what is it you wish to report?"

Relaxing a little now, Duris smiled slightly before replying, "Prince Helios has been captured, your majesty."

And all three of looked up at Duris in surprise simultaneously exclaiming, "What?" Then after a second, I asked, "How?"

Lowering his arm, Duris replied, "This is what Captain Hyllus told us, your majesty. At first light this morning, a group of thirty or more Wild Ones appeared outside the city and approached the gates. Which as you can imagine created quite a commotion. And Captain Hyllus's had his Archers man the battlements while his Spearmen formed up inside the gates. But after brandishing their weapons and howling taunts for a few minutes, the Wild Ones turned and left again. But they left a body behind lying on the ground. After the Wild Ones disappeared, Captain Hyllus took a squad of Spearmen out to see who it was. And reaching the body, Captain Hyllus found the body of a beaten, unconscious male Wild-one. But on closer inspection, they discovered the gold insignia of the royal family beneath the furs covering his chest. And the unconscious Wild One was none other than Prince Helios himself. So, Captain Hyllus immediately arrested him and had him brought to the palace in a stretcher. And Prince Helios is locked up down in the palace dungeon under double guard now being treated by the physicians. General Aetolus sent me here to inform your majesties before going to consult with the Consul of Elders on the Helios's punishment."

Surprised, I managed to say, "Wow!" That was good news, and I wasn't exactly sure how to respond at the moment. But I wondered if Prince Helios would receive the death sentence that he deserved now.

Then Duris continued adding, "Captain Hyllus believes that once Helios's bio-suit changed, the Wild-ones had no further use for him. So, after their massive defeat at the Caves of Mephisto, the Wild Ones beat Helios and dumped him off outside the gates for us to punish."

And I asked Duris, "Sounds about right, don't you think Captain?"

Nodding his head now, Duris replied, "Yes, your majesty. General Aetolus and I both agree with Captain Hyllus's assessment."

Suddenly Sandra sat bolt upright and blurted out, "My father isn't the one treating Helios, is he? I mean, he is the royal physician!"

Turning to face Sandra, Duris nodded his head before replying, "No, your majesty. The Elders and General Aetolus have forbidden your father from treating Helios. Our two royal guard physicians are down in the dungeon treating Prince Helios now, your majesty."

Relaxing now, Sandra breathed a sigh of relief and regaining her composure, smiled before replying, "Thank you, Captain Duris."

Speaking up now, I said, "Tell General Aetolus that I agree about the Senior Physician, Captain. Under no circumstances should the Senior Physician's safety be put in danger. In fact, have General Aetolus inform the Elders that it is my wish now that my future in-laws be given residence here within the palace. Is that understood, Captain?"

Slapping his hand to his chest and nodding his head, Captain Duris smiled as he replied, "Yes, your majesty. With your permission, I shall inform General Aetolus immediately, your majesty?"

Returning his salute, I gave him a quick nod and said, "Yes. Thank you, Captain Duris" Backing up five paces, Duris turned and strode out the room like a man with on a mission now.

Smiling gratefully now, Sandra said, "Thank you, your majesty."

Which drew a frown from me, as I replied, "We are all equal here now, Sandra. I think it's time you start calling me Andrew?"

Sandra nodded her head and answered, "Yes, your majesty . . . I mean Andrew" And we all chuckled now at Sandra's little slip and quick recovery.

Then taking Sandra's hand now, Amy asked Sandra earnestly, "What do you think Helios's punishment will be, Sandra?"

Sandra thought about it for a moment, before replying, "If history serves me right, Attean Law does not permit the Consul of Elders to execute a member of the royal family. So, Helios will either be sentenced to spend the rest of his days in the palace dungeon or be exiled to the outlands. Which as far as I know, has never been done before. So, I'm fairly certain that Prince Helios will be condemned to rot in the palace dungeon. Which is far better than he deserves."

And Amy and I both nodded to Sandra now thanking her for the information. Then thinking about it for a moment, I said, "That doesn't make sense. Logically speaking, the Elders should order Prince Helios be given a snake venom injection and end the threat to crown and our family once and for all."

Realizing I was referring to our future children, Amy and Sandra both nodded in agreement now. Then Amy said, "Yes, I agree Andrew, it's an unnecessary risk. But if it weren't for those same laws, Sandra wouldn't be sitting here having breakfast with us now either!" And bowing to Amy's logic now, I took each of their hands in mine, and kissed Amy's hand then Sandra's. Which made Amy smile, and Sandra blush. And seeing Sandra's blush, Amy broke out into a gleeful laugh teasing Sandra now, which I wasn't sure was the best tact. But Amy knew Sandra far better than I did, and Sandra did need to lighten up a little and relax. So, still holding both their hands, I smiled at Sandra and gave her hand a small squeeze now in support.

The next two days passed without much happening other than Nestor and Sophia coming over for dinner the second night. On the third morning after breakfast, Agis stepped into the room and informed us that Nestor was waiting outside to see us. And after bowing twice and taking as seat, Nestor told us, "The Consul of Elders had reached a decision on Prince Helios's punishment. And Prince Helios is to spend the rest of his days locked up down in the palace dungeon." And pausing to take a sip of his tsia, Nestor added,

"I informed the Elders that is was your majesty's wish that Helios be given a lethal injection. And the reasoning behind your majesty's request. But the Elders stated that Attean Law clearly forbids executing a member of the royal family. No matter how heinous his or her crimes against Attea and the throne may be."

It was Amy who spoke now, frowning and stating, "Well, let's hope Attea and our family doesn't end up regretting that decision."

And Sandra spoke up now, adding, "I agree with their majesties, Father. The Elders have made the wrong decision this time. As this affects not only us but could one day endanger the lives of our children, your grandchildren, and the future of all Attea!"

Nodding his head, Nestor replied, "I know your majesty. And I have argued this point with the Elders at length. But they are not willing to make an exception to Attean Law now, not even for Helios. The Elders agree with your majesties. But pointed out, that once you start making exceptions to the law, where does it end!"

And we were all silent now, knowing the Elders were right. And none of us were up to arguing that point with Nestor or the Elders now. Then I wondered how much trouble I would get into if I were to sneak down to the dungeon tonight and separate Helios's head from his shoulders? But the thought of killing an unarmed man chained to a wall, let alone a cousin whom I had never met, stuck in my craw and seemed cowardly. Even though he had tried to have Amy and me killed more than once. Putting that thought out of my mind, I turned my attention back to Nestor and my beautiful fiancées here at table.

After a second cup of tsia, Nestor rose and excused himself now on the grounds he had much to do if Amy and I wanted our wedding to proceed on schedule. And after saying our goodbyes, Nestor bowed and left the royal chambers.

The next few days passed quickly as we were all busy preparing for the wedding. The ladies consumed with the completion of Amy's wedding dress. While in my dressing room, Agis and the stewards struggled now to find something a little less gaudy that I was willing to wear to the wedding. The south end of the hallway outside our chambers having been walled off by construction workers now as they remodeled the northeast corner of the second floor into Sandra's new chambers. Though Amy and Sandra had already decided we would continue sleeping together until our wedding day.

At least with Helios locked up in the dungeon, we could move around the palace freely now without having to wear armor. But thinking of Ajax now, I decided that we would still wear our armor at all the public events and viewings. Who knows how many of Helios's supporters or henchmen were still lurking about. And my gut telling me that this wasn't over yet, and Helios still had another card to play.

Finally, the day of the wedding arrived, and the whole palace was abuzz with activity. And a cheerful mood seemed to float about the palace now, as if carried on the air. After breakfast, Nestor and Lady Sophia entered our chamber. Then after a cup of tsai, Sophia, Sandra, and Petra whisked Amy off into her private chambers to begin getting ready.

While Nestor and I took lingering over another cup of tsia. After which, Agis and the stewards entered ushering me into my chambers for a bath and to get me dressed for the wedding. This time there were three entirely new attractive female bathers. And after another overly obvious display of their finer attributes, they set to work washing me. Honestly, I couldn't complain, having these three lovely young ladies clean my nether regions now was preferrable to having the stewards come in and attempt it.

Once I had my robe on again, Agis escorted me back into the dressing room. And to my surprise, I stepped into the room to find Nestor waiting inside. And when Nestor bowed, I noticed he was holding an intricately carved wooden box in his hands now. After returning Nestor's and the stewards nods, Agis indicated for me to step up onto the podium. And Nestor sat down on the couch with the box on his lap now as he waited for Agis and the stewards to finish dressing me. Once the stewards had finished decking me out in the medium blue below the waist tunic with gold seahorses on the shoulders, a gold sash, and one of the extravagant over the shoulder jeweled swords. Agis and the stewards stepped back to double-check their work, and finding no fault with my attire now, they all bowed in unison. And receiving my return nod, they turned and filed out of the dressing room now leaving me alone with Nestor.

Rising from the couch, Nestor bowed before saying, "You look very regal, your majesty." And clutching the wooden box in front of him now, Nestor added, "It is Attean custom for the groom to present his new wife with a token of his love and devotion on their wedding day. And knowing that you are new to Attea, I have brought a selection of the crown jewels now for you to choose her majesty Amy's wedding gift from, your majesty."

Smiling at Nestor, I replied, "Thank you, my friend. Though I am surprised that Agis didn't bring this to my attention earlier."

Chuckling now, Nestor said, "Yes. Knowing that your majesty is new to Attea. First Agis, then Petra, both contacted me to make sure that I would provide your majesty with an appropriate gift for her majesty Amy today."

And I chuckled along with Nestor now, he opened the box and held it out to me. Carefully looking over the contents of the box, there were many attractive items inside. But most were gaudy and too heavy or cumbersome for daily use. Then a small necklace in the corner caught my eye, and reaching into the box now, I picked it up and held it up for a closer inspection. The necklace had a two-inch long, slender, tear shaped gem. The gem was clear, except for an aqua-blue tint. And mounted on a thin finely wrought silver chain now. And closing my eyes for just a second, I pictured this necklace hanging around Amy's lovely neck. And smiling at Nestor now, I nodded my head and said, "This one, Nestor."

And Nestor hesitated for a moment, seeming puzzled slightly by my choice now before replying, "Excellent choice, your majesty. I am sure her majesty Amy will love the necklace."

And sensing his curiosity, I asked him, "What is it, my friend?"

Smiling now, Nestor answered saying, "That necklace is the only item in this box which belonged to your great-grandmother, Princess Helena. I find it interesting now that you choose that particular piece for her majesty Amy."

Holding the necklace up admiring it again. I looked over at Nestor and said, "That is interesting, my friend. And I am sure that fact will make this necklace even more precious to Amy."

Then Nestor spent the next couple of minutes going over the wedding ceremony. And having me practice saying, "Ποιῶ" which meant "I do" in Attean. And after I could pronounce "Ποιῶ" sufficiently to pass the Elders and the Attean court, Nestor asked for Amy's necklace back, and he tucked it into a small pouch attached to the sash now, before buttoning it shut again. Then Nestor informed me that he would be standing on my right during the entire ceremony translating for Amy and me. And that he would hand me the necklace at the appropriate time.

About then, Agis entered the room again with two royal guards, and Agis stopped to bow as the two guards saluted. Then the older guard stepped forward and nodded his head to Nestor, before accepting the box of jewels from Nestor's hands. Then saluting us again, the two guards turned and left the room now with the box of jewels. Then bowing again, Agis gestured towards the main chamber with his hand and stated, "If your majesty is ready? I have an excellent bottle of wine open in the main chamber for your majesty and the Senior Physician to try while you wait for her majesty Amy."

Agis didn't need to ask us twice, as I glanced over at Nestor. Who nodded his head now and turning back to Agis, I said, "Lead the way Agis, we're right behind you!" And we followed Agis back into the main chamber now, where a carafe of wine and two cups waited for us on the coffee table in the sitting area. Once we were seated and had our cups filled, Agis bowed again and left us alone to test his claim. It was some time before Amy and the ladies were ready, and since there was a reception after the ceremony, Nestor and I limited ourselves to just one bottle of the excellent wine Agis had provided for us now.

And when the ladies finally brought Amy out of her chambers, she was breathtaking. She had on a full-length white slip underneath, over which lay some sort of woven gold dress that almost covered the whole shift and sparkled in the light as she moved. Her fiery red hair was tied back into a single braid down the middle of her back now, with blue and gold ribbons woven into the braid. On her head sat a slender gold crown with diamonds tips on its four-inch-spikes, and a long sheer white train with gold stitching around the edges now trailing out behind her crown. Amy was absolutely stunning, and I was struck speechless now, all I could do was bow to her beauty.

And realizing that her beauty had rendered me speechless. Amy smiled now as she addressed the woman, saying, "I guess this is the best compliment of all. Looking so good that it renders your betrothed dumbfounded and speechless." Then Amy laughed, and Sandra, Sophia, and Petra all joined her in having a chuckle.

Still chuckling, Sandra asked, "I hope his majesty will still be able to say, I do later?" And the women burst into another round of laughter now.

Ignoring their laughter, I finally regained the power of speech, and bowing now said, "I would say you look amazing my love, but that doesn't cover it. Because you are absolutely mesmerizing now, my love." And that ended their laughter, as Amy, Sandra, Sophia, and Petra all returned my bow now.

Then Sophia spoke up, saying, "We thank your majesty, and are glad you approve." Then turning to Nestor, Sophia asked, "And what about you husband, don't you have anything to say to her majesty?"

Nodding his head to Amy now, Nestor replied, "You are a vision of beauty your majesty. Even the goddess Aphrodite herself would be envious of you today, your majesty." After which, Sophia smiled at Nestor and gave him a quick nod of approval.

Graciously returning Nestor's nod now, Amy replied, "Thank you my friend. That is a true compliment. And thank you Petra, Sophia, and Sandra for all your hard work. I am grateful, and these compliments are for you as well, not just me."

Agis entered the room now and bowed before saying, "Captain Duris is outside with the royal escort now, your majesties."

And nodding to Agis, I turned to Amy and asked, "Are you ready to get married, my love?"

Amy hesitated for a second, looking around the room like she'd forgotten something or left the stove on. Then looking into my eyes, Amy nodded her head now replying, "Yes, I am Andrew."

And turning to Agis now, I said, "Please show the captain in, Agis." Nodding again, Agis moved to the front doors and opened them. Revealing Captain Duris waiting on the other side now, his black armor all polished and his blue crested helmet neatly tucked under his left arm.

Stepping in room ten paces, Duris stopped, slapped his hand to his chest, and bowed his head now, as I said, "Good day Captain Duris."

Smiling in return, Duris replied, "Good day to you, your majesties, and congratulations. We are ready whenever you are, your majesties."

Looking at Amy now, I got a smile and nod from her before saying, "Okay my love, let's go get married!" And I held out my arm out to Amy now, who stepped forward accepting my arm as Petra and Sophia quickly moved in picking Amy's train up off the floor. And Nestor bowed to Sandra now before offering her his arm. And all set now, we followed Captain Duris out the doors with Petra and Sophia holding Amy's train, and Nestor and Sandra behind them.

Once we cleared our chambers doors, we picked up our twelve-man escort. Captain Duris leading us down the south stairs and into the south hallway now. And as we neared the doors to the throne room, the two guards stepped forward opening the doors and bowed their heads. Our procession neither slowed nor stopped now, as we walked out into the throne room.

The throne room was packed full of courtiers, officials, and guests now. In the front of which stood the four Consul of Elders. And everyone bowed as we entered the room and followed Captain Duris up onto the podium. I covered Amy's hand on my arm now as I guided her up onto the podium before we turned around to face the room again and returned everyone's bows.

Petra and Sophia quickly straightened out Amy's train before bowing and backing away to the left. And Nestor led Sandra up onto the podium now and over on Amy's left side, before nodding to the three of us. And receiving our return nods, Nestor moved to right taking up position on my right side now.

Once everyone was settled and the crowd was upright again. The four Elder took two steps forward and bowed. And receiving our nods in return, the Elders climbed the stairs. And reaching the top of the stairs, the four Elders spread out slightly facing us now.

Then Tydeus began to speak now in a loud voice so that everyone in the room could hear. And Nestor leaned in on my right quietly translating Tydeus's words into English now for Amy and me. As Tydeus asked me, "Do you, Andrew Tallfer take her majesty Amy Ryan as your lawful wife and Queen, your majesty?"

And smiling at Amy now, I replied in Attean, "Ποιῶ." Or "I do" and nodded my head.

Then Tydeus asked, "And do you, your majesty, promise to love, honor, and protect her majesty Amy Ryan, all the days of your life?"

And again, I responded, "Ποιῶ."

Smiling, Tydeus turned to Amy now and bowing first, asking her, "Do you, Amy Ryan, take his majesty Andrew Tallfer as your lawful husband and King, your majesty?"

And looking into the eyes now, Amy smiled and replied, "Ποιῶ!"

And still smiling, Tydeus asked, "And do you, your majesty, promise to love, honor, and obey his majesty Andrew Tallfer all the days of your life?"

Amy hesitated as Nestor quickly correcting his translation now, saying, "Obey his majesty in matters of state, your majesty."

And squeezing my hand hard now, Amy gave me a tight smile before replying, "Ποιῶ." Only easing up her grip on my hand after having said the second "I do."

Then turning to me again, Tydeus asked, "Does your majesty have a gift to present to his wife and seal this promise?" And Nestor gently pressed Princess Helena's necklace into my right hand now.

Facing Amy again, I nodded and replied, "Ποιῶ," And smiling at Amy, I let the necklace drop down and dangle from my hand now for Amy to see Then after a moment, I opened the clasp on the necklace and leaned forward, gently fastening it around Amy's lovely neck now. As I leaned back, Amy picked up the little blue jewel admiring it for moment. Then raising the jewel to her lips, Amy gently kissed it before smiling at me.

Then, with tears glistening in her eyes, Amy leapt forward kissing me on the lips, as Tydeus announced, "I now pronounce your majesties, husband and wife." And everyone in the room turned their heads away whether out of courtesy or embarrassment now. And

Tydeus chuckled now as he added, "You may kiss and seal the promise now." And the whole room chuckled with Tydeus now for a moment before their chuckling turned into cheering.

As Amy and I finished our kiss, the whole room fell silent again. And I smiled at Amy for a moment before turning my attention back to our audience. Who I found were all had their heads bowed now silently waiting. And returning their bows now, the Elders each step forward to shake our hands and congratulate Amy and me. Nestor happily translating now for the two Elder who didn't speak English. Then stepping back, all four Elder bowed in unison before going down the stairs and going directly into the open doors on the north side of the room followed by their four scribes. And Sandra, who had been standing beside Amy the entire time, gave me a quick nod before stepping forward all watery eyed now to give Amy a big hug.

And after Sandra and Amy finished hugging each other and wiping the tears from off each other's face. Nestor leaned in and said, "Same as the last time, your majesty. Your majesties are expected to receive the congratulations of the court at the base of the stairs." And nodding to Nestor, I stepped around to Amy's and smiled now as I held my right arm out to my bride. And nodding, Amy accepted my arm now. Then turning, I smiled and held my left arm out to Sandra now. Who nodded and smiled now as she wrapped her hand around my left arm. Then I guided my two ladies down step to the bottom, as Nestor followed us, and Sophia and Petra stepped forward taking hold of Amy's train again now as we descended the stairs. The courtiers having formed a line on the left this time as they came forward to congratulate us now.

After the congratulations petered out, the courtiers all bowed again. Then Duris and the royal guards escorted us through the open doors on the north side of the room into a large banquet hall.

Stepping into the banquet hall now. There was another podium on the east side covered by a wide table and chairs. And the four Elders were seated there now two on each end. And they rose and bowed to us now as we entered the room. There was a ring of white cloth covered tables now with dinner settings already set up, starting here on the South wall and running clear around the room to the east edge of the two-story stained-glass windows on the north wall. And as we turned towards the podium, I noticed a group of musicians up on the balcony above the west side, their heads bowed, and holding their instruments now.

Captain Duris led us to the podium before stopping to salute us while we took our seats now. And once we were seated with Amy and Sandra on my left, and Nestor and Sophia on my right. Duris nodded again before barking out an order causing our royal guards to split and take up positions on either side of the podium.

Then our silver-haired herald entered the room and nodded to us. And retuning his now, he signaled for the courtiers to enter the room in small groups. And walking into the room and they all stopped to bow briefly before moving to the tables and standing beside the cushioned chairs waiting now. And once the last of the courtiers filed in, bowed, and moved to the chairs at the tables. Our regal-looking herald took two steps forward and bowed his head again waiting. And returning his nod, the herald struck his staff on the stone floor twice loudly now and said, "κάθιζε" or "sit" in Attean. And the courtiers pulled out their chairs now and sat down.

Rising from his chair, Tydeus picked his wine cup up and bowed to us first. Then raised his cup into the air for the whole room to see now, and said in Attean, "I speak for the Consul of Elders and all of Attean when we wish your majesties a long happy life, and the blessing of many children now." Nestor quickly translated Tydeus's words, as the courtiers all picked up their cups now and stood up shouting, "μακρὰ ζωή!" Which Nestor explained meant "long life!"

Standing up now, I raised my cup of wine to Amy first, then to the courtiers around the room before down the entire cup now and slam it down on the table afterwards. Which brought on another cheer now from all the courtiers, servants, and royal guards in the room. Amy and Sandra had raised their cups when I did, and both took a generous drink now. Though neither of having any intention of emptying their glasses or slamming them on the table. After the commotion of the toast had died down and cheering subsided. Everyone took their seats again as the herald raped his staff on the floor again and the double-doors opened as he proclaimed, "Δεῖπνον παρέστη." Or "dinner is served." And dozens of servants in blue and gold heraldry began pouring in through the doors now pushing carts of steaming food into the room. And once our table was covered with food, the servants began moving around the room serving the courtiers now. And there were stewards roaming around the room with carafes of wine looking for empty cups to fill now.

And Nestor rose and signaled to the musicians to begin playing, as the courtiers began talking amongst themselves now. The food was fabulous as always, though the music they played now reminded me of one of those old cheesy black and white Italian movies.

Done eating, I looked left to find Amy and Sandra lost in conversation now. No big surprise there. So, turning back to Nestor on my right, I found him sitting back enjoying his wine and looking at me now. So, I asked him, "Nestor, I noticed many things here in Attean seem to be stuck in the past and haven't advanced much over the centuries, like your farming, weapons, and music. Why is that?"

And to my surprise, it was Tydeus on the other side of Sophia who had been listening in and answered me now, saying, "Yes, you're right your majesty. History has taught us of the many wonders and advancements that our ancestors achieved during the time of the six staves. Also, how it nearly destroyed all Attea." And Tydeus paused now to take a sip of his wine before continuing, adding, "Don't misunderstand, your majesty. Our science and medicine here in Attea has far surpasses that of the outlanders. But we have learned from our mistakes and chose to live a simple life here in Attean now. And all the advancements that we make and discover are weighed heavily by the Consul of Elders against that idea now, before being put into use."

And leaning towards Nestor and Tydeus now, I replied, "Thank you, Tydeus. I find no fault in your logic, and I agree."

Nodding his head to me, Tydeus said, "Thank you, your majesty. I am sure the other Elders will be pleased to know your majesty isn't looking to make any radical changes to our daily lives here in Attea."

Smiling at Tydeus now, I added, "Though I still feel it's a mistake not to give Prince Helios the sea snake venom injection. I know their majesties and I would all sleep a lot better if you did!"

And Tydeus nodded his head now, replying, "We see your majesties point. But that law was made when there were only a couple of people with royal blood in the kingdom. Also, to our knowledge your majesty doesn't have an heir on the way yet either?"

Chuckling now, I whispered back, "Yes, but I plan to spend the next couple of weeks rectifying that situation, Tydeus." And Nestor and Sophia who had been quietly listening to our conversation up to this point, chuckled now.

Smiling, Tydeus said, "And we sincerely thank your majesties."

Then Nestor leaned in and whispered, "If your majesties are finished with dinner? It's time to change for your public appearance in the palace courtyard, your majesty."

Nodding to Nestor, I leaned over and put my hand on Amy's arm and gave it a gentle squeeze now to get her attention. And finishing her sentence, Amy turned to look over at me lovingly now. And I whispered, "Nestor says it time to go change for our public appearance, if you and Sandra are finished eating now?" And Amy leaned over to ask Sandra, and Sandra nodded her head that she was ready, while Amy just smiled and nodded now. And turning back to Nestor I said, "We're ready, my friend." Rising from his chair, Nestor signaled the herald now that we were ready to leave.

Cleared his throat loudly now the herald rapped his staff on the ground now three times before proclaiming in Attean, "Their majesties are leaving." And the musicians stopped playing as the room fell silent and everyone rose from their chairs before turning to face us and bowing now.

Captain Duris and the guards moved to the south side of the podium as the guard in front opened the hidden door now leading into the north hallway. Rising from my chairs, I took Amy's hand now before pausing to return everyone's nods and leading Amy out into the north hallway. Sofia and Petra stepped forward to pick up Amy's train again as Nestor bowed to Sandra and offered her his arm now before falling in behind us. And we returned to the royal chamber in the same order as we had left in, except Duris lead us up the north stairs this time back to our royal chambers.

Chapter - 11

Agis was waiting inside with the stewards and handmaidens, and they all bowed in unison and shouted, "μακρὰ ζωή!" Long life as we entered the room.

Amy spoke first, nodding her head to them and saying, "Thank you, my friends." Which made the handmaidens and stewards all smile and bow to Amy again. Then the closest handmaiden stepped forward opening the door into lady's private chambers as the ladies and the handmaidens all followed Amy in through the door and disappeared.

At the same time, Agis opened the door to my chambers and held it while the three stewards filed inside to go prepare my armor. Turning to Nestor and Captain Duris behind me now, I said, "Gentlemen, please sit and have some wine, as today is a day of celebration" and then adding in a hushed tone, "And no telling how long their majesties will take getting ready!"

Chuckling, Nestor bowed and replied, "Thank you, your majesty."

Duris saluted me again, and smiling now repeated, "Thank you, your majesty. And congratulations!" I returned Duris's salute, then turned and followed Agis down the hallway to my dressing room.

This time I walked directly up onto the little podium, and the stewards nodded then set to work removing my wedding outfit and fitting me into my armor. My archer's robe had long since been replaced with a new pale blue colored robe with gold epaulets on the shoulders and a large gold seahorse on the back. Of course, I wouldn't dawn the robe until right before we stepped out onto the balcony. The armor was hot enough by itself here inside the confines of the palace. And after fitting me into my armor, the three stewards bowed and left the room. Then Agis picked up my robe and laid it over his arm before bowing and swinging his free arm out now indicating for me to lead the way back to the main chamber. Nodding to Agis, he followed me back out into the main chamber again. And upon reentering the room, I saw Nestor and Duris on the sofas enjoying a cup of wine.

Both quickly rising to bow now as I entered, and I waved my hand at them saying, "Sit my friends, I'll join you."

Nestor and Duris remained bowed now as I moved forward and sat down on the nearest sofa. While Agis lay my robe across the top of an empty chair before picking up the carafe now and quickly filled a cup of wine for me. Then Nestor and Duris both sat back down and picked their wine cups again. Agis set the cup of wine down in front of me before bowing and asking, "Is there anything else that you require, your majesty?"

Taking a quick look at the coffee table, I leaned over to Agis and said, "Better bring us some more wine please, Agis."

And nodding, he quietly replied, "Immediately, your majesty." Then bowing again, Agis backed away before turning and leaving the room. Agis returned shortly with another carafe and an extra bottle of wine. Setting the carafe down on our table first, Agis put the extra bottle of wine on one of the small side tables for later. Then bowing again, Agis asked, "Will there be anything else, your majesty?"

Smiling at Agis now, I nodded and replied, "No. Thank you, Agis." Agis backed away again before turning and going back into my chambers shutting the door behind him. Turning my attention to my guests now, I asked Nestor, "Do I need to ask how the wine is?"

Nestor smiled before replying, "Agis has outdone himself again, your majesty." Smiling now, I nodded to Nestor and tried my wine. And it was excellent as Nestor claimed. While Nestor and I were liberal in our wine consumption now, Captain Duris was prudent with his. We knew he dared not get intoxicated while on duty.

We spent the next twenty minutes casually talking about Prince Helios's punishment, during which, they both subtly hinted at my need to produce an heir tonight. And I made a mental note to invite Duris and General Aetolus to dine with us after the honeymoon when they were off duty sometime. Which reminded me now of Lady Ophelia. And feeling my wine now, I asked Duris, "So Captain Duris, how are things progressing with the Lady Ophelia?" And Nestor burst out laughing, while Duris, caught off guard by my question now snorted wine out his nose and turned visibly red under his bio-suit.

Trying to cover his red face with his hand now, Duris replied, "It's going well, your majesty." Then regaining some composure, Duris added, "That is to say, now that the entire kingdom knows, your majesty!" And Nestor and I both chuckled now at Duris's reply.

Suddenly the door to lady's chambers opened, as Amy and Sandra entered the room again. Amy was wearing Queen Hera's black and gold armor. And though her long train had been removed, she still had the gold crown on top of her head. Sandra was wearing an older set of black armor. Similar to that of the royal guards but decorated with gold trim and gold seahorses on the shoulders.

Rising from our seats, Nestor and Duris bowed to Amy and Sandra as they entered. And rising a little too quickly I started to feel my wine, and I simply nodded my head to the ladies, fearing I might tip over if I tried to bow now.

Amy and Sandra both entered the room now and stopped to return Nestor and Captain Duris's bows. While Petra, Sophia, and the handmaidens moved in behind them and spread out before bowing to me. Then Amy asked, "We heard laughter. What were you men laughing about, my love?"

Smiling widely and still enjoying Duris's embarrassment now, I replied, "Oh, I was just asked Captain Duris how things were going with the Lady Ophelia."

And the ladies all chuckled now, before Amy sarcastically said, "You're so bad! You should be ashamed, husband!" And the ladies all giggled now at Amy's reprimanded.

Captain Duris just wanting to escape now, and said, "Whenever your majesties are ready?" Quickly bowing again to hide his red face, as he swung his arm out indicating the front doors.

Apparently Amy and Sandra felt sorry for Duris too, as we all answered "yes" at the same time. Moving forward, Amy accepted my arm now as Nestor bowed to his daughter and offered Sandra his arm. Sophia and Petra falling in behind now carrying Amy's and Sandra's robes. And our little troop joined by Agis carrying my robe. Amy's and Sandra's robes were similar to mine, except theirs were pale gold trimmed in royal blue, instead of my pale blue one trimmed in gold.

Passing through the doors, we picked up our escort and went down the south stairs. Then, going through the south hallway, we crossed the throne room into the foyer before taking the north stairs up to the second floor balcony. Once we reached the terrace doors, Agis stepped forward to put my robe on over my armor. While Petra and Sophia moved forward putting the robes on Amy and Sandra now.

Once our robes were on and checked for coverage, Duris signaled to the guards by the doors. And as the guards opened the doors we were engulfed by the sound of the drunken rivalry out in the courtyard. I nodded to our grey-haired herald now, who had been waiting next to the doors head bowed while we got our robes on. He raised his head now and walked out through the open doors onto the balcony stopping by the rail. Then striking his staff on the balcony three times loudly now the noise outside quickly died. Then the herald announced, his majesty King Andrew, her majesty Queen Amy, and her majesty Lady Sandra, from the limited Attean I had been able learn since arriving here in Attea.

Taking Amy's hand now, we walked across the balcony to the stone balustrade together. And looking out, we could see the palace courtyard was completely packed with Atteans. Their heads all bowed now as they waited to catch a glimpse of their new queen.

And once Amy and I had returned their nods, the crowd stood up and began cheering "μακρὰ ζωή! μακρὰ ζωή!" Long life, though I got the feeling this was directed more at Amy than me. Two minutes later, Nestor appeared on my left and bowing first, gently offered me Sandra's hand. Smiling and nodding to Nestor, I took Sandra's hand from him and wrapped it around my left arm. Today was about Amy and me, but Sandra was family too and belonged here beside us now.

Once Sandra was beside me, Amy reached across in front of me and took Sandra's other hand in hers and the two smiled at each other briefly, which drew another huge cheer from the crowd below. Then letting go of their hands, Amy and Sandra began waving to the crowd below but remembering to keep elbows down and their underarms protected now. And I noticed a half dozen wagons laden with casks of wine now on either side of the courtyard and a dozen stewards standing in front them, busily refilling the cups of the cheering

Attean's below. So, this truly was a day of celebration throughout the kingdom. And the tremendous noise rising up from the courtyard now literally was drunken revelry.

After five minutes, I heard Nestor clear his throat behind us. And our regal looking herald spoke to us for the first time in perfect English, asking, "If your majesties are ready now?"

Without checking with Amy or Sandra now due to the sheer volume of the noise out here, I nodded and answered the herald now, saying, "Yes, we're ready." Nodding again, the herald stepped up to the balustrade now and rapped his staff three times loudly on the balcony announcing that we were leaving. Once again the crowd fell silent as they all stopped now to bow their heads. And all three of us nodded to the crowd now as we turned and walked back in through the glass doors. And after the guards closed the doors behind us, we heard, "μακρά ζωή!" Long life rising up from the crowd again outside as they went back to celebrating.

Once we were inside and the doors closed, we all chuckled at the enormous celebration going on outside. And Nestor, Sophia, Petra, Agis, and even Captain Duris joined us now in having a chuckle. After which, Sophia, Petra, and Agis stepped forward and removed our robes. And Captain Duris slapped his hand to his chest and bowed his head now waiting. Glancing from Amy to Sandra now, I got a quick nod from them both before turning to Captain Duris and returning his salute first, before saying, "We're ready, Captain."

Nodding now, Duris barked an order, then turned and led the way downstairs. And forming up behind the front half of the twelve royal guards now we followed them down the stairs.

And safely back at our main chambers, Captain Duris congratulated us again before saluting and leaving with the royal escort. And once we shed our armor and were back in casual clothes again, we all sat down in the sitting area and had a glass of Agis's wonderful wine. And we had another laugh about the enormous celebration going on out in the palace courtyard now, and of course Captain Duris's love life. Then the three women huddled together and had some sort of private conversation, while Nestor told me that my schedule was clear and for the next week and not to expect to see him or Sophia unless there was a problem. As he would be busy overseeing the preparations for my upcoming marriage to his daughter. And their little chat finished now, Sophia and Sandra hugged each other, then they rose and bowed to Amy before turning and bowing to me. Then Sandra very formally said, "Congratulations, your majesties. If you will excuse me now, I will retire to my chambers for the night?"

Amy and I both smiled and nodded to Sandra, then Amy took the lead now, replying, "Certainly, Sandra. And thank you all for making this a wonderful and special day." Then Sandra bowed again before following Petra and the handmaidens into the lady's chambers. And rising now, Nestor and Sophia congratulated us again, before bowing and taking their leave now retiring for the night.

A few minutes later, Petra and the handmaidens returned along with Agis and the stewards. And they quickly set to work turning down the bed, cleaning up the sitting area, and laying out our sleepwear before Agis stopped to ask if there was anything else we required tonight. And receiving a "no" from both of us, the stewards and handmaidens all bowed before exiting and leaving Amy and me alone for the first time today. Rising now, Amy moved over onto the couch next to me, and I put my arm around her as we snuggled up together relaxing over a final glass of this amazing wine.

The next morning, we woke up late, unlike all the previous mornings here in the palace. And no one entered our chamber this morning to wake us up for breakfast. It wasn't until we had dressed, and I pulled the ribbons on the wall that Agis and Petra appeared with the servants. And after ordering some tsia and what Amy wanted for breakfast this morning, Amy disappeared with Petra and the handmaids into her private chambers. In their absence, the stewards remade the bed and set the table for breakfast. And remembering my request this morning that Amy be seated on my right from now on, rather than at the far end of the table.

After relieving myself of last night's wine, I sat down over a cup of tsia and waited for my wife to return. I was halfway through my second cup of tsia before Amy and Petra returned. Amy looking amazing as always, dressed into what we called "casual" attire now, and her lovely red hair braided back up into a bun behind her head again. After Petra seated Amy next to me, the woman whispered something back and forth privately. After which, they both looked in my direction briefly with straight faces before Petra bowed and left again. Picking up the pot of tsai now, I leaned over and filled Amy's cup as I asked, "Should I be worried about that look, my love?"

Looking over the top of her tsia cup now, Amy grinned and replied, "No, my love. That was just women's' talk, not intended for the ears of men." We took our time over breakfast this morning. And when we finished, the servants came in and cleared the table. After which, we sat back over another cup of tsia. I was fairly sure what Amy and I would be doing during our nights this week. But I wondered what we were supposed to do during the day and said as much to Amy now. To my surprise, Amy got up, walked over to the bed, and threw the covers back. Then removing her sash and tunic now, let then dropped to the floor before climbing into the bed and looking at me and saying, "Who says we had to wait until night?"

Smiling, I wasn't going to argue with my wife, so I just took her at her word now and climbed back into bed. Nobody disturbed us and we spent the rest of the day making love. And when the light from the Staff of Attea started to dim in the stained-glass windows overhead, we decided it was time for a break and some food. And after another wonderful dinner and two bottles of Agis's best wine. We found ourselves back in bed again, both of us giving it our best effort to produce the heir that the entire kingdom expected. Though neither of us was thinking about that at the time. And this was our routine for the better part of the next two weeks. And if Amy wasn't pregnant by now, it wasn't for lack of trying.

We finally seemed to have gotten enough of each other and made up for all the lost time during our trip here. And we were both starting to feel a little worn out, honestly. Not to mention, we were starting to get cabin fever after having been locked up inside this room for over a week now. I know I was ready for some fresh air and different surroundings, while Amy was eager to see how things were going with the wedding preparations and Sandra's wedding gown now.

Pulling both ribbons now, summoning Agis and Petra. And after they had entered and approached. I asked Agis to inform the Senior Physician we would be pleased if he and Lady Sophia could join us for dinner tonight. While Amy quizzed Petra now on their progress with Sandra's wedding dress. Shortly after which, Amy leaned over and kissed me now and lingered over the kiss. Before whispering that she was going with Petra to Sandra's chambers now, but she would be back with Sandra for dinner. After the ladies left, Agis stepped forward and suggested that I use this time to take a bath and change before dinner. And while I was bathing, Agis would find out whether Nestor was available to come and try the new wine that Agis had recently acquired. It sounded like a good plan, and giving Agis a smile now, I nodded in agreement.

The same three lovely bathers came in to wash me. But this time they didn't get carried away showing me their wares now before setting to work washing me. And when I reached the dressing room again, Agis informed me that Nestor was currently with the Elders and wouldn't be free for another hour. So, Agis suggested that I dawn my armor now and go out into the garden for some fresh air while I waited for Nestor to arrive. And I agreed.

After the stewards dressed me in my armor, Agis led me back out to the double doors of the main chambers. And opening the doors, I found six royal guards standing ready to accompany me now. Going down the south stairs, we crossed the atrium and out into the palace garden. And I walked around the perimeter of the garden before stopping in front of the white stone building on the far end. Where the senior guard, who spoke English, informed me that this was King Atlas's tomb. And continuing around the garden, I stopped by the large seahorse fountain in the center and sat down there for a while. The royal guards spreading out around me facing outwards now with their blue capes gently rustling in the breeze. They were a little closer than I would have liked and partially blocked my view. But I decided against saying anything. I was sure, this was dull enough task without having to deal with some nitpicky royal. Sitting back, I closed my eyes and listened to the water flowing in the fountain now and drank in the fresh air. And absorbing the heat coming down from the Staff of Attea at the top of the cavern now. After twenty-five minutes or so, I rose and headed back into the palace again.

My escort all saluting me once when we reached my chamber doors. And to their surprise, I returned their salute and their nods now before raising a hand in thanks and walking back into the royal chamber again. Agis and the three stewards waiting by the door to my private chamber with their heads bowed now as I came through the doors. And returning their nods, I waved them ahead and followed them into the dressing room. After they removed my armor and dressed me for dinner, I moved back out to the sitting area in the main chamber where I found a bottle of Agis's latest acquisition open and waiting for me. And filling my cup now, Agis and the steward bowed before leaving me to try Agis's new wine while I waited for Nestor.

I was halfway through my second glass of the delightful new wine when Agis entered the chamber again and pausing to bow, said, "The Senior Physician is outside now, your majesty."

Eager to talk to Nestor now, I nodded to Agis and replied, "Good, show him in please! And thank you for the wine, you've outdone yourself again, Agis."

Smiling at the compliment now, Agis bowed and said, "Right away, your majesty. I am glad your majesty likes the new wine. I shall make sure we have a sufficient quantity stocked in the royal cellar for your majesty." Then Agis turned and moved to the inner doors and opened the right-hand door now before bowing to the Senior Physician and gesturing for Nestor to enter.

Smiling as he entered, Nestor walked in ten paces and stopped to bow. But I stopped him before he could finish his bow, waving him forward now with my hand, as I said, "Good to see you, my friend. I need your opinion on Agis's latest acquisition." And before he could respond I filled the second cup on the tray from the wine carafe.

Smiling, Nestor finished his bow, then giving me a wink, replied, "With pleasure, your majesty." And Nestor rose before quickly moving forward to receive the cup of wine from my hand. And waiting for me to sit down again, Nestor sat down in the single chair on my left now, before taking a sip of the wine now and saying, "Oh, that is wonderful, your majesty." And turning to Agis now, Nestor said, "My compliments, Agis."

Agis bowed again, before replying, "Thank you, I am pleased that you like it. I shall get you another carafe, your majesty."

Nodding, I smiled at Agis and replied, "Thank you, Agis." And bowing curtly now, Agis turned and left the room to get the wine. Nestor and I were still tasting the wine and hadn't said anything yet when Agis appeared with the second carafe of wine. Bowing, Agis set the wine down before turning and leaving again.

Holding his cup up admiringly now, Nestor said, "This really is good wine!" Then turning his attention back to me, he asked, "And how are you doing your majesty, if I may ask?"

Smiling at Nestor, I replied, "Fine, my friend. It's good to see your face though." And taking another sip of my wine, I added, "I assume the kingdom is getting along fine without me now?"

Leaning back, Nestor chuckled as he replied, "Yes, your majesty. I am happy to report there is nothing in the kingdom requiring your majesty's attention at the moment. Other than the necessity of producing an heir. And your majesties have the whole kingdoms best wishes in that endeavor." After which, Nestor set his empty cup down and reached for the carafe again before adding, "It's been a long time since I delivered a baby. And I'm looking forward to it with anticipation now, your majesty."

"So does her majesty Amy. Her majesty and I both want children, though we had planned to wait a couple more years until we were done traveling and had a home of our own." I replied. Then taking another sip of my wine, I continued added, "But since coming to Attea, getting married, and living here in the palace, we agree there is no reason to wait any longer."

Smiling now, Nestor said, "Her majesty Sandra is and has always been the joy in our lives. And her accomplishments are constant source of pride and honor for Sophia and me, your majesty." And just as Nestor finished his statement, the door to the Lady's chambers opened. And in walked Amy, followed by Sandra, Sophia, Petra, and the handmaidens. Nestor and I both rose now to nod to their majesties as they entered.

And receiving their nods in return, I swung my arm out inviting the ladies to join us now in the sitting area. And Agis appeared bearing another carafe of wine and three more wine cups now for the ladies. Which he deposited on the coffee table in front of the women. Then Petra whispered something to Agis which made him smile before nodding his head now and leaving the room again. Petra bowed again now before moving forward to fill the ladies' cups with wine. And I noticed that Petra only filled Amy's cup halfway. Which struck me as odd, but I ignored it since this was the first time in over a week that it had more than just Amy and me here in the chamber.

Then Agis appeared carrying another pitcher now, and bowing first, he stepped forward and topped Amy's wine off with water. Which got my full attention, as not only was Amy not having her usual scotch, but now she was drinking watered down wine. Something was definitely up, so I asked Amy, "Okay, what's going on, my love?"

All four women grinned now as Amy calmly replied, "I'm late. That is to say my period is overdue. And we may be on the way to making you a father, Andrew" And smiling widely, Amy batted her eyes flirtatiously at me now.

Jumping to my feet, I looked at Amy for a second, and still smiling, Amy nodded her head now confirming my silent query. And dropping down beside Amy now, I gave her a big hug and kiss on her cheek, before exclaiming, "That's wonderful, my love!" Then letting go of Amy, I rose again and grabbed the wine carafe now quickly topped off everyone's' cup except for Amy's. Then picking up my cup, I held it up to Amy now, before saying, "To my beautiful wife, I know that any child of yours will be nothing short of amazing! So, here's hoping, my love!" And we all drank a toast to Amy now.

After which, we talked about whether we were hoping for a little prince or princess now. And it turned out neither Amy nor I cared which it was, as long as it was healthy. Being an only child myself, I knew how lonely it had been growing up an only child and still was to this day. And I didn't want our child to grow up alone like I had. Amy on the other hand was the fourth of eight children, and had grown up in a large family, and never even considered having just one child.

The next morning after breakfast, when I pulled on the gold ribbon for Petra and the handmaids, Sandra led the way into our chamber. Nodding to us first, Sandra walked directly up to Amy and leaning down whispering something into Amy's ear. At which point, Amy rose from her chair, and turning to me, leaned in and quickly kissed me on the lips before saying, "Excuse us husband, Sandra and I have important business to attend to this morning!"

And stepping back, Amy, Sandra, Petra, and the handmaids all nodded to me. And smiling curiously, I returned their nods now as they turned and filed back out of the room without another word. Leaving me staring after them wondering what this important business they had to attend to this morning.

Leaning over, I pulled the blue ribbon for Agis and the stewards now. After a moment, the door to my private chambers opened and Agis and the three stewards entered the room before stopping to bow. Returning their nods, I waved Agis forward. And moving up to my side now, Agis bowed his head before asking, "Yes, your majesty?"

Returning his nod, I said, "We're done with breakfast, Agis." And Agis nodded in acknowledgement as I whispered, "Any idea what the women are up this morning, Agis?"

And glancing at the door to lady's chambers now, Agis shook his head negatively before whispering back, "I am sorry to say I have no idea, your majesty."

To which I replied, "Hmm!" And looking over at the door to lady's chamber again, I said, "Okay. Well, how about a bath and a change of clothes, Agis?"

Nodding his head again, Agis grinned as he replied, "Very good, your majesty. Both are ready and waiting for you." Returning Agis's nod, I rose from the table now and moved to my private chambers. Agis and the stewards turning to following me. And after the three lovely young ladies had finished washing me again. Agis and the stewards presented me with a brand-new tunic. The color of which matched the blue of my bio-suit now to a tee and had a small gold seahorse on the chest, and I nodded my approval. Having figured out my preference for simple, less gaudy clothes now, Agis was having new outfits added to my wardrobe. I wasn't complaining now as the stewards wrapped a gold sash around my waist completing my outfit.

Then Agis pointed to the mirror on the wall now as the four men bowed their heads and waited. Looking in the mirror, I smiled and returned their nods now before saying, "I like it, Agis. Thank you, and thank you stewards, too." Bowing again, Agis gestured to the door now as we were done in here. And turning, I walked back out into the main chamber with Agis and the stewards following behind.

Chapter - 12

Just as I stepped back into the main chamber, the door on the other side of the room opened and Amy, Sandra, and Petra followed by the three handmaidens walked in. All of which were smiling now as they stopped to nod their heads. And I could tell something was up by the excited look on Amy's face now as I returned their nods. As soon as I returned their nods, Amy ran forward and leapt into arms, kissing me, and whispering, "It's confirmed, my love. I'm pregnant!"

Cradling Amy's face in my hands, I looked down into her beautiful blue eyes now waiting for her to visually confirm what she had just said. And looking up at me now Amy nodded her head. And pulling Amy to me, I kissed her lips and held her tightly, as we celebrated the news of Amy's pregnancy and our first child.

Then leaning back, I smiled proudly at wife and noticed every head in the chamber was turned away to avoid looking at us. And Amy joined me now in having a chuckle at their antics. I didn't care, I was just overjoyed that Amy was pregnant, and that I was going to be a father soon.

Still holding me, Amy said, "Sandra gave me the pregnancy test me this morning and it came back positive." Taking my attention off Amy for a moment, I looked over at Sandra now, who smiled and nodded her head confirming Amy's news. Then grinning, Amy whispered, "Let's have your wedding to Sandra as soon as possible. I want Sandra to know this incredible feeling I have now too, my love!"

And nodding my head to Amy, I bent down and kissed her on the lips now before whispering, "As you wish, my love. I'll speak to Nestor about it as soon as he arrives." Releasing Amy, I kept hold of her hand now as turned to Petra and asked, "Petra, have the Consul of Elders been notified of the Queen's glorious condition yet?"

Stepping forward, Petra nodded her head replying, "No, your majesty. Such matters require your majesties permission, first."

Nodding to Petra, I acknowledged her response. Then looking directly at her now, I said, "Please inform the Consul of Elders of her majesty's glorious condition now, Petra. And let Nestor know that we wish to speak with him at his earliest convenance, please."

Nodding in response, Petra replied, "Immediately, your majesty!"

Then raising my eyebrows, I chuckled at Petra adding, "Oh, and Petra! I suggest you hurry and get her majesty Sandra's wedding dress finished." Both Sandra and Petra grinned now understanding my meaning. Then Petra turned to go and report the glorious news to the Consul of Elders, as Amy opened her arms to Sandra. Who quickly crossed the room to accept Amy's open arms now.

And after Agis brought us tsia, Amy and Sandra sat together on the couch while I sat in the single chair. As they discussed the second wedding and Amy's pregnancy now while continuing to hug each other. And Amy had been right at the Inspection, I did feel a little left out now as the two of them joyfully chatted away none-stop. Luckily, thirty minutes later, we heard, and then saw, a huge barrage of pink and blue fireworks exploding above the palace now through the ring of stained glass in the ceiling. And Sandra explained, this was just the Consul of Elders announcing to Attea that the Queen is pregnant now.

And we all stood up now to watch the fireworks through the ring of stained glass in the ceiling. Then Agis stepped into the room and stopped to nod his head and wait.

Smiling at Agis, I returned his nod and Agis stated, "The Senior Physician is outside now, your majesties."

Still smiling, I replied, "Good Agis, show him in, please." And nodding again, Agis moved to the inner doors, opening the righthand door before nodding to Nestor and gesturing for him to enter.

Grinning widely, Nestor walked in five paces and stopped to nod to the three of us now. And we all eagerly returned Nestor's nod as we waved him forward now to join us in celebrating the good news. Approaching the three of us, Nestor stopped to nod again, and we returned his nod as I shook my head and frowned at all this pointless protocol as I indicated for Nestor to take a seat.

Taking a seat on the other couch, Nestor smiled and nodded to Amy, before saying, "Congratulations on the wonderful news, your majesty." Then he added, "As you can see, the whole city is celebrating the joyous news now too, your majesties!"

Smiling, Amy returned Nestor's nod before replying, "Thank you, my friend. And I am happy to be fulfilling my royal obligation now." Then Amy and Sandra both giggled and hugged each other again.

Speaking up now, I said, "The reason I sent for you today Nestor, is now that her majesty pregnancy has been confirmed. It is her majesty's wish that Sandra and my wedding take place as soon as it can be arranged. So that Sandra may know the immense joy she feels now too!" After I finished speaking, Amy took Sandra's hand and held it to her stomach now, smiling at Sandra and nodding her head. And both women, their eyes watery now hugged each other again. And when I looked back at Nestor, he was dabbing his eyes now too, apparently moved by his daughter's tears of joy.

It was still early, and Agis entered the room now bearing a single tsia cup and saucer for Nestor before pausing to nod. And I waved Agis forward as Nestor and the ladies tried to recover. Stopping at the edge of the carpet to Agis nodding again, and I returned Agis's nod. Then Agis set the cup down in front of Nestor, and quickly filled it with tsia before nodding and asking, "Is there anything else your majesties require?"

Looking around the room everyone shook their head no, so I replied, "No, but will be five for dinner again tonight, Agis."

Smiling, Agis nodded his head again, replying, "Very good, your majesty." And I returned Agis's nod as he turned and left the room.

Turning to Nestor, I asked, "I hope you and Lady Sophia will be able to join us for dinner tonight?"

Grinning confidently, Nestor replied, "Even without this joyous news, I know my Sophia would never pass up the chance to dine with your majesties." Then pausing for a moment, Nestor added, "Plus, we need Sophia input so we can move the wedding up and figure out how quickly it can take place. Sophia is great at pointing out the little details that I tend to overlook." And we all nodded to Nestor as Amy and Sandra discussed the second wedding amongst themselves now.

And I took this opportunity to lean over to Nestor and whisper, "Maybe you could get the Lady Sophia's help in choosing the right wedding gift for Sandra too?"

Nodding his head, Nestor whispered back, "Yes, I'll definitely have her do that, your majesty." Finishing his tsia, Nestor stood up now and nodded before saying, "If your majesties will excuse me now? I shall go inform the Consul of Elders that is your majesties wish the second wedding take place as soon as it can be arranged."

And Sandra who spoke now, returning her father's nod, and saying, "Thank you father. We look forward to seeing you and mother at dinner tonight." Nodding to Sandra now, Nestor backed away five paces before turning and walking back out the door.

And since we had several hours until dinner, I suggested that we take a walk in the palace garden now and get some fresh air before dinner. Especially, since we were no longer required to put on amor before stepping outside the royal chambers now. Amy and Sandra both eagerly agreed as we had all spent the last two weeks basically couped up here inside the royal chambers.

Moving to the wall, I pulled the blue ribbon now. And Agis and the stewards appearing a moment later, stepping into the room and nodding their heads. Speaking to Agis now, I said, "Their majesties and I would like to take a walk in the garden before dinner, could you notify Captain Duris please, Agis?"

Nodding, Agis replied, "Immediately, your majesty" Then Agis turned and left again taking the stewards with him.

Ten minutes later Agis returned, and bowing first, announced, "Captain Duris is outside now with your escort, your majesties."

Rising now, I moved in front of Amy and Sandra before returning Agis's nod and replying, "Please show the captain in, Agis." As Agis moved to the door, I offered Amy my right hand and Sandra my left now to help them up off the couch, which both gratefully accepted. And Captain Duris walked into the room stopping to salute and nod his head. With both ladies on their feet again, I returned Captain Duris's salute as Amy and Sandra returned his nod. Then holding my right arm out to Amy and my left arm out to Sandra, they wrapped their hands around my arms and Agis opened the lefthand door now before bowing again.

With a genuine smile on his face, Captain Duris nodded to Amy now and said, "Congratulations, your majesty."

And smiling at Duris now, Amy replied, "Thank you, Captain Duris. We are incredibly happy about it too!"

To which, Captain Duris nodded again and gestured with his hand saying, "The royal guard is ready whenever your majesties are?" And with Amy and Sandra hands wrapped around my arms now we headed out the doors. Leading the way now, Captain Duris went down the south stairs, across the atrium, and out the glass doors onto the garden's terrace. Where, to our surprise, we found another dozen royal guards standing there waiting. Two holding the doors and ten more standing on the terrace at attention, with their heads bowed.

Turning to look at Duris, he answered our question before we could ask it, saying, "The Senior Physician informed us that your majesties require more privacy. The guards are here so we can cover the garden's entire perimeter now and give your majesties a little more privacy."

Amy and Sandra responded before I got a chance, smiling and saying, "Thank you, Captain Duris."

Captain Duris nodded to us then turned and barked out an order as all twenty royal guards split now and took off at a quick jog down both sides of the garden before two of them appeared in front of Atlas's tomb at the far end. Then the two guards behind us closed the doors before taking position on either side of the doors. Duris snapped us another salute and nodded his head as he swung his arm out now, saying, "The garden is yours, your majesties."

Nodding to Duris, I lead Amy and Sandra down the stairs into the garden now. And we suddenly heard explosions in the distance, and we all turned to look to the southwest now. As Captain Duris cleared his throat from the top of the stairs and said, "That's just Captain Hyllus and the city guard setting of the defensive rockets in celebration of the joyous news, your majesties. Our messengers reported on their return that the city guard and the people were going wild in the streets down there now drinking and celebrating in the joyous news.

Amy gave my butt a squeeze now. Then Amy and Sandra chuckled at my surprised reaction as Amy calmly replied, "You may pass the word along now Captain, that we all equally overjoyed in learning that we are expecting our first child."

Snapping another salute and bowing to Amy now, Duris replied, "I shall gladly pass that information along, your majesty."

Turning now, we left Captain Duris standing on the terrace as I led Amy and Sandra across the garden to the blue seahorse fountain in the center. Guiding the ladies to the edge of the pool now, I sat them down on the stone coping around the edge of the pool. And since they didn't scoot together, I sat down between them now to relax and enjoy the view. To my surprise, they both scooted up next to me and leaning their heads over on my shoulders now. Then Amy took hold of my right arm before looking over at Sandra, who followed suit taking hold of my left arm now. Then Amy began pointing at various items on the palace before looking at Sandra, who calmly answered Amy's questions now as they leaned on me. And I sat there quietly listening to their conversation sandwiched between the two most beautiful women in all of Attea, thinking being the King really isn't so bad!

After thirty minutes by the fountain, we got up and took the ladies on a lap around the garden to see everything. Also, to get a little exercise now after being couped up inside the royal chambers for weeks. The guards all snapping to attention and nodding now as we passed their stations.

Returning to the stairs again, Captain Duris saluted and bowed his head before barking the order recalling the guards as we climbed the stairs up onto the terrace. Returning the captain's salute, I nodded my head to him and said, "Thank you, Duris. We are ready to go back in now." Nodding again, Duris gave the order, and the two guards opened the atrium doors as three guards passed us on either side now and took up position inside the atrium. Then Duris stepped to the front and barked the order to move out as six more guards fell in behind and we climbed back up the stairs.

Back inside our chambers again, Petra and the handmaids were waiting for Amy and Sandra. And Petra suggesting their majesties follow her now so they could freshen up before dinner. While Agis simply opened my chamber door and bowed his head. Agis leading me to the restroom first, figuring I had downed a fair amount of tsia this morning. Afterwards, Agis led me into the dressing room, where the stewards were waiting now to comb my hair and brush my teeth.

We had a pleasant dinner that night. And Nestor and I showed a little self-control now by limiting ourselves to just two bottles of wine tonight, since Amy wasn't drinking. And after Sophia finished congratulating Amy, we learned from Nestor that the Elders had agreed to hold Sandra's and my wedding the day after tomorrow. Which was sooner than any of us expected, but after discussing it with Sophia, Petra, and Agis, they agreed it was doable, and we began planning accordingly.

Later that night Amy and I discussed it privately in bed. And Amy told me she was fine sleeping by herself in the "spare bedroom," which is what Amy and Sandra had dubbed Sandra's new chambers. But Amy was too excited to sleep now after having her pregnancy confirmed today. And quickly reminded me that even though she was pregnant, and I was marrying Sandra in two days, that didn't excuse me from my husbandly duties now.

Chuckling at Amy, it didn't take me long to convince her I had no intention of shirking my husbandly duties tonight, or any night for that matter. Finally nodding off in my arms, I looked down at my wife for few minutes, and the smug little smile she had on her beautiful face as she slept all snuggled up here on my left side, and closing my eyes now, I joined her in sleep.

The next day seemed to drag on, as the women disappeared into their private chambers right after breakfast, only returning briefly for lunch before disappearing again until dinner time.

My only duties today consisted of verifying for Agis and the stewards that my new blue wedding outfit met with my approval. And choosing a wedding present for Sandra now from the box of royal jewels that Nestor and Lady Sophia had picked out. And I found two that I liked, the first one being an octagon shaped ruby with three diamonds and mounted on a fine silver chain. The second was a heart-shaped emerald, whose gold mounting made two turns before passing over the finely wrought snake-scale gold chain. And tiny leaves etched into the surface of its gold mounting. I was leaning towards emerald but held them both up now to get Nestor's opinion. Nestor stated the ruby necklace was beautiful and slightly larger, but Sophia had told Nestor earlier that if it were up to her, she would choose the emerald heart for Sandra. And we both agreed with Sophia, so I laid the ruby necklace back in the box and handed the emerald heart to Nestor now for Sandra's wedding gift.

Tonight, it was just Amy, Sandra, and me for dinner. And it was a little quieter than usual at the table tonight. As we were all excited about the wedding tomorrow, and all a little cautious in choosing our words tonight, fearful of saying the wrong thing now and spoiling the event tomorrow.

We didn't dawdle after dinner, knowing Petra expected Sandra and Amy to both get a goodnight's beauty sleep. And before Sandra said goodnight and turned to leave, Amy called Sandra to her side, giving Sandra a hug and peck on the cheek before saying, "After tomorrow, you we will officially be family and my sister, Sandra!"

Tears glistening in their eyes now, Sandra nodded to Amy, then wiping her eyes, Sandra replied, "Thank you, Amy. I always wanted a sister!" And turning to me now, Sandra smiled and looking at me in the eyes before nodding and saying, "Goodnight, your majesty." And I got the impression that Sandra chose to call me "your majesty" now because after tomorrow, it would be Andrew or husband from now on. Amy grinned at Sandra's choice of words too, as we bid each other goodnight now.

Once Amy and I were in bed again, Amy rolled over and put her elbows on my chest now, which meant Amy had something she needed to discuss or wanted to tell me. I knew it was about tomorrow night with Sandra, but I had no idea what Amy was going to say or tell me now. Brushing a lock of Amy's lovely red hair back now, I looked her in the eyes and asked, "Okay, my love. What is it?

And I got the feeling that Amy knew what she wanted to say, but wasn't quite sure how to phrase it now, as she hesitated for a moment before saying, "Being a physician, Sandra knows more about biology and procreation than both of us combined, right?"

And nodding my head to Amy, I replied, "Yes, but your gonna tell me that it's all theory and no practice right?"

Nodding her head now, Amy said, "Yes, how did you know?"

Shaking my head at Amy, I replied, "It's not hard to spot, my love. Sandra is nervous and blushes easily. Rather than confident and sure of her femineity."

And thinking about it for a moment, Amy nodded her head and replied, "Yeah, I noticed that. I just didn't know that you noticed it too, husband?"

Looking Amy in the eyes, I frowned as I added, "I am planning to take it slow and careful tomorrow night. And have a second bottle of wine so Sandra is relaxed. Does that sound okay, my love?"

Frowning now, Amy's Irish started to flare up as she flatly stated, "I love Sandra like a sister. So, you'd better make this first time special for her. Or so help me god Andrew, I swear I'll never forgive you, and I mean that!"

Shaking my head now, I replied, "I swear I will do my best to make special. But you realize how weird it is discussing this with you now, my love?"

Grinning ironically now, Amy leaned in and kissed me on the lips for a moment before sliding into her normal spot on my left side and saying, "Yes, it's weird for me too! But I have accepted it now because it is Sandra. And she has been my friend and comfort since arriving here in Attea. Not to mention her shielding me with her body in the Cave of Mephisto!"

Kissing Amy on the forehead, I wrapped my arms around her now replying, "I know. And because I love you so much, I would never mess that up for you, Amy." And laying back on the pillows now, we both closed our eye's knowing tomorrow was going to be a busy day.

The next morning, Petra and the handmaids whisked Sandra and Amy off into their private chambers right after breakfast. And I learned later that Lady Sophia was waiting for them when they stepped through the door. Then while Amy bathed, Sandra, Petra, and the handmaids got Lady Sophia's ready. And while Sandra bathed, Sophia, Petra, and the handmaids did Amy's hair and got her dressed. Then when Sandra finished her bath, the ladies all worked together getting Sandra dressed and ready for the wedding.

Fortunately, my day was much simpler. After I finished my second cup of tsia, Agis led me in for my bath. And I almost felt sorry for the three attractive female bathers now, as I was marrying the second most beautiful woman in Attea today. After my bath, I followed Agis back into my dressing room where the stewards combed my hair and cleaned my teeth before dressing me in my new blue tunic with matching sash and one of the ceremonial swords again. After which, they stepped back to check me over before Agis and the stewards all bowed. And after returning their nods, Agis led me back out to the main chamber again. Then stepping out, Agis returned with a fresh pot of tsia and two cups. Agis chuckled lightly as he filled my cup and told me that Nestor had informed him yesterday that he would be joining me for tsia this morning, while we waited on the women. Nodding gratefully to Agis, I was relieved to hear my future father-in-law was coming now to help me pass the time.

Agis returned about fifteen minutes later, nodding and informing me that Nestor was outside waiting. Returning Agis's nod, I asked him to show the Senior Physician in. And impeccably dressed now, Nestor walked into the room five paces and stopped to nod his head. Receiving my return nod, Nestor smiled now as he moved forward to the sitting area. And after Nestor was seated with a cup of tsia, I had to say something, so I asked, "I am glad to see you're in a good mood this morning, Nestor?"

Smiling, Nestor beamed, "And why not, your majesty? I am a man who is about to have all his wishes for-filled."

Curious now, I asked, "Oh, and what might those be, if I may ask, my friend?"

Grinning, Nestor held up his hand up and touched his index finger before listing them out for me now, saying, "One, that my daughter fall in love with and marry a man worthy of her. Two, that in marrying that man, my daughter's future is secured. And three, that my daughter provide Sophia and I with grandchildren one day. That covers it, what more could a father wish for really, your majesty?"

Nodding my head to Nestor, I replied, "Thank you, Nestor. I am honored that you think so highly of me. And I promise to do my best to make sure Sandra feels loved and I live up to your expectations." Then chuckling, I added, "Which by the way, is the exact same thing her majesty Amy made me promise last night!"

And nodding his head now, Nestor replied, "And I sincerely thank both your majesties." Then we were silent for a minute, as each of us paused to sip of our tsia now. Then Nestor continued adding, "Unfortunately, those wishes and concerns for your child's future are like a torch. That I pass to you now, your majesty. As you are about to become a father soon yourself."

Nodding in agreement with Nestor, I answered him now confessing, "Yes, but I have been preparing to accept that torch since the first time I saw her majesty Amy. So, I've had a little time to get used to the idea."

Then Nestor spent some time telling me what Sandra was like as a child. And how she followed him around, curious about everything to the point of being annoying at times. That, and how Sandra decided at an early age she wanted to be a physician like her father and help people. Then some of the more humorous things Sandra had done as a child. And we were still chuckling about Sandra's antics when the door to the Lady's chambers opened.

Then Amy, Sophia, Petra, and the handmaids walked in, before stopping to nod and holding their hands out towards the chamber door as Sandra stepped into the room now. Completely dressed in white from head to toe, Sandra had a slender gold crown like Amy's atop her lovely head now. But this one's eight points were half emeralds and half diamonds now and seemed to be made for Sandra. And Sandra had a transparent white veil covering her face and a ten foot white train flowing out behind her, making Sandra a stunningly beautiful bride now.

Rising from our seats, Nestor and I bowed to Sandra. And Amy spoke now, saying, "Isn't she beautiful Andrew? I told them this is what my wedding dress would have looked like had we gotten married in the outlands."

Smiling and nodding my head now, I said, "You look truly amazing Sandra, and take my breath away."

Confused, Sandra leaned over and asked Amy, "Is that a good?"

Smiling at Sandra, Amy chuckled replying, "No, that's extremely good! It means Andrew is stunned now by your beauty, Sandra."

Smiling shyly and blushing a little, Sandra nodded to me, as she said, "Thank you, your majesty. I'm glad you are pleased."

It was at this point, Sophia cleared her throat while looking over at Nestor now. And bowing to his daughter, Nestor said, "You are an absolute vision of beauty my daughter, and we are both very proud of you, your majesty!" And stepping forward now with tears of joy in her eyes, Sophia gave Sandra a hug, saying, "Your father is right, you look absolutely stunning now, and we are so happy for you, your majesty." And Sandra started to get watery eyed, but Nestor spoke quickly now saying, "Careful Sophia, you're going to make her majesty cry, and you don't want ruin your daughter's dress on her wedding today!" And letting go of Sandra now, Sophia stepping back and wiped her eyes before bowing formally to her daughter again. And dabbing her own eyes, Sandra returned her mother's nod now.

Agis's timing couldn't have been better, as he stepped into the room and bowed to us now. After returning his nod, Agis said, "Captain Duris is outside with the escort now, your majesties?" Looking from Sandra to Amy, they both gave me a quick nod now letting me know they were ready.

And smiling at them both now, I said, "Then we should go." And turning to Agis, I said, "We're ready, Agis. Would you show the captain in now please?"

Nodding in acknowledging, Agis moved to the inner doors and opened the righthand door revealing Captain Duris now, helmet in hand waiting patiently in the entryway. And taking five steps into the room, Duris stopped snapping hand to his chest and nodding his head. And returning his nod, Duris turned and took a step towards Sandra now before smiling and slapping his hand to his chest again and nodding a second time, complementing Sandra on her beauty now soldier fashion. Blushing, Sandra graciously smiled as she returned Captain Duris's nod and complement.

Then turning to me again, Duris nodded and said, "Whenever you're ready, your majesty?"

Returning Duris's nod, I held my left arm out to Sandra now, as I replied, "We're ready, captain." Sandra hesitated for a second before stepping forward and smiling as she wrapped her hand around my arm now. As soon as I had Sandra hand was around my left arm, I covered it with my right hand. Giving it a small squeeze now as I looked into her eyes and smiled at her. Then turning the other way, I smiled at Amy now and held my right arm out to her. Grinning and giving me a quick nod now, Amy stepped forward accepting my right arm as we moved to the doors. Sophia and Petra quickly stepped forward picking up Sandra's train now as Nestor fell in behind.

Chapter - 13

Captain Duris led us down the south stairs and through the south hallway to the throne room again. This time the throne room was completely full of courtiers and officials. And when we reached the podium, I noticed a group of younger guests huddled in the rear with their heads bowed. Which I assumed now were Sandra's classmates from the medical university.

Leading Sandra and Amy up onto the podium, we turned around to face the room again. Nestor moving to my right, as Sophia and Petra quickly straightening out Sandra's long train now, folding it in half on Sandra's left before bowing and backing away. Then the three us nodded returning everyone's bows now and getting a look at their smiling faces.

Releasing my arm now, Amy stepped forward and made a big show of placing Sandra's hand in mine before holding our hands between hers. Then looking at both of us, Amy smiled and winked. And we had to grin as Amy tried to lighten things up a little now. After which, I interlocked my fingers with Sandra's, making her smile now. Then releasing our hands, Amy took two steps back and nodded to us both. And as Sandra and I returned Amy's nod, Amy moved to the left taking hold of Sophia's arm as they watched and waited now.

The four Elders in front nodded their heads now, and Sandra and I returned their nods. Then the Elders moved forward climbing the three steps up onto the podium in front of us. And reaching the top, the Elders nodded again, and we returned their nods. Then Tydeus smiled and speaking loudly in Attean, asked, "Do you Andrew Tallfer, King of Attea, take the Lady Sandra now as your lawful wife and Queen, your majesty?"

To which I smiled and replied, "Ποιῶ," I do, as I nodded my head.

Returning my nod, Tydeus continued now, asking, "And do you Andrew Tallfer, King of Attea, promise to love, honor, and protect the Lady Sandra all the days of your life?"

Turning to look at Sandra, I responded, "Ποιῶ," I do, and smiled at Sandra now as nodded my head.

And returning my nod, Tydeus turned to Sandra now and nodded his head. And getting her return nod, Tydeus asked Sandra, "And do you, Lady Sandra, take his majesty Andrew Tallfer as your lawful husband and King?"

Nodding her head, Sandra answered, "χάριν!" And the whole room suddenly burst into a mirthful chuckle, even Nestor and Sophia joining in now. Tydeus and the three Elders covering their mouths with their hands now, trying to hide their chuckling.

Realizing her mistake now, Sandra quickly said, "Ποιῶ!"

Still chuckling, Nestor leaned over now and whispered, "Her majesty said 'gladly' instead of I do!" And turning to look at Sandra now, I could see her face was beet-red under her bio-suit. So, raising Sandra's hand to my lips, I kissed it sweetly now, silencing the room as everyone turned and looked away. And out of the corner of my eye, I saw Amy smile now and nod her head in approval.

His mirth under control now, Tydeus nodded to Sandra and continuing the ceremony, asking, "And do you, your majesty Sandra, promise to love, honor, and obey his majesty Andrew Tallfer, all the days of your life?"

Smiling now, Sandra looked into my eyes and replied, "Ποιῶ!"

And nodding his head to Sandra again and getting a nod in return. Tydeus turned to me now and asked, "Does your majesty have a gift to present to his wife and seal this promise now?"

Nodding my head to Tydeus, I replied, "Ποιῶ." And holding my hand out to Nestor now. He carefully placed the jade heart necklace in my hand and gave my hand a small squeeze as he smiled and nodded now. And turning to Sandra, I opened my hand and held the necklace up so she could get a good look at it. And judging by the smile on her face now, I'd say the jade heart was definitely the right gift for Sandra. Then opening the clasp, I leaned forward raising the two halves of the necklace up around Sandra' lovely neck. And Sandra leaned forward slightly lifting her hair up out of the way now to receive her wedding gift.

And smiling brightly now, Tydeus said, "I now pronounce your majesties, husband and wife." Then nodding to us both again, Tydeus added, "You may kiss now and seal the promise!" And the entire room cheered now as they looked way. Except for Amy, who was jerking her head to right now telling me to hurry up and kiss Sandra, who was standing there waiting. And stepping closer, I put my arms around Sandra now and pulled her to me. And as Sandra closed her eyes as I leaned forward and kissed her for the first time on lips. And after what seemed like five seconds, I pulled back and looked down at Sandra's closed eyes and puckered lips. Apparently Sandra had been expecting a much longer kiss, and I saw Amy frowning now.

Opening her eyes, Sandra joined me now as we turned to face the Consul of Elders again. Who, along with the rest of the room, stood heads bowed waiting. And quickly returning their bows, Tydeus was first to step forward and congratulate us. Followed by Kallinos, who was beside himself now, congratulating Sandra and bowing to us both. Then Sippas and Thestor each stepped forward congratulating us. After which, Amy stepped forward accepting Sandra's open arms as the two of them hugged each other now. Followed by Lady Sophia and Nestor, who bowed to Sandra first, before stepping forward to hug their daughter.

Wrapping Sandra's hand around my arm, I turned to Amy now and held out my right arm. And once I had both my wives' hands around my arms again, we turned to face the room. Then I checked with my wives to make sure they were ready now to go greet the line of people who were forming up on the left to congratulate us.

Nestor and Sophia moved up on Sandra's left now to receive their congratulations along with their daughter's. Amy on my right now as the courtiers, officials, and Sandra's classmates and teachers came forward to congratulate us now. The men bowing to Sandra, while the women bowed then stepping forward shaking Sandra's hand and giving her their best wishes.

After the line petered out, we moved into the banquet hall to have some food and wine. And it was Kallinos who stood up now and made the first toast this time instead of Tydeus. And Kallinos took a bit longer, proudly wishing one of his star pupils a long and happy life. Followed by Nestor, who, watery eyed now wished us the blessing of healthy children, and a long, happy life. Before stating how proud he was with his daughter's choice of husbands. And everyone stood up and cheered now as they downed their goblets of wine to Nestor's toast. I thought it was a bit much, considering all I had really done so far is show up here in Attea. Looking around Sandra at Amy now, I held my hands up and shrugged my shoulders. Understanding me, Amy smiled and gave me a quick nod before going back to her conversation with her new sister Sandra.

After two hours of food, drink, and conversation with Nestor and Elders. Captain Duris walked up behind Nestor and whispered something into his ear, followed by Nestor nodding in return. Then leaning over to me, Nestor nodded before saying, "It's time to let all Attea see their new Queen, your majesty."

And turning to the left, I lifted Sandra's hand up to my lips and kissed it. Ending her conversation with Amy, as Sandra blushed and smiled. And having their attention now, I asked, "It's time to let the city to see their new Queen, if you two are ready?" Amy and Sandra quickly glanced at each other now, then turned to me and nodded their heads. And turning back Nestor, I replied, "We're ready."

And Nestor signaled the herald, who nodded his head to Nestor and us before taking two steps forward now and rapping his staff three times loudly on the floor. Causing the music to stop abruptly and everyone in the room to rise and bow to us now as the herald announced we were leaving.

Rising, we returned everyone's bows before Captain Duris led us out the secret door into the north hallway again. Once the door closed, we heard the herald strike his staff on the floor three more times and the music faintly begin to play again. And Nestor informed me now that the reception would go well into the wee hours of the night as the court celebrated this joyful event and Attea's bright future.

Back in our royal chambers, Petra and Sophia ushered Sandra and Amy into their private chambers now to get their armor on. While Agis and the stewards led Nestor and me to my changing room where there was a tray of cups and a carafe of wine waiting for us. I told Nestor to sit and have a cup wine while the stewards dressed me in my armor and used "Father" this time instead of Nestor, catching Nestor by surprise now, but putting a grin on Agis's face. Fully changed, Agis picked up my robe and led us back into the main chamber where he deposited my robe across the back of one of the chairs while one of the steward moved the wine to the coffee table. And Agis paused to fill my cup and top of Nestor's before nodding and leaving with the stewards.

I took my time with the wine now, as I was planning to have wine with Sandra later tonight after everyone had left. Nestor on the other hand was celebrating now. And he downed two full glasses of wine before the ladies returned from their chambers in their armor. And Sandra looked especially nice in her new midnight blue amor with a gold seahorse on the center of her cuirass and matching seahorses' greaves. I paused to complement Petra on Sandra's new armor now. And Petra informed us that Amy's, and my new armor would be finished soon, and we thanked her for the update.

Then Agis stepped into the room to let us know that Captain Duris was outside now with our escort, whenever we were ready. And after Agis showed Captain Duris in. Duris walked in ten paces stopping to salute and bow to us. Then turning to face Sandra, Duris saluted a second time soldier fashion, obviously impressed with Sandra's new armor now like the rest of us.

Taking the south stairs and hallway now, we crossed the throne room into the west foyer. And we all chuckled as we passed the banquet hall and heard the revelry going on inside now through the doors. Taking the south stairs, we climbed up to the second floor balcony again. And we could hear the celebration going on out in the palace courtyard too now. Stopping at the top of the stairs, Agis, Petra, and Sophia stepped forward to get our robes on over our amor. While our herald and the two guards waited by the door with their heads bowed. Ans ready now, we returned their bows. And the two guards stepped forward and opened the doors, as our herald strode out onto the balcony and stopped to rap his staff three times loudly on the terrace before announcing us.

Taking Sandra's and Amy's hands again, we stepped outside into silence now as we moved up to the balcony railing. And returning the crowds bows, the courtyard suddenly burst into an enormous cheer as the Atteans' looked up now and saw their new Queen Sandra. Amy and Sandra raised their forearms now and began waving down at the cheering crowd below. Then Amy and I took two steps back and applauded Sandra as she stood alone at the railing now with thousands of her fellow Atteans cheering her. And I noticed a small group in front were waving red, white, and grey banners now instead of the traditional blue and gold colors of Attea. Half of them were wearing the white robes of physicians, so the red, white, and grey banners must be their university colors, as they shouted wildly and cheered their new Queen and fellow physician now. After about five minutes of this, I led Amy up beside Sandra again before turning and nodding to our herald. And returning my nod, the herald moved forward facing the crowd below now and rapped his staff three times loudly on the balcony's deck again. And the courtyard fell silent now as everyone stopped and bowed their heads.

And facing the crowd now, we returned their bows before I led Amy and Sandra back in through the glass doors onto the second floor balcony. Stopping in front of Captain Duris and our escort, as Agis, Petra, and Sophia bowed and stepped forward to remove our robes. Then turning to Duris. I returned his salute letting him know we were ready to go back to our chambers now.

Nodding, Duris turned and gave the order. And we followed him down the stairs, across the throne room, and back up to the royal chambers again. Parting ways with Duris outside our chamber.

Once inside, Petra and Sophia leading Amy and Sandra into their private chambers followed closely the handmaidens. And I invited my new father-in-law to sit and have some wine now, while I followed Agis and the stewards changed me out of my armor. Agis presented me with a brand new green tunic now in the style I preferred. And nodding my approval, the stewards quickly removed my armor and dressed me in the green tunic for dinner. After which, I called Agis to my side and whispered into his ear now. Informing him that we will be five for dinner again tonight. And after the others had left, I would like two bottles of wine for her majesty Sandra and I later tonight.

Nodding, Agis acknowledging my request, then swung his arm out now indicating that we were done. And Agis followed me back to the main chamber. Where I could see my new father-in-law had some color showing in his cheeks now as the wine was beginning to catch up with him. Which made me chuckle as Nestor rose from his seat now, bowing as I entered the room with Agis. Returning Nestor's nod, I indicated for my father-in-law to sit down so I could join him in celebrating Sandra's and my wedding now. Agis stopping at the edge of the carpet and nodded to Nestor before moving forward and picking up the wine carafe to fill Nestor and my cups again.

Nestor and I had time to finish a full glass of wine before the women reappeared. Sandra, Amy, and Sophia stepping out of the lady's chambers having changed into something comfortably now for dinner. Amy plainly dressed now, had her lovely red hair braided into a bun on the back of her head again. While Sandra's had on a thin, emerald-green tunic now, down to the middle of her shapely thighs, and a gold sash around her slender waist. Sandra's long blonde hair having been braided down the middle of her back now, with a matching green ribbon woven into the braid and securing the end. And Sandra's wedding gift sparkled in the center of her tunic. Nestor and I scrambled up off the couches now, smiling and returning their bows. Then I gestured for the ladies to join us on the couches now for a drink before dinner.

And all three smiling at us now, they moved forward to join us in the sitting area. Amy leading now and taking the single chair between the two couches. While Sophia bowed and took a seat on the couch next to Nestor. Which left the spot beside me on the other couch open for Sandra now. And offering Sandra my hand, as I seated my new wife on the right side of the couch next to Amy before sitting down on the left side next to Sandra.

A few seconds later Agis entered the room again carrying another carafe of wine while one of the stewards followed him bearing a tray with a water pitcher and three cups. And stepping into the room, Agis and the steward bowed before moving to the edge of the carpet and bowing again waiting to be acknowledged. Smiling, I returned their nods, and they waved them forward now. After the steward set the tray down on the coffee table, Agis proceeded to fill the first two cups full of wine. Then setting the wine carafe down, Agis picked up the water pitcher and filled the third cup with water before handing it to Amy now. Then Agis proceeded to hand the other cups of wine to Sandra and Sophie. Whom both nodded to Agis now as they received their wine. The Agis and the steward back up and bowed again waiting. Returning their nods now, I said, "Thank you Agis. Please let us know when dinner is ready?"

Nodding again Agis replied, "Gladly, your majesties." Then Agis and the steward turned and left the room again.

Frowning now, Sandra slid forward on the couch and held her hand out to Amy. And taking Amy's cup, Sandra dumped half the cup back into the water pitcher before setting it down and picking up the carafe now and filling Amy's cup with wine. Then handing the cup back to Amy now, said, "As your physician, I am recommending a small amount of wine once or twice a week during the first half of your pregnancy to help you relax!" Then turning to Nestor now, Sandra asked, "Don't you agree, father?"

And nodding his head now, Nestor answered, "Yes, her majesty Sandra is right, your majesty." Amy smiled and nodded to Sandra now. Who turned and nodded to her father before resting her hand on my shoulder and sitting back in the couch with me.

Smiling, Amy replied, "Thank you, Sandra. I've been wanting to properly toast your wedding since it finished!" Then to our surprise, Amy rose and held her glass out towards us, and we all rose now from our chairs. As Amy put her hand on her stomach, saying, "To Andrew and my new sister, Sandra. May you join me tonight in having the glorious feeling of your child growing inside you! To Andrew and Sandra, best of luck!"

And Amy glared at me none to subtly before drinking her toast. And I nodded to Amy before drinking the toast, having received my orders from my lovely wife now. Sandra noticed our little byplay and let a small giggle slip out now. And as we all looked at Sandra, she raised her cup and took a drink now before nodding to her new sister.

Luckily Agis stepped into the room right then. Nodding and letting us know dinner was outside before Sophia or Nestor could ask any questions. Nestor was well lubed from all the wine now and needed a little help getting to the dinner table. And Agis stepped forward now offering to help. But I waved him off, preferring to help my new father-in-law to the table myself. Sandra offered to help, but I tilted my head towards Sophia, hinting that her mother might require some help now in reaching the dinner table too. Sandra and Amy moved to Sophia's side now taking her arms and guiding her to the table.

As we migrated to the dinner table, Petra and the handmaids entered and stopped to bow. While Agis and the stewards opened the front doors revealing the cooks and the carts of food on the other side. Amy, Sandra, and I returned Petra and the handmaid's nods as Nestor sat Sophia down at the table. Then I seated Amy on the right before seating my lovely bride next to her mother on the left again. And pulling out the chair on the end, we sat down to dinner now.

The food was fabulous. And we started dinner off with a round of laughter. As Nestor brought up Sandra's little slip again during the ceremony, to Sandra's dismay and embarrassment. Taking Sandra's hand in mine, I smiled at her adoringly now. Which made Sandra forget her embarrassment and chuckle along with the rest of us now.

During dinner, Amy quizzed Sandra about all her classmates who had shown up for the ceremony. And Sandra, Amy, and Sophia chatted for quite a while after dinner over their wine. While Nestor did what he usually did when his wife was busy chatting. He leaned back with his wine and quietly listened. And when I looked back at Nestor again, I found him tilted back in his chair, out cold. And noticing my grin now, the three women all turned to look at Nestor.

Lady Sophia started to apologize for her husband, but I raised my hand cutting her off now, before saying, "No need to apologize, Sophia. I am well aware of how busy we've kept Nestor these last couple of months. And how hard Nestor has worked to make sure everything went off smoothly and on schedule. And my new father-in-law Nestor, is more than welcome to celebrate as much he wants and nod off anytime he wishes at my table!" Then I smiled at Sophia.

Lady Sophia didn't say anything, she just smiled now and nodded her head. And reaching out, Sandra and Amy put their hands atop of mine now as they nodded in agreement. Realizing it was getting late, Amy leaned back now and covered her mouth faking a yawn. And I grinned as Amy said, "It's late, and I think I'm ready for bed now."

Taking the hint now, Lady Sophia said, "Yes, It's past time I took my husband to bed!" And the three of us turned to look at Sophia in surprise now. Realizing her mistake, Lady Sophia let out a small giggle before correcting herself, and saying, "I mean, it's past Nestor and my bedtime." Amy and I chuckled as Sandra face turned all red again, embarrassed now by her mother's little slip.

Rising from the table now, Amy and Sophia moved over to Sandra side to give her a hug and kiss on the cheek. As I pulled the blue and gold ribbons on the wall now summoning Agis and Petra again. Both of which entered the room now and stopped to bow. And while I waved Agis forward now, Sandra and Amy waved Petra forward. Agis and Petra both stopping a couple of feet short of the table now to bow their heads again.

Grinning at Agis, I said, "My father-in-law asked me to compliment you on the wine again, Agis. Can you and the stewards make sure he makes it back to his room safely?"

Nodding his head, Agis smiled and replied "Certainly, your majesty!" And Agis turned now signaling the other stewards to come forward and assist the Senior Physician. Turning, I saw Petra signaling to the handmaids to come forward and assist my new mother-in-law back to her room now too. Then Petra bowed and swung her arm out for Amy, indicating they should proceed to the guest room. Smiling at me, Amy stepped forward and gave me a quick peck on the cheek before turning to follow Petra and shouting over her shoulder redneck fashion now, "Get'er done!"

Sandra stood next to me now watching Amy disappear into the lady's chambers, turned and asked me, "What did Amy say?"

Grinning at Sandra, I replied, "That was your sister's humorous way telling me that we need to consummate our marriage tonight."

Blushing now, Sandra slid her hand into mine and leaned in whispering, "I want that too, Andrew!"

Smiling at Sandra now, I whispered back, "No hurry, I'm sure we will get to that tonight." And as Sandra nodded in agreement the remaining steward and handmaid moved forward to begin clearing the table as Agis set a fresh carafe of wine and two cups on the coffee table now. Then the two stewards having delivered Nestor safely back to his room walked back in now, and pausing to bow first, they quickly moved forward to help clear the table.

Looking into Sandra beautiful face, I asked, "Why don't we move to the couch and have another glass of wine while we wait for the servants to finish up?" And I led Sandra to the couch and seated her before sitting down next to her now.

Looking at the wine carafe and cups, Sandra leaned in and whispering, "You're not trying to get me drunk are you, Andrew? Because I am a full grown woman and have no intention of being intoxicated or passing out the first time in I get to put all this theory and knowledge to use!"

Grinning at Sandra now, I whispered back, "I wouldn't do that, my wife. We have days to consummate our marriage. And if you were to pass out, I would simply wait until tomorrow. But being relaxed the first time is a good idea, physically and mentally."

Sandra whispering, "oh," and laid her head over on my shoulder now as two of the handmaids stepped back into the chamber having delivered Lady Sophia back to her room. And stopping inside the doors, they bowed to us on the couch before moving forward and giggling quietly as they turned the covers down on the bed. Reaching for the wine carafe on the coffee table, I filled the two cups before picking up the first one and handing it to Sandra. Then picking the second cup, I held it up to Sandra, who raised her own cup and held it there. Smiling at Sandra, obviously clinking your glasses together wasn't a custom here in Attea.

Smiling softly at Sandra, I said, "In the outlands, its customary for family and lovers to clink their cups together before drinking." And clinking my cup to Sandra's now, I took a sip of the wine.

Sandra raised an eyebrow before replying, "Hmm, interesting!" As Sandra downed her entire cup in the one shot now. And held her cup out to again, saying, "One more please, husband." Nodding my head,

I grabbed the carafe off the coffee table and filled Sandra's cup again. And she held it up waiting for me to clink our cups together before taking a smaller drink this time.

When the table cleared, the bed turned down, and those ghastly nightgowns laid out across the end of the bed again. Agis approached us, and stopping at the edge of the carpet now to bow, Agis politely asked, "Is there anything else your majesties require?"

Smiling now, I said, "Yes, I have a question for you, Agis."

Nodding again, Agis replied, "Certainly, your majesty."

Returning Agis's nod, I asked, "Have you and the other servants had a chance to celebrate her majesties and my wedding yet?"

Grinning now, Agis replied, "No, your majesty."

Looking Agis in the eyes now, I said, "Take a couple cases of the wine for yourself and the servants and properly celebrate her majesty Sandra's and my wedding now, please. I am certain that we won't need you or the servants again until late tomorrow morning."

Nodding again, Agis replied, "Thank you, your majesty!"

And grinning at Agis now, I added, "And Agis, consider that a royal order now, my friend!"

Smiling and nodding now, Agis replied, "My congratulations to you both your majesties again. And I will bid you a goodnight now, your majesties." And we both returned Agis's nod now as he turned and exited the room closing the door behind him.

Alone now, I smiled at Sandra and put my arm around her pulling her to me. And Sandra smiled now as she snuggled up against me. After our third glass of wine, I looked into my empty wine cup. And seeing me staring at my empty cup, Sandra tipped her cup up and emptying it now. And I calmly asked her, "Have you had enough wine yet, my love."

And nodding her head now, I rose from the couch and turned around offering Sandra my hands. Smiling up at me, Sandra accepted my hands as I gently helped her up off the couch. And keeping hold of Sandra's hand now, I led her over to the bed.

Chapter - 14

Still holding Sandra's warm soft hand, I led her around to the right side of the bed. Then gently pushing her back against the bed, I pinned her there now against the bed. Kissing her on the neck and mouth while softly sliding my hands over Sandra's body and pressing my hips against her. And reaching up, Sandra tossed her emerald heart necklace out of the way now so that I could kiss her neck freely. And taking the hint, I spent the next several minutes gently kissing her lovely neck, mouth, and ears before sliding down to her cleavage at the neckline of her tunic and branching out from there. While I was caressing Sandra's hips and backside, Sandra struggled to get the sash loose around her waist. And finally succeeding, Sandra pulled her tunic off now as I slowly worked my way further south now. After several equally pleasant minutes, I reached under Sandra's legs and slid her up onto the bed.

And it wasn't too long before Sandra slid back onto the pillows and held her hands out to me. Sandra pulled me on top of her as soon as our hands closed around each other. And I gave Sandra that long kiss now that she had been looking for at the wedding ceremony. After which, Sandra looked up into my eyes and nodded her head letting me know that she was ready now.

And going slow, me made love for the first time. After which, Sandra informed me all that book learning and theory was useless and fell far short in the describing how she felt now after making love for the first time. Smiling shyly at me, Sandra added that she couldn't be sure though without having something to compare her first time to now. And she wondered if I was up to trying that again for the sake of research. The light from the Staff of Attea was showing through the window above before Sandra finally decided that we had done enough research for our first night. And pulling Sandra to me, I wrapped her up in my arms now and we drifted off to sleep together.

It was noon before Sandra, and I awoke. And slipping our clothes back on, I checked to make sure Sandra was ready before pulling the ribbons on the wall. Smiling at Sandra now, I crossed the room to meet Agis by the door to my private chambers. And returning his nod, I indicated for him to back up and give the ladies the chamber and some privacy now. And as I pulled the door closed, I glimpsed Petra and the handmaids entering the room and stopping to bow.

After a cup tsia in my changing room, I went into the bathing room and the three young ladies entered to washed me. And when they flaunted their wares this time, I knew none of them came close to Sandra's wholesome beauty. And I found myself now looking forward to the Staff of Attea going dark again.

The steward's dressing me in a navy blue tunic with gold trim today, before Agis showed me back out into the main chamber. The entire process taking about an hour, and I sat on the couch drinking tsia now as I waited for the lovely wife to return. And it was a good forty minutes before Sandra reappeared with Petra and the handmaids. All washed now, and her blonde hair combed and tied back with a light blue ribbon that matched the short tunic she was wearing. And as soon as I returned the ladies' bows, Agis opened the front doors, and the stewards brought our breakfast in and set the table.

When the table was set, Agis asked us if there was anything else that we required. Then bowing again, Agis relayed a thank you from the stewards and handmaids now for the wine and the time off to enjoy it last night. And I took a moment to remind Agis that Amy, Sandra, and I had all been regular people the same as them until recently. So, we appreciated everything that he and the servants did for us each day. And smiling, Agis nodded before leaving the chamber again.

Pulling out the chair on the left now, I held it for Sandra as we sat down to have breakfast. During which we had a small chuckle over Nestor passing out at dinner. Then a slightly larger chuckle over Sophia's slip last night when she said it was past time she bedded her husband. Over her embarrassment now, Sandra found it hilarious and was able to laugh along with me about it.

Finished with breakfast, Sandra looked around the chamber curiously, then asked me what Amy and I had alone in here for a week? And chuckling, I winked at Sandra now replying, "Research!"

And raising her eyebrows now, Sandra asked, "Really?"

Grinning now, I nodded my head and replied, "Really!"

Getting up from the table now, Sandra moved to the bed and threw the covers back before asking, "Well, I am up for that, if you are?" And smiling at Sandra, I dropped my head dolefully in feigned submission now like it was an unpleasant task as I rose from the table and moved to the bed. And removing her sash easily this time, Sandra let it fall to the floor before pulling her tunic off revealing her amazing body again. Confident that she had my attention now, Sandra slid into the bed. Then sitting up on one elbow, Sandra patted the open bed beside her now and said, "Well?"

Chuckling, I removed my sash and tunic as I joined Sandra in bed. Then, leaning over I looked into Sandra's green eyes as she smiled up at me now inviting me to do a little more research. And bending down, I kissed Sandra on the lips as she closed her eyes and enthusiastically kissed me back now. After a minute of this, I moved down kissing her lovely neck which I knew she enjoyed. Before working my way further down and pulling the covers up over my head. And Sandra suddenly asked, "Where are you going?" Followed shortly thereafter by Sandra exclaiming, "Oh!" And we made love the until the Staff of Attea went dark again before finally deciding to take a break and have dinner.

Once we were both dressed again, I smiled at Sandra and got her nod before pulling both the blue and gold ribbons on the wall. Summoning Agis and Petra, who entered the chamber individually this time without the stewards or handmaids. And each taking five steps into the room before stopping to bow.

And speaking to Agis now, I said, "Her majesty Sandra and I are ready for dinner now please, Agis."

Nodding in acknowledgement, Agis replied, "Very good, your majesty." Then Agis added, "Dinner will be a few minutes, if your majesties would like to freshen up now and change your clothes before dinner?" Nodding to Agis, I looked over just in time to see Sandra whispering in Petra's ear. Petra smiled and bowed to Sandra before turning and leading the way back into the lady's chambers. Glancing back at me, Sandra flashed me a smile now before disappearing into the lady's chambers with Petra.

I turned my attention back to Agis, who was standing by the door with his head bowed and his arm out now indicating for me to lead the way. And returning Agis's nod now, I strode into my private chambers as Agis closed the door behind us. The stewards bowed as I entered the room, one of which was holding my bathrobe over his arm. And quicky returning their bows, the three stewards stepped forward now removing my sash and tunic before putting the bathrobe over my shoulders and stepping back to bow again. Then Agis led the way across the hall into the bathing room. And to my surprise, the three female bathers were already inside waiting now with heads bowed. Returning their bows, the three attractive young ladies didn't waste any time in removing my bathrobe and guiding me down into the hot water. After retrieving the desired items from off their trays while blatantly displaying their finer attributes, they set to work cleaning me up. Then leading me back out of the bath, they dried me off with towels and put my robe back on before picking up their trays and bowing again. And returning their bows, Agis entered the room again immediately after the three women left. Bowing and gesturing for me move back into the dressing room. And we crossed back into the dressing room again, where the three stewards stood ready and waiting.

After having my hair brushed and my teeth cleaned, Agis presented me with two completely new tunics, holding them up now for me to choose from. The first one being crimson red, and the second one being a dark plum color. And picking the plum-colored one now, the stewards dressed me again choosing a cream colored sash now to go with my plum tunic. And I'd bet less than forty minutes had passed before Agis led me back out into the main chamber again.

Stepping back into the main chamber, I noticed three things immediately. First, that the table was set for two, and dinner was already on the table. Secondly, our bed had been remade and the sheets probably changed too. And thirdly, Sandra wasn't back yet, which wasn't a big surprise.

And bowing now, Agis asked, "Is there anything else that I can get your majesty?"

Smiling at Agis, I returned his nod and replied, "No, everything looks wonderful my friend, thank you." And bowing again, Agis backed up a couple of steps before turning and leaving the room.

Moving to the table, I picked up my wine cup and took a sip now as I looked over tonight's dinner. Smiling, as I could never get enough lobster, though Attean butter, being made from goat's milk, was a little different compared to our Maine butter.

I had just finished my first glass of wine and was about to reach for the wine carafe again when the doors to the lady's chambers opened. And turning to face the door, I was surprised to see Amy walking through the door now arm and arm with Sandra. As Petra and the three handmaids filed in behind them and spread out. My beautiful wives stopped, then they all nodded and bowed together now. Returning their nods, I gave my wives a smile as I bowed to their beauty. And while Amy and Sandra moved forward, Petra and the handmaids having delivered their Queens now, turned and filed back out of the room again.

Reaching the table, Amy released Sandra's arm and moved to the end of the table grabbing my arm before leaning in and kissed me sweetly on the lips for a moment. Then sliding left, Amy whispered, "Thank you, my love." And letting go of my arm now, Amy moved back to Sandra's side again and winked at Sandra. Who chuckled at Amy now as she turned and walked right back out of the room closing the door behind her. Leaving me standing there with my mouth open and a flabbergasted look on my face. After Amy left, Sandra turned to look at me, and her chuckle turned into full blown laugh as she saw the stunned expression on my face now.

Recovering from my surprise about the same time as Sandra got her laughter under control. I shook my head at Amy now before moving forward to pull Sandra's chair out. Moving to the table, Sandra caught me by surprise too, as she leaned in kissing and me on the lips suddenly. Then lingered over the kiss before taking her seat now.

Smiling at Sandra, I pulled my chair out before sitting down to the wonderful dinner which was getting cold now. After loading our plates, I filled Sandra's and my wine cups from the carafe before setting about eating dinner. During dinner, Sandra told me that Petra had taken Sandra straight into the spare room where Amy was waiting for her with tsia. And Amy asked her a series of questions about our wedding night. Asking first if we had properly consummated our marriage. And asking Sandra for her impression of my performance in my husbandly duties. Followed by Sandra's level of satisfaction with her first sexual experience. Before asking Sandra about her overall satisfaction with her wedding night. To which I replied, "Wow!"

Chuckling now, Sandra added, "My teachers at the university weren't that tough!" Which made us both laugh and nod our heads. After which, I jokingly asked Sandra if she had given me passing grade on my performance last night. And Sandra said that she had but required a few more days' research before giving me my final grade on performance of my husbandly duties.

Taking our wine over to the couches after dinner, I sat in the corner of the couch while Sandra lay back against me and we relaxed for a few minutes to let our dinner settle. Gently stroking Sandra's hair as she snuggled up against me and we finished our wine. After a few minutes, Sandra looked up at me and asked, "More research?"

And nodding my head, Sandra rose and took my hand leading me back to bed again. It was midnight before Sandra said she was ready to sleep. And snuggling up against my chest, I put my arms around my new wife now. Then I kissed the top of her pretty head one last time as we closed our eyes and drifted off to sleep.

And after five days of making love, eating, and making love again. Sandra said she was beginning to miss her mother, father, and new sister Amy's faces. And asked if we could invite them for dinner, to which I happily agreed. Then I suggested we take a walk out in the palace garden after breakfast, and our morning research. To help us get rid of our cabin fever after being couped in the royal chambers for five days straight. Blushing now, Sandra quickly agreed to both ideas.

And after our long first kiss of the day, Sandra and I almost decided to do our research before breakfast. But my stomach growled loudly, reminding both of us of how hungry we were.. And rising from the bed, we quickly dressed before stepping over and pulling the ribbons on the wall summoning Agis and Petra again. And while I informed Agis that we were ready for breakfast, Petra led Sandra off into the lady's chambers to freshen up now before breakfast.

Following the plan, we ate breakfast together then moved back to bed and spent a good hour enthusiastically completing our morning's research. Then dressing again, I pulled both ribbons calling Agis and Petra back, informing them we were ready for a bath and a change of clothes. And that we wished to invite her majesty Amy, Nestor, and Lady Sophia to join us for dinner tonight, so we would be five for dinner. And to notify Captain Duris that her majesty and I wished to take a walk in the garden after we washed and changed.

Petra and Agis smiled as they nodded, and Agis answered for both of them now, saying, "Very good, your majesties. We will see to it at once."

And nodding to Agis first, and then to Petra, I said, "Thank you, my friends." And rising, Petra held her hand out now gesturing for Sandra to enter the lady's chambers, followed by Agis holding his arm out for me to lead the way into my chambers. And holding hands to the last second, Sandra and I parted ways now. Sandra glancing back over her shoulder, smiling, and batting her eyes at me now as she stepped through the doorway into the lady's private chambers. And shaking my head, I chuckled as I walked into my private chambers and Agis closed the door behind us now.

The stewards were lined up against the closets on the right with heads bowed, as we entered the room. And stepping up onto the little podium, I returned their nods, as they moved forward and quickly changing me into my bathrobe before stepping back and nodding again. And Agis led me across the hall into the bathing room. And we stood there with me until the three lovely young ladies entered to give me my bath. Then nodding, Agis turned and left. I'm sure now to go oversee the clearing of the breakfast table, having the sheets changed and the bed remade while the three lovely ladies were cleaning me up.

Once I was dry and my robe on again, the three young ladies lined up and politely bowed to me before taking their trays and leaving. A few seconds later Agis reappeared, and nodding first, gestured for me to move back into my dressing room.

And choosing the crimson tunic with light gray sash today, Agis showed me back out into the main chamber again. And no surprise, Sandra was still in lady's chambers. So, nodding now, Agis asked, "Would your majesty care for some tsia or wine now while he waits for her majesty Sandra?"

Nodding my head to Agis, I replied, "Yes, some tsia would be wonderful right now Agis, thank you." Nodding again, Agis backed away before turning and disappearing into my chambers. Only to return a few minutes later, with a steaming tsia pot and two cups on the tray now. The second cup I assumed was for Sandra, in case she wanted tsia before going out into the garden.

And stopping at the edge of the carpet, Agis nodded again waiting to be acknowledged. And returning his nod, Agis stepped forward sitting the tray down on the coffee table and filling the first cup with tsia before setting it in front of me. Then nodding again, Agis asked, "Will there be anything else, your majesty?"

Giving Agis a quick nod, I replied, "No, and thank you Agis."

And Agis replied, "Your very welcome. I will come back and let you know when Captain Duris arrives, your majesty."

Nodding to Agis again, I replied, "Thank you." And Agis backed away again before turning and exiting the room closing the door behind him now. Sitting there casually sipping my tsia, I knew it took a time to dry and braid Sandra's hair, not to mention makeup and possible even having her fingernails and toes redone. I chuckled ironically trying not to imagine what they gossiped about during that time. Certain I would be embarrassed if not shocked if I could hear their conversation now. Then I remembered being a physician, Sandra didn't paint her fingernails.

I had just poured myself a second cup of tsia when the door to the lady's chamber opened and out walked Sandra followed by Petra as they stepped into the room and stopped to nod their heads. And smiling at my lovely wife, I gladly returned their nods. And Sandra moved forward to join me on the couch while Petra nodded before turning and leaving again.

Rising as Sandra approached, I offered her my hands to help her get seated. Sandra's beautiful blonde hair had been braided down the middle of her back again with a white ribbon this morning to match the bright white tunic she was wearing now. And both seated now, I leaned in and quickly kissed her smiling face before reaching for the tsia pot and filling her cup. Smiling, Sandra accepted the cup of tsia from my hands. And just as she took a sip, the door opened behind us opened as Agis stepped back into the room and bowed.

Turning, I returned Agis's bow, and he said, "Captain Duris is outside with your escort, whenever you're ready, your majesties?"

Sandra took another quick sip of her tsia before rising and smiling at Agis now and saying, "Please show the captain in, Agis." Then smiling at me, Sandra took my hand giving it a small squeeze and whispered, "I heard a rumor from the handmaids this morning that we need to confirm."

Nodding to Sandra, Agis quickly moved to the door and opened it now, revealing Captain Duris waiting on the other side with his helmet under arm as usual. And taking five steps into the room, Duris stopped and smacked his fist to his chest as he bowed his head now.

Her eyes sparking mischievously, Sandra said, "Good morning Captain Duris," as she smiled and returned Duris's nod.

And smiling back at Sandra, Duris nodded to Sandra before replying, "Good morning, my Queen." And nodding to me, Duris added, "And good morning to you, your majesty."

Then still having that mischievous look in her eyes now, Sandra asked, "I heard a rumor this morning from the handmaids that you and the Lady Ophelia are betrothed now. Is that true?"

And a little chuckle slipped out of my lips as I watched Captain Duris's cheeks turn all red now inside his bio-suit. And after a couple of seconds of surprise, Duris nodded his head to Sandra again and replied, "It's true, your majesty. I asked Lady Ophelia to marry me, and she accepted, your majesty.

Smiling brightly, Sandra said, "Congratulations, Captain Duris. And please be sure to give our congratulations to Lady Ophelia too!"

Nodding again, Duris replied, "Glady. Thank you, your majesty."

Standing up now, I returned Duris's salute and nod before saying, "Well done Duris, my congratulations to the both of you!"

And nodding again, Duris replied, "Thank you, your majesty."

Bowing his head too, Agis said, "Congratulations, Captain."

Returning Agis's nod, Duris warmly replied, "Thank you, Agis."

Turning back to Sandra and me now, Duris held his arm towards the door, saying, "Your escort is ready whenever you are, your majesties?" Nodding to Duris, I took Sandra's hand and gently wrapped it around my arm. Keeping her warm soft hand covered with mine as I tilted my head towards the door to see if Sandra was ready now. And giving me a smile, we started for the doors as Captain Duris turned and led the way out. And Agis bowing now as we passed him on our way out.

There were twelve royal guards waiting outside in the hallway, and I could see another ten on the terrace outside the atrium doors now as Caption Duris lead us down the south stairs and out into the garden. Stepping onto the terrace Duris stopped and barked orders as royal guards quickly spread out along both sides of the garden. And when the two guards appeared in front of King Atlas's tomb at the far end. Captain Duris slapped his hand to his chest and nodded his head again before holding his arm out indicating the garden was ours now to enjoy. And Sandra and I both gratefully returned Duris's nod before walking down into the garden now.

We decided to walk around the garden before sitting down by the fountain this time. And I led Sandra along the north side of the garden to Atlas's tomb. Where we paused for a minute in front of the tomb to admire the ten-foot-high marble statue of King Atlas holding his trident. Before casually walking around the south side of the garden until we reached the blue crystal seahorse fountain in the center.

And taking Sandra's hand off my arm now, I guided her down onto the stone coping around the pool. Then I sat down next to Sandra, and she leaned back into me taking my hand in hers as we sat there now enjoying the fresh air looking up at the north slope of the cavern behind the palace. Sandra relaxing, while I tried to imagine how many feet of rock lay between the cavern wall and the ocean above. After a few minutes of silence, Sandra and I chuckled about Captain Duris's and Lady Ophelia's betrothal. And I jokingly commented that Duris must have finally stopped running long enough for Ophelia to corner him. And received an elbow to the ribs from

Sandra for my remark. Though both of us agreed that their marriage probably wouldn't take place now until after Captain Duris returned, since Duris was scheduled to rotate to the West Cavern's garrison in a few days. Which meant Ajax would be back at the palace soon too.

And I decided right then and there, to have Ajax teach me how to use a "xiphos" or short sword when he got back. So, I could properly defend myself, and my beautiful wives if the need should arise. And I told Sandra about it now too. The thought of something so terrible ever happening that I needed to defend her and Amy with a sword frightened Sandra. But being as smart as she was, Sandra looked at it from my perspective and agreed that having Ajax teach me how to properly use a xiphos was a good idea. And trying to lighten things up now, I asked Sandra if her father had said anything to her lately about cousin Pylos's recovery? Sandra said no, but she wished to know Pylos's condition now too, since I mentioned it.

Which made me chuckle at her now, before saying, "You are a Queen of Attea now, my wife! Who's going to stop you, or tell you, you can't go visit cousin Pylos? Better yet, all you have to do is request that Pylos's and Cressida join you for tsia, and they will come to you!" Then thinking about it for a second, I added, "Though I would check with your father tonight before making such a request."

Thinking about it for a now, Sandra smiled and replied, "Yeah! I guess the Queen part just hasn't sunk in yet, my love. I am still enjoying the wife part." Then Sandra added, "And you're right about checking with father first before requesting they join us for tsia."

Nodding to Sandra, I bent down and kissed the top of her head before looking up at the cavern walls again. Stirring some idea or notion in the back of my mind that I couldn't quite get a grip on yet.

Having had enough fresh air now, Sandra sat back up and I rose offering her my hands to help her up. And taking my hand, Sandra rose now brushing her body up against mine in a very seductive manner. And I got the impression that having refreshed herself in the garden now, Sandra was ready for a little more research. Shaking my head, I looked at Sandra's grinning face now and nodded my head. And still having hold of Sandra's hand, I wrapped it around my arm now before leading my lovely wife back up to our chambers.

Stopping outside our chamber doors, we thanked Duris for the walk in the garden and congratulated him again on his betrothal to Lady Ophelia. Then we both smiled and returned his nod before turning and entering the royal chambers. Holding the door for Sandra, we found Agis and Petra waiting heads bowed on the other side now. And Agis asking us if there was anything we required before dinner? And looking around the room, I saw the pot of tsia was gone from the coffee table and had been replaced with a carafe of wine and two glasses now. Then looking at Sandra, she shook her head "no," and I told Agis and Petra we had everything we needed as we returned their bows. Then Agis and Petra both nodded again before turning and leaving the room shutting the doors behind them.

And taking Sandra's hands in mine now, I held them as I slowly looked from the wine carafe on the coffee table over to the bed before looking back at Sandra's lovely face. And smiling shyly at me, Sandra tilted her head towards the bed. And letting go of Sandra's hands, I swung my arm out palm up towards the bed, indicating for my lovely wife to lead the way now.

After a good hour of research, we decided that we were thirsty. So, getting up we remade the bed, and as Sandra bent over straightening out the blanket. And I snuck up behind her and let her know that I was still interested in doing more research. One thing led to another, and we ended up having another round of research right there. And with her cheeks all flushed now, Sandra quickly dressed and gave the bed a wide berth as she moved to the couches now to get some wine. Then she stayed at the other end of the couch me until she finished her wine. Only after Sandra's was one her second cup of wine did Sandra move over next to me blushing as I sheepishly grinned at her.

After finishing her second cup of wine, Sandra leaned back against me. And I put my arms around my wife and brushed aside the strands of her blond hair that had come loose during our research. Then bending down, I kissed the top of Sandra's head as she pulled her feet up onto the couch. And snuggling up against me now, Sandra closed her eyes for a little pre-dinner nap. Leaning back, I closed my eyes too, joining my beautiful wife in a short nap before dinner.

Chapter - 15

It was Agis lightly clearing his throat by my chamber door that woke me from my nap on the couch with Sandra. Leaning down, I kissed the top of Sandra's head again waking her from her nap on my chest. Smiling at her, Sandra looked up at me sleepily in anticipation of more kisses. And grinning at the look on her face now, I whispered "Agis is here, it's dinner time my love."

Sitting up now, Sandra glanced over at Agis standing by the door with head bowed before saying, "Good evening, Agis."

Grinning now, Agis kept his head bowed as he replied, "And a good evening to you, your majesty." Then he added, "Your father and mother are outside waiting now, your majesty."

With a genuine smile of joy on her face now, Sandra replied, "Please show them in, Agis." And nodding his head again, Agis moved to the doors as Sandra asked, "And her majesty Amy?"

Stopping, Agis turned to face Sandra again before nodding and answering, "Waiting on you, my Queen. You need only to pull the gold ribbon, your majesty." Then continuing to the front doors, Agis opened the righthand door now as Nestor and Lady Sophia entered.

Equally eager to see Amy and her parents, Sandra turned to me and asked, "Could you pull the gold ribbon, my love?" And nodding my head to my wife, as I rose from the couch as Sandra smiled brightly and turned to greet her parents now as they entered the chamber. Nestor and Sophia stepped into the room, then stopped to nod to Sandra first before nodding to me. And I returned their nods as Sophia and Sandra held out their arms now, and mother and daughter moved to hug each other.

And giving the gold ribbon a tug to summon Amy, I turned to greet my new father-in-law now. Who, after the women finished their hug was getting a hug from his daughter now too. Nestor and Sophia both nodded again as I approached them. And the door behind me opened as Amy and Petra entered from the lady's chambers now and stopped to nod their heads. Returning Nestor's and Sophia's nods, I turned around and smiled now as I returned my lovely wife Amy's nod.

All of us smiled at our little reunion now. And turning to face Agis on the right again, he read my mind, saying, "Dinner will be ready in a few minutes, your majesty. Would your majesties care for a glass of wine first?"

Nodding my head to Agis, I smiled and replied, "Yes, thank you, Agis." Then turning to face everyone again, I held my hand out indicating the couches now and asked, "Shall we sit and have a glass of wine before dinner?" Agis and Petra quickly nodded again before leaving the room. Everyone in agreement, Sandra, Sophia, Nestor, and Amy all moved to the couches now.

Following behind, Nestor seated Sophia on the second couch, while I took Sandra's hand guiding her back down onto the first couch again. Then turning to Amy, she stepped in front of me and faked an elbow to my ribs before dropping down beside Sandra on the first couch now. Leaving me the single chair in the middle. The four of them quickly turning their heads away trying to hide their snickering faces. Frowning at them, I happily took the single chair in the middle and sat down.

Agis reentering the room with one of the stewards now, each carrying a tray with a carafe of wine or water and two cups. And pausing by the door to nod first, they both moved forward to the edge of the sitting area before stopping again to nod and wait. I quickly returned their nods, and they stepped forward now setting their trays down on the coffee table, Then Agis carefully filled each of the four cups before backing up to the other steward and nodding again waiting to be dismissed. Returning Agis's and the steward's nods now, I grinned and said, "Thank you. Agis."

The women immediately striking up their own conversation with Sandra, curious about Sandra's satisfaction with the wedding and of course her wedding night. And it only took about a minute before Amy gestured for Sophia to move over next to them. And Sandra patted the empty spot on the couch next to her signaling her mother she was too far away for a proper gossip, and that she needed to move over next to Amy and her now on the couch. Quickly rising, Sophia moved to her daughter's side now pausing to briefly nod at Sandra and Amy before sitting down on the far side of Sandra. Sandwiching Sandra in the middle now so they could whisper back and forth.

Luckily, Nestor had sat down on the left side of the second couch by me, so he was right next to me now on my left. Nestor and I downed our first glass of wine as we watched the woman on the other couch chatting away non-stop, oblivious to our presence now. And reaching out, I picked up the wine carafe and holding it up, asked Nestor, "Are you ready for another, father?"

And grinning at me, Nestor nodded his head before replying, "Definitely! Thank you, your majesty."

Carefully refilling Nestor's glass and my own glass again, I set the carafe back down on the table and picked up my cup holding it up towards Nestor and saying, "You are most welcome, my friend." And grinning back at me, Nestor held his cup up towards me, then we both took a drink of our wine. Both of us relaxing for a moment, enjoying the peace and serenity of the women being completely pre-occupied in their own private conservation now.

I was just about to reach for the wine carafe again when Agis stepped back into the room informing us that dinner was outside waiting. Returning Agis's nod, I signaled for him to go ahead and serve the food. We stayed on the couches until the stewards and handmaids had the table set and the dinner laid out for us.

Rising now, I offered Amy and Sandra each a hand to help them up. And they both accepted my hands, as I leaned back slightly to help them to their feet again. Once we were all seated at the table with Amy and Nestor on my right and Sandra and Sophia on my left again. I picked up my wine cup and held it aloft for a toast now.

And when everyone had their glass's up, I said, "To my new family, may everyday be as pleasant as this one!" And clinking my glass to Amy's first, I then clinked my glass to Sandra's. And Nestor and Sophia quickly followed our lead now as they clinked their glasses to ours. And smiling at them all, I proceeded to down the entire glass of wine now celebrating the toast. Which made the women shake their heads, while Nestor simply chuckled and followed my lead emptying his entire glass. Then we set about the wonderful feast before us.

The women started out gossiped about Captain Duris and Lady Ophelia's betrothal, and how their wedding was scheduled to take place in six months when Duris's returned to the palace. Then they switched to Pylos's and Cressida's wedding, which was supposed to take place in just over a week. And remembering our earlier conversation, Sandra asked Nestor, "And how is Pylos's recovery going father?"

Grinning now, Nestor nodded to Sandra and replied, "Captain Pylos is up and back to his duties again, your majesty. But I had a talk with General Aetolus and suggested that he keep Pylos in the office doing paperwork for another week or two. Just to be sure he doesn't have a relapse, and we're sure he's fully recovered. Aetolus agreed, if only to appease Cressida and make sure that their wedding takes place on schedule. And Captain Duris agreed, as he would rather do most anything than sit behind a desk doing mundane paperwork, your majesty!" And we all had a chuckle now at Duris's reason.

Then Sophia said, "Lady Calista, Cressida's mother, mentioned to me that she and Cressida are both unhappy with the choices of wedding locations down in the capitol now, which is delaying the preparations."

And looking at Nestor now, I asked, "You told us Pylos is my cousin, right?"

And curious now, everyone turned to look at me as Nestor nodded his head and replied, "Yes, he is, your majesty!"

Then I said, "Well, since he is my cousin, and of royal blood. Why don't they just get married here in the palace garden, and have their wedding reception here in the banquet hall?"

Nodding in agreement with me, Nestor replied, "That's a good point, your majesty!" Then turning to Sophia now, Nestor asked, "Do you think Cressida and Calista would agree to having the wedding here in the palace, Sophia?"

Nodding her head now, Sophia replied, "Thank you, your majesty. I will speak with Cressida and Calista first thing tomorrow. I am certain they will accept your generous offer, your majesty."

Smiling at Sophia now, I replied, "Bah, nothing generous about. Pylos is family, and he risked his life to save her majesty Amy!"

And reaching over taking hold my hand now, Amy added, "Andrew's right. This is the least we can do for Pylos, to whom I will forever be in debt." And Sandra, Nestor, and Sophia all nodded their heads now agreeing with Amy.

And we talked on for an hour after that, the women mostly about Cressida wedding and helping to make sure it was the best day of her life. And having finished dinner along with all the wine on the table, I suggested we move back to the couches and get comfortable, while Nestor and I polished off another carafe of wine. During which Nestor informed me that Ajax was due to arrive tomorrow. And Helios, fully recovered now, was back to his usual arrogant, unpleasant self.

It was getting late when Nestor and Sophia rose and excused themselves now as they had lots to do in the morning. And I was impressed that Nestor could still stand now, let alone walk. As I had a decent buzz going now myself from all the wine. And pulling ribbons on the wall, I summoned both Agis and Petra now to assist my in-laws back to their rooms here in the palace. And once the servants had finished cleaning up, they turned down the blankets and left the room again. Then Amy walked right up to me and grabbed the front of my tunic, before pulling me down and kissing me soundly on the lips. Then letting go of my tunic again, Amy turned and opened her arms to her new sister Sandra. Hugging and kissing Sandra on the cheek before waving goodnight and walking back into the lady's chambers shutting the door behind her, leaving Sandra and me alone again.

Sandra and I were both a little tired but content after having some wine, a wonderful dinner, and a pleasant conversation with Nestor, Sophia, and Amy. The only thing missing to make this a perfect day now was a little research. And we both moved to the edge of the bed, kissing, and chuckling as we scrambled to get our clothes off and round out the evening. After an hour of research, Sandra snuggled up on my left, and we settled in for a good night's sleep.

The next morning, we woke up at a decent time and I gently persuaded Sandra to have our morning research before breakfast. It didn't take much persuading, and we made love again, while we were both rested and able to give our full attention. Smiling and declaring that she was satisfied now, Sandra rose from the bed and stretched her beautiful body before grabbing her clothes. And joining my lovely wife now, I rose and quickly dressed, then smiling at her, I checked to see if she was ready to start our day. And nodding her head that she was, I stepped over and pulled the ribbons on the wall now for Agis and Petra.

To our surprise, several minutes passed before the doors opened and Agis and Petra stepped into our chamber. Obviously surprised to see Sandra and me up this early now. Grinning at them, we returned their nods and informed them we were ready for a bath, a change of clothes, and breakfast, in that order if they could manage it. Grinning back, they replied that they could. And I took the time now to inform Agis that it is her majesty Sandra's wish for Captain Pylos and the Lady Cressida to join us today for tsia after lunch. And I asked him to make sure that they were both informed of her majesty's request? Agis smiled and nodded his head, saying he would personally make sure they were both notified now. At the end of which, Sandra stepped up and quickly kissed me now before turning and walking into the lady's chambers, and Petra closed the door behind them.

Turning back to Agis, he nodded his head and held his arm out now for me to lead the way. Walking down the short hallway, I entered the dressing room where my three stewards stood waiting. We all knew the routine. But this morning, it honestly felt excessive. As I was quite capable of changing into my bathrobe myself. And stepping up onto the podium in the center of the room, I called Agis to my side now and whispered, "This really is a bit much, Agis. I'm quite capable of changing into my bathrobe and dressing myself!"

Nodding his head, Agis leaned in and whispered back, "We are all aware of that, your majesty. But this is the way it's been done since the time of King Atlas. And we do it gratefully, your majesty. Happy to be serving you now rather than Prince Helios, your majesty!"

Grinning at Agis, he had a point, and I really couldn't really argue with him. So, I whispered, "Maybe if you and stewards nodded instead of bowing all the time, I wouldn't find it so unsettling, Would that be possible, Agis?"

Nodding his head and grinning now, Agis replied, "Certainly, your majesty. I will see to it immediately. But please forgive us if we occasionally forget and bow, your majesty."

Smiling at Agis, I replied, "It's already forgiven, my friend."

Nodding his head solemnly, Agis held out his arm now indicating for me to cross into the bathing room. And leading the way, I crossed into the bathing room where the three attractive young ladies bowing as I entered. Looking at Agis, he nodded and said, "I take care of it, your majesty!"

In a good mood now this morning, I nodded in return and smiling at the three young ladies, said, "Good morning ladies!"

And they all smiled back now, and bowed in unison again, replied, "Good morning, your majesty." Then they set their trays down and removed my bathrobe before leading me down into the hot water.

After my bath, I noticed that when I returned to the dressing room, the steward nodded their heads instead of bowing, and I smiled at them as I returned their nods and stepped up onto the podium now so they could dress me. And Agis presented me with a shiny pale blue tunic and bright yellow sash today, to which I nodded in approval, and they quickly dressed me. After which, Agis informed me that Captain Ajax had arrived last night on schedule replacing Captain Duris. And knowing my fondness for Ajax, Agis asked now if I wanted him to request that Ajax join us for tsia today as well with Pylos and Cressida. To which I eagerly agreed.

Following Agis back into the main chamber, the bed had been made, and breakfast was on the table, though Sandra hadn't returned yet. Delivering me to the table, Agis paused long enough to fill my tsia cup before nodding again and leaving me to enjoy my breakfast. Quickly checked out what was on the table this morning, I decided to wait for Sandra and just have tsia for now. Ten minutes later, the door to the lady's chambers opened and out walked Petra followed by Sandra. And stepping into the room, they both paused by the door to bow now. Rising from my chair, I returned their bows before moving to get Sandra's chair. Smiling, Sandra nodded to Petra then moved to the table to take the chair I was holding for her.

Touching my hand briefly as she took her seat, Sandra whispered, "I asked Amy to join us for breakfast this morning. But she said it was still too soon, and that she had already had her breakfast. But she will be joining us for tsia with Pylos and Cressida later."

And remembering Ajax now, I replied, "Good. Because Agis just informed me that Ajax arrived last night, and he suggested that I invite Ajax as well for tsai today. I know Amy will be thrilled to see Ajax again!"

Nodding her head and chuckling, Sandra added, "Amy told me we have six more days until it's a full two weeks. And that if you haven't gotten me "knocked up" as she put it, by then. There was going to be hell to pay when she got back!"

Shaking my head, I had to chuckle at this bizarre situation. Where my wife, and love of my life, was insisting that I get my second wife pregnant now! It was almost as crazy as our boat capsizing and waking up on that table to Nestor's grey bio-suited face and being told that we were in the mythical land of Attea and could never leave.

Then Sandra said, "I informed Amy that my cycle is due any time. And six days from now, we could officially consider me late. Which seemed to make Amy extremely happy."

Chuckling again, I was still trying to get my head around this crazy situation and Amy's attitude, as I replied, "Well, we best finish our breakfasts so we can get back to our research. We wouldn't want to disappoint your lovely sister now would we!" And grinning shyly at my reply, Sandra started to eat a little faster now in anticipation.

After finishing breakfast, we had a couple of hours before Pylos, Cressida, and Ajax were due to for tsia. So, we happily spent it now doing the extra research to make Amy happy. And we kept at it until we were both pleasantly exhausted. Then we lay there together for twenty minutes recovering afterwards before getting up and dressing again. Though this time, Sandra pointed at the couches and told me to go sit while she remade the bed.

After the bed was made, Sandra joined me on the couch. Sitting next to me wanting some cuddle time now, since she only had me to herself for six more days. And cuddling up on the couch together, I caressed Sandra's hair as we swapped stories about our youth.

It was Agis's knock on my door that ended our cuddle session, as Agis stepped into the room now and stopped to nod. At the same time, the south door opened, and Petra followed Amy now walked into the room, and stopped to nod briefly to us. I quickly nodded to Amy and Petra before turning to Agis, and acknowledging his nod, waved him forward now. Stepping up to my side, Agis nodded and said, "Captain Ajax, Pylos, and the Lady Cressida are outside now, your majesty."

Rising from the couch, I nodded to Agis before replying, "Please show them in, Agis." Then turning, I offered Sandra my hands to help her up off the couch as Amy crossed the room now to embrace her new sister. Having delivered Amy, Petra nodded again and stepped back into the lady's chambers closing the door behind her.

Agis opened the inner doors, and Cressida, Pylos, and Ajax entered the room now. Stepping in five paces, Cressida bowed, while Pylos and Ajax both grinned now before snapping a salute and bowing their heads. Returning Cressida's bow first, I smiled at my cousins and returned their salutes before moving forward exchanging the two-handed clasp of friendship with them both now. Amy and Sandra smiled now as they returned their nods. And while I greeted my cousins, Sandra and Amy moved forward latching onto Cressida now before guiding her to the second couch and having her sit between them. Moving back to my chamber door, Agis opened it as two stewards entered now bearing trays with tsia pots and cups. Once Cressida was seated on the second couch, Sandra sat down beside her, while Amy moved around to Cressida's other side and sat down on the first couch. The three of them were already engrossed discussing Cressida's wedding now and the problems she was having.

Once the formal greetings were complete, I smiled at both my cousins and gestured for them to take a seat. Nodding again, they moved to join the ladies in the sitting area. But before they could reach their seats, Amy stood up and catching Pylos by surprise now, gave him a hug and asking, "How are you, Pylos?" Then releasing him, Amy added, "I will never be able to thank you enough for your courage and sacrifice, Pylos."

Embarrassed by Amy's hug and praise now, Pylos's face began to turn red as he managing to nod and reply to Amy, "Thank you, my Queen. I gladly would do it again, your majesty!"

Ajax tried to go around them, but Amy stepped in front of him now, and looking up at Ajax's face, smiled and said, "Where do you think you're going, Ajax?" And before Ajax could answer or move, Amy stepped forward grabbing hold of Ajax now and gave him a hug too, saying, "We have missed you, cousin!"

More than a little embarrassed now, Ajax nodded his head and tried to hide his red face as he shyly replied, "It's good to be back in the palace guarding your majesties again." Sandra, Pylos, Cressida, and I all turned our heads away now trying to hide our grins.

Point to the single chair between the two couches now, Amy said, "Sit here by me please, Ajax." As Amy sat back down on the end of the first couch by singe chair. Leaving me at the other end of the couch with Amy. And Pylos took the single chair next to Sandra on the right. And sitting down beside Amy, I signaled for the stewards to serve the tsia now. Nodding their heads, they quickly moved forward setting down their trays on the coffee table and carefully filling the three cups on each of their trays nodded again and stepping back next to Agis again nodding their heads and waiting to be dismissed.

And Agis stepping forward now asking, "Do you require anything else, your majesties?"

Shaking my head negatively now, I returned their nods and replied, "No, but thank you all."

Then the four of them nodded again before filing back into my private chambers. Turning back to the table, I started to reach for the nearest tsia cup when Cressida nodded her head and excitedly blurted out, "Thank you for allowing us to get married in the palace garden, your majesty. It's perfect!"

Smiling at Cressida, I returned her nod, replying, "You're very welcome, Cressida. It's the least I can do for my cousins and family." Then giving Ajax a sideways glance now, I added, "How often does one of my cousins get married anyway?" And Pylos, Amy, and Sandra all picked up on my subtle hint and turned to look at Ajax now to his dismay. And we all chuckled at the sour look on Ajax's face.

Still looking at Ajax, I said, "As a matter of fact, I was thinking that after our tsia, we might all go out and take a walk in the garden together to get some fresh air. Then Cressida and their majesties will have a better idea of what they have to work with, if that's not a problem, Ajax?"

For which I received a nod and smile from all three ladies and a nod from Pylos, before Ajax nodded his head and replied, "Certainly, your majesty." And Amy leaned over and took hold of my hand now giving it a squeeze. I couldn't tell whether Amy was just pleased with my suggestion or starting to miss me now. As she kept hold of my hand for several minutes while our new family drank their tsia and chatted back and forth in a mix of Attean and English now.

His tsia finished, Ajax stood up and bowed to Sandra and Amy before saluted me, saying, "If your majesties will excuse me now, I shall go see to the escort for your walk in the garden, your majesties?"

Returning Ajax salute, I replied, "Thank you, cousin." Then Ajax backed up five paces before turning and leaving the room. While Amy, Sandra, and Cressida went back to talking about the wedding again. Outnumbered now, Pylos wisely choose to sit back and just nod and smile occasionally to the ladies as they continued to chat excitedly about Cressida's and his upcoming wedding.

Ten minutes later, Agis stepped out of my private chambers and stopping to nod before saying, "Captain Ajax is outside with the royal escort now whenever you're ready, your majesty."

Having been expecting this, I rose from the couch and offered Amy my hand to get up. Then I returned Agis's nod and said, "Please show Captain Ajax in now Agis, thank you." And once Amy was on her feet, I turned to smile at Sandra as I extended my right hand out to her now to help her get up. And smiling back at me, Sandra graciously accepted my hand giving it a little squeeze now as she rose from the couch. Then Pylos stepped forward offering his hand to his fiancée Cressida to help her up off the couch. And moving around the coffee table, we all turned to face Ajax as he strode into the room now and stopped to salute and nod his head, before proclaiming, "Whenever you are ready, your majesties?"

Returning Ajax's nod, I held out my right arm out to Amy now, who nodded as she wrapped her left hand around my arm. Then looking at Sandra, I held my left arm out now. And Sandra nodded and smiled as she stepped forward wrapping her hand around left arm now. Then looking at Ajax again, I replied, "We are ready, cousin."

Snapping us another salute, Ajax wheeled around and led the way out of the chamber now, as Amy, Sandra, and I followed him. As Pylos and Cressida followed behind us. Our twelve man escort waiting for us in the hallway as Ajax led us down the south stairs, across the atrium, and out onto the garden terrace where another dozen royal guard stood at attention now heads bowed and waiting. Pausing on the terrace, Ajax gave the order and the guards quickly split up spreading out along the north and south sides of the garden. Then Ajax saluted us again now, before swinging his hand out and inviting us to proceed down into the garden.

Once we had descended the stairs, Amy and Sandra flashing me a smile before letting go of my arms now and commandeering Cressida from Pylos. And oblivious to us men now, the woman proceeded out into the garden pointing at this and that and giggling as they walked arm in arm towards the fountain in the center now.

Ajax and Pylos both shaking their heads now as they stepped up on either side of me. Turning to Pylos on my right, I leaned in and asked, "Pylos, would you mind keeping an eye on the woman for a minute while I have a word with Cousin Ajax?'

Taking a step back, Pylos snapped his hand to his chest and nodded his head to me, replying, "Certainly, your majesty!"

And smiling at Pylos, I returned his salute and said, "Ajax can tell you about later, Pylos." And returning my smile now, Pylos took two steps back before turning and trotting off after the women.

Once Pylos was gone, Ajax saluted me and nodded his head again, saying, "I am at service, your majesty."

And returning Ajax's nod, I put my hand on Ajax's shoulder now replying, "Walk along with me for a moment, Ajax." And nodding his head again, Ajax and I slowly started moving towards Pylos and the ladies in the center of the garden. And I continued, adding, "I have discussed this her majesty Sandra. And she agrees that you should teach me how to properly use a xiphos now, cousin."

Grinning now, Ajax nodded his head replying, "It would be an honor, your majesty."

And returning his nod, I added, "Thank you. And if you are wondering why, cousin? It's because as you are aware, I won't be long before I'll have more than just their majesties to protect. And if someone should manage to get into the royal chambers, I need to be able to do more than just stand there waiting for the royal guard to arrive."

Nodding his head now, Ajax replied, "I understand, and I agree, your majesty. It's a good idea." Then thinking about it for a moment as we walked, Ajax added, "How about an hour or two each day here in the palace garden, starting after Pylos's wedding, your majesty?" And nodding my head that I agreed, Ajax briefly pointed to the right of Atlas's tomb now and added, "How about over there in the corner by Atlas's tomb? I can have a training post installed there without it drawing much attention. And I can stash the equipment in the bushes. But protocol requires that you have at least six guards with you if we are going to spare. But I will handpick six of my tighter lipped men and assign them to your personal guard. If you agree, your majesty."

And nodding to Ajax, I replied, "That sounds good, Ajax. I trust your judgement, cousin." Then grinning at Ajax as we neared my lovely wife's, I continued adding, "Now that's settled. Let's join the ladies and see what trouble their majesties have gotten me into now."

Chapter - 16

When Ajax and I reached the fountain, Amy and Sandra left Cressida's side and moved up on either side of me taking my arms again. Then they took turns telling me what they had decided so far. Ruling out holding the ceremony at Atlas's tomb first for obvious reasons, as well as holding it here at the fountain with Atlas's tomb looming behind them. Which left the terrace and the stairs outside the East Atrium, facing the palace. And since Pylos was a royal, they would ask Elders to perform the ceremony and hold the reception here in the great hall.

Finished looking at the garden for now, we turned and headed back into the palace. Pausing to say goodbye to Pylos and Cressida in the East Atrium, as Amy and Sandra exchanged bows and hugs with what was soon to be their new cousin Cressida. While I received another salute and nod from Pylos. After which, Ajax led us back up to the royal chambers before thanking us for the tsia and saying goodbye outside the doors.

Back in our chambers again, Amy teased Sandra now, telling her, "You'd best make the most of remaining time, sister. Because in five days, you have to start sharing our husband again." Then pausing in the doorway to the ladies' chambers, Amy looked back and gave Sandra a wink now before turning and closing the door behind her.

After dinner and a couple of glasses of wine, Sandra suggested that we move to bed and do the additional research that her sister had recommended. And we gave it our best effort now until we were both exhausted and ready to sleep. Then Sandra curled up in my arms, and I kissed the top of her head before asking, "So, how exactly is this going to work, the three of us in here?"

Snuggling back against me, Sandra replied, "I don't know either, my love. But there's plenty of room in this bed. So, I'll discuss the research arrangements with Amy privately tomorrow over tsia and let you know what we decide at dinner." Then after a moment, Sandra added, "Though, I suspect that after two weeks in the guest room alone, Amy will be ready for a little research of her own. So, you should be prepared for that, husband." Agreeing with Sandra now, we closed our eyes and drifted off to sleep.

The five days later, I had resolved to spend my afternoon alone again and had just stretched out on the couch, when Agis stepped into the room and informed me that my father-in-law Nestor was outside waiting now. Rising, I smiled and asked Agis to show Nestor in.

Agis opened the door, and Nestor walked in five paces before stopping to nod. Returning Nestor's nod, I waved him forward to join me in the sitting area. And moving into the sitting area, Nestor nodded again before taking a seat in the single chair on my left. And moving up to the edge of the sitting area now, Agis nodded his head and asked, "Would you like some tsia or wine now, your majesty?"

Returning Agis nod now, I replied, "I think tsia now, Agis. It's still a little early in the day for wine."

And glancing at Nestor and getting a nod from my father-in-law now. Agis nodded again and said, "Very good, your majesty."

Then turning to Nestor, I asked, "Is everything okay, Nestor? What brings you here this morning?"

Grinning wryly now, Nestor replied, "I received a note this morning from her majesty Sandra. Informing me that your majesty would be alone all day in case I had any affairs of the state or business to discuss with you, your majesty."

Smiling now at my lovely wife Sandra's foresight, I asked, "And are there any affairs of state or business that we need to address?"

Smiling and shaking his head, Nestor replied, "No, your majesty. With Prince Helios safely locked up in the palace dungeon, the Wild Ones in hiding licking their wounds, and your majesty's first heir on the way, the kingdom is at peace finally." And as I nodded to Nestor, Agis stepped back into the room carrying the tray with our tsia. And stopping by the door, Agis nodded his head and waited now.

Returning Agis's nod, he moved forward, pausing to briefly nod again before setting the tsia on the coffee table and filling Nestor's and my cups. And nodding afterwards, Agis asked, "Is there anything else that you or the senior physician require, your majesty?"

Turning to smile up at Agis, I replied, "No, I think we're good Agis, thank you." Nodding again, Agis turned and left the room now.

After Agis had closed the door, Nestor continued, saying, "As far as kingdom news, there isn't anything other than Pylos's and Lady Cressida's wedding in the palace garden tomorrow. Tydeus and the Elders happily agreed to perform the ceremony for your cousin Captain Pylos, the hero of Attea." And I assumed Nestor was referring to Pylos risking his life to save Amy's with the latter part.

Picking up my tsia cup, I took a sip before replying, "Good, thank you Nestor." To which Nestor dolefully nodded his head before reaching for his cup and taking a sip of his tsia too. And grinning at Nestor now, I continued adding, "Now, that I have one of my cousins married off. I'm wondering what I can do about the other one?"

And raising his eyebrows now, Nestor shook his head and replied, "Ew, I don't know about Ajax? That's not going to be easy, your majesty?"

And chuckling lightly, I nodded my head to Nestor before replying, "Yes, I know." Then thinking of my previous idea about candidate number four Lady Kassandra now, I said, "You know if her majesty Sandra hadn't been one of the candidates that day, the Lady Kassandra would have been our second choice, Nestor?" And looking at me now, Nestor waited for me to explain, and I did, adding, "What do you think of matching cousin Ajax up with Lady Kassandra?" And not waiting for Nestor to respond, I asked, "How well do you know Lady Kassandra?"

Thinking on it for a moment, Nestor replied, "Actually, I know of more of Lady Kassandra, than I know her personally. As my friend and mentor Kallinos, keeps me informed of Kassandra's academic achievements and progress." Then pausing for a moment, Nestor continued adding, "Your majesty has a good eye though, I think Captain Ajax and the Lady Kassandra would be a good match, your majesty." Then grinning mischievously, Nestor added, "You know as King of Attea now. You could just simply order the Lady Kassandra's and Captain Ajax's marriage don't you, your majesty?"

Chuckling for a moment, I shook my head now before replying, "Interesting? But I like Ajax far too much to order him to marry Lady Kassandra or any other woman for that matter. Out of respect for Ajax, I would prefer that he marries the woman of his choosing.

Though in cousin Ajax's case, a little nudge or assistance in the right direction may be required."

Chucking and nodding his head, Nestor held his tsia cup up like a toast now before replying, "I agree, your majesty."

Later that night, while I was having dinner with Sandra and Amy, I thanked Sandra for her little note to Nestor. And I told Sandra about Lady Kassandra being our second choice had Sandra not been one of the candidates. Then I told Amy and Sandra of my idea of matching Kassandra up with Ajax now. And I wasn't surprised by the look of dismay on their faces when I told them that Nestor had informed me, as the king, I could just order their marriage. Sandra spoke up now, informing us that she knew Kassandra from school, and she agreed with me that Kassandra was a good match for Ajax. And my wives quickly volunteered to help as our little plot began to take shape now.

After which, Amy and Sandra informed me that they had decided we would all sleep in the enormous bed together. And that they would just take turns doing research. To which I simply nodded now agreeing with their decision. Only to find out later what they meant by taking turns was who went first that night. And after satisfying both Amy and Sandra, I ended up alone on the left side of the bed, as my two lovely wives preferred to snuggle up together on the right after having been apart for two weeks.

The next day, we were sitting in the front row of chairs in the palace garden with Nestor, Lady Sophia, and Lady Callista, Cressida's mother beside us facing the terrace. The rest of the garden packed full of brightly dressed Atteans. And the entire garden strung with row after row of white and pink flowers now.

As we watched now as General Aetolus gently kissed Cressida's hand before exchanging nods with Pylos and passing his daughter's hand to Pylos. Then Tydeus, with Sippas, Kallinos, and Thestor standing behind him, performed the marriage ceremony on the terrace. And after giving Cressida a long kiss on the lips and taking Cressida's hand, Pylos and Cressida, along with the four Elders, all turned to face Amy, Sandra, and me in the front row and bowed.

And rising from our chairs now, Amy, Sandra, and I returned their bows before applauding and cheering for our cousins. Ajax by our side as Amy, Sandra, and I moved forward to congratulate the happy couple now as they descended the stairs. General Aetolus moving up on his new son-in-law's left. While Lady Callista moved forward hugging and kissing Callista before standing on her right now as they prepared to receive congratulations from all the guests and courtiers lined up behind us.

After Amy and Sandra exchanged bows and congratulated the Lady Callista, they exchanged bows and moved in hugging our new cousin Cressida for a minute before moving on to Pylos. Following my two wives,' I exchanged bows with Lady Callista, congratulating her with Nestor doing the translation. Then moving on to the smiling Cressida, I briefly exchanged bows with her before shaking her hand and congratulating her. And to the surprise of the other guests, Amy and Sandra returned Pylos's bow, then they both stepped forward giving our embarrassed cousin a quick hug now congratulating him on his marriage to Cressida. Then they stepped over exchanging bows with General Aetolus and shaking his hand congratulating him.

Sandra and Amy were waiting at the end of the line when I stepped in front of Pylos and returned his salute. Then stepping forward, I exchanged the two-handed clasp of friendship with my cousin and congratulating him on his marriage to Cressida. Then stepping to the right, I returned General Aetolus's salute and congratulated him now before joining my two beautiful wives on the end.

Then quickly exchanging bows with the line of guests waiting to congratulate the Pylos and Cressida, Ajax led us back into the palace and down the north hallway into the banquet hall for the reception.

Two days later, I began my xiphos training with Ajax. After my breakfast with my beautiful wives and a bath, I returned to my dressing room, where the stewards changed me into my new armor. Then I returned to the sitting area for tsia with my lovely wives while I waited for Ajax and my escort to arrive.

And once Agis announced Captain Ajax was here, I gave Amy and Sandra both a quick kiss before bidding them goodbye and following Ajax out into the hallway where my six handpicked personal guards waited for us. And all six men resembling Ajax in a way, though I doubt that Ajax had noticed it. All six men having stern faces, tank like builds, and numerous battle scars showing through their green and brown bio-suits now in the places their black cuirasses didn't cover. Ajax led us down the south stairs, across the atrium, and out into the garden now. And we followed Ajax out to the southeast corner of the palace garden by Atlas's tomb, where Ajax had the thick wood training post buried and set up already.

Then Ajax had five of the guards spread out in a semi-circle, then do an about-face and stand watch now, while keeping the older guard by his side. I later learned that this was squad leader Peleus, who Ajax considered the best swordsman in all of Attea and a true artist with a xiphos. Not to mention Peleus was Ajax's sparring partner.

Reaching into the bushes in the corner now, Ajax withdrew two short swords from their wood cases hidden there and handed one of them to me. Then Ajax had me spend a ten minutes getting used to the feel of the 24-inch long flat sword or "xiphos," as it was called here in Attean. The sword only weighed about 2-1/2 pounds and was heavier on the front. Where the flat blade was nearly three inches wide before tapering down to about half that width by its six inch wood hilt. Then Ajax demonstrated the correct way to stand and swing the sword now before showing me how to properly slash and thrust with it.

Nodding his head each time, Peleus quietly and modestly made the occasional suggestions to Ajax as they began my training. After correcting my grip on the hilt and adjusting my stance, Ajax had me practice what I had learned on the wood training post. Explaining that I should be cutting into the post or driving the tip in roughly an inch but no more, to correctly wield the short sword. Then Ajax had me practice my swings and thrusts now for a good twenty minutes, while he and Peleus circled me watching. Making suggestions and correcting my stance and technique as I practiced.

Luckily, just as my arm was ready to give out from swinging at the post, Ajax had me stop. And taking the xiphos from me now, Ajax returned the two swords to their cases in the bushes before taking out two slightly thicker wood practice swords from the bushes. Ajax walked me through parrying the various swings and thrust now with the practice swords and correcting my blocking technique.

After thirty minutes of demonstrating how to properly block or parry the various attacks. Ajax and Peleus were both fairly satisfied with my defensive technique. And Ajax had me defend myself now, as he circled to the left and we began the first of many sparring matches to come. Starting out at half speed, Ajax waited until he was convinced of my ability to parry his attacks, before gradually beginning to increase his speed. And after fifteen minutes of parrying the majority of Ajax's attacks, Ajax saluted and nodded, signaling the end of our training session for today. And taking the wooden practice sword from my hand, Ajax stuck them back into the bushes again. Then Ajax barked out the order for the guards to reform, and they escorted me back up to my chambers.

Back inside my royal chambers again. I informed Agis that I required another bath before my lovely wives, who were busy turning the guest room into a nursery now returned. And I informed Agis that from now on, I will take my daily bath after sword practice. Agis quickly agreeing to my request, as the stewards removed my armor now to find me completely drenched in sweat underneath.

And the next two weeks went by the same way. After breakfast with my lovely wives, Agis and the stewards would dress me in my armor, then I would have tsia in the sitting area unit Ajax showed up. Once we were out in the garden, Ajax would have me practice on the training post for a good twenty minutes. While Ajax and Peleus circled me making suggestions and giving me advice. Then we would switch to the wooden practice swords. And I would spare with Ajax for a close to an hour. While Peleus circled us making suggestions, which Ajax calmly translated as we continued to spare. And at the end of the second day, I suggested to Ajax that we end our session with a two-handed clasp of friendship to put the guards at ease. As I noticed more than one of the guards glancing over their shoulders the noise of our sparring increased. And while we exchanged the two-handed clasp of friendship, Ajax leaned in now and whispered, "Your right, your majesty. And once we switch from these wood swords to the xiphos, the guards will definitely be watching to make sure I don't attempt to injure you or kill, your majesty."

Surprised now, I asked, "Why would they think that Ajax?"

And grinning at me now, Ajax replied, "Because after cousin Helios, I am next in line for your throne, your majesty!"

Chuckling at Ajax, I asked, "Does that interest you cousin, if I may ask?"

Shaking his head emphatically now, Ajax replied, "No, my King. Just the thought of being couped inside the palace with the Elders forcing me to get married, then telling me who to marry would drive me insane! I don't know how you handle it, your majesty." Then after a moment, Ajax added, "Also, if I may say so? Being raised in the outlands as a commoner gives you a unique perspective. Which is something the throne has been missing for too long, your majesty."

Nodding to Ajax now, I replied, "Well, thank you cousin. And yes, being stuck in the palace isn't much fun. But I am in love with her majesties Amy and her majesty Sandra. And I couldn't imagine leaving their sides, which makes up for that feeling now." Then chuckling, I added, "I'm more like a willing prisoner now, cousin."

Grinning and nodding now, Ajax said, "Though I have never felt that way about a woman myself. I can understand it, your majesty."

Putting my hand on Ajax's shoulder now, I said, "I think we better go back now, cousin. So, I can get cleaned up before my lovely wives return for lunch!"

Nodding his head now, Ajax slapped his hand to his chest and replied, "Immediately, your majesty." Then turning, Ajax barked the order to reform and escorted me back into the palace again.

After nearly two full weeks of training on the practice post and sparing with Ajax every day. Ajax tossed his training sword to Peleus now, who caught it mid-air with a big smile, before planting his 8-foot long spear in the ground. Then slowly drawing his xiphos from the leather baldric on his chest, threw the sword into the ground sticking it there. And saluting me with the practice sword now, Peleus nodded his head before grinning wryly at me. Returning Peleus's salute with my wood sword, I took up position. Unsure what to expect now from the best swordsman in all of Attea.

Peleus began his attack now, at what I guessed was three-quarter speed for him, and I could see why Ajax considered him the best swordman in all of Attea. Peleus attack was smooth and graceful, almost effortless on his part. Probing for weakness as he repeated several moves watching my reaction as I parried his blows. And out of the corner of my eye, I saw Ajax cover his face in anticipation now. But I knew what Peleus was up to, and when he repeated that same move again, instead of parrying the blow like I had done before. I suddenly stepped forward right on top of Peleus's sandaled foot and gave him a hard elbow to the cuirass now knocking over backwards onto the ground, much to the surprise of both Peleus and Ajax.

Grinning at them both, I stuck my practice sword in the ground, then stepped forward extending my hand to Peleus to help him up now. Accepting my hand with a smile now, Peleus rose and saluted me again with his practice sword. And walking back to my practice sword, I drew it out of the ground and returned salute before swinging my arms up indicating I was ready for another go. This time Peleus didn't hold back, and after he got the drop on me a half dozen times, knocking me to the ground twice. Ajax signaled that this was enough for today. And after passing the practice swords to Ajax, I exchanged the two-handed clasp of friendship with Peleus now. Who smiled and spoke to Ajax now, who told me that Peleus was impressed with how quickly I learned and my progress so far.

A four days later, Ajax switched from the wood swords to the steel xiphos. And Ajax started out slow with the short swords, giving me time to get adjusted to the additional weight and heavier front of the xiphos now. And he was right, it took some time for me to adjust, the xiphos being a little harder to swing quickly but requiring less force to achieve the desired impact of my blows. But by the end of the session, I began to feel a little more confident with xiphos. And after exchanging the two-handed clasp of friendship with Ajax. We turned around to find cousin Pylos standing next to Peleus now discussing my training. And seeing we were done, they both saluted and nodded their heads now. Returning their salutes with a tired smile now, I walked over to greet cousin Pylos. And exchanging handshakes with Pylos now, I asked, "What brings you out here today, cousin?"

Nodding his head, Pylos replied, "The guards at the East Atrium reported that you were out in the garden and that they heard the sound of sword fighting now, your majesty." And pausing to grin now,

Plyos added, "Ajax had informed me you were training out here now, your majesty. So, after calming the two guards by the door down. I came out to see for myself. Though, I had no idea your training had progressed so far already, your majesty!"

Standing beside me, Ajax replied, "Yes, his majesty is a quick learner, Pylos." And Peleus put his hand on his chest and nodded his head now agreeing with Ajax's comment. Then Ajax said, "Maybe you can come out and spar with his majesty one of these days, Pylos."

Shaking his head negatively now, Pylos replied, "As you are well aware Ajax, I am fair hand with a sword or a spear. But my true skill lies with the bow. And if his majesty is able to successfully spar against Peleus and you cousin, then I am afraid his skill with a xiphos is already beyond that of my own!" At the end of which, Pylos translated his words to Peleus before nodding to Ajax.

Ajax and Peleus chuckled as they returned Pylos's nod now, then jokingly Ajax replied, "Oh, I wasn't suggesting that you spar with his majesty to now work on his skill!"

After which, Ajax and Peleus both patted the embarrassed Pylos on the shoulder, and we all had a chuckle now. And not passing up an opportunity to tease my cousin, I asked Pylos now, "Speaking of skills, cousin. Should General Aetolus expect to be a grandfather any time soon?" And as Pylos's face began to turn red, Ajax and I both burst out laughing and thumping Pylos on the shoulder now as we congratulated him again on his marriage to the lovely Cressida.

Recovery from his embarrassment, and overcoming some of his shyness now, Pylos snapped me a salute and nodded his head before replying, "Rest assured, I gave it my best effort, your majesty!" And we all chuckled as I returned Pylos's salute now, then Ajax gave the order to reform so we could return to the palace. Pylos walked along with us as we returned to the royal chambers. Both saluting me again outside my chamber doors before bidding me farewell.

Agis and the stewards were lined up by my chamber door awaiting my return. And after a quick bath and a change of clothes, I walked back out into the main chamber to find lunch on the table and my beautiful wives there talking with Petra now while they waited for me. Nodding to the three ladies, I moved forward and seated Amy on my right, then Sandra on the left before taking a seat at the head of the table now. Once Petra nodded and left again, I told my wives that Pylos was back from his honeymoon now and had come out to watch our training session today. After which, Amy and Sandra agreed to invite Cressida, Lady Callista Cressida's mother, and Sophia for tsia tomorrow afternoon.

That night after the servants left, we climbed into the enormous bed together. And Amy smiled as Sandra gave me her good news now. Which was that Sandra tested positive today and was pregnant. Amy was just as excited as Sandra and me at the wonderful news, as we took turns now hugging Sandra and congratulating her. After which, Sandra and I each took a turn touching the bulge showing in Amy's belly. And I spent several minutes kissing my beautiful wives telling them again how much I loved them both and how proud I was of them now. Then wrapping my arm around Amy, I pulled her in on my left, before reaching around Sandra now and pulling her in on my right. After which, I gently kissed each of their lovely heads as they snuggled up together on my chest and continued chatting back and forth, too excited now to sleep. After twenty minutes of this, I realized that they were too worked up and excited now for anyone to get any sleep tonight unless we did a little research first. Which I was happy to do since I was excited by Sandra's joyous news now too.

We decided before we even sat down for breakfast the next morning to have Agis send for Nestor now. As Sandra wished to be the one to inform her father she was pregnant. Nestor showed up just before Ajax came for our daily sword training. And Nestor was truly overjoyed when the three encircled him now and Sandra calmly informed her father that she was pregnant. And after hugging his daughter and getting a hug from Amy too, Nestor nodded to me solemnly before shaking my hand thoroughly. And when Ajax showed up, I excused myself now as Nestor, Sandra, and Amy continued to celebrate the wonderful news.

It wasn't until I had finished my training post practice, and Ajax and I were sparring that Ajax asked me, "What was the commotion was in the royal chamber this morning with Nestor?"

Smiling at Ajax now as we circled each other, I calmly replied, "Oh, her majesty Sandra wanted to be the one to inform her father that she is pregnant now."

And Ajax hesitated for a second now and I got the drop on him, besting him as he stood there frozen with my sword at his throat. Then dropping his sword as I withdrew mine, and Ajax snapped me a salute and nodded his head, saying, "That's wonderful news your majesty, congratulations!" Then Ajax quickly translated what had happened to Peleus. And Peleus turned to saluted me too before saying something in Attean. Which Ajax quickly translated, saying, "Peleus congratulates your majesties on the wonderful news now too, your majesty."

Returning their salutes, I replied, "Thank you cousin, and thank Peleus for me too. I am actually quite happy about it too, cousin."

To which, Ajax added, "I am sure the entire kingdom will share in your joy too, your majesty. Once they learn of her majesty Sandra's glorious condition."

Nodding my head to Ajax again, I replied, "Thank you, Ajax." And giving my sword a couple of spins, I pointed at Ajax's sword sticking in the ground and added, "Now, shall we continue making sure that I am able to defend my new family properly, cousin?" And nodding his head again, Ajax picked up his sword and grinned at me before beginning to circle to the right now.

After my training session, we were sitting down to lunch, and Sandra and Amy informed me that Nestor had rushed off after I left to give the Elders the good news. And that Nestor, and the Lady Sophia would be joining us for dinner tonight. Sandra and Amy planning now to give Sophia the good news over tsia shortly with Cressida and the Lady Callista, if Nestor hadn't told her already.

And when had finished our lunch, I kissed Amy and Sandra on the lips before giving each of their backsides an affectionate squeeze now and sending them off with Petra to their little tsia party. Once everyone was gone again, I stretched out on the couch now for a nap before dinner. Knowing that my new father-in-law would expect me to celebrate the good news with him tonight over a half dozen bottles of Agis's best wine.

Chapter - 17

This time it was Petra who cleared her throat as she entered the chamber, stepping to the side and nodding as Amy, Sandra, and Lady Sophia entered behind her now. I must have been pretty tired because Petra's attempt to wake me now failed. And seizing their opportunity, Amy and Sandra shushed Petra before sneaking up on me as I slept on the couch. Both of whom crossed the room quietly and gently sat down on the edge of the couch next to me. Then, smiling at each other, they proceeded to tickle me without mercy now. Startled from my nap, I sat up and grabbed wildly for my wives as they continued to tickle me. And pulling them in tight now, I proceeded to kiss them repeatedly. Which embarrassed them and our guests sufficiently that they stopped tickling me and returned my hug now. Which was cut short by Petra clearing her throat again to get our attention as she and Lady Sophia stood by the door to the lady's private chambers looking up. And letting go of my beautiful wives again, I rose from the couch and smiling at Petra and my mother-in-law now, I returned their nods, saying, "Lady Sophia, is good to see you again. Welcome, and I'm sorry about that, but we are still newlyweds."

Bowing now, Lady Sophia, replied, "Nothing to forgive, your majesty. I am just grateful to see that her majesty Sandra is happy and loved by your majesties."

I returned Sophia's bow now, but it was Amy who answered her, smiling and saying, "As you can see, Sophia. We both love Sandra. So please, come join and us now."

Nodding again, Sophia smiled and moved forward to the other couch, briefly nodding again before sitting down. And rising, Sandra moved over to the other couch with her mother, giving Sophia an affectionate hug and smile now. After which, Sandra smiled at Petra and said, "I think his majesty would like some tsia now Petra, as would the rest of us, please."

And nodding her head, Petra replied, "Immediately, your majesty." Then Petra turned and went back out of the door.

Turning to look at Sandra and Sophia on the other couch, I asked, "And where is my new father-in-law, Nestor?"

Sophia spoke up now, answering, "My husband is still with the Elders, planning the announcement and celebration tomorrow of her majesty Sandra glorious condition. But he should be here shortly, your majesty."

The doors to the lady's private chambers opened again as Petra and one of the handmaids entered the room carrying the trays with the tsia pot and cups. Pausing by the door to nod before proceeding forward to the seating area and stopped to nod again. And smiling at them, Sandra returned their nods and indicated for them to serve the tsia now. The handmaid quickly setting her tray of cups down on the coffee table followed by Petra. Who picked up the tsia pot now, quickly filled the four cups before moving the cups one at a time in front of us. Then the two ladies nodded again before turning and leaving the room again.

We all reached for our cups, as Agis entered the room behind us pausing to nod his head and quietly clear his throat before saying, "The Senior Physician is outside now, your majesty.

Turning, I returned Agis nod replying, "Show my father-in-law in please, Agis." Then I added, "Oh, and Agis! I think my father-in-law will be wanting something a little stronger than tsia now to celebrate her majesty Sandra's glorious condition."

Grinning, Agis nodded his head and replied, "Understood, your majesty. And congratulations, your majesties."

Nodding my head solemnly in return now, I smiled at Agis now knowing he meant what he said, as I replied, "Thank you, Agis." And rising again, Agis moved to the front doors to open them for Nestor. Who strode into the room smiling now as he stopped to exchange nods, and we motioned for him to join us in the seating area. While Nestor moved forward and took a seat, Agis disappeared back into my private chambers. And taking the single chair between the two couches now, Nestor looked at our tsia cups for a second and I could tell he wasn't in the mood for tsia. And as I grinned at Nestor, Agis entered the room again carrying a tray of wine cups and a carafe of wine. And briefly nodding by the door, Agis moved forward to the sitting area before stopping to nod and wait. Returning Agis's nod, he moved forward setting the tray down on the coffee table before filling one of the cups with wine for Nestor and setting it in front of him.

Looking up at Agis now, Nestor said, "Thank you my friend, you're a mind reader." And nodding to Nestor, Agis turned and grinned now as nodded to the rest of us. And returning Agis's nod, he backed up five paces before turning and leaving the room again.

Picking up his cup off the table, Nestor held it out to his daughter Sandra for a second, then over at Amy, before Nestor made a toast now, saying, "May your majesties children be healthy, and always make you as proud as Sophia and I are today, to your majesties!" It was wonderful toast, and we all drank our tsia as Nestor proceeded to empty his cup of wine and smack it down on the table now in celebration. Then after expressing his pride and joy to Sandra and Amy again. Nestor proceeded to tell us about the public viewing tomorrow in the courtyard and the fireworks. As the whole city turns out to congratulate her majesty Sandra and Amy again.

And Nestor managing to polish off a whole carafe of wine before Agis returned to announce dinner was ready. And nodding to Agis, we all rose from our seats as the Agis opened the front doors, and the servants quickly set the table.

Escorting my two wives over to the table, I seated Amy on my right and Sandra on my left. And grinning, I watched Sophia guide Nestor to the table and get him seated, as Petra poured Sandra and Amy each a glass of watered down wine now. Then she set them in front of Amy and Sandra before nodding and lining up by the door with the handmaids. When Agis and the stewards finished setting up dinner. They lined up by my door again, all eight of them nodded again before turning and filling out of the room.

Dinner was wonderful, and after Nestor had congratulated Sandra and told her how proud they were of her, several time. I changed the subject to cousin Ajax's and his marital status now. Asking my new mother-in-law if she knew Lady Kassandra's mother. To which she replied that she had spoken to Lady Ismene on more than one occasion. And that Lady Ismene had confided in Sophia that she was extremely proud of her daughter's many accomplishments, except one. Which was providing her with a grandchild. So, Sophia felt sure Lady Ismene would be more than willing to assist us in our little scheme to get Ajax and Lady Kassandra together. And Sophia volunteering to pay Lady Ismene a visit tomorrow to confirm her approval of the match now. And to let Lady Ismene know that this is their majesties wish.

At which point Sandra spoke up, saying that we should invite Cressida, Pylos, and Ajax to dine with us tomorrow night, which would seem normal, since Amy and Sandra haven't seen our cousins since they returned from their honeymoon. And Sandra would send an official invite to Lady Kassandra to join us for dinner as well. After which, the fairly plastered Nestor leaned in and whispered, "And the plot thickens!" And we all had a good chuckle at Nestor now.

Dinner was running a little longer than usual as Nestor and I polished off another carafe of wine. And the ladies had an endless list of topics to discuss now. With both Amy and Sandra pregnant now and Amy starting to show. Plus, the renovation of the guest room into a nursery. That, and the amusement of plotting Ajax's demise now.

After dinner two of the stewards helped Nestor back to his room, while Petra insisted on helping Lady Sophia back to her room personally. And once the Agis and the servants had cleared away dinner and left again. I climbed into bed with my two lovely wives. Luckily, they were both still tired from last night. And curling up together on the right side of the bed, giving me the night off now. And feeling the wine a little myself, it wasn't long before we were all fast asleep. And I began to dream. . .

After dinner and several glasses of wine, I was more than a little sleepy. And while Amy and Sandra went to the nursery to feed the babies for the night. I slipped off my clothes and climbed into the enormous bed by myself. I had just nodded off when suddenly I heard a bloodcurdling scream coming from the lady's chambers.

Jumping up, I grabbed my xiphos from its scabbard by the bed and ran into the lady's chambers now. And going to the last room on the right, I threw the door to the nursery open. And the first thing that caught my attention was a dark hooded figure kneeling in the open windowsill holding a bloody sword. And he glanced back at me before leaping from the window, it was Prince Helios.

The room was a bloodbath. Amy, Sandra, and two of the handmaids lay slaughtered on the floor now. Blood streaked the walls and pools of blood spread out beneath the lifeless forms of my two wives. Kneeling down, I quickly checked Amy and then Sandra, desperately hoping to find a pulse, but there was none now. Then I saw the blood on the cribs. And stepping forward, I hesitated afraid to look in the cribs now, fearing I would find my innocent children slaughtered in their beds. And I did, both my children having been stabbed to death as they lay sleeping. Bright red blood covering their white nightgowns. Dropping to my knees between the cribs, my sword slipped out my fingers and fell to the floor now as shock and grief overwhelmed me.

Gasping, I suddenly sat bolt upright in the bed, drenched in sweat and wide awake. Then looking to my left, I confirmed that my two lovely wives were still sleeping safe and sound next to me now.

Then laying back down on my pillow, I tried to shake off the nightmare and go back to sleep. But after lying there for fifteen minutes, I gave up and climbed out of bed now. And dressing, I moved over to the couches and sat down, hoping the nightmare would fade and my sleep return. Finally realizing this wasn't going to happen anytime soon. So, I decided to go out for a walk in the palace garden and get some fresh air.

And entering my private chambers, I passed the open door to the stewards' room on the right. Agis wasn't there, but the three young stewards were all sound asleep in the chairs lining the left wall. Continuing down the hall to my dressing room, I quickly dawned my armor and sword. Then I opened the closets one at a time, until I found a dark blue hooded robe in the fifth closet. And pulling it up over my armor now, I fastened the clasps to small rings on my cuirass. Then going back down the hallway to the steward's room. I used the steward's entrance now, sneaking past the three sleeping stewards to the door out into the hallway outside. And quietly opening the door, I stepped out into the hallway trying to avoid drawing the attention of the royal guards stationed in front of my chamber doors.

And when I glanced back to check if the guards had noticed me, I was surprised to find the guards missing from in front of our doors now.

Turning my attention back to the stairs, I went down south stairs into the East Atrium now. The atrium was dark, but I didn't find that surprising since I had never really been outside the royal chambers this late at night before. And there was a small amount of light coming in through the atrium windows now from battlements outside.

Reaching the bottom of the stairs, I started across the atrium for the garden doors when I noticed a dark mass lying on the floor in the corner. And moving to the dark mass, I discovered one of the royal guards lying dead on the floor now, a pool of blood spread out around him. My eyes adjusting to the dim light, I looked around the atrium now and spotted four more bodies lying in the dark area on the far side of the atrium. I was about to shout and raise the alarm, when out of the corner of my eye, I caught the glint off a sword outside as it moved away from the terrace. The assassin standing by the bottom of the terrace was just making his escape now across the palace garden.

And stepping over the dead guard, I watched the assassin as he fled east across the garden now. Passing through the open doors, I went down the terrace steps and crouched down behind the nearest bush. Then carefully began working my way forward through the manicured hedges of the garden now from bush to bush. Trying not to alert the assassin to my presence now and get ambushed somewhere ahead in the dark.

Staying on the center walkway, the assassin skirted the seahorse fountain in the center now and continued straight on to King Atlas's tomb on the far end. And as I worked my way closer, I watched the assassin climb the steps of the tomb and stop in front of the two large stone doors.

And I watched in fascination, as the assassin began reading the symbols on the doors now like he was searching for something. Then suddenly the assassin stepped forward and pushed four of the carved symbols on the righthand door. And there was a loud mechanical sound from inside the tomb as the two doors unlocked, followed by a low grating noise. As the two doors slowly parted and began moving outwards to the left and right now.

Pausing in the doorway while he waited for the doors to open. The assassin turned his head around to check the garden behind him before entering Atlas's tomb. And in that brief instant, I caught a glimpse of the assassin's face in the dim light. To my astonishment now, the assassin was none other than Prince Helios.

Stepping away from the hedges, I paused at the base of the stairs now to listen. And straining my ears, I heard the faint grating noise coming from down inside the tomb. Which was followed suddenly by an enormous crashing sound from inside the tomb. Like a stature or some large piece of stone had tipped over and crashed to the floor. Whatever it was, it was heavy enough that I felt with my feet now.

Quickly climbing the steps, I was surprised to see a light coming up the stairwell from the tomb below now. Drawing my xiphos out, I slowly crept down the stairs along the left wall into the tomb. And reaching the bottom of the stairs, I leaned forward peering around the corner checking the tomb for Helios, but I didn't see him now. Suddenly Helios stepped out from behind the statue of King Atlas on the other end of the sarcophagus, holding what must be King Atlas's gold trident in his hands. And seeing me now, Helios pointed the trident at me. Then a look of frustration came over his face, like he had expected the trident to shoot our lightning bolts or something, but the trident didn't work. And Helios frantically wrung the trident with his hands now. Suddenly he gave up and dropped the trident at his feet with a loud metallic clang that echoed through the tomb now.

His eyes filled with hatred, Helios pulled his blood stained xiphos out, and stepping around Atlas's sarcophagus now, charged. I just stood there, sword in hand, waiting. Hoping that Ajax's and Peleus's training had been sufficient enough now for me to survive a one-on-one swordfight with Prince Helios.

We were both wearing armor now, me in my new lighter king's armor, and Helios in the black cuirass and helmet of the royal guard. Apparently stolen during his escape from the dungeon. And with his helmet on, I knew the only exposed or fatal spots on Helios were his throat, under his arms, or up under his cuirass now.

Reaching me, Helios didn't waste any time swinging at my unprotected head. And I parried his blow now, returning strokes of my own. As we quickly exchanged two dozen blows back and forth now trading stroke for stroke. Neither able to gain the advantage now, as Helios slowly circled to my left. And I quickly realized Helios was either better trained or more experienced than me now. But I was stronger, quicker, and had a reach advantage over the shorter Helios.

Suddenly Helios changed direction, jumping back to the right and attacking. And I was hard pressed for a moment blocking and parrying Helios's blows. But after a few minutes of this, the momentum changed as Helios was apparently beginning to tire. And I quickly put him on the defensive. Pressing him hard now as I tested the limits of his stamina, and it was beginning to fail. As I rained down blow after blow now down on Helios, driving him back to the wall. And reaching the point where my blows were starting to make it through his defenses, striking his helmet and cuirass now.

Realizing he was losing, Helios suddenly stepped back and threw his sword straight at my head now. Ducking, I managed to deflect Helios's blade away with my sword. His sword missing my head by inches now before hitting the wall and loudly landing on the floor.

Wheeling now, Helios ran back to Atlas's trident again snatching it up off the floor. But this time he didn't waste time trying to use its power, he just leveled the trident at me and charged again. Stepping to the left at the last second, I knocked the pronged head of the trident's away with my sword. And off balance after his thrust, I caught Helios backhand with my sword, slicing into his right bicep just below his armor now as I brought my sword back across. Recovering his balance, Helios tried to raise the trident again, but his right arm failed him now, and he nearly dropped the trident.

Having stepped to the left to avoid Helios's charge, Helios was now closer to stairs than me. And realizing that he had lost, Helios suddenly turned and bolted for the stairs now, trying to escape with King Atlas's trident.

I started up the stairs after Helios when suddenly I saw the flash of a sword as it came out from behind the column on the right and passed clear through Helios's neck. Causing his head to come off and fly back down the stairs at me. And I froze now as I felt Helios's blood splash my legs as his head bounced back down the stairs past me. Mesmerized, I watched Helios's head as it tumbled down the stairs and came to a stop a few feet from the bottom of the stairs.

And turning to look back up the stairs, I saw Ajax step out from behind the column now on the right into the light. A smile on his face now as he calmly bent down and wiped his sword off on the blue cape covering the Helios's headless body. Then standing up, Ajax slid his sword back into its sheath before bending down and prying Atlas's trident out of Helios's dead hands now, as I climbed the stairs and exited the tomb.

Sheathing my sword, I stepped over Helios's dead body to greet my cousin now. And Ajax held the trident out to me now, determined that I should take it for some reason. Looking at his grinning face now, I accepted the trident from Ajax's hand.

I immediately felt an enormous surge of power from the trident running through my body now like an electrical current. As hundreds of images suddenly began flashing before my eyes, so fast that I couldn't comprehend or grasp what I was seeing. Startled, I let go of the trident now, letting it drop to the ground at my feet again with a clang as the visions in my head stopped coming and I snapped out of the trance.

When I finally regained my sight, Ajax had back up and stood there staring at me now with a look of fear and concern on his face. Still a little dazed, I asked him, "What happened?"

Recovering from his shock, Ajax replied, "As soon as you touched the trident. The crystal began to glow bright blue, and your eyes turned the same color as the crystal. And for the first time in my life, I knew what it means to be afraid. Are you okay, your majesty?"

Smiling to reassure Ajax now, I put my hand on his shoulder and said, "I'm fine, Ajax. Don't worry." Then continuing, I added, "As soon as I touched Atlas's trident, I felt an enormous surge of power, and hundreds of images began flashing through my mind. But they were coming so fast that I couldn't comprehend what I was seeing. It was a little unnerving, so I dropped the trident." And we both paused to look down at trident now as it lay there on the ground between us.

Apparently Ajax had no intention of touching the trident again. And turning to Ajax now, I stated, "Well, I am not going to touch that thing again either." And drawing my sword out, I moved over to Helios's dead body and quickly cut the lower half of his cape off now. Then sheathing my sword, I folded the piece cape in half and wrapped it around the Atlas's trident before slowly picking the trident up again. This seemed to work, as there was no surge of power when I touched Atlas's trident this time. And with trident in my hand, I was just about to say something to Ajax when the guards in the palace sounded the alarm now. Then there was a flurry of shouts and the sound of running feet, as every light in the palace slowly came on. Then there was more shouting, and Pylos followed by a dozen guards now came sprinting across the garden towards Ajax and me here atop King Atlas's tomb.

Reaching the top of the stairs, I could tell Pylos wasn't happy upon seeing the headless body of one of the royal guards lying here at our feet. And snapping me a saluting now, Pylos nodded his head and asked, "Are you okay, your majesty?"

And grinning at Pylos to put him at ease, as I replied, "I am fine Pylos, thank you. In fact, I am better than fine. Since the headless body you see here before you now is none other than cousin Helios's. Which Ajax most appreciatively separated from its head, ending our throne issues once and for all!"

Smiling, Ajax nodded his head now replying, "Thank you, your majesty. It was as pleasurable as it was overdue, your majesty!!"

With a huge smile on his face, Pylos turned and saluted Ajax now. Then Pylos surprised both of us by stepping forward putting his arm around his cousin now and congratulating him, saying, "Well done, Ajax!" Caught off guard, Ajax looked embarrassed now by Pylos's hug and the words of praise. And I couldn't help but laugh at the startled expression on Ajax's face. Ajax's smile returned after a moment though, and he put his arm up around Pylos now returning his cousin's hug.

Then Pylos noticed the guard's cape I was using to hold Atlas's trident now and pointing to the piece of cape, asked "Why the cape, your majesty?" Looking from me to Ajax now as he spoke.

And answering his question, I said, "Helios opened Atlas's tomb to get the trident. Then he tried to use it on me, but the trident wouldn't work for him. But once Helios was dead, Ajax handed the trident to me. And it reacted immediately as soon as I touched it. The crystal started to glow blue, and hundreds of visions started flashing through my mind. It was unnerving so I dropped the trident, and it stopped. So, I wrapped trident up I the cape now so that I can hold it safely." Bringing Pylos up to speed now.

Pylos nodded at my explanation, then after a second, asked, "But what was your majesty doing out I the garden? And how did you know that Prince Helios's had escaped, your majesty?"

Grinning as I answered now, I replied, "I didn't. I had a bad dream and couldn't go back to sleep. So, not wanting to disturb anyone, I put my armor on and come outside for a walk in the garden. I discovered the dead guards when I came down into the atrium. Then I caught the glint off the assassin's sword as he fled through the garden. So, I followed him here to Atlas's tomb. I didn't know it was Helios until he stopped to open the tomb doors. Luckily, thanks to Ajax's and Peleus's training. I was able to best Helios in a swordfight, then Ajax showed up just in time to prevent Helios from escaping with Atlas's trident." Then turning to look at Ajax now, I asked him, "Which reminds me, how did you know I was out in the garden, Ajax?"

Grinning now, Ajax answered, replying, "Agis, your majesty. When Agis returned to your chambers. He went into your dressing room to hang up some clothes and noticed that your armor was missing. And he immediately pulled the red ribbon, notifying the night guards that something was wrong in the royal chambers, and they came running and notified me. I just figured you went out for a walk in the gardens. But after finding the slain guards in the atrium, I ran out into the garden to search for you. And seeing the tomb's doors open, I came to find your majesty."

Shaking his head and frowning at me now, Pylos said, "Well, I am relieved that your majesty was skilled enough to defeat cousin Helios in a swordfight. But disturbed that your majesty would take such a risk, rather than raising the alarm and letting us do our duty."

Chuckling now, Ajax put his hand on Pylos's shoulder nodding in agreement with his cousin, before turning to face me and saying, "Pylos is right, your majesty. Your death would have thrown the kingdom into a state of chaos! Not to mention, finally have a King worth serving, and losing him! It would have broken everyone's hearts, your majesty." And both cousins nodding again now after Ajax's declaration.

And returning their nods, I replied, "Thank you, cousins. I will do my best not to put the crown in jeopardy again. And thank you both now for keeping it safe. And I command you both from now on cousins, to speak your minds freely about any safety concerns or mistakes I make. Understood?" To which they both saluted and nodded their heads now acknowledging my order.

Returning their nods again, I smiled and said, "Well, I'd best get back before their majesties begin to worry. As you will find out Pylos, pregnant women tend to be emotional and prone to worrying if left alone too long." Then I added, "I think its best if I hold onto Atlas's trident for now, until I have a chance to speak with Nestor and the Consul of Elders." And they both nodded their heads, then the three of us walked back down the steps to the royal guards waiting below. The guards snapping to attention, but each giving Atlas's trident an awed look before nodding their heads and taking up their escort positions around us. With Atlas's trident in my hand, we walked back across the garden and into the now well-lit East Atrium. Where I noticed the dead bodies had been removed, and a half dozen stewards and handmaids were busy trying to clean the blood off the floor. But they all stopped and bowed now as we entered. And the six guards by the doorway snapped to attention as we entered. All of which gawked starry-eyed at King Atlas's legendary trident as they bowed their heads now.

Saying our goodnights. I left Ajax and Pylos at my chamber doors and walked back into the main chamber. And I was surprised to find my lovely wives still sound asleep in the bed. Apparently, even all the shouting and commotion inside the palace having failed to wake them from their slumber.

Taking Atlas's trident with me, I quietly entered my private chambers. And I was just as surprised to find Agis and the stewards waiting for me in my dressing room, as they were to see me carrying Atlas's trident now. And since no one dared ask, I related tonight's events to them while they removed my armor and dressed me for bed again. Telling them of Helios and his accomplice murdering the royal guards, then of Helios defiling Atlas's tomb, and our fight inside the tomb. And of Ajax abruptly ending Helios as he tried to escape. Which is how I came to be in possession of King Atlas's trident.

Agis was the only one to speak now, and his thinking was the same as Pylos's, as he said, "You were extremely lucky, your majesty. And we are relieved to hear that the throne issue has been resolved. But if you will forgive me, your majesty? You should never have taken such a risk with your life, or the crown, your majesty."

Nodding to Agis, I replied, "Yes, I know, Agis. In hindsight, it probably wasn't one of my better decisions. Luckily, Ajax always seems to have my back, so it turned out for the best. And from now on please feel free to speak your mind, if you see me making a mistake. Don't forget that her majesty Amy and I have only been in Attea a few months, okay?"

Nodding now, Agis replied, "Thank you, your majesty. We will all do our best. And know we consider it an honor to serve your majesties in any way we can, your majesty."

Dressed for bed now, I returned Agis's nod, then picking up the trident again, I said, "Thank you, Agis. Now let's see if I can sneak back into bed without waking their majesties?" Agis and the stewards quickly lining up against the wall before nodding in unison. And returning their nods, I walked out the door headed back to the main chamber where my beautiful wives lay sleeping now.

Chapter - 18

It was no surprise that Sandra and Amy awoke before me the next morning. And seeing the golden trident leaning against the wall on my side of the bed. They were both dying of curiosity for me to wake and explain its presence. After twenty minutes of waiting and I still hadn't woken up yet. Curiosity got the better of them, and they devised a plan to wake me up. Climbing back into the bed on either side of me now, they began lightly brushing their bodies against mine in an attempt to wake me.

Which woke me almost instantly, but I kept my eyes closed now. Wanting to see exactly how far my beautiful wives were willing to take this new form of research. Though they thought I was still asleep, they noticed my body reacting to their attentions and lifting the covers up now both started to giggle. Of course, their mirth made me grin. And spotting my grin, they realized I was faking it and dove on top of me now tickling me until I opened my eyes. And wrestling my two wives onto their backs, I kissed them both soundly on the lips. Then taking a moment to return my affections, Amy and Sandra rolled to the outside making a space in the middle now for me before rolling back up against me again. And sitting up on their elbows now, they rested their chins on their hands and smiled as Amy asked, "Where did the trident come from, husband?"

I hesitated for a moment, trying to decide how much of last night's events I could share with my lovely wives now without getting into trouble. And noticing my hesitation, Amy bluntly said, "Okay Andrew, out with it!" And Sandra giggled at Amy's quick perception and stern response.

So, with the three of us lying there in bed, I related last night's events to them, starting with my nightmare and ending with Ajax removing Helios's head.

After which, Sandra looking over at the trident again and gasped, "So, that really is King Atlas's trident?"

And nodding my head to Sandra now, I replied, "I couldn't just let Helios kill five guards and escape with King Atlas's trident."

At which point, Amy interrupted now frowning and stating, "So, all alone, you decided to stop the assassin who just finished slaying five royal guards?"

Shrugging my shoulders, I replied, "Probably wasn't the smartest move, but I didn't see any other choice at the moment." And Amy and Sandra both shook their heads now in disbelief and frowned at me.

Relieved now, Sandra asked, "So Prince Helios really dead now?" And Sandra's and Amy's smiles quickly returned as I nodded my head confirming that Prince Helios was indeed dead now. And the last threat to our children and family was finally gone.

Turning to look at the trident again, Amy asked, "Why didn't you just put the trident back in Atlas's tomb, my love?"

Frowning slightly, I replied, "For two reasons. The first one being that Helios broke the cover to King Atlas's sarcophagus when he opened it. So that will have to be replaced. And secondly, when Ajax handed Atlas's trident to me, unlike Helios, the trident reacted."

Worried, Amy quickly asked, "What happened?" And Sandra nodded her head too now, curious to know what had happened.

Smiling at them, I replied, "As soon as I touched the trident, I felt an enormous surge of power. Then hundreds of images began flashing before my eyes, so fast that I couldn't understand them or even see them clearly." And they both looked at me with concern on their faces now, as I added, "Ajax was standing beside me, and he said the crystal in Atlas's trident began glow blue, and so did my eyes. It was a little unnerving, so I dropped the trident, and it stopped. Afterwards, Ajax said he afraid for the first time in his life."

Rising from the bed now, Amy and then Sandra both dressed and moved over to have a closer look at King Atlas's trident. Though neither one of them tried to touch the trident after my warning. Getting out of bed, I dressed and moved over to the wall pulling the gold ribbon now. Remembering that I had kept Agis and the stewards up most of the night.

A few moments later Petra stepped into the room and stopped just inside the door now to nod and wait. Smiling at Petra, I returned her nod and said, "Good morning Petra. We're ready for breakfast now whenever its ready, please." Then I added, "Oh, I'm afraid that I kept Agis and the stewards up most of the night, Petra."

Smiling and nodding again, Petra replied, "Yes, your majesty. You were right to use the gold ribbon this morning. Agis is taking a nap as we speak." Then Petra added, "Breakfast will be ready in a few minutes, but I'll send in a some tsia in now, your majesty."

Returning Petra's nod now, I said, "Thank you Petra, that's perfect." And nodding again, Petra turned and stepped back into the lady's private chambers. Two minutes later, Petra returned carrying a tray of cups and a pot of tsia. And nodding by the door, Petra moved forward setting the tray down on the table before picking up the tsia pot now and filling the three cups. Then nodding again, Petra turned to leave. Seeing Petra dropping off the tsia now, Sandra and Amy ended their examination of Atlas's trident and moved back around the bed to the table. Smiling at Petra as they rounded the bed. And Petra paused to nod to Amy and Sandra before continuing out of the room.

I held the chair for Amy on my right and then Sandra on my left again before taking a seat at the head of the table. And we all reached for our tsia cups at the same time. Taking a sip of her tsia, Sandra said, "It's amazing, after hearing and knowing "The Legend of the Six Stave's" most of my life, to actually see King Atlas's trident now. And if wasn't for your warning Andrew, I surely would have picked it up for a closer look."

Nodding to Sandra, I replied, "That's understandable." Then grinning, I said, "And if it weren't for Amy's and your glorious conditions. I would have let you hold the trident." Then gently reaching down I put my hands on both their stomachs before adding, "But it not worth the risking the future of Attea, my loves." And they both nodded their heads now in agreement.

After breakfast, Petra led Amy and Sandra into lady's chambers again. As Agis and the stewards entered the room from the other side and stopped to nod. And returning their nods, the stewards set to work clearing the breakfast table, making the bed, and tidying up the room now before lining up by my private chambers again and nodding their heads. Returning their nods, I signaled Agis forward now. And moving up next to me on my right, Agis nodded his head and asked, "What can I do for you, your majesty?"

Grinning at Agis, I replied, "First, I've had enough sword practice for one day, so I wish to bathe as soon as its ready. And secondly, after my bath, can you let my father-in-law Nestor know I wish to speak with him as soon as he is free?" And thinking about the trident for a moment, I added, "Also, warn the stewards and handmaids not to touch King Atlas's trident, as it's dangerous and they could get injured."

Nodding again, Agis replied, "Understood, Your Majesty. I took the liberty of ordering your bath when I awoke, so it's ready and waiting, if you will follow me, Your Majesty?" And turning, Agis led the way into my private chambers now as I followed behind.

After my bath and the stewards dressed me, Agis led me back out to the sitting area where a pot of tsia and two cups sat on the coffee table now. Then Agis informed me that Nestor had been notified and would be here shortly. And before I could finish my first cup of tsia, Agis reappeared informing me that my father-in-law was outside. Returning Agis's nod, I asked him to show my father-in-law in now.

Nestor's bowed after he entered, and I waved him forward now as I reached over and filled the other tsia cup. Crossing to the sitting area, Nestor quickly nodded to me then paused for a moment looking at Atlas's trident leaning against the wall before taking a seat. I was sure that Nestor had already been inform of last night's events and Prince Helios's death from Ajax.

Grinning at Nestor, I said, "Your welcome to go over and have a closer look, Nestor. I can understand your fascination in seeing King Atlas's trident. Though, I wouldn't recommend touching it."

Nodding his head, Nestor returned my grin and replied, "Thank you, your majesty. But after listening to Ajax's report this morning of last night's events and his description of your majesty's reaction to the trident. I have no wish to touch Atlas's trident now!" And absently scratching his cheek as he stared at the trident now, Nestor asked, "And Prince Helios attempted to use the trident but failed, your majesty." Then turning to looked at me again, Nestor added, "After Ajax finished his report. The Elders and Aetolus all expressed their dismay at your decision to follow Prince Helios out into the garden. However, Ajax defended you. Stating that he has been training you how to use a xiphos in the garden at your majesty's request for over a month now. And your majesty is a very quick learner. Also, your majesty was wearing his armor. Then Ajax reminded them that, as a result of your choice, the last threat to the Attean throne and your majesty's children has been eliminated. Which silenced the room, your majesty."

Grinning at Nestor now, I replied, "Yes, I agree in hindsight now, it probably wasn't the wisest of choices. But you can inform the Consul of Elders, that this morning both their majesties were far more displeased with my choice, than they are!"

Chuckling lightly, Nestor said, "That must have been interesting, your majesty?"

Nodding to Nestor now, I replied, "Luckily, the death of Helios and the knowledge that their children were now safe, outweighed their majesties anger at my choice."

Chuckling again, Nestor to a sip of tsia before asking, "Though I assume your majesty have something else on his mind this morning?"

Smiling at Nestor's intuition, I said, "Yes. First I would like to properly reward Ajax for ridding the kingdom of Prince Helios finally, and making it safe for our children, and your grandchildren. And for his crushing victory over the Wild-ones, which resulted in the Wild-ones turning Helios over to us. Is there some special honor or reward that I, or we, can bestow upon him now?"

Taking another sip of his tsia, Nestor thought about it for a minute before replying, "I think promoting Ajax to 'ταξίαρχος,' or brigadier, would be a great honor, and show the entire kingdom what your majesty thinks of Ajax. And I'm sure General Aetolus, and Consul of Elders would eagerly agree with your majesty."

And thinking about it for a few seconds, I said, "That sounds good, how do we go about that? And how long will it take?"

Giving me a curious look now, Nestor replied, "I can draw up a royal decree for Ajax's promotion this afternoon and have it ready for you to sign by dinner tonight. And if you wish, I can have the Elders add their signatures to yours tomorrow morning, your majesty?"

Smiling deviously at Nestor now, I said, "Good, because I'd like to present it to Ajax tomorrow night at dinner, while the Lady Kassandra is present!" Grinning, Nestor realized the reason for the urgency on the promotion now and chuckled at the deviousness of my plan.

That settled now, I moved on to the other reason I had asked Nestor here this morning. And I began by saying, "Ever since you told me about the Wild-ones, and they attack us after Medina. I've been wondering how to resolve the problem with the Wild Ones." And pausing to take a sip of my tsia, I continued now adding, "And rest assured, I have every intention of making sure that King Atlas's trident is returned to his tomb where it belongs. But now that King Atlas's trident is out of his sarcophagus temporarily. If I could master the power of the trident, I could use it to defeat the Kraken and repair the breach in the North cavern. And if we successfully reclaimed the North cavern, we could strike a truce with the Wild Ones. And offering them the North Cavern and a pardon, in exchange for them living in peace and ending their raiding once and for all?"

After which, Nestor looked at me in surprise replying, "It's a very noble idea, your majesty. But I can't see the Elders agreeing, as the danger to the kingdom far outweighs the benefits, your majesty."

Frowning, I said, "I am not asking for their permission to repair the North Cavern. And as King, I don't need their permission. But neither will I ignore the Elders advice either. What I am asking for is their blessing and help now in finding out any information we can about the use of the trident in the ancient scrolls. So, we can experiment with trident somewhere safe, and see if I can master its power, that's all." And letting Nestor think about that for a moment, I added, "As far as the North Cavern, if I succeed in mastering the tridents power. I will have to defeat the Kraken and repair the cavern from the outside. Otherwise, I would endanger my lovely wives and the entire kingdom. Which, you can tell the Elders I would never do!"

Still a little skeptical, Nestor nodded his head now before replying, "Well, I can discuss the testing of Atlas's trident with the Elders tomorrow, after they sign Ajax's promotion. But give me a few days to sway the Elders over to your side please, your majesty."

And returning Nestor's nod, I replied, "Very well. And speaking of days, how long before King Atlas's sarcophagus can be repaired?"

To which, Nestor replied, "The senior stonecutter was notified this morning. And he has already been out to inspect King Atlas's sarcophagus. He stated, assuming that your majesty wants an exact replacement, that it will take a couple of weeks for them to find a stone slab of the same size and quality. After that, it will take his apprentices and him another two weeks to carve the new cover. And the apprentice stonecutters are out in the tomb right now moving the broken pieces of the sarcophagus cover back to their shop."

Thinking aloud now, I said, "So, we have roughly one month to figure out if and how to use Atlas's trident before it goes back into the tomb. That's not much time." And Nestor smiled as he nodded, convinced now that I was serious about King Atlas's trident going back into his tomb where it belongs.

Finishing his tsai, Nestor rose and asked if there was anything else I required, and I replied that there wasn't. So, Nestor excused himself now to go check on the preparations for our public appearance today.

Shortly after Nestor had gone, the doors to the lady's chambers opened as Petra, Amy, and Sandra entered the main chamber again. Petra stopped to nod by the door, while Amy and Sandra continued forward joining me in the sitting area. Rising as they approached, I returned Petra's nod before offering a hand to each of my lovely wives to help then get seated, and they had opted to sit together on the other couch now. After which, Petra left closing the door behind her again. Then Amy and Sandra spent the next few minutes telling me about the progress on the nursery renovations.

Though, after their bathes and dressing, my wives confined themselves to their dressing room, knitting baby clothes with Petra. To prevent contractors from constantly having to stop and bow, slowing down the progress on the nursery. And Sophia, who was usually in attendance, was absent this morning. Due to the fact she was having tsia with Lady Ismene, to get her thoughts and blessing now on our plot to match her daughter Kassandra up with Ajax. And I spent a few minutes telling them about Nestor's visit, and the Elders dismay at me confronting Prince Helios on my own. And of Ajax defending my choice and silencing the Elders' grumbling by reminding them of the result of that choice. And then of my plan to promote Ajax to Brigadier, and spring it on him tomorrow night at dinner with Lady Kassandra. Which made both my beautiful wives grin and nod now at the deviousness of my plan. But I left out my idea of experimenting with the trident to see if we could use it to reclaim the North Cavern.

But before Amy and Sandra could ask me any question about my conversation with Nestor. Agis entered the room and nodded, informing us that our lunch was outside. And rising from the couch, I returned Agis nod and told him that we were ready. Then stepping in front of my lovely wives, I offered them each a hand to get up before leading them over to the table and seating them both.

The stewards quickly transferred our lunch from the carts to the dinner table, while the handmaids set the table. Then the handmaids lining up beside Petra on the left and the stewards lined up on the right beside Agis, before all eight nodded in unison and waited. Nodding to the left and the right, I said, "Thank you." And they all turned and filed out of the room again. Leaving Amy, Sandra, and me to enjoy a quiet lunch together before our public appearance today.

Our conversation quickly switched to our little plot and the impending dinner tomorrow night with Pylos, Cressida, Kassandra, and the unsuspecting Ajax. And Sandra informed me she had written a personal invitation to Kassandra now, while Amy had written the invitations to our cousins Cressida, Pylos, and Ajax for dinner tomorrow. All of which Petra was having hand-delivered today.

After we finished lunch, Petra entered and informed their majesties that it was time to begin dressing for our public appearance. And after Petra had escorted Amy and Sandra into their private chambers. Agis and the stewards entered to clear the table before escorting me into my dressing room to get my armor on for the public appearance.

Once I was dressed in my armor. Agis escorted me back out into the main chamber again, carrying my robe over his arm as we waited for my wives to come out of their chambers. And ten minutes later, Amy and Sandra stepped out of their chambers in full armor followed by Petra and one of the handmaids now carrying their robes over their arms. And after nodding at me, Petra walked directly up to me before nodding her head again and waiting to be acknowledged. And quickly returning Petra's nod now, she leaned in quietly saying, "This is the last time her majesty Amy can wear this armor, your majesty. Even now it a little tight for her majesty Amy and the baby, your majesty."

Nodding my head to Petra now, I asked, "I assume new armor has been ordered for their majesties already?"

To my surprise, Petra chuckled now as she replied, "Yes, your majesty. The Senior Physician and her majesty Sandra discussed it at some length, and it was decided that a second set of armor for up to five months should be made. But after five months it's medically unsound to expect their majesties to wear armor or make any public appearances. The Senior Physician Nestor offered to procure the molds for their majesties new amor from the city's hospital. And when word got out that they were making molds their majesties new armor. It was utter chaos at the hospital the next day, as every pregnant woman in the city showed up proudly volunteering their stomachs in hope that theirs would be chosen as the mold for their majesties new armor!" And chuckling with Petra now, Petra added, "Please keep a firm grip on her majesties Amy today, as she is basically holding her breath inside that armor now, your majesty."

And nodding to Petra, I replied, "Thank you Petra. Rest assured I will keep a good hold onto her majesty the whole time." And Nodding her head now, Petra moved to stand next to the other handmaid while we waited for Ajax to arrive with the royal guards. And moving over to Amy's side now, I took hold of her arm. And smiling at me now, Amy leaned over putting her weight on me. Seeing Amy leaning on me, Sandra moved up on Amy other side taking her sisters arm in hers now and smiling at Amy.

Luckily, Agis entered the room to announce that Ajax was outside now. And after exchanging salutes and nods with Ajax, Sandra and I kept a firm grip on Amy now as we followed Ajax across the keep and back up to the second floor balcony. Pausing at the top of the stairs, we got our robes on over our armor now, before Ajax signaled for the guards to open the terrace doors. And we were immediately emersed in the sound of the merriment going on out in the courtyard.

And returning our herald's nod, he turned and strode out the doors onto the terrace now. Sudden hush fell over the crowd as the herald stepped up to the balustrade and rapped his staff loudly three times on the balcony before announcing us now. Then bowing his head, the herald backed up several steps to the left.

With Amy on my right arm, I offered my left arm to Sandra now, and we crossed the balcony to the balustrade. Once we returned their bows, everyone raised their heads and began to cheer now. Lifting my arm up slightly up, I let Sandra have her hand back. And placing her right hand on her stomach now, Sandra smiled and waved at the thousand cheering Atteans with her left. And keeping hold of my right arm, Amy put her left hand on her stomach now and began waving down at the cheering Atteans with her right hand.

After five minutes of this, Sandra turned and looked over at Amy for a moment before furling her brows at me. Then Sandra gently tilted her head towards the doors now, letting me know it was time for us to go. And I turned to look over at our herald, who nodded his head now. Then stepping forward, our herald rapping his staff three times on the balcony again causing a hush to fall over the courtyard now as everyone stopped to bow. And I returned their bows, before leading my wives back through the doors. Once we were inside and the doors shut again, Sandra quickly moved around to Amy's other side to help support her. While Petra and the handmaid stepped forward quickly removing their robes. Then Agis stepped forward removing my robe as I held onto Amy. Who was smiling now, though I knew Amy disliked being a burden to anyone.

Suddenly a shadow came over us and I looked up to see Ajax standing beside us with a look of concern on his face now as he looked down at Amy. Reaching out now, I touched his Ajax's arm to get his attention.. And turning to salute me, I grinned at him and said, "Her majesty is fine Ajax, this armor is just a little tight for her and the baby." And seeing me grinning at him now Ajax relaxed slightly. Then I added, "Best thing we can do is get her majesty is get her back to the royal chambers now, so she can get out of this armor."

Nodding again, Ajax didn't wait for my return nod as he turned and barked out the order to reform now, so we could head back to the royal chambers. And with Sandra holding Amy's right and me holding her left arm now, we walked back across the keep and back up into the royal chambers. Once we were inside our chambers, Petra, Sandra, and the handmaids whisked Amy into the lady's chambers to get Amy out of the armor now. And it wasn't long before Sandra and Petra returned, assisting a relieved looking Amy back into the room. And quickly nodding their heads, they helped Amy over to the couch now and got her seated.

Once Amy was seated, I sat down beside her taking her hand in mine as I asked, "Are you okay, my love?"

Smiling now, Amy patted my hand replying, "I am now. Though that armor was surprisingly uncomfortable."

Nodding, Petra said, "I am so sorry, your majesty. I should have realized it was too tight and never put it on you, your majesty."

And apologizing too now, Sandra said, "Yes, I am sorry too Amy. We should have waited for the new armor to arrive before making the announcement and the public appearance. Or just left our armor off since Helios is dead now."

Smiling, Amy extended her hand to Sandra, who quickly moved forward accepting Amy's hand and giving her sister a hug. And looking up at Petra, Amy said, "If I could get a cup of tsai now, Petra. All is forgiven!"

Understanding Amy's meaning, Petra smiled as she nodded her head, replying, "Right away, your majesty!" And Petra took off at an actual jog now for the lady's chambers to get Amy her tsia.

A few moments later, Petra returned carrying a tray with a pot of tsia and one cup. And pausing to nod first, Petra moved forward and set the tray down on the table. Then Petra quickly filled the cup and handed it to Amy now before taking two steps back and nodding her head again. Smiling at Petra, Amy returned her nod and said, "Thank you, Petra."

And nodding again, Petra replied, "You are most welcome, your majesty." Then one of the handmaids entered the room carrying a tray with two more cups. And nodding by the door first, the handmaid moved forward and nodding again handing the tray to Petra now, then turned and left the chamber again. Setting the tray down on the table,

Petra filled the other two cups before setting the pot back down on the tray and handing the first cup to Sandra, and the other cup to me. Then looking at Amy, Petra asked, "Is there anything else I can get for you, your majesty?" Smiling up at Petra, Amy shook her head negatively, and Petra nodded again before turning and walking back out of the room.

Sandra and I were sitting on the couch with Amy in the middle now, as we drank our tsia and talked about the enormous crowd of cheering Atteans in the courtyard. And how odd it was now to have the whole kingdom fascinated with every aspect of our lives.

Then Agis entered and stopping to nod, announced that Nestor and Lady Sophia were outside now Sandra returned his nod and asked Agis to show her parents in, before turning to me now and saying, "Oh, sorry. I forgot to mention that I invited mother and father to dinner tonight. Amy and I were dying to know what Lady Ismene thought of the match between Ajax and her daughter Kassandra."

And smiling at Sandra, I replied, "No apology necessary. Mother and father are always welcome." And Sandra looked at Amy, who nodded her head in agreement now.

Agis opened the door and nodded his head as Nestor and Sophia as they entered the room and stopped to bow now. All three of us noticed the rolled scroll in Nestor's hand as we returned their nods. As we waved them forward to join us in the sitting area now. Nestor and Sophia moved to the other couch before nodding again and sitting down together. And turning to Agis, Nestor held up the scroll in his hand, saying, "Agis, could you please bring a quill and the royal seal for his majesty?" And nodding to Nestor, Agis turned and left the room again. Then turning to Sandra, Nestor nodded and handed the scroll to Sandra now. Returning her father's nod, Sandra accepted the scroll and opened it quickly reading it now as Amy and I waited. And smiling now, Sandra said, "It's reads, for exceptional acts of courage and valor in service of the kingdom of Attea, Ajax Marinos is hereby promoted to the rank of ταξίαρχος, "brigadier" by royal decree, on this day. And it's dated for today, and has your full title, King Andrew Tallfer, Ruler of Attea, written below it, husband."

As I nodded my head now and Amy smiled, Agis entered the room again carrying tray with a feather tipped quill, bottle of ink, a red candle, and a small wood box which I assumed contained the royal seal. And pausing to nod briefly by the door, Agis moved forward now before stopping to nod again and placing the tray down on the coffee table. Sandra spread the scroll out on the table now, and Amy leaned forward holding of the other side of the curly scroll. As Nestor took the quill out of ink bottle, gently dabbing the quill on the edge of the bottle now before handing it to me.

And leaning forward now, I carefully signed my name to the scroll in the space above my title. After which, Nestor leaned forward picking up the scroll and gently blew on my signature to dry the ink. Then opening the box, Nester removed the gold seal, and looking at the bottom, rotated it slightly before handing me the royal seal in the correct position. Next, Nestor picked up the red candle from off the tray and held it up to Agis, who produced some sort of small lighter from the sash around his waist now and lit the candle for Nestor. And after dripping a small pool of hot wax onto the scroll next to my signature, Nestor nodded his head to me indicating for me to put my royal seal on it now. And it was done, and we all sat back smiling at each other, everyone happy about Ajax's promotion.

Agis nodded his head now, then stepped forward with a grin on his face as he collected the royal seal and picked up the tray again. Agis apparently agreeing that Ajax's promotion was well deserved now.

After which, Agis disappeared for a minute, then reappeared a few moments later followed by two of the stewards' bearing carafes of wine and water, and a tray of cups. And pausing to nod by the door, they moved forward now nodding again before setting the trays down in front of us. And nodding again, the two stewards turned and left the room. While Agis stepped forward pouring the first two glasses half full of wine before switching to the water pitcher and filling them the rest of the way up. Then Agis set them out in front of Amy and Sandra, before filling three glasses with wine, before setting them in front of Sophia, Nestor, and me now. And leaning in, Agis quietly whispered to me that dinner would be ready in a few minutes.

Returning Agis's nod, I thanked him now, then Agis turned and left the room, leaving us to enjoy our wine.

We were through with our wine about the same time as Agis, Petra and the servants entered the room to let us know that dinner was outside waiting. And nodding to Agis and Petra, they quickly moved forward now opening the doors as the servants worked together getting the dinner set on the table. And rising from the couch, both Sandra and I turned at the same time now to help Amy up off the couch as we moved to the table for dinner. After the table was set, Agis, Petra, and the servants lined up on either side of the room and nodded their heads. Smiling and thanking them, we returned their nods, as they turned and filed out of the room again.

After we were seated and had a few bites to eat, Sandra turned to her mother and asked, "So what did Lady Ismene think of his majesty's idea of matching Kassandra up with Ajax?"

Waiting until her mouth was empty, Sophia dabbed her mouth with her napkin before smiling at Sandra now and replying, "Lady Ismene was thrilled and honored by your majesty's idea. And offered to help in any way possible to make the match. Having seen Ajax on more than one occasion, Lady Ismene thinks Ajax is extremely attractive. She also informed me that in her younger days, Kassandra had been smitten with Ajax when they were in school, though Ajax was a couple of years Kassandra's senior, your majesties."

Amy, Sandra, and I all smiled now as Sandra turned to her mother and said, "Thank you mother. That is good news."

And shook his head now, Nestor said, "If Ajax knew what we up to right now, he would ever forgive us! Though it's with the best of intentions, and for his own good really." We all chuckled at Nestor's remark, and Nestor joined us now in having a small chuckle.

After dinner and another carafe of wine, Nestor and Sophia rose to say goodnight. And Sandra, Sophia, and Amy exchanged hugs by the door. Then Agis, Petra, and the servants returned to clear the table, tidy up the room, and turn down our bed. After which, they lined up against the walls again and nodded their heads. And returning their nods, they turned and filed out of the room.

I was the first one into bed tonight and sliding across to make room for my two lovely wives to climb in together. And I lay there getting comfortable on my pillow as I watched Sandra and then Amy climbing into bed with me. And once they were both in bed, they looked at each other for moment, then turned to look at me on the pillow, and stated, "Tonight is not your night off, husband!"

Chapter - 19

The next day after breakfast with my wives and a bath, I returned to the sitting area for a quiet cup of tsia by myself. Then shortly before lunch, Agis entered the room informing me that Nestor was outside requesting an audience, and I asked Agis to show him in please. Holding the royal decree in his right hand now, Nestor walked into the room five paces and stopped to nod. And smiling at my father-in-law now, I returned his nod as I waved him forward to join me in the sitting area. And Nestor paused to nod again before handing me the tan scroll and taking a seat on the other couch.

As I opened the scroll to have a look, Agis asked Nestor if he would like some tsia, and Nestor replied that he would. And after Agis took off to get another cup, as Nestor turned his attention back to me. I couldn't read the four Elders signatures, nor could I figure out which signature was General Aetolus's as it was all in Attean.

And once Agis delivered the cup and left again. Nestor smiled and said, "The four Elders were pleased with your decision to promote Ajax to Brigadier but sent for General Aetolus. Aetolus to one look at the royal decree, then smiled and said that Ajax's promotion was overdue. Then the Elders and General Aetolus all signed below your signature, your majesty."

Rolling the scroll back up again, I replied, "Good, I'm glad they approve."

Nodding again, Nestor added, "Also, promoting Ajax to brigadier takes him out of the captain's rotation and keeps him here in the palace from now on, your majesty."

Smiling now, I replied, "Thank you Nestor. Their majesties and I will sleep better now knowing that Ajax is here in the palace guarding us." Nestor nodded his head in agreement, and I could tell Nestor was relieved too that Ajax would be here in the palace from now on.

Sitting back now with his tsia, Nestor casually said, "That was the easy part. Now I have to try and sell your other idea to the Elders, your majesty." And thinking aloud now, Nestor continued adding, "I think Kallinos and Tydeus would be open to your majesty's idea. But

Sippas and Thestor are always a hard sell on any new idea. The good news is though, if the Elders split on supporting of your idea, it's the same as a win, your majesty."

And nodding to Nestor now, I asked, "So where do you think the safest place to do our tests is, Nestor?"

Nodding now, Nestor scratched his head for a moment before replying, "I have been thinking about that since you mentioned your idea yesterday, your majesty. And have ruled out a half dozen places, due to lack of secrecy. And I think that down in King Atlas's tomb now would be the safest and most private place to do the tests, your majesty. Since the whole palace is aware now that Brigadier Ajax has been training your majesty to use a xiphos out in the garden. It will provide the perfect cover for the tests, your majesty."

Nodding in agreement with Nestor, I replied, "I agree. Very clever, my friend."

His tsai finished, Nestor rose and sighed now saying, "Ah, and now for the Elders. If you will excuse me, your majesty?" And rising from the couch, I shook hands with Nestor now as he left to go try and win the Elders over to my side.

Once Nestor was gone, I rolled the scroll with Ajax's promotion on it back up. And moving around to the right side of the bed now, I carefully tucked it under the pillow for later tonight. And I had just sat back down to finish my tsia, when the door to my chambers opened as Agis and the steward entered the room and stopped to nod. Followed by Amy, Sandra, Petra, and the handmaids on the left, signaling that it was lunch time.

Returning their nods, Agis and the stewards moved to the front doors to transfer our lunch to the table. As I rose from the couch and nodded to my lovely wives before moving forward to seat Amy and Sandra at the table. And once lunch was set up and the servants left again, our conversation switched to our dinner tonight with Ajax, Pylos, Cressida, and Lady Kassandra. And we decided now that Amy would ask Ajax to sit by her, while Sandra would ask Kassandra to sit next to her, leaving our Pylos and Cressida at the end of the table. Which seemed a little odd since they were family. So, I suggested that Sandra send a little note now to Cressida after lunch. Letting Cressida and Pylos know that they would be sitting at the end of the table tonight. As we have something special planned, that she and Pylos should thoroughly enjoy. And my wives agreed.

After lunch, my wives retired to their chambers to write Cressida a note, while I stretched out on the couch. And as the afternoon dragged on, I grew sleepy, which seemed to be happening a lot lately. And closing my eyes now, I took a little nap before dinner. Grinning and blaming it on doing double-duty last night with my beautiful wives.

And knowing me fairly well now, Agis stepped into the main chamber about five minutes before my wives were due to return. And nodding his head, Agis cleared his throat a couple of times now to wake me up for dinner. I was still rubbing my eyes when the doors to the lady's chambers opened and my lovely wives stepped back into the room. Rising from the couch, I returned their nods, then helped them get seated on the couch with me.

Pylos and Cressida were the first to arrive. And we all rose now and moved to greet our cousins as they entered. After exchanging bows, Amy and Sandra moved forward giving Cressida a hug and steered Cressida to the couch as they all sat down together. And after returning Pylos's salute, I exchanged the two-handed clasp of friendship with my cousin before inviting him to sit with me on the other couch now. Amy and Sandra had Cressida sandwiched between them now and were already busy filling Cressida in on tonight's little plan to match Ajax up with Kassandra. Pylos and I sat on the other couch and watched the women absorbed in their gossiping now.

After a couple minutes, I turned to Pylos and asked, "With Ajax and you both here for dinner, who's guarding the palace?"

Grinning now, Pylos replied, "The General volunteered to stand my watch tonight. Claiming he had a bunch of paperwork he needed to get caught up on, your majesty."

Overhearing Pylos's words now, Cressida spoke up correcting her husband saying, "You mean mother told him to volunteer?"

And I chuckled as Pylos frowned at Cressida on the other couch. Realizing that even the General was no different than the rest of us when it came to who was really in charge. Amy and Sandra joined me in having a chuckle too, once they realized how hilarious that was.

Kassandra was the next to arrive, and Agis stepped back into the room and nodded, announcing the Lady Kassandra was outside. Cressida and Pylos remained seated, as Sandra, Amy, and I rose to greet Lady Kassandra as she entered the room and stopped to bow. The Lady Kassandra was dressed very elegantly and alluringly now, her raven-black hair intricately braided on the sides of her head.

And returning her bow, we all welcomed Kassandra now. Then Sandra stepped forward latching onto Kassandra's arm and making small talk as she steered Kassandra to the couches. Excited about the plan now, Cressida moved over next to her husband on the other couch. While I took the single chair in the middle now as Sandra and Amy sandwiched Kassandra on the other couch to the left. At which point, Sandra formally introduced Kassandra to Pylos and Cressida. And Sandra and Kassandra began chatting about the university and finding out that Kassandra was fluent in English, they graciously switched to English now. As Sandra quickly got caught up on the latest gossip at the university. After which Sandra confessed to Kassandra, though we were slightly couped up in the palace, she was incredibly happy with her new life. And she and her new sister Amy were both eagerly awaiting the arrival of their first little prince or princess now.

Then Agis reappeared again, nodding his head, and announcing that Captain Ajax was outside now. And nodding to Agis, I asked him to show Ajax in as we rose from our chairs again. And Amy, Sandra, and I all moved towards the front doors to greet Ajax. Walking in, Ajax stopped and bowed to Sandra and Amy before saluting and nodding his head to me. Amy and Sandra quickly returned Ajax's bow smiling at him, as I returned his salute and nodded. Then stepping forward, I quickly exchanged the handshake of friendship with my cousin.

After which, Amy and Sandra stepped forward latching onto Ajax and steered him to the sitting area. Before pausing, as Sandra formally introduced Ajax to Lady Kassandra in Attean. Then Pylos and Ajax exchanged salutes and handshakes, and I indicated for Ajax to take the single chair in the middle by Amy. Stepping up behind me, Agis nodded and leaned in whispering that dinner would be ready in a few minutes. After returning his nod and thanking him, Agis turned and left the room again, only to return a few minutes later with the three stewards as Petra and the three handmaids all stepped into the room from the other side now and nodded their heads. Amy, Sandra, and I quickly returned their nods as they moved to the front doors and began transferring dinner from the carts in the entryway to the table.

Slowly rising from out seats, we hung back for a minute so we wouldn't be in the servant's way while they worked setting up the table now. And Amy latched onto Ajax's arm as Sandra latched onto Kassandra's arm now as agreed earlier, and we lingered in the seating area until the stewards and handmaids finished setting the table.

Once the servants finished, and lined up along the walls again, we quickly exchanged nods with them. Then they turned and filed out of the room. And I let Ajax seat Amy now, while I went around to the other side of the table to get Sandra's and the Lady Kassandra's chairs. Pylos seating Cressida next to Kassandra before moving back around and standing next to Ajax waiting on me.

Once all four ladies were seated, Ajax, Pylos, and I quickly exchanged nods and took our seats. Amy was on my right followed by Ajax and Pylos. And Sandra was on my left, followed by Kassandra and Cressida now. I think everyone at the table except Ajax understood the seating arrangement, and I caught Lady Kassandra sneaking a peek across the table at the oblivious Ajax now. And Amy smiled at Kassandra now and nodded her head, which made Kassandra smile and blush slightly. As Amy and I had noted at the Inspection, Lady Kassandra was quite beautiful and smart too. And if Ajax didn't notice Kassandra tonight, then this was going to be a lot harder than I had figured.

Holding my hands out palms up now, I said, "Welcome my friends, please help yourselves." And Amy and Sandra smiled at me as they both reached out touching my outstretched hands before proceeding to look over the choices on the table tonight. As always, dinner was fabulous. And Kassandra started the conversation off tonight. Noticing the trident on the wall behind our bed now, she asked, "What's the trident for, your majesty?"

Grinning at Kassandra now, I replied, "Oh, you mean King Atlas trident?"

With a stunned look on her face now, Kassandra asked, "What is Atlas trident doing out of his tomb, if I may ask, your majesty?"

And I spent the next few minutes telling Kassandra about Prince Helios's escape, following him out to Atlas's tomb, and Helios breaking the cover on Atlas's sarcophagus to get the trident. Then of our swordfight, and Ajax's gratefully removing Prince Helios's head.

After which, Kassandra nodded and replied, "Wow! That was brave of your majesty but not very wise, if I may say so, your majesty."

And we all burst into laughter at Kassandra reply now, much to her surprise and embarrassment. Until Sandra leaned over and informed Kassandra that it was exactly what the four Elders, General Aetolus, Ajax, Pylos, and their majesties all said to me when they found out what I had done. Which made Kassandra relax and laugh now too, lighting up her face and catching Ajax's attention.

Grinning at Sandra and then Amy, I said, "Which reminds me of the reason for our little dinner and celebration tonight!" And Sandra and Amy both smiled brightly at me as I rose and held my hand out now for our guests to remain seated. Then, moving to the bed I retrieved the tan scroll from underneath the pillow. And all eyes on me now as I moved up next to Ajax's and said, "If would stand now please, Ajax?" And I waited for Ajax to rise before saluting him and nodding my head now. A look of surprise coming over Ajax's face now as he immediately returned my salute and nod, then I handed him the scroll and said, "For unwavering service to the crown and the kingdom of Attean, cousin!" Ajax nodded as he accepted the scroll from my hand slightly stunned as he opened the scroll now and read it. And the look on Ajax's face was priceless, as Amy and Sandra rose from their chairs now and clapped and cheered Ajax loudly. While Cressida, Kassandra, and Plyos all sat there dumbfounded now by our reaction to Ajax reading the scroll, before Pylos asked, "What is it cousin?"

And Ajax nodded to Amy, Sandra, and me again before answering Pylos, saying, "I've been promoted to Brigadier!"

Overcome with joy, Pylos rose from his chair and clapped Ajax on the back now, before saying, "You deserve it Ajax, Congratulations!" Then taking a step back, Pylos formerly saluted and nodded his head to Ajax now.

Grinning at Pylos, Ajax returned his salute, then turning to face Amy, Sandra, and me, nodded his head again before saying "Thank you, it is my great honor to protect and serve your majesties."

At which point, I returned Ajax's salute, and added, "And it is my great honor to reward you cousin for your valiant service. And their majesties pleasure to learn now, that this promotion will keep you here in the palace permanently from now on!" And Amy's and Sandra's faces both lit up now as they learned that Ajax's promotion would keep him here in the palace. After Amy, Sandra, and Cressida finished congratulating Ajax. Kassandra offered her congratulations to Ajax on his promotion, and news that he would be stationed here permanently in the palace from now on.

Stepping over to the wall, I pulled the blue ribbon and Agis appeared a few seconds later. And I informed Agis that we required more wine to properly celebrate Ajax's promotion to Brigadier. Agis nodded his head at my request, then pausing Agis nodded to Ajax now, congratulated him on behalf of the entire staff. And returning Agis's nod, Ajax thanked him, then Agis left to get more wine.

Our dinner finished, Agis and the stewards returned with the wine and water, and I suggested we move back to the sitting area now. And grabbing onto Plyos, Amy had Pylos and Cressida sit with her on the first couch now, while Sandra latched onto Kassandra and had her sit on Sandra's right in the other couch. And I dropped into the single chair on Sandra's left, leaving Ajax the single chair in the middle between Kassandra and Amy. And Sandra asked Kassandra a variety of questions now while we drank our wine. Trying to get to know Kassandra better by having her tell us a little bit about herself.

And after a half dozen glasses of wine on my part, I had a crazy idea and blurted it out, saying, "Why don't we all go out in the garden and walk this wine off now. And I will show you the spot where Ajax removed Helios's head?"

Amy and Sandra were the only sober ones left, both turned to look at me now in surprise, before Amy replied, "Ew yuk! I have no desire to see some blood stain at King Atlas's tomb." But understanding my hidden agenda, Amy lightly put her hand on her stomach now, and said, "But a walk in the garden before bed would be good for the babies, don't you think Sandra?"

Smiling and touching her stomach, Sandra nodded and replied, "Yes, a short walk in the garden would be perfect before bed."

Rising from the couch now, Amy looked over at me and asked, "Well, husband?"

Giggling, Sandra rose from her seat and copied Amy now, repeating, "Well, husband?"

Rising from my chair, I grinned and said, "Well, cousins?" And Ajax and Pylos, who were just as sloshed as me now, both stood up shakily and saluted me. And returning their salutes, I pointing to the door and said, "Shall we?" And holding my arm out to Ajax, he accepted it, then I held my other arm out to Pylos, who stepped forward accepting my other arm now. And the three of us arms joined now and walked out the front doors into the hallway before having to back up slightly to make the turn to the south stairs.

Chuckling, Amy offered Cressida her arm as Sandra offered her arm to Kassandra, and the four of them following us outside giggling and laughing now as they watched our drunken antics. Once we reached the atrium floor, we crossed to the doors and passed through the doorway while the guards stationed by the door struggled to keep a straight face. And we crossed the terrace and went down the steps into the garden before I suddenly stopped realizing that something was missing. And having an epiphany now, I said, "The women!" And we turned around to face the terrace again. Amy and Sandra were standing at the top of the stairs now between Cressida and Kassandra, with their arms folded and frowns on their faces. And I did what any sane man would do after messing so badly. I slapped my hand to my chest saluting and nodded my head solemnly now to my two wives. Seeing the wisdom of my action, Pylos and Ajax both followed suit now, saluting and bowing to the women.

I was slightly surprised when I looked up again to see smiles on my wives faces now, as they returned our nods and Amy said, "Sandra and I will take the one in the middle."

And grinning now, Cressida said, "I'll take the one on the right, your majesties."

Then the three women turned to look at Kassandra now, as Sandra said, "That leaves you the big one on the left Kassandra, if you think you can handle him?"

Smiling and nodding to Amy and Sandra now, Kassandra replied, "I can handle him, your majesties." And returning Kassandra nod the ladies came down the stairs to collect us.

Stepping forward, I raised my arms now as my lovely wives took hold of me, and Pylos raised his right arm for Cressida. And Ajax having sufficient wine in him now, overcame his shyness, and raised his right arm for Kassandra. Then turning with Amy and Sandra on my arms now, I said, "Shall we?" And we all moved towards the seahorse fountain in the center of the garden. Pylos and Cressida fell in behind us now as Ajax and Kassandra brought up the rear.

Reaching the fountain, I used a commanding tone now as I jokingly said, "We'll take the center. Brigadier Ajax, you take the left flank. Captain Pylos can take the right flank. And we will regroup again in front of Atlas's tomb!" Everyone chuckling now as Ajax and Pylos quickly saluted having received their orders. And following my instructions we split up now. And once the others were out of sight, I bent over kissing the top of Amy's head and then Sandra's, as we started walking towards the lighted area in the front of Atlas's tomb.

And since we had the center path through the garden, we reached the base of Atlas tomb before the others did and turned around now to look back at the palace keep while we waited for the others to join us. And Amy whispered, "I wonder who will show up first?"

Then Amy and Sandra giggling, as Sandra whispered, "Very clever, husband." Which caused them both to giggle even more.

To our surprise, it was Pylos and Cressida who stepped out first and walked towards us. Stopping a few feet from us now to nod their heads. And returning their nods with a smile, they moved up next to us as we waited at the base of the Atlas's tomb. Pylos and Cressida were just as surprised as we were now that they had beaten Ajax and Kassandra here.

Just as the women started to gossip, Ajax and Kassandra stepped out into the open and began walking toward us. As they got closer, I let a small chuckle slip out when I noticed that Kassandra's hair wasn't as neat or tidy as it had been when we parted at the fountain. Sandra and Amy both immediately leaning in and asking, "What's was so funny?"

Whispering back, I said, "Look at Kassandra's hair." And seeing what I was talking about now, Amy and Sandra both covered their mouths as they giggled. Feeling left out now, Cressida leaned over touching Sandra's arm and raising her eyebrows. And putting her hand over Cressida's ear, Sandra whispered, "Take a look at Kassandra's hair."

And seeing it now too. Cressida covered her mouth and giggled as she leaned over and whispered into Pylos's ear now, and the light of understanding suddenly coming on in Pylos's face as he looked at Kassandra hair and grinned. As Ajax and Kassandra drew near, I could see Kassandra face was flushed and she was blushing now.

Once Ajax and Kassandra reached our side. We exchanged nods, and I turned my wives around to face Atlas's tomb again to take some of attention off the Kassandra now. From our position here at the base of the stairs, we could see the top half of the opening and the two stone doors. And pointing to the column to the right of the doors, I said, "That column on the right is where Brigadier Ajax was standing when Prince Helios fled the tomb, and where Ajax stepped out and removed his head!" And pausing for a second while everyone looked up at the column, I added, "I think removing Helios's head, and your crushing defeat of the Wild Ones at the Caves of Mephisto have earned you a place in the Attean history books now, cousin."

And we all turned to look at Ajax and Kassandra. And nodding his head now, Ajax humbly replied, "Thank you, your majesty."

Returning Ajax's nod, I asked, "Shall we head back into the palace?" And getting a nod from Amy and Sandra now, I lead them back down the center of the garden to the palace beyond. Opting not to take the scenic route back to the palace this time, as Pylos and Cressida stepped in behind us followed by Ajax and Kassandra.

All four of them followed us up the stairs, as Ajax and Plyos made sure we reached our chambers safely. And having had enough wine for one day, we said our goodnights in the hallway outside our chambers. Since it was late, and Ajax was starting to suber up now. I asked him to escort Kassandra and make sure she reached home safely now. Which Ajax gladly agreed to do. And after exchanging nods and salutes with my cousins again, Amy and Sandra exchanged hugs with Cressida and Kassandra. Then the guards opened the doors, and my lovely wives guided me into our royal chamber for the night.

Undressing, we all climbed into bed, with Amy on my right and Sandra on my left. And they giggled back and forth now about Kassandra's disheveled hair and the success of our little plot tonight.

After twenty minutes of this, Amy and Sandra suddenly stopped talking and turned their attention to me in the middle. Too excited after success to sleep, I realized what my lovely wives wanted, and grinning now, I nodded my head.

The next couple of days seemed to drag on, my beautiful wives busy in their chambers happily preparing for the arrival of their babies. While I was stuck waiting for Nestor to let me know the Elders opinion on testing Atlas's trident. Though as king, I had already basically made up my mind now to test the trident. I was just waiting on the Elders' blessing and any information they may find.

I spent the first day napping on the couch recovering from my beautiful wives' attentions the previous night. But the next day I was fully rested and bored out of my mind. So, I asked Agis to contact Ajax after breakfast and let him know I could use some sword training today, if he was available. Understanding the problem, Agis nodded his head and said he would contact Ajax immediately. Fifteen minutes later Agis returned to let me know Brigadier Ajax was on his way and that I should move into the changing room so the stewards could get my armor on now. And after the stewards finished dressing me, Agis informed me that Ajax and my personal guard were waiting out in the hallway for me.

Leaving Agis at my chamber door, I moved to the inner doors and stepped into the entryway now to greet Ajax. Slightly surprised when the door opened, Ajax quickly recovered, saluting and nodding his head. Returning his salute, I stepped forward exchanging handshakes with my cousin as he smiled at me. And I said, "Thank you cousin, I was dying of boredom waiting for the Elders to respond to my idea."

Curious now, Ajax calmed asked, "Idea, your majesty?"

Grinning at Ajax, I put my hand on his shoulder now before saying, "I will tell you all about it after we finish sparring. Right now, I need a little exercise and a lot of fresh air, cousin."

Grinning back Ajax replied, "Right away, your majesty." And taking my hand off Ajax's shoulder, he opened the outer door where my six guard escort stood waiting now with their heads bowed. Not wasting any time, Ajax barked out an order as he led the way down the south stairwell, across the East Atrium, and out into the garden now. And briefly pausing at the base of the terrace to make sure we were still behind him. Ajax proceeded across the garden to Atlas's tomb before turning into our training area in the corner of the garden.

Reaching the spot, Ajax barked out another order, and the five guards fanned out encircling us. Though they no longer faced outward anymore, having been given permission now to watch Ajax and Peleus spar with me. Which they thoroughly enjoyed, and they were learning from too. Peleus took a few steps forward before they all bowed their heads and saluted me. And I returned their salutes as Ajax leaning over into the bushes and pulled the short swords out before nodding to me and tossed one of the xiphos to me, tip upwards and spinning in the air. Catching the sword in the air, I slapped the xiphos to my chest now returning Ajax's salute and motioning with my other hand for Ajax to begin.

After sparring with Ajax for fifteen minutes, Ajax got the drop on me three times to my one time. And saluting me again, Ajax tossed his xiphos to Peleus now, who caught it in the air and saluted me with the sword. Holding my left index finger up, I took a moment to catch my breath before returning Peleus's salute and motioning for Peleus to begin. Though I couldn't best Peleus today, and he managed to get the drop on me four times. I did feel a whole lot better now than being stuck in my chambers alone all day. Ajax stepped forward nodding first before taking the swords from Peleus and me now and returning them to their hiding place in the bushes. And when he returned Peleus and Ajax both saluted me again and grinned now.

Nodding, Peleus spoke first in Attean, and Ajax smiled as he translated Peleus's words now, saying "Peleus says though the outcome didn't reflect it today, your skill with a sword has greatly improved, your majesty."

Returning Peleus's nod now, I replied to Ajax, "Tell Peleus, thank you. And that I appreciate his help."

And grinning wryly now, Ajax translated my words to Peleus. Then looking back at me again, said, "Oh, and that's Captain Peleus, with your permission, your majesty?"

Grinning at Ajax now, I replied, "Yes, I agree cousin."

Turning to Peleus, Ajax smiled and informed Peleus he was promoted to Captain now. And caught off guard, Peleus humbly nodded his head and saluted again before replying in Attean, "It is a great honor, your majesty. And I pledge my sword and my life in your defense, your majesty," which Ajax translated before saluting and nodded his head.

Returning Peleus's and Ajax's salutes and nods, I stepped forward and exchanged the two-handed clasp of friendship with Peleus now. As my five royal guards smacked their spears three times on the ground now in approval of Peleus's promotion and his pledge. And as we exchanged handshakes, I said, "Thank you Captain Peleus. Their majesties and I need as many friends as we can get here in Attea," which Ajax translated to Peleus.

And to which Captain Peleus nodded his head again. Then stepping back, I returned his salute before asking Ajax, "Could you have Captain Peleus take the royal guards and wait by the terrace now? I have something to discuss in private with you, cousin."

Nodding his head, Ajax turned and translated my request to Peleus. Who snapped Ajax a salute, then turning, Peleus barked the order out to the guards now. Who turned and quickly formed up as Peleus stepped in front now and led them back to the terrace steps.

And once the guard had left for the terrace, Ajax leaned in and said, "Peleus is a good man, and someone I would trust with my life, your majesty."

Nodding to Ajax now, I leaned towards him replying, "I figured as much. Let's go sit on the steps cousin, as my idea will take a few minutes to explain?" And Ajax nodded in agreement as we walked the short distance over to the stairs in front of Atlas's tomb now and sat down. And then I spent the next several minutes telling Ajax of my idea to test the Atlas's trident and see if I could master is power. Then use the Atlas's trident to defeat the Kraken and repair the North Cavern from the outside to protect Attea from any danger. Then offer the Wild Ones the North Cavern and a pardon, in exchange for their promise to live in peace from now on.

At first, Ajax was appalled by my idea of testing Atlas's trident out myself, fearing the incredible power of the trident and for my safety. Though he admitted my idea of giving the Wild Ones the North Cavern in exchange for their promise to live in peace was ingenious. And I informed Ajax that I would have the Nester with me the whole time while conducting the tests. Also, the response I mentioned earlier was the elders' blessing of my idea. Afterwards, Ajax still felt that it was too dangerous. But agreed we should my personal guard now to cover tests, as they were all trustworthy. And having seen firsthand what kind of person their new king was, they were all completely loyal to me now.

Chapter - 20

The next morning, I had breakfast again with my lovely wives, and Amy's appetite seemed normal this morning. Unlike lunch and dinner, where Amy was definitely eating for two now. After breakfast, Petra appeared and whisked Amy and Sandra off into their private chambers again. While Agis, anticipating my needs, showed up a few moments later with a fresh pot of tsia for me. Thanking him, I moved to the sitting area with nothing to do now other than wait for lunch. After cup of tsia, I stretched out on the couch and closed my eyes. Shortly after which, I heard Agis clearing his throat by the doorway to my chambers. And opening my eyes again, Agis said, "Sorry to disturb your majesty. But the Senior Physician is outside now and wants an audience with you, your majesty."

Sitting up, I returned Agis's nod and replied, "Please show my father-in-law in. And bring another cup if you would please, Agis?"

Nodding his head, Agis answered, "Right away, your majesty." And moving to the double doors now, Agis opened the right-hand door and nodded to Nestor as he gestured for him to enter.

Walking in five paces, Nestor was grinning as he stopped to nod his head now. And standing up, I returned my father-in-law's nod and held my arm out inviting him to join me in the sitting area. Moving to the other couch, Nestor nodded again before taking a seat. And judging by his expression on his face now, I guessed things had gone better than we had expected with the Elders. At the same time, I saw Agis duck into my private chambers to get another cup for Nestor. Nestor and I both grinned at each other as we waited for Agis to return with the cup. And Agis returned a few seconds later bearing a second cup and saucer in his hands. Nodding briefly at the edge of the sitting area, Agis set the cup down on the table in front of Nestor and quickly filled it with the tsia pot. Then nodding again, Agis turned and went back out of the chamber closing the door behind him now.

Hearing the door close behind us, I asked Nestor, "Judging by your expression. I take it things went better than expected with the Elders?"

Nodding his head, Nestor replied, "Yes, your majesty. Three of the Elders agreed with your majesty's idea of testing Atlas's trident." And pausing for a second to take a sip of his tsia, Nestor continued adding, "I was able to sway Tydeus and Kallinos over to your side relatively easily. As they both feel as you do, we should test the trident now and find out if it's even possible before returning the trident to Atlas's tomb. Sippas agreed because for years he's had to listen to the merchants complain about the Wild one attacks on their caravans. And it's been a constant source of aggravation for him. Of course, Thestor still thinks the risks far outweigh the rewards, and there was no changing his mind about that. Though, the Elders all wish to appease your majesty now, having secured the throne and brought peace to Attea again."

Smiling wryly at Nestor now, I replied, "Well, I am glad they trust me enough to give me their blessing. Though I must admit, I had already decided to do the tests with or without their consent. As this is a once in a millennium opportunity, that shouldn't be wasted."

Nodding in agreement, Nestor replied, "Like Thestor, I was against it at first too, feeling that the danger far outweighed the benefits. But after arguing on your behalf, your majesty. I slowly came to believe as Tydeus, Kallinos, and you do, your majesty. That this is a once in a millennium opportunity that we may never come again, and we should at least find out if it is possible now."

Grinning at Nestor, I replied, "Well now that we're on the same page. Let's plan on beginning our tests tomorrow morning at my normal sword practice time. And if you would please Nestor, let Ajax know to be ready to begin tomorrow morning at our normal time?"

Nodding his head again, Nestor glanced over at the door to their majesty's chambers before asking, "Do their majesties know of your plans, your majesty?"

Frowning, I leaned towards Nestor and quietly replied, "No, and I don't see any reason to tell them until we find out whether or not I can master the trident's power." And pausing for a second as I glanced at the door to my wives' chambers, before adding "I have no doubt that my beautiful wives will side with Thestor now. Saying that the risks outweigh the benefits."

Frowning and nodding now, Nestor said, "Understood, your majesty." Then finishing his tsia, Nestor rose and nodded again, adding, "If you will excuse me, your majesty? I shall go and speak with Brigadier Ajax now."

Getting up, I returned Nestor's nod now and walked the short distance to the inner doors with Nestor before exchanging nods again with my father-in-law as he exited the chamber.

Moving back to the couch, I poured myself another cup of tsia and sat there sipping it now as I looked over at Atlas's trident. Then stretching out on the couch again, I closed my eyes thinking of tomorrow's all important tests.

Stepping into the main chamber again five minutes before the ladies were due back for lunch, Agis stood by the door now and nodded as he cleared his throat.

Sitting up, I returned Agis's nod before saying, "Thank you, Agis."

Nodding again, Agis replied, "Your most welcome, your majesty."

Thinking ahead now, I said, "Agis, I am taking the trident back out to King Atlas's tomb tomorrow and I wish to conceal it. Could you provide me with some heavy cloth to cover the trident with?"

Nodding again, Agis replied, "Certainly, I will see to it at once, your majesty."

No sooner than Agis had left, than the door to the lady's chambers opened, and in walked Amy, Sandra, and Petra now. All three women smiling as they stopped to nod. And rising from the couch, I returned their smiles and nods now as I moved to the table to greet my wives and seat them for lunch. After the servants left, Sandra took my hand and gently placed it on her stomach where I could feel a small bulge now. And Amy smiled and nodded, indicating that Sandra was starting to show now too.

After lunch, the ladies returned to their chambers for tsia and to continue their preparations for our expected bundles of joy. And Agis returned with a fresh pot of tsia, a bolt of thick blue cloth, and three lengths of gold cord to wrap up the trident in tomorrow. Which I had Agis put under my side of the bed out of sight. And with nothing to do all afternoon except wait, I had another cup of tsia before stretching out on the couch again to wait for dinner. And even though

I was a little nervous about tomorrow's tests, I eventually nodded off again. Stepping back into the chamber ten minutes before the ladies were due to return, Agis bowed his head and cleared his throat again.

After dinner, and the servants had cleaned up and left again, Amy and Sandra were tired and ready for bed. And I have to admit, I wasn't disappointed now when they informed me that tonight was my night off. Climbing into bed, I scooted over as Amy climbed in first, informing us now that sleeping on her left side was more comfortable. So, Amy and Sandra ended up sleeping together on the right side of the bed with Sandra's arm lightly draped over the top of Amy. I was a little nervous about tomorrow's impending test of Atlas's trident and unable to sleep at first. So, I just lay there for a while watching my beautiful wives as they slept beside me. Focusing on the enormous felling pride I had for them both now, and I eventually nodded off with a small grin on my face.

The next morning, I awoke before my beautiful wives. And I spent a few minutes lying there admiring their sleeping forms. Then I carefully slid out the left side of the bed before dressing and moving to the sitting area. And I noticed that they both had a small grin on their faces now as they slept together peacefully.

Sandra awoke first, gently lifting her arm off her sister now, which woke Amy like someone removing her blanket. Then, smiling at each other in a silent good morning, they turned to look for me at the same time. And seemed surprised to find me over on the couch smiling at them now.

Getting out of bed, Sandra casually asked, "How long have you been up, husband?"

And grinning at Sandra, I replied, "Oh, about an hour, my love."

Rising from the bed now, Amy wryly asked, "Doing what for the last hour, if I may ask?"

Smiling now, I replied, "Watching the two women I love peacefully sleeping together. And thinking how proud I am of you both now, my wives."

Leaning over and giggling to Sandra now, Amy said, "See, we give him one night off, and he's already getting all melancholy and missing us?"

Giggling shyly now, Sandra replied, "Well, maybe we shouldn't give him anymore nights off?" Then arm in arm, they giggled again before turning to look at me and grin mischievously.

Rising from the couch, I crossed the room and hugged and kissed Amy before gently touching the bulge in her stomach and smiling at her now. Then turning to Sandra, I pulled her to me and kissed her now as I gave her backside a squeeze. Then releasing Sandra, I stepped back and nodded "good morning" to my beautiful wives. And receiving their smiles and nods in return, I stepped over and pulled the two ribbons on the wall now.

Petra and the handmaids were the first to enter, lining up along the south wall and nodding their heads. Then a moment later, Agis and the stewards entered on the right, lining up along the north wall and nodding their heads. Two of the steward's bearing trays with a pot of tsia on one, and the thee cups on the other. And I caught Agis's wry grin now, having out thought Petra this morning. Amy and Sandra noticed this little byplay now too, the three of us trying to hide our smirks now as we returned Petra's and the handmaids' nods then those of Agis and the stewards. Then nodding again, Agis said, "Breakfast is outside waiting, your majesties."

Returning Agis nod, I replied, "Thank you all. Their majesties and I are ready for breakfast now." Agis moved to open the front doors now, as the two stewards with the tsia moved forward quickly nodding again before setting their trays down on the table. Then briefly nodding again, the two stewards turned to get our breakfast from the carts in the entryway. Pulling out the chair on the right, as the servants set the table, I held it for Amy now as she took her seat. Then moving around to the left, I pulled out the chair for Sandra now and held it as she took her seat. Sandra lightly touched my arm now silently thanking me as she took her seat.

Once breakfast table was set, the handmaids and the stewards lined up along the walls again. And we smiled in gratitude now nodding our heads now, as the servants turned and filed back out of the chamber.

Amy and Sandra informed me over breakfast that having finished knitting three sets of baby clothes now, they were starting on the babies' quilts. But since both had decided to wait to find out whether the little bundle of joy they were carrying was a prince or princess. They had decided now that Amy would make a girl's blanket, while Sandra made a boy's blanket. Which they would switch later if necessary since both blankets had been made with love.

Once we finished breakfast and the servants cleared the table. I rose and nodded to my two lovely wives before turning and following Agis to get changed into my armor. As Petra stepped up nodding Amy and Sandra, waiting for them to move into the lady's chambers.

Returning to the main chamber, Agis removed the bolt of cloth and cord from underneath the bed. And unwrapping a dozen feet cloth from the bolt, Agis handed it to me now. Covering the front of the trident with the cloth, I lifted the trident up and wrapped the cloth around the back. Then I turned and laid the trident down on top of the bed. And seeing how cautious I was being, Agis stood back, content just to hand me the cords. Once Atlas's trident was wrapped and tied shut, I moved it to the couch to wait for Nestor' and Ajax's arrival.

Going back into my private chambers, Agis returned a few moments later with a fresh pot of tsia. And nodding at the edge of the sitting area, Agis moved forward and quickly refilled my cup from the new pot. Then setting the new pot down on the table, Agis picked up the old pot before nodding again and exited the room leaving me alone with Atlas's trident to wait now.

I was halfway through the cup of tsia from the new pot, when Agis reappeared, nodding his head and informing me that Nestor and Ajax were outside now. Quickly returning Agis's nod, I told him to open the doors now as I picked up the cloth covered trident from the couch and followed Agis to the doors. And quickly exchanging nods with Nestor and salutes with Ajax in the entryway. Nestor remained by my side as Ajax turned and led the way back out into the hallway where Peleus and my personal guard stood waiting now with heads bowed.

Going down the stairs, we crossed the East Atrium out into the garden. And Ajax silently led us across the garden to the base of steps in front of Atlas's tomb now. Then stopping, Ajax signaled Captain Peleus forward before informing Peleus that he, Nestor, and I would be going down into Atlas's tomb with trident, and that we needed Peleus and the men to stand guard here at entrance now. And Captain

Peleus slapped fist to his chest and nodded his head acknowledging Ajax's orders now.

And climbing the steps of the tomb, Peleus and his men spread out across top of the stairs while Ajax, Nestor, and I descended down into the tomb now. Stopping to grab the first torch out of its socket on the wall, Ajax removed a small lighter from the pouch on his belt and lit the torch. And reaching the bottom of the stairs, Ajax quickly lit the torches on both sides. Then Ajax went around the chamber lighting the torches on the north side before crossing and lighting all the torches on the south side as he checked to make sure the tomb was empty. And returning to Nestor and me by the stairs, Ajax stopped and saluted letting us know the tomb was ours now.

Turning to face me, Nestor spoke up now saying, "The Elders stayed up until midnight last night going through the ancient scrolls again for your majesty. But they were only able to find two things that might be of use now. The first thing the Elders found was that your eye's turning blue is normal and happens to all the staff bearers when using their staves. And the second thing they found was that King Atlas and his advisors had formed a large, blue, impenetrable shield around themselves when they defeated the General and his follows. Afterwards, Atlas and his advisors had used that same blue shield to completely cover and protect the city of Attea as it sank beneath the waves. Which is helpful, don't you I think, your majesty?"

Taking a quick look around the tomb, I turned to Nestor now and replied, "Thank you, Nestor. Yes, that's good to know. Okay. I think you two should stay here by the stairs while I begin the tests at the far end of the tomb." And with a look of concern on their faces, Nestor and Ajax both nodded their heads agreeing now.

Grinning at them, I lightly patted my father-in-law on the shoulder now before walking the sixty odd feet to the back of the tomb with Atlas trident. Pausing to nod to King Atlas briefly as I passed his open sarcophagus. Laying his trident down on the floor now, I untied the three cords and flipped the cloth back exposing Atlas's trident. Then glancing at Nestor's and Ajax's nervous faces for a moment. I bent down and picked up the trident now before standing up facing Nestor and Ajax again.

I instantly felt the surge of power flow through me as the visions began flashing through my mind again. I saw Nestor gasp and take a couple of steps towards me before stopping. While Ajax on the other hand, just stood there with his mouth agape, too stunned to move now. Raising my left hand, I signaled for Nestor to remain where he was, as thousands of images continued to flash through my mind.

And suddenly I understand what the images were, and shouted, "I understand what the images are now. Their King Atlas's memories recorded here on the crystal. Even weirder, I can understand what they are saying now even though I knew they are speaking Attean. It's like an enormous slideshow, here in front of my eyes. And I can reach out and touch it now and move forwards or backwards through King Atlas's life with my hand. Everything we needed to know about the trident is right here, recorded on the crystal. Showing me the step by step the things Atlas's advisors had learned about the crystal's power and passed on to King Atlas."

Suddenly the slide show stopped. And reaching out now, I touched the slideshow with my finger and slid it to the right from the end now. Where Atlas said his final fair well to his family gathered around his bed to where Atlas's advisors showed him how to make the blue defensive shield. Then I simply envisioned the shield around me now in my mind and suddenly felt it appear. Opening my eyes, I saw Nestor and Ajax backing away now from the glowing blue shield around me in surprise. And slowly opening my left hand outwards, I increased the size of the blue shield. Then closing my hand again, I shrunk the blue shield down until it just barely surrounded me now. Then I envisioned the shield being gone again, and felt it disappear.

Nervously taking a few steps forward, Nestor and Ajax both asked, "Are you okay, your majesty?."

Grinning at them now, I replied, "I'm fine. There's nothing to worry about, my friends." Then I added, "And now we know for sure that I am the great grandson of Princess Helena. Because the Trident is genetically coded to only work for King Atlas and his descendants. But only if their intentions are peaceful. The trident can only be used for defense, which explains why the trident wouldn't work for Prince Helios now."

Looking at Nestor and Ajax again, they finally began to relax, and I added, "Take a seat, my friends. The knowledge of how to use the trident is spread out over several years and is going to take me a little time to go through and learn now."

And we spent three hours a day for the next few days down in Atlas's tomb. As I went through Atlas's memories, learning the various powers of the trident. Along with the tragic bits of Atlas's life and Attean history now. Which I passed onto Nestor and Ajax, saying, "King Atlas was sad and lonely after the Battle of the Six Staves where he lost his beloved wife, Queen Pleione. After which, Atlas's four loyal advisors convinced him that the staves were just too dangerous, and they had a plan to save Attea from starvation. Though the tale of the 'Six Staves of Attea,' leaves out the fact that the Atlas's four advisors each willingly surrendered their own life to make the lights atop the four caverns. Their spirits trapped forever inside the staves providing the light needed to save their beloved Attea. And leaving Atlas alone in the palace afterwards. Only in Atlas's last few years after the birth of his grandson Hyrieus was Atlas cheerful again." Nestor promised to pass this information on to the Elders now, so their history books could be amended.

On the second day, I used the trident to collect all the small shards of stone left behind from Atlas's broken sarcophagus cover. And forming them into a small cone, I used fire from trident to melt and fuse them together. In the same way as Atlas and his advisors had formed the rock dome over Attea to save it from the ocean above.

On the third day, I tested a small lightning bolt from the trident. And Nestor and Ajax nearly wetting themselves in surprise. I quickly apologized for not warning them first. Then turned around to hide my snickering.

By the end of the fourth day, I was ready to tackle the Kraken and repair the North Cavern. So, I asked Nestor to inform the Consul of Elders that I had mastered the power of Atlas's trident. And that I was sure I could defeat the Kraken now and repair the breach in the North Cavern safely, which was the easy part. And I asked Ajax to go along with Nestor to confirm everything Nestor told the Elders. Then chuckling, I told Nestor to inform the Elders I would be ready to go and do this, once I got permission from their majesties. Which would be the difficult part.

Now it was time to tell my lovely wives about my idea, and of successfully mastering the trident's power, and see how they reacted. And I considered inviting Nestor and Sophia over to dinner tonight to help mediate. But I liked my new father-in-law and mother-in-law too much to involve them in such a hostile endeavor. And after dinner was cleared away and the servants had left for the night. I asked my beautiful wives to join me on the couch as I had something important I needed to tell them now.

Curious, they both quickly agreed before moving to the couch, and sandwiching me between them now. And I started by saying, "First I'd like to apologize for deceiving you both slightly."

Surprised, they both looked at me now and Amy asked, "How's that, Andrew?"

And grinning at them sheepishly now, I replied, "Well, for the last four days I told you I was out in the garden doing intensive sword training with Ajax. Which is why we had Nestor join us. The truth is, we were testing Atlas's trident to finding out whether or not I could master its power."

And they both frowned at me showing their disapproval, before Sandra asked, "Well, since your still alive! Should we ask you how the tests went, husband?"

Smiling at Sandra, I replied, "Yes, my beautiful wife." And turning to Amy, I added, "It turned out to be easier than I expected."

Surprised, Amy asked, "How's that?"

Taking both their hands in mine now, I replied, "Those images that I had first seen when I touched the trident, were in fact, King Atlas memories recorded on the trident's crystal. And like an enormous slideshow, showing me every one of Atlas's memories until his death. And by moving my hand left or right I could browse through Atlas's life. But that's not the weird part, the weird part was even though they were speaking in Attean. I could understand everything that was being said."

Curious now, Sandra spoke to me in Attean for a second, before asking, "Did you understand what I just said, husband?"

And thinking about it for a moment, I replied, "Yes, you said that tonight is not my night off." Which made Amy chuckle now at Sandra's choice of phrases.

Then Amy face suddenly got serious, and she asked, "But you're leaving the important part out, Andrew. Which is, why would you risk your life, and Sandra's and my happiness to find out if you could master the power of Atlas's trident?"

Then I spent the next hour explaining my idea of repairing the North cavern. Striking a truce with the Wild Ones and giving them a full pardon and the North Cavern in exchange for them living in peace from now on. And Amy and Sandra did side with Thestor at first. But after telling them getting the Elders blessing first, and the information they had found in the ancient scrolls. And of all the abilities that I had mastered. Plus, the interesting and unknown things I learned about the "Battle of the Six Staves" and King Atlas's life. I was finally able to win them over as far as the testing of the trident.

They both agreed that my plan to end the Wild one's raiding was ingenious. But they weren't thrilled with the idea of me battling the Kraken inside the North cavern. So, I told them both of seeing King Atlas and his four advisors standing outside the city gates using the blue shield to protect Attea from the tidal wave that poured over the city as it sank beneath the waves. I was able to convince my wives now that I would never attempt this unless I was one hundred percent sure that I could do it safely. And grinning and speaking in Attean now, Sandra suggested that we finish this discission in bed.

And sensing that Sandra had said something amusing again, Amy smiled and asked, "So, what did my sister say, husband?"

Rising from the couch, I turned and offered Amy my hand now. And smiling, Amy accepted my hand as I replied, "Sandra suggested since tonight is not my night off, that we finish this conversation in the bed." And Sandra blushed as I translated her words to Amy.

Once Amy was on her feet, I offered my hand to the red-faced Sandra, who quickly accepted my hand rising from the couch now. Amy grinned at Sandra, and said, "I agree with Sandra, get your butt in bed, husband!" Sandra and I chuckled as we moved to the bed now.

After which, I slept in the middle with Amy on my right and Sandra snuggled up on my left.

I spent the next few days in the royal chambers with Nestor and Ajax, getting ready to repair the North Cavern. And it wasn't just defeating the Kraken and sealing the breach in the cavern wall. We had to devise a way to pump the salt water out while filling the cavern with air again. And Ajax was a big help now having studied engineering before going into the army.

Ajax assured me that the pumps on the glide-subs could do the job. But it would require both glide-subs working together to avoid drawing the attention of the outworlders. And the two split hoses we needed to do the job would have to be manufactured. The first hose long enough to reach from the glide-sub bottom of the cavern to the glide-sub outside the breach. And a second hose long enough to reach from the ocean floor up to the glide-sub at the surface. Then it would take several weeks to pump out the cavern. As the second glide-sub would have to lie submerged during the day. Then raise its air-intake at night, while watching out for outworlders with their periscope.

As a secondary precaution, I recommended that we build an airlock inside the entrance of the North Cavern now. That way, if the cavern wall somehow failed after we opened the tunnel, the rest of Attea wouldn't be flooded and remain safe. Ajax and the Elders quickly agreed to my suggestion and the added safety precaution.

Then Ajax brought up a valid point, that it will be tough to get the workers we need, once they find out the job is inside the Caves of Mephisto. Even with the Wild one's numbers drastically reduced. The workers would be an easy target in the Cave of Mephisto. I had originally planned to offer the Wild Ones a truce once the North Cavern was repaired. But I decided to go out now and meet with the leader the Wild Ones outside the city gates.

So, I instructed Ajax to have a large canopy set up out on the flat in front of the city gates now. Far enough out so that the Wild Ones wouldn't fear an attack, but close enough that we could walk there and back in an hour. And put a table and four chairs in the center of the canopy with a couple of cases of wine, and some cups. Then to have a two large white flags planted on either side of the canopy. And finally, write a note and leave it on the table. The note saying that the new King wishes to speak to the leader of the Wild Ones, face to face, and in peace. As I have an offer now I think he should hear in person.

Both Nestor and Ajax started to object to the meeting, stating the obvious safety concerns. But I assured them that as I was holding King Atlas's trident in my hand, ten thousand Wild Ones wouldn't be enough to injure me. And it was agreed that Pylos would go with me to translate now instead of Ajax. As seeing Ajax again might make the Wild Ones nervous. Then Nestor and I both had a small chuckle at the frown on Ajax's face.

And following my instructions, Ajax had the canopy and flags pitched out on the flat outside the city gates. Then stopped to inform Captain Hyllus why I had ordered it done. So that Captain Hyllus could post a 24-hour watch on the canopy now. Also, so Hyllus could inform all the nosey merchants and farmers that this was the King's canopy.

And it worked. Three days later, Agis stepped into the room while Nestor, Ajax, and I were discussing the North Cavern plans. And nodding his head, Agis announced that Pylos was waiting outside. And returning his nod, I asked Agis to please show Pylos in now.

Chapter - 21

Agis opened the door and Pylos promptly stepping into the room stopping to salute and nod. And after returning my cousin's salute. Pylos informed us that Captain Hyllus's lieutenant had just arrived at the palace to notify his majesty that the Wild Ones were out at the canopy now.

Asking Pylos to wait now. I signaled to Agis, then followed him into my changing room. Where the stewards quickly dressed me in my armor now. And grabbing Atlas's trident, Ajax, Nestor, and I followed Pylos back out of my chambers.

Reaching the courtyard, we found a full squad of palace guard with shields and spears standing ready and waiting. And as we reached the bottom of the steps, Pylos barked an order out causing the rear half of the guards to part outwards now in the middle as we started across the courtyard. Then reaching the center of the formation, Pylos barked out two more orders. The first one, closing the rear formation behind us, and then the second causing the entire formation to begin marching out the palace gates down to the city.

And just before we reached the edge of the city, Pylos barked another order, and the royal guards formed a phalanx around us now as we entered the city. And I saw two of Captain Hyllus's Spearmen stationed in the openings of every street, while a dozen more city guards were busy clearing the street ahead for us. Though the appearance of a full squad of royal guards in battle formation now seemed to be sufficient to clear a path through the busy streets. The Atteans quickly stepping out of the way now before stopping to bow as our formation passed them.

Reaching the main gates, Captain Hyllus had one quad Spearmen formed up in the street to the north. While his second squad of Spearman having formed up behind us as we passed them in the street. And looking up through the shields now, I could see Hyllus's Archers manning the battlements above. Then Pylos gave the order, and the phalanx came to an abrupt halt. As Captain Hyllus and his lieutenant stepping up to our phalanx to salute and nod their heads.

And getting a nod from me, Pylos barked out the order and the guards on the norths split now, making a hole in the phalanx for Hyllus and his lieutenant to enter. And stepping into the phalanx, Hyllus and his lieutenant saluted and nodded again. And smiling at them now, I returned their salutes before saying, "Good to see your again, Captain Hyllus. I would shake hand, but no one here feels comfortable holding Atlas's trident. And I can't say that I blame them either!"

Nodding his head again, Captain Hyllus replied, "Thank you, your majesty. And thank you for the warm greeting though I feel unworthy of it, your majesty."

Grinning at Hyllus now, I replied, "No need to apologize, Captain Hyllus. We were expecting an assignation attempt that day and were prepared for it. If you still feel the need to apologize, then apologize to Captain Pylos here, he got the worst of it that day!"

Nodding his head to me, Pylos said, "Captain Hyllus has apologized several times already, your majesty. And I have told him there is nothing to forgive. Though Captain Hyllus seems to be a little hard of hearing apparently, your majesty."

At which point, Ajax, Nestor, Pylos, and I all let a chuckle slip out. And I rested my hand on Pylos's shoulder now as I tried to regain my composure. And seeing us all laughing, Hyllus's face got a little red at first, before it finally clicked, that there weren't any hard feelings amongst us over the assassination attempt Pylos's injury. And Hyllus finally relaxed and joined us now in chuckling at Pylos's reply.

With my hand on Pylos shoulder, I turned to look at him now and before asked, "Shall we go out and speak to the Wild Ones now, cousin?"

Snapping me another salute and nodding his head, Pylos replied, "Whenever you're ready, your majesty!"

And taking my hand off Pylos's shoulder now, I returned his salute and his nod. Then stepping out of the phalanx into the street, I turned around to face Ajax and said, "Don't come out of the gates unless you see me vaporize the Wild Ones under the canopy. The rest of the Wild Ones are hiding behind that hill to the northwest. Feel free to come out and finish off the survivors if they decide to charge."

Hyllus, his lieutenant, and Pylos all raised their eyebrow now in surprise, as Ajax saluted me, replying, "Understood, your majesty."

Walking towards the gates now, Pylos hesitated for a moment quickly saluting Ajax again, who returned his salute and gestured with his head for Pylos to hurry and catch up with me now. The canopy with the four Wild Ones in it was a fair distance out from the gates. And it took Pylos and me a good twenty minutes to walk out to the canopy now. During which time, Pylos asked the obvious question, saying, "There are four Wild Ones under that canopy and only the two of us, your majesty. Aren't your concerned for your safety, your majesty?"

Smiling over at Pylos, I calmly replied, "You weren't there when I mastered the power of King Atlas's trident, cousin. So, haven't witnessed the power of the trident." And lifting the trident up slightly now as we continued to walk, I added, "I hold the power of ten thousand soldiers in my hand now. Be assured cousin, as long as I am holding the trident in my hand, we vastly outnumber the Wild ones!"

And nodding his head, Pylos remained silent until we reached the canopy. Stopping five feet from the canopy, Pylos took two steps forward now before asking in Attean, "Who is the leader here?"

And the enormous man in the center, who looked a lot like Hyllus or one of his relatives, rose now and replied, "I am Lycus, leader of the Wild Ones. And I'm here to listen to the king's offer. But I think your king must be a fool, to come all the way out here alone now."

Turning to face me, Pylos nodded and translated Lycus's words now, saying, "This is Lycus, Leader of the Wild Ones. And he is here to hear your offer. Though he thinks you are a fool to come out here alone now, your majesty."

Nodding in return to them both, I replied, "Tell Lycus, I come here with peaceful intent. But not alone." And raising Atlas's trident up now, I added, "Ask Lycus if he is familiar with the story of the 'Six Staves of Attean?' Then inform Lycus that I now hold King Atlas's trident in my hand."

Turning to Lycus and the others, Pylos quickly translated my words to them. And the surprised, terrified look on their faces was plain to see. And Lycus waved his arm at the other Wild Ones now silencing their frightened mumbling.

Nodding his head, Lycus realized that I had the advantage, and grinned now before replying, "So, his majesty is no fool. Good, let's hear this offer now?" Nodding to Lycus, Pylos turned and quickly translating Lycus's words. And stepping forward, I pulled out a chair with my left and sat down across from Lycus, planting the trident beside me now but not letting go of it. After which, Lycus quickly nodded his head and sat down again.

Looking up at Pylos now, I said, "Tell Lycus, I am planning to use the power of Atlas's trident to repair the breach in the North Cavern now. And I am willing to pardon all the Wild Ones and give them the North Cavern to live in. If they swear to live in peace and obey Attean law from now on?"

Turning to Lycus, Pylos quickly translated my words to Lycus and the other Wild Ones. And they huddled together now whispering back and forth before Lycus signaled for them to be quiet. Then turning to Pylos now, Lycus asked, "What about the Kraken?"

And not waiting for Pylos to translate, I replied, "Tell Lycus, if I was worried about the Kraken, we wouldn't be sitting here now talking!" And Lycus seemed slightly surprised now as Pylos quickly translated my words.

Lycus was silent for a moment as he thought something over, then he said, "I am wondering why the King has come out here to meet us now? Rather than after doing the things he claims he can do with Atlas's trident. And has nothing to offer us now really other than his word. What is it that the king wants from us?"

Pylos started to translate, but I held my hand stopping him and grinned across at Lycus now. Who I had to admire, as he quickly saw the missing piece of the puzzle and I cut straight to the point now. And I replied, "Tell Lycus he's right. And tell him we need to build an airlock in the entrance of the North Cavern, and it will take several weeks. And what I want from Lycus and the Wild Ones now, is their promise not to attack our workers in the crossroads, or the Merchants carrying food and supplies back and forth from Attea to the airlock. But only in those two places now, not the entire kingdom?" Then after

Pylos had translated my word to Lycus, I added, "And tell Lycus, there is no place in the kingdom his people can hide that I can't find them with the trident now."

And after Pylos finished translating my words, Lycus and the three Wild Ones formed another huddle whispering back and forth before Lycus turned to face us again, and replied, "Agreed. You have my word now that neither the airlock workers in the Caves of Mephisto nor the Merchants wagons travelling back and forth between the workers and the Attea will not be attacked for one full month."

Nodding my head to Lycus now, I told Pylos to translate, "Thank Lycus for me. And tell him that we will lower the white flags tomorrow and raise them again after I have defeated the Kraken and repaired the North Cavern. Then we can meet again to discuss the North Cavern, the Wild one's pardons and Lycus's appointment as mayor of the North Cavern, and his duties as the new mayor."

After Pylos translated my words, Lycus nodded his head and we rose from the table together now, our meeting concluded. Then Lycus and his three chiefs turned and walked away leaving Pylos and me standing there under the canopy watching them go.

Grinning now as he watched Lycus and the Wild Ones walk away, Pylos said, "That went better than I expected, your majesty." Then Pylos added, "And you understand Attean now, your majesty?"

Looking at Pylos, I replied, "Yes, it's a side effect of using Atlas's trident. Though I have a ways to go yet before I can speak Attean." Pylos nodded his head now, and we stood there for another minute watching Lycus and the Wild Ones walking away, then I turned to Pylos and said, "Let's head back, cousin." Saluting and nodding again, I returned Pylos's salute as we turned and began the long walk back to the city gates.

As we drew closer to the gates, I could see Ajax, Nestor, and Captain Hyllus out in front of the gates waiting impatiently for our return. And Pylos and I both grinned at them as we reached the three men now. And exchanging salutes and nods with them, and Nestor asked, "How did it go, Your majesty?"

Nodding my head now, I grinned at Hyllus and replied, "Good. Lycus, the leader of the Wild Ones, who by the way, looks a lot like

Captain Hyllus here. Has given me his word that the Wild Ones will neither attack our men at the airlock, nor our wagons carrying supplies between Attea and the crossroads for the next thirty days."

And Captain Hyllus hung his head now, replying, "Yes, I'm sorry to admit it, your majesty. Lycus is my cousin, much to my family's humiliation, and my aunt's and uncles' shame, your majesty."

Grinning at Hyllus now, I replied, "Well, tell your family to expect that to change soon. As I was fairly impressed with Lycus today, and he is the logical choice for the new mayor of the North Cavern."

And thinking out loud, Hyllus mumbled, "Oh no, if Lycus is appointed mayor, he will out rank me, and I'll never hear the end of it!" And we all burst into laughter now at Hyllus's words and the look of dismay on his face. Then grinning wryly, Hyllus replied, "Well, I guess it's better than his current status?"

And putting my hand on Hyllus shoulder now, I said, "Let's go back into the city, my friend. I need to get back to the palace before their majesties start to worry and have me summoned!" And we all chuckled as they saluted me again. And I returned their salutes, as we turned and all walked back in through the gates.

Pylos and Hyllus exchanged the two-handed clasp of friendship, then Hyllus and his lieutenant saluted again as we said our goodbyes and the royal guards closed the phalanx around us. Then Pylos gave the command, and we set out for the palace again. Once we were back inside the palace courtyard and the guards closed the gates, Pylos gave the command for the phalanx to open up. And I saw Captain Peleus standing by the foot of the palace stairs with my personal guard now, ready to take me back to my chambers.

I quickly exchanged salutes with my cousins, then asked Nestor if he and Sophia could join us for dinner again tonight. And never turning down a chance to dine with his lovely daughter, Nestor graciously accepted on behalf of Sophia and himself now before thanking me. And crossing the courtyard to Peleus and my guards now, I returned Peleus's salute. Then Captain Peleus turned and led Nestor and me back up to the royal chambers. Where Nestor and I said our goodbyes at the doors. And entering the royal chambers, I found Agis and the stewards ready and waiting again.

Returning their nods, I followed them into the changing room. After a bath and changing clothes, I felt a whole lot better. Then leading me back out the sitting area, Agis nodded and asked, "Would you prefer tsia or wine before dinner now, your majesty?"

Grinning at Agis, I replied, "Wine please, it was hot on the flat outside the city. Oh, and Nestor and Lady Sophia will be joining us for dinner again tonight, Agis. So, you should have more wine ready, thank you."

After two cups of wine, I stretched out on the couch to relax before dinner. And no surprise, it was Agis clearing his throat by the door to my chambers that woke me later. Sitting up, I returned Agis's nod, as he said, "Nestor and Lady Sophia are outside now, your majesty."

To which smiled and replied, "Thank you, Agis. Show them in please and bring two more glasses."

Nodding, Agis grinned and replied, "Immediately, your majesty."

Rising from the couch, I stood there waiting to greet my mother and father-in-law as Agis moved to the inner door and opened the right-hand door. Quickly returning Agis's nod, Nestor and Sophia walked into the room and stopped to nod their heads. And smiling at them, I returned their nods before moving forward to shake hands and welcoming them both. And I held my arm out inviting Nestor and Sophia to have a seat in the sitting area, as Agis disappeared into my chambers only to return a moment later with a tray with two cups on it. Agis paused at the edge of the sitting area to nod, before stepping forward to set the tray down on the table. Then he took a quick peek into my wine carafe and quietly said, "Dinner will be about twenty minutes. Is there anything else I can get you, your majesty?"

Grinning at Agis, I shook my head negatively and replied, "No, thank you Agis. I think we're good for now" Nodding again, Agis turned and went back into my chambers closing the door behind him.

Reaching for the wine carafe, I filled Nestor's cup before looking at Sophia and asking, "Wine, Sophia?" And smiling now, Sophia nodded her head "yes", and I filled the second cup for Sophia.

Picking up his cup, Nestor took a sip before saying, "I am surprised their majesties are haven't returned yet?"

And reaching for her cup now, Sophia calmly replied, "Their majesties each have a divan in their dressing room and lately have been nodding off in the afternoons after tsia and knitting. And Petra is quite adamant that no one makes any noise or wake their majesties during their naps." Then pausing to giggle slightly, Lady Sophia continued, added, "Which is an endless source of speculation and gossip amongst the handmaids now as to his majesty apparent prowess in bed."

Turning to stare at his wife in dismay, Nestor replied, "Really Sophia, you go too far."

And chuckling to calm Nestor down, I grinned and asked Lady Sophia, "And what do my lovely wives say?"

Grinning now, Sophia replied, "Nothing, your majesty. Her majesty Amy just grins and touches her stomach. While her majesty Sandra, turns all red when the subject comes up, your majesty,"

Chuckling again, I replied, "I assume that's takin as a good sign, Sophia?"

And nodding her head, Sophia smiled and replied, "A very good sign, your majesty."

Returning Sophia's nod, I said, "Well, I am happy to be a source of speculation and help you ladies pass the time more pleasantly." Which made Nestor chuckle, while Sophia grinned and nodded her head now.

Then the doors to Lady's private chambers opened now and my two beautiful wives stepped into the room followed closely by Petra. All three pausing to nod briefly, before Sandra and Amy both smiled at Nestor and Sophia sitting here next to me. Returning their nods, they quickly moved forward exchanging hugs with Nestor and Sophia greeting them now. And Amy sat down on my right, while Sandra sat down on the other couch now with her mother and onto Sophia's arm. As Nestor moved to the single chair in the middle. And taking my arm now, Amy touched her stomach before whispering, "I'm really hungry, Andrew?"

Leaning over to Amy, I whispered back, "Any minute now, my love." And just as I finished saying it, the door to my private chamber opened as Agis and the stewards filed out into the room from the left.

Then the three handmaids entered from the right taking up position next to Petra. And nodding first, Agis said, "Dinner is outside, if your majesties are ready?"

Rising, Amy answered now, saying, "We're ready Agis, thank you!" Then rising, we all moved to the table as Agis, Petra, and the servants moved to the front doors to get dinner and set the table.

Reaching the table, I pulled out Amy's normal chair. But Sandra stepped forward now touching my arm before whispering, "Amy and I decided to switch places tonight husband, so that I can sit with my father for a change, and Amy could sit with Sophia." And nodding my head, I seated Sandra on the right now then moved around the table seating Amy on the left. Once the ladies were seated, Sophia and Amy exchanged hugs as the servants finished setting the table.

And when the servants lined up along the walls and bowed their heads again. I returned their nods, and said, "Thank you all." And nodding again, they all turned and filed out of the room.

While we ate dinner, Nestor and I listened to Amy, Sandra, and Sophia filled us in on the completion of the new nursey, and how pleased they were now. Then my wives spent a minute telling me about their progress on the baby blankets. At the end of which, Nestor wryly asked, "Has his majesty filled you in on his little victory today, your majesties?"

I frowned at Nestor now as Amy stared at me and asked, "And what have you been up to all day husband, if I may ask?" Causing a small chuckle to escape from Sandra's and Sophia's mouths now.

Gently patting Amy's hand, I looked into her lovely face now and replied, "Pylos and I had our first meeting with the leader of the Wild Ones outside the city today."

Amy looking me over now, before asking "Well, you look unscathed, so I assume the meeting went off as expected, my love."

Grinning at Amy now, I replied, "It was a little dicey for a minute, as there was four of them, and only Pylos and myself. And their leader Lycus, who it turns out is Captain Hyllus's cousin. Thought I was a fool to meet him out there in person, two against four. Until I had Pylos inform Lycus that the trident I was holding now was King Atlas's trident. And that he and his comrades were in far more danger than Pylos and me." And pausing to take a sip of my wine now, I continued adding, "After which Lycus and I sat down at the table and had a nice little chat. Where I informed Lycus of my plan, and he gave me his word that the Wild Ones would neither attack our workers at the airlock nor our supply wagons from the city for the next 30 days. And as I told the embarrassed Captain Hyllus on our return. I was fairly impressed by Lycus today, he is sharp and intelligent, and neither crude nor common as I expected from the leader of the Wild Ones."

Nestor spoke up now, saying, "I know Lucus's story, your majesty. Lycus was the longtime rival of a wealthy man for Lady Amara hand. And the two men had several public brawls over her. But Lady Amara eventually chose to marry for money. After which, unhappy and realizing her mistake, Lady Amara began an affair with Lycus. Shortly after which, Lady Amara's husband was found murdered, the obvious suspect being Lycus. Lady Amara ran to warn Lycus and begged him to flee the city before he was arrested. Nine months later Lady Amara gave birth to a son, which as you might guess, bears a striking resemblance to Lycus, and not the Lady Amara's husband." And taking another sip of his wine, Nestor continued, adding, "Rumor has it. Though it has never been proven, every year when the Lady Amara travels to Actium to celebrate her son's birthday with her older sister. She is secretly meeting Lycus there."

And Amy spoke now, saying, "That's a sad and interesting tale, Nestor." Then Amy squeezed my hand afterwards, obviously affected by the tragic story of Lycus's and Lady Amara's love.

Smiling at Amy and then at Sandra, I said, "Well, that is going to change soon. Once I repair the breach and we recover the North Cavern. Lycus is the logical, and only choice really for the new mayor. Since he is the only the Wild one's trust, and the only one we can trust to keep the peace."

Nodding now, Nestor replied, "I agree with your majesty."

Sandra and Amy both looked at me now before Sandra asked, "So you think that Lycus and Lady Amara's tragic tale will finally have a happy ending, my husband?"

Thinking about if for a moment, I nodded my head now and replied, "I do, my loves." Which made Sandra and Amy both smile.

After dinner, we lingered at the table for a while, taking our time before saying goodnight to Nestor and Sophia. Then the servants came in to clear the table and turn down the bed again before leaving.

My two beautiful wives apparently touched by Lycus's and Lady Amara's love story now, informed me that they were in the mood and expected me to fulfill my husbandly duties again tonight. Nodding my head to my beautiful wives, I swung my arm out indicating they need only get into bed now.

The next morning after breakfast and a bath, the stewards dressed me, and Agis escorted me back out into the main chamber. And I wasn't surprised to find that my lovely wives had disappeared into their private chambers. And Agis brought me tsia now, while I waited for Nestor's and Ajax's arrival.

After Ajax and Nestor sat down and I filled their tsia cups. Nestor informed me that securing the promise from the Wild Ones had done the trick, and the construction crew was on their way out to the Caves of Mephisto now. And Ajax informed us that Captain Peleus and a half squad of volunteers from the royal guards had gone with the workers. To alleviate their fears and help with the construction.

After which, Ajax informed me that the armored hoses that he had designed and requested were ready now. And Captains Theron and Orius were standing by at the east airlock with their glide-subs whenever I was ready. That, and it was a several-hour hike from the palace to the east airlock. Then from there, it would take about four hours for the glide-subs to travel to the breach in the North Cavern.

Everything seemed to be coming together now, and it was time for me to do my part. As we only had a week left before the cover for Atlas's sarcophagus would be finished, and King Atlas's trident was scheduled to return to its proper resting place. Though I worried after being submerged in salt water for so long, would anything actually grow inside the North Cavern now? As that would kill our plans, and I brought it to Nestors and Ajax's attention now.

And I suggested that once I repaired the breach, we explain the problem to the Elders and ask their blessing to keep the trident for another twenty days. So that I can use it to remove the salt from inside the North Cavern before returning it to Atlas's tomb. And considering the size and scope of the problem, Nestor and Ajax both agreed that it wasn't an unreasonable request. Not to mention, the time it would take to pump out the North Cavern and to finish the airlock. I wasn't happy about it, since I promised that King Atlas's trident would be returned to his sarcophagus as soon as the new cover was ready. However, I couldn't see any other choice at the moment.

So, we decided to set out for the east airlock tomorrow after lunch. And Ajax made his plans, accordingly. Sending runners out to notify Captain Theron and Orius to expect us tomorrow night. We could sleep on the glide-sub while they travelled within a few miles of the breach. Ajax informed us now that the Kraken came out at night to feed. And that in the dark, our glide-subs look like a whales to a hungry Kraken.

I explained the plan to Amy and Sandra over dinner later that night, and I could tell they were still worried. So, going into my dressing room, I grabbed the trident and returned to the main chamber. Then I had them both stand by the bed, as I moved to the front door. Then closing my eyes, envisioning the shield around me. And when I felt it appear, and I opened my eyes again before asking them, "Can you see that now?" Slightly startled, they both nodded their heads, then I told them, "This is what King Atlas, and his advisors used to protect the entire city of Attea when it sank beneath the waves. And I will be inside this shield the whole time I face the Kraken." Then I added, "I would show you the lightning bolt now, but I don't want to level the palace." And seeing them both relaxing a little, I envisioned the shield being gone again and felt it disappear. Then I walked forward standing the trident up against the wall on the left side of the bed. And we crawled into bed, with Amy on my right side and Sandra on my left again. After kissing both of them. I reminded them now how much I loved them again. And that I had no intention of ever leaving their sides. Then closing our eyes now, we all went to sleep.

Chapter - 22

Amy and Sandra were unusually quiet during breakfast the next morning. Aware that I was leaving after lunch, and there was a chance that today would be the last time they ever saw me. And both lingered over their breakfast now, reluctant to go and work on their baby blankets. Waiting until Agis finally entered to let me know my bath was ready, before calling for Petra. And rising from the table, they watched me follow Agis into my chambers before Sandra rose and pulled the gold ribbon for Petra.

After my bath, the stewards dressed me into a fresh tunic and sash before sending me back out to sitting area for more tsia. And I asked Agis now to wake in time to get my armor on before lunch. That way, Ajax and Nestor wouldn't have to wait for me when they arrived after lunch. Agis nodded and agreed to my request, I returned his nod and thanked him, then Agis left again. And after another cup of tsia, I stretched out on the couch and eventually nodded off.

Stepping into the chamber, Agis bowed his head and cleared his throat again letting me know it was time to change into my armor. And sitting up, I rose from the couch and returned Agis's nod before following him into the dressing room. Returning the stewards nods, I stepped up podium as they put my armor on again now. Finished, the three stewards lined up against the wall again and nodded their heads. And returning the stewards nods, Agis led the way back out to the sitting area before nodding and leaving me alone again.

Which wasn't long, as ten minutes Amy and Sandra returned. Followed shortly thereafter by Agis and the stewards letting us know our lunch was outside. Rising from the couch, I returned everyone's nods before moving to the table and seating my wives. As Agis, Petra, and the servants quickly set the table and transferred the food. Even the servants looked a little nervous now, as they lined up and nodded their heads. Aware that I was leaving after lunch to go battle the Kraken in the North Cavern. So, I smiled trying to reassure them now as I returned their nods, and they filed back out of the room again.

I was surprised that Amy and Sandra didn't have any questions for me during lunch. Confining their conversation to their baby blankets and the fact that Sandra's was really starting to show now.

After lunch, I got my wives' chairs helping them up. Then stepping up to Amy, I leaned in and kissed her on the lips before leaning back looking her in the eyes and telling her that I loved her. And receiving a nod from Amy now, I stepped over to Sandra. And kissing her on lips now, I leaning back making eye contact with Sandra before telling her that I loved her too. After which, I pulled them both to me and hugged them as I kissed the top of their heads. Then I told them we were all being overly dramatic now, since I already knew that I could defeat the Kraken, and that everything would be fine. Then stepping over to the wall, I pulled the gold ribbon now summoning Petra. A few seconds later, Petra stepped into the room and stopped to nod by the door. Then I nodded to my wives again before returning Petra's nod. And Amy and Sandra returned my nod before joining arms and following Petra back to their private chambers. And both pausing to glance back at me now before disappearing into their chambers with Petra.

I was right to have changed into my armor before lunch. As Agis stepped back into the room informing me that Nestor and Ajax were outside now. As the stewards moved forward to begin clearing clear the table. Moving around the bed, I picked up Atlas's wrapped trident as Agis returned from the dressing room bearing the cloak of a regular Spearmen now over his arm. And nodding first, Agis stepped forward quickly putting Spearmen's cloak over my cuirass and fastening the clasps by my neck. Then taking two steps back, Agis nodded again to me. And nodding to my friend in return, I thanked Agis and crossed the room to the inner doors now.

Exchanging nods with my father-in-law and salutes with Ajax at the door, I bid Ajax lead the way now. Where I found five Spearmen waiting out in the hallway instead of my personnel guard. Quickly recognizing their faces, I realized these were my personal guards, but like me, they were all dressed as regular Spearmen now. And reading my mind, Ajax said, "A lone patrol of foot soldiers won't draw any attention, your majesty." And Nestor and I both nodded to Ajax now.

Though to my surprise, when we reached the atrium, Ajax went out into the garden doors now rather than heading for the front gates. But trusting Ajax, I remained silent as he led us across the garden now over to the southeast corner where we had been training. Then stopping in the corner, Ajax ordered to the five guards, "Halt. Attention. About-face." And as the guards turned around, Ajax walked up to the palace wall and began searching for something. And finding it now, Ajax counted down four stones with his finger, before stepping forward and suddenly pushing on the stone.

And to Nestor and my surprise, the right side of the fourth stone slid inward a couple of inches, followed by a low grating noise as a small section of the palace wall suddenly opened inward. And stepping forward, Ajax put his shoulder against the section of the wall and pushed inward, slowly opening the secret door. And stepping into the dark passageway, we heard the same low grating noise again followed by light shining in through the small passageway now. And stepping back out into the garden, Ajax ordered the guards to do an about-face. And our five guards turned around obviously surprised as they saw the secret passageway now. Then Ajax ordered the guards to go through the passageway and make sure it was safe on the other side. And we waited as the five guards moved through the passageway single file and spread out on the other side. Then we heard on one of the guards outside say, "Clear!" And turning to me and Nestor now, Ajax held his arm out indicating for us to enter the passageway as he nodded and said, "It's clear, your majesty."

Quickly returning Ajax's nod, I led the way through the passageway out of the palace with Nestor following behind me. And stepping down onto the ground outside, I looked up to find we were standing in a large apple orchard now covering the hillside here. The apple orchard stretching up the hillside about fifty yards before ending on dry barren hillside above. And looking down the hill to the right, I could see the apple orchard ended about fifty yards below, before changing into row after row of purple grapes.

Our five guards spread out in a semi-circle twenty-five feet out from the secret entrance intently watching the hillside. And I heard the solid thud behind us now as Ajax closed the inner door to the garden, followed by his footsteps in the passageway. And stepping outside, Ajax ordered the guards back to attention. Then putting his shoulder against the section of the wall, Ajax pushed it shut. It locked now with an audible clunk, and I saw one of the stone on the wall move slightly as the door locked. And counting up four stones, I saw the small triangular notch in the corner of the stones marking the location of the secret entrance. Which to anyone passing by, would simply look like a chipped corner in one of the thousands of stones making up the palace walls.

Then ordering the guards to reform, Ajax said, "If we meet any of the farmers up here, you and Nestor just stand behind the other men. While I will ask the man if he has seen any Wild one's lurking about, your majesty." And nodding my head to Ajax, he returned my nod then ordered our patrol to move out to the east.

It was a pleasant walk through the apple orchard and finding a well-worn path on the shady side of the apple trees now, we moved east at a steady pace. After about two hours we reached the end of the apple orchard, and I could see olive trees covering the hillside ahead. And taking a seat beneath one of the large apple trees now. We all ate an apple and got a drink of wine from the bota bags as we passed them around. Ajax ordered the guards not to bow or draw attention to me and just treat me like one of their fellow soldiers now.

Leaving the apple orchard now, we moved into the olive grove as we continued east along the hillside. Ajax informed us during our break that we could walk a little easier down on the valley floor, but we were far less likely to run into any people up here on the hillside.

After walking for another hour, we topped a small rise and I saw a large ravine ahead, on the far side of which was the massive east wall of the cavern. Looking at the base of the wall now, I saw six enormous stone columns with a large opening between the columns in the center of the cavern. And a wide road running west clear through the valley to the east gates of the city. On which I could see a half dozen wagons traveling back and forth now on the road. And there were several small carts parked along the side of the road at various places, and we could see the farmers out working in the fields there. And in the northeast corner, I saw four small columns with an opening between them. The doors stood open, but the heavy steel portcullis was lowered, blocking the entrance. And reaching a point on the hillside about 45-degrees from the small opening, Ajax turned downhill now and moved directly towards it.

Passing down through the olive trees now. Ajax found a set of overgrown stone steps leading down through the grapevines and out onto the rutted wagon trail running along the northern edge of the fields. Here, Ajax had the guard's fan out into flanking position as we followed the wagon trail east. The wagon trail following the base of the north hillside before curving to the south, passing the four small columns and the entrance to East Glide-sub Airlock.

Reaching the four columns and portcullis, I could see the cut stones inside the tunnel went back about sixty feet before ending at a set of large wood doors. Walking up to the pillar on the left, Ajax took hold of the knotted rope hanging there now and gave it a good tug. And down at the far end of the tunnel I heard the faint jingling of a bell. Moments later the doors opened, and a dozen Spearmen poured out into the tunnel facing the entrance. Stopping to form up, as an older, grey-haired soldier circled the squad, quickly inspecting the men and barking out orders. Then he ordered them to move out. And barking the order for them to stop again when they reached the portcullis. The older squad leader stepped forward salute before smiling wryly at Ajax. Who grinned back at the older man now and asked, "How are you Hektor, my old friend?"

Grinning, Hektor replied, "The same my young friend, old and bored. But rumor has it now that the new King has promoted you to Brigadier? If that's true, then congratulations, Ajax. The new king must be a wise man, as you were always my best student!"

Chuckling loudly, Ajax stepped to the side now and swung his arm out as he said, "Well, why don't you just ask his majesty yourself, Hektor?"

And reaching up, I pushed the hood back on my cloak as I smiled at Hektor. Stunned and surprised, Hektor looked like he was about to have a cow, as he snapped me a salute and bowed his head solemnly now, before saying in Attean, "I apologize for my rudeness, your majesty."

Chuckling, Ajax quickly translating Hektor's words, saying, "Hektor would like to apologize for his rudeness, your majesty."

Smiling at Hektor, I replied, "Well, tell Hektor I will forgive him, if he can open this gate for us now, cousin!"

Chuckling again, Ajax nodded as he translated my words to Hektor. Who quickly saluted and nodded again, before barking out, "Don't just stand there you fools, open the gate for our King!"

Hektor's formation suddenly split in half as they disappeared into the small passageways on either side of the tunnel. And a moment later, we heard the creaking protests of the portcullis as it slowly began to rise. Once the portcullis was raised, we all stepped into the shade of tunnel now and out of the heat of the East Cavern's staff.

And Ajax moved forward exchanging the two-handed clasp of friendship with Hektor, who smiled at Ajax like a proud father now. Once the two men separated, I added, "And yes Hektor, I did promote Ajax to Brigadier, for his crushing defeat of the Wild Ones at the Caves of Mephisto and for finally ridding Attea of Prince Helios once and for all!" And slightly embarrassed now, Ajax saluted and nodded before translating my word to Hektor.

And stepping forward now, Hektor thumped his huge fist on Ajax shoulder three times before stepping back and slapping his fist to his chest smartly and nodding his head to Ajax, smiled and said, "Well done, Brigadier Ajax."

Returning Hektor's salute, Ajax replied, "Thank you, my friend."

Then turning to Nestor, Ajax said, "And let me introduce you to the Senior Physician Nestor now, Hektor. His majesties Chief Advisor, and father of her majesty Queen Sandra!"

Hektor turned now saluting and nodded to Nestor, who smiled back at him graciously returning Hektor's nod. Then Hektor said, "I forget myself though, Captain Theron and Caption Orius are waiting impatiently inside for your arrival, your majesty." Then chuckling, Hektor added, "Those two have been sculking around down here all day like they were drydocked or something, your majesty." Then walking over between the two passageways, Hektor shouted, "Okay, you can close the portcullis now." Then saluting us again, Hektor asked, "If you will follow me, your majesty." And held his arm out now indicating the doors at the end of the tunnel. And returning Hektors salute, we all nodded and turned to face the doors at the end of the tunnel. Once the portcullis was closed, and Hektor's men were back in formation. Hektor barked out about face, then forward march, to his men standing at attention in the tunnel now. And Ajax, Nestor, and I started walking side by side towards the wood doors with our five guards following behind.

Reaching the doors, Hektor stepped forward now opening the doors for us and his men. And we discovered the tunnel continued for another forty feet before opening into the large room or hall now. Here there were two wide twenty-foot long tables with benches stretching down either side of the room. Then there were a half dozen doorless openings on the left side, with unmade bunks inside each. Beyond the openings there were two more openings with wood doors. And at the far end of the hall, there was a wide set of stairs led up out of sight. And on the right was another large room. Where I could see a two cooks in white aprons moving about now as they added ingredients and stirred steaming pots of food on the stoves lining the far wall.

Seated in the left corner of the two tables were two men in polished silver cuirasses and gold trimmed blue capes. Tsia mugs sitting on the table in front of them now, and I assumed these were my two glide-sub captains. Rising as we entered the room, both captains, seeing the gold crown atop of my blue bio-suit immediately saluted and nodded their heads now. Even the cooks in the kitchen stopped what they were doing now and turned to bow. Returning the Captain's salutes first, I turned to the kitchen and quickly nodded to the cooks, who stared at me for a moment before turning and going back to work on the food.

Walking directly up to the older of the two captains at the table, I asked, "Which one is Captain Theron?"

And the older one with a little grey showing in his hair beneath his dark green bio-suit spoke up now, replying, "I am, your majesty."

Returning the captains' salutes and nods now, I said, "I didn't get a chance to thank you last time for rescuing her majesty Amy and me. And I wish to do so now formally Captain Theron. Thank you."

Smiling, Theron nodded his head and replied, "It was my crews' and my honor, your majesty." Then hesitating for a moment, Captain Theron asked, "I was told you intend to repair the breach in the North Cavern now? And I have to warn your majesty that my men and I have attempted this four times previously without success. And I lost several good men in the attempts, your majesty."

Nodding my head to Theron now, I set the trident down on top of the table in front of the two men. And untying the three cords, I folded the cloth back exposing King Atlas's trident now, before saying, "Yes, I am aware of that, Captain Theron. But you weren't in possession of King Atlas's trident or the knowledge of how to use it, as I am now!" And they both stared in awe and amazement at Atlas's trident on the table, as I added, "Though I wouldn't recommend touching Atlas's trident, as it's a little unnerving at first!"

To my surprise, Caption Theron suddenly smiled and snapped me another salute as he nodded his head and said, "My men and our glide-subs are at service, your majesty." And following Theron's lead, Captain Orius snapped me a salute and nodded his head too.

Returning their salutes, I turned to Ajax now and asked, "Should we eat here first cousin, or continue to the glide-subs?"

Cutting in now, Captain Theron nodded and whispered, "I think you'll find the food up at the glide-subs base far superior to the food here, your majesty." Then turning to Orios, Theron said in Attean, "Would you run ahead please Orius, and inform the cooks that we shall be five for dinner tonight, one of which being his majesty?"

Orius saluted Captain Theron acknowledging the order, then turning to me, saluted me again and said in near-perfect English, "If you'll excuse me now, your majesty?" And after I returned Orius's salute, he strode over to the wide stone stairs and began climbing them two at a time now, disappearing in seconds.

Watching Orius leave, Theron shook his head and smiled now saying in Attean, "Ah, to be young again!"

Walking up to Hektor, Ajax and Hektor smiled at each other and exchanged the two-handed clasp of friendship again, before Ajax said, "I will see on our return, old friend." Then stepping back, the two exchanged salutes.

And grinning wryly at Ajax, Hektor pointed to the floor now replying, "I will be right here, Brigadier Ajax." And the two men chuckled for a moment. Then Hektor saluted me again, and said, "It was a great honor to meet you, your majesty."

Returning Hektor's salute, I replied, "And it is my honor to meet you Hektor, or any man cousin Ajax thinks so highly of." And Ajax translated my words.

Saluting again, Hektor replied, "Thank you, your majesty." And returning Hektors salute, I turned and wrapped Atlas's trident back up again before picking it up off the table. And the cooks in the kitchen and all the soldiers in the room bowed and saluted again. As Captain Theron held out his hands indicating the stairs leading up. And I went around the room returning everyone's nods and salutes before crossing the room to the foot of the stairs. Pausing at the base of the stairs for a second to let Nestor and Ajax catch up, while Theron passed us now and took the lead.

The stairs were twelve feet wide and the steps leading up out of sight were of moderate height. And studying the stonework of the semicircle now, I was impressed by the craftsmanship and the amount of work that it must have taken to make the stairwell. The steps lead up for forty feet before reaching the first small landing. Then you walked twenty feet across the landing before starting up the next set of stairs to the next landing above. After twenty-five minutes of this, Captain Theron stopped for a moment to rest, nodding his head, and saying, "I'm sorry, your majesty. I am used to standing at the helm of my glide-sub for hours on end, not climbing stairs."

Waving my arm at Theron, I replied, "No need to apologize captain. I spend most my time couped up in the royal chambers sitting on the backside." And looking over at Nestor, he looked a little paler than usual, so I quickly moved to his side taking hold of his arm as we both leaned on each other momentarily to catch our breaths. Then I looked over at Ajax and the guards, who, as expected, looked completely unaffected by the climb, and seemed confused now as to the reason for the delay.

Straightening up again, Captain Theron nodded and said, "Just another ten minutes. We are two-thirds of the way up now, your majesty." Then turning, Theron started up the next flight of stairs. Nestor and I silently nodded to each other before following Captain Theron up the stairs.

And Theron was right, ten minutes later we reached the landing at the top where a large glass and metal door greeted us at the other end. Pausing for a moment to catch his breath, Theron walked over to the panel on the south wall with two small lights on top and three gold seahorses below. And Theron turned the seahorse to the left, and we heard the faint hiss of seals breaking on the steel-rimmed glass semicircle of the airlock door. As it slowly rotated clockwise stopping at 90 degrees. Captain Theron glancing back at us briefly before walking into the airlock.

Once all nine of us were inside thirty-foot chamber, Theron stepped up to the two control panels on the right, where one of the small lights was out now. And Theron rotated the center seahorse on the right panel, and the outer door slowly swung counterclockwise and shut again. Followed by the sound of the door resealing now, and the second small lights above the two panels coming on again.

Then Theron turned the first seahorse on the left panel now, and we heard the seal on the inner door break as the door slowly rotated clockwise and opened. And reaching 90 degrees, the inner door stopped. And Captain Theron turned and nodded now before saying, "I am sorry to say this is the first of two airlocks, your majesty. The second airlock being installed for added safety."

And returning Theron's nod, we followed him into the thirty-foot section of tunnel between the two airlocks. Theron immediately stepping up to the panel on the right and rotating the second seahorse now closing the airlock behind us. Then walking across the section of tunnel to the control panel by the second airlock. Theron waited for the inner door of the first airlock to fully close and the lights on the top on the panel to come on again before rotating the first seahorse there and waiting as the outer door of the second airlock slowly rotated 90 degrees and came to a stop. And following Theron into the second airlock now, we watched as Theron closed the outer door and waited until both lights lit again before turning the first seahorse on the lefthand panel opening the inner door. Then nodding his head,

Captain Theron swung his arm out now indicating for us to exit the airlock. And following us out of the airlock, Theron paused at the control panel on the wall just long enough to close the inner door again before stepping to the front now lead us down the tunnel.

The tunnel continued east for a good two hundred feet before opening up into an enormous cavern with a cobblestone road running north to south, and a steel railing on the other side. Beyond the railing, I could see water glistening and stretching out for eighty yards to the far side of the cavern. On the other side of the railing, I could see eight large rusty steel posts jutting up from what appeared to be a large drydock. On either side of the drydock here in the center were two wide floating docks, with large dark grey glide-subs tied off to each dock. And in front of their glide-subs on docks now, stood two rows of men in dark blue tunics, quietly chatting amongst themselves as they waited. Suddenly Captain Orius appeared by the railing on the left and snapping us a salute, nodded his head now and loudly shouted in Attean, "Attention!" And I watched as the men on both docks suddenly ceased talking and snapped to attention facing forward.

Crossing the small road to the railing now, we all stopped as Theron, Ajax, and I returned Captain Orius's salute, and Nestor nodded his head. And looking around the enormous cavern, which was easily a hundred yards wide by fifty yards high in the center. The stone walls of the cavern glistened, and dark grey stalactites hung down everywhere covering the ceiling. To the left, was a large opening in the wall where two forty-foot-long wood tables sat with rows of benches beneath them. To the right, there was several opening or hallways, then two arched stone doorways with wood doors. And across the water on the south side of the cavern, there were four more wide, arched-stone openings or passageways, where they led I had no idea. All and all, the glide-sub base here was quite impressive.

Holding his arm out to the right now, Captain Orius nodded before saying, "If you will follow me please, dinner will be ready in a few minutes, your majesty?"

Returning Orius's nod, I replied, "I would feel better if you dismissed the men first and let them return to their duties?"

And saluting again, Orius turned to face the men down on the docks before barking in Attean, "Dismissed! Return to your duties." Then holding his arm out, Orius smiled before turning and leading the way to the tables. Which, I noticed now had five dinner settings on the north end of the table, and a padded chair at the end. There were five more dinner settings in the center of the table, which I assumed now were for our guards. Theron and Orius split off now walking down the right side of the tables with three of our guards. Our guards, assuming the place settings in the center of the table were for them too, stopped in the center of the table now and bowed their heads. Nestor and Ajax stayed with me and as Theron and Orius stopped on the right side of the table facing their glide-subs, as Nestor and Ajax stopped on my left, leaving me the padded chair on the end now.

And reaching the chair on the end, I turned around to face them again, as Nestor nodded and the other eight men all saluted now. Grinning at them, I returned their salutes and nods before holding out my hand indicating for everyone to sit. All nine waited for me to sit first. So, pulling out the chair with my left, I sat down now. Laying the trident in my lap and sliding the butt of the trident under the table.

Looking at the table now, I spotted a wine carafe in front of me. I don't know about the rest of them, but I was thirsty after the long climb up here to the glide-sub base. So, reaching for the wine carafe now, I picked it up off the table, which seemed to surprise Theron and Orius. And turning to my father-in-law now, I asked, "Wine Nestor?"

Grinning at me, Nestor nodded his head, replying, "Yes, thank you, your majesty." And after filling Nestor's cup, I looked over at Ajax now, who nodded his head, and I leaned forward filling his cup now as I returned his nod.

Then turning to look at Captain Orius, he nodded his head now and said, "Yes, thank you, your majesty."

And returning Orius's nod, I proceeded to fill his cup before looking at Captain Theron. Who nodded his head now and said, "Yes, thank you, your majesty." And smiling at Theron, I leaned over and filled his cup as I returned his nod. Then filling my own cup now, I set the carafe back on the table again.

And picking up my wine cup now, I held it aloft before saying, "To King Atlas, and a successful endeavor tomorrow!" As Nestor quickly translating my toast into Attean, as the entire table lifted their cups now and repeated my toast before nodding their heads and taking a large drink from their cups. Returning their nods, I took a large drink of the wine myself. The wine was decent being as thirsty as I was but couldn't compare to Agis's wine. And Nestor and I both looked at our cups for a moment before grinning at each other, thinking the same thing.

Looking past Nestor, I saw five cooks in white aprons come out of the openings on the other side of the airlock tunnel. Each pushing a food laden cart now as they approached our table. The two cooks in the rear stopped by our guards, while the three cooks in front continued forward. And stopping beside Nestor and Ajax now, they bowed in unison. Then the older cook in front snapping his hand to his chest and bowing now as he said in Attean, "I, Acumus, the head cook, do hereby swear under penalty of death, I that have personally tested all the food being served here tonight in the presence of my fellow cooks, and that it is safe to eat now, your majesty."

Then the other two cooks replied, "I swear that I have witnessed Acumus test all the food with my own eyes, your majesty."

I had forgotten about the oaths, as Agis or Petra received the oaths for us at the palace. And returning the cooks nods now, I replied "σ' ευχαριστώ," or "thank you" in Attean. Smiling now, the cooks quickly began moving the steaming dishes of food from their carts onto the table. And when they were done, they bowed again before rolling their empty carts back towards the kitchen. Turning my attention back to the table again, I said, "Let's eat, I am hungry!" and they all grinned and nodded now as we began loading their plates.

Captain Theron was right about the food being better here, as it was all fresh and tasted wonderful, which made up for the mediocre wine.

Chapter - 23

After dinner Nestor, Ajax, and I sat back over another glass of wine, though Captain Theron and Orius abstained now switching to tsia. And Theron informed me that his cabin had been prepared for me to sleep in while he and Captain Orios moved the glide-subs as close as they dared at night to the breach in the North Cavern.

After finishing our wine, we all rose and moved to the glide-subs now. And Ajax stopped to speak to our guards briefly, telling them to wait here until our return. Giving them the night off to rest and drink as much as they wanted tonight. But reminding them now that they were guests here. And we would be back tomorrow, so they had best all be sober and ready to move out when we returned. All five guards grinning now as they snapped Ajax a salute and nodded their heads acknowledging his orders.

Then Captain Orius paused to salute us and excuse himself now before nodding to Captain Theron and going down the north ramp to the Poseidon. After which, Theron held out his arm now indicating the south ramp before leading Nestor, Ajax, and me down ramp onto the dock to where the Neptune was moored.

Stopping at the foot of the gang plank up onto the glide-sub, Theron saluted and nodded again before holding out his arm and saying, "Welcome aboard the Neptune, your majesty," in Attean. And going up the gangplank first, I turned left towards the stern where four of Theron's men stood at attention now on either side of the Neptunes main entrance. Like the Poseidon on the other dock, the bow of the Neptune was completely covered with armored hose. The enormous mound of coils lashed down to the bows of the two glide-subs now.

Reaching the four sailors in the stern, they snapped us a salute as we waited for Captain Theron to catch up. And passing us, Captain Theron quickly returned his men's salutes before leading us down into the glide-sub. Theron pausing at the bottom of the stairs, as Ajax and I returned the crewmen's salutes now before following Theron down the stairs onto the second deck of the glide-sub. And Theron proceeded to proudly explain the Neptune's layout to us now. The glide-sub had three decks and was divided into two parts. The stern third of the glide-sub, containing the engine room, reactor, and propulsion systems. The front two-thirds, containing the control room and navigations system on the main deck and the second deck where we were standing now, containing their sleeping quarters, dining area, and the galley. The third deck, containing the min-sub, airlock, torpedo room, and defensive systems now.

Stopping at the first door on the left in the passageway, Theron informed me this was his quarters where I would be sleeping. Then he asked me if I wished to sleep now or preferred to have some more wine or tsia before bed. And looking at Nestor and Ajax, they both nodded, and I replied tsia would be good. Continuing forward, the cooks in the galley nodded to Theron as he passed them, then stopped to salute as Ajax, Nestor, and I stepped into the dining room. Returning their salutes now, Theron said, "Tsia, please."

I could hear the two cooks in the galley quickly setting up the tsia and cups now to bring out to us. And nodding solemnly, they stepped forward setting the tray down in front of us before leaving again. Remaining standing, Captain Theron indicated the table in front of us, before saluting and saying, "Please sit your majesty. And if you will excuse me now, I will get the Neptune underway and return in a few minutes, your majesty?"

Returning Theron's salute, I replied, "σ' ευχαριστώ," or thank you in Attean. And turning now, Theron disappeared back down the passageway as Nestor, Ajax, and I all took a seat and poured ourselves a cup of tsia.

And being a man of his word, Captain Theron returned a few minutes later. And exchanging nods again, Theron took a seat with us before stating, "We've cleared the base now and are enroute to the breach. My lieutenant is getting some much-needed time at the helm now, your majesty."

And sipping our tsia, I explained to Theron some of the amazing things that I learned from King Atlas's trident now. And to our surprise, Theron had heard of my meeting with the Wild Ones and the promise I had gotten from their leader Lycus at the meeting.

After my second cup of tsia, I informed the three of them I was ready for bed now, and Captain Theron rose from the table to show me to his cabin. Informing Nestor and Ajax his lieutenant given up his cabin now which had two beds in it. And that we had about six hours now until sunrise and be able to see underwater clearly again.

Taking the trident with me now, I followed Theron back down the passageway to his cabin. And stepping into the room for a moment, Theron quickly showed me the light switches and the alarm button inside his cabin. Then exchanging salutes again, Theron bid me goodnight and left closing the door behind him.

Hours later, I awoke to a light knocking on the door, and Ajax's voice, saying, "It's light enough to see outside now, your majesty."

Sitting up in bed, I replied, "Be out in a moment, cousin." Wiping the sleep from my eyes now, I rose from Theron's bed and picked up the trident again. Opening the door, Ajax saluted me now as I stepped out of Theron's cabin into narrow passageway.

Then grinning, Ajax held out his arm now saying, "There's tsia and breakfast ready for you in the dining room, your majesty."

Returning Ajax's salute, I replied, "Some tsia would be good, but breakfast would seem like the condemned man's last meal now. But lead the way, cousin." Chuckling at my response, Ajax turned and led the way back down the passageway to the dining area.

And stepping into the room. Theron and Nestor both rose from their chairs as I entered, quickly nodding their heads to me before sitting down again with their tsia. And reaching for the tsia pot now, Nestor filled me a cup as he said, "Good morning, your majesty."

And taking a seat, I nodded to both men now and replied, "Good morning, Nestor, Captain Theron."

Returning my nod, Theron said, "You will be happy to know, your majesty. That since sunrise, we have moved within sight of the breach. And my crew uncoiled Ajax's hose and laid it out across the seabed while the Neptune and Poseidon stood guard. So, all the preparations have been made, your majesty."

Taking a sip of my tsia now, I replied, "σ' ευχαριστώ," thanking Captain Theron now. Then looking at Nestor's with a worried face, I sarcastically said, "I'll just stick with tsia this morning Nestor, as

breakfast would feel too much like the condemned man's last meal."
Unfortunately, Nestor didn't find my little joke amusing and
continued to look worried now. Ajax, on the other hand, had a little
more faith that I could do what I said I could do, and grinned now.

Finishing my tsia, I rose and said, "Let's do this my friends." And
Captain Theron rose and nodded his head now before leading the way
back down the passageway with Nestor and Ajax following behind.
We followed Theron to a set of spiral stairs on the starboard side, next
to the same stairs we used to enter the Neptune last night. And
descending the spiral stairs now we followed Theron forward across
to the third deck of the Neptune to the airlock. Passing a large
rectangular glass tank on the starboard side containing the Neptune's
mini sub.

And Captain Theron stopped at the hatch to their circular airlock
on the port side now next to the large hatch in the forward bulkhead.
Which I assumed was their torpedo room. Stopping by Theron, I
untied the cords covering the King Atlas's trident, letting them fall to
the deck as I held the King Atlas's trident now and nodded to Theron.
And Theron turned and spun the handwheel on the airlock
counterclockwise, before Ajax stepped forward now to help Theron
pull the heavy hatch open.

And stepping into the airlock with the trident, Theron stuck his
head inside the airlock pointing to the control box with two buttons on
the wall, before saying, "The red button floods the chamber and the
green one empties it. But neither will work unless both hatches are
fully closed, your majesty."

Then leaning back, Theron and Ajax saluted me, as Nestor nodded
their head. And returning their salutes and nods, I smiled at them now
and said, "Okay!" Then Theron and Ajax closed the hatch again, and I
watched now as the handwheel rotated clockwise until it came to a
stop. And Nestor moved to the observation window to watch. Once
the handwheel stopped, I reached over and hit the red button to flood
the chamber. And I suddenly realized that Nestor had said that the
bio-suits allowed us to breath underwater. But I had never actually
tested that statement now to verify whether it was true or not. So,
when the water in the airlock reached my chest, I knelt down to

confirm that I could actually breathe underwater. And I was pleasantly surprised to discover that I could indeed breathe underwater normally now. And standing back up again, I gave Nestor the thumbs up. Which, to my surprise, made my father-in-law grin now, having figured out what I was doing.

Once the chamber was flooded, I leaned the trident up against the wall, then bent down and cranked the handwheel on the floor hatch counterclockwise until I felt it stop, then using both hands, I pulled the heavy hatch open now. And picking up the trident again, I held it against my chest. As I stepped into the opening and let the weight of my armor and the trident pull me down through the opening now.

Landing on the ocean floor ten feet below the Neptune. I found that I could see clearly and quickly spotted Ajax's armored hose on my right now, stretching north out of sight. Following the hose out past the bow of the Neptune, I spotted the gaping hole of the North Cavern breach on the east slope now. And swimming towards it, the weight of the trident and my armor pulled me down. And looking back at my feet, I could see that my bio-suit had extended itself out past my toes now forming fins. And spreading my webbed fingers out on my left hand now, I found I could keep myself level as I swam towards the breach.

Reaching the opening, I used the trident to show me the breach now. And the breach ran down a quarter mile before opening up into the North Cavern. Closing my eyes, I envisioned the blue defensive shield around me, and when I opened my eyes again found my shield sending up a shower of bubbles now partially blocking my view above. Closing using my left hand now, I shrunk the blue shield down to ten feet in diameter before moving to the center of the breach and floating there.

Then turning to the right, I lifted the south half of the Ajax's hose up off the seabed. And curling the end of the hose back on itself now, I brought it back to me and guided it down into the breach at my feet. And when that half of the hose was inside the breach, I turned and faced north now. Then I picked up the rest of the armored hose and continued feeding it down into the breach until the trident showed me the hose was laying on the cavern floor. And I had about two hundred feet of hose remaining here now outside the breach. Then I picked up a couple of large rocks and set them on top of the hose now, pinning it in place so it couldn't slide into the breach.

And the trident began projecting images in my mind of the dozen or more enormous Kraken lying in the corners of the cavern. Who had begun to move now, alerted by the sound and movement of the armored hose. Confident in the trident, I entered the opening of the breach and began my descent down into the North Cavern now to battle the Kraken. Once I cleared the other end of the breach and entered the cavern, it was completely dark. The only light coming from my glow of my blue shield. And six or seven young 40-foot Kraken, being faster than their larger elders, immediately attacked me thinking I was a free meal. And using my left hand now, I quickly doubled the size of my shield, making it harder for them to grab onto me. One by one, they all tried grabbing my blue shield to eat me before quickly releasing it again, as the blue shield burned their tentacles. And each of the young Kraken had to try it for himself, before retreating to the edges of the cavern to lick their wounds as I moved south towards the head of the cavern.

Next, four 100-foot-long adult Kraken attacked me. And though they each held onto my shield a little longer now, they too eventually withdrew, retreating back to the edges of the cavern again. By that time, their two 150-foot-long grandparents with shells on their backs had moved up under me now and reached up grabbing onto my blue shield and keeping hold of it. Seeming indifferent to the fact that my defensive shield was slowly turning their enormous tentacles into calamari. And they began pulling my shield down now towards their enormous beaks. Those beaks easily large enough to fit my entire shield inside of them now.

And pointing the trident at their open beaks in desperation now, I shot lightning bolts out of the trident into their mouths. The lightning bolts passing clear through the enormous Kraken and their shells now and plowing furrows in the cavern floor behind them. Two blasts into each of the enormous Kraken's open beaks doing the trick. As they released me now and expelled a large cloud of ink before retreating.

I had no wish to kill these mythical creatures. I just needed to drive them out of the North Cavern now and back out into the open sea. But neither was I going to stand by and let myself be swallowed now by one of those enormous Kraken either. Unsure if this shield would hold up under that kind of pressure. And now that I had the Kraken on the run, I began shooting lightning bolts at the bottom of the slopes around the cavern. Basically, using the trident to herd the Kraken towards the breach now. Forcing the Kraken to either exit or be cut to pieces by my lightning bolts.

It took a couple of dozen blasts of lightning from Atlas's trident before the Kraken got the message and began exiting through the breach out into the ocean above. And I kept at it until the trident showed me that the last of the Kraken was fleeing out of the breach. And I followed the last Kraken's enormous shell back out of the opening now from a safe distance.

And what I saw when I cleared the breach was utter chaos. The first of the enormous Kraken had latched onto the Neptune and getting ready to eat it bow first now. While two of the hundred foot adult Kraken had grabbed onto the Poseidon now and were trying to crack it open to see what was inside. Shooting a lightning bolt at the gigantic Kraken on the Neptune first, it released another cloud of ink before letting go of the Neptune now and fleeing south. And while the Neptune righted itself again, I pointed the trident up. And I quickly rose to the aid of the Poseidon now, expanding my shield to twice the size of the adult Kraken as I moved towards them. Fearing they were about to be eaten, the two adult Kraken released the Poseidon now. Shooting out black ink, before fleeing south with the other Kraken. And with both glide-subs out of danger now, I shrunk my shield back down before moving back to the opening of the breach again.

And floating thirty feet above the opening now, I checked to make sure none of the Kraken had gone back into the North Cavern or were still lurking about nearby. Once I was sure the Kraken were gone, I closed my eyes now and used the trident to burn a two foot deep groove straight down the bottom of the breach. And after the salt water had cooled it again, I moved Ajax's armored hose into the groove now. Then picking up several yards of sand from the ocean floor around me, I used it to fill the groove now. Then I melted the top of the sand, holding Ajax's hose in place, and protecting the armored hose from the next step.

Then I pictured the enormous mound of stones on the cavern floor below in my mind. And using the trident now, I lifted the stones up off the muddy bottom. Then I began rotating the pieces of stone around, and the trident helping me now. As I slowly moved the pieces up inside the breach fitting them back together like some gigantic mechanical puzzle now as I filled the breach. And when I had all the pieces fitted together again, I heated the stones with the trident and fused them back together again. Then using fire from the trident again I heated up the surrounding rock everywhere except in the bottom, where the armored hose lay. And I fused the cone-shaped piece in the breach to the surrounding rock, permanently sealed the North Cavern. And hovering there now, I used the trident to check for leaks or any other issues as the rock slowly cooled.

My task completed, I checked the surrounding area for Kraken again but didn't sense any. Obviously, the Kraken haven chosen to go in search of safer waters now. And lowering my shield, I turned and started back to the Neptune, figuring they were probably in need of help now. As I swam back to the sub, I saw the glide-sub suddenly start moving towards me. And I could see three men in the front window clapping each other on the backs now, probably relieved that I was still alive.

Ducking under the Neptune now, I had to push the hatch open again before I could climb back into the airlock. And leaning the trident up against the wall, I closed the floor hatch and cranked it shut again. Then I hit the green button by the door and waited as the water slowly drained out of the airlock and the light above the door changed from red to green.

Picking up the trident, I reached for the handwheel on the inner hatch, but Ajax and Theron were already cranking it open from the other side. And pulling the hatch open, they both grinned and saluted me now in disbelief. Still grinning, Ajax handed me a towel, as Theron asked, "Well, how did it go, your majesty?"

And grinning back at them, I returned their salutes before replying, "Well, there were thirteen Kraken in the North Cavern. Starting at about forty feet and going up to the one hundred and fifty foot ones, as you saw for yourselves. Apparently, I looked like food to the smaller ones because they attacked me immediately. But they quickly let go again as my shield cooked their tentacles." And letting that sink in for a moment, I continued adding, "But those enormous ones didn't care that their tentacles were getting burnt and tried to swallow me whole. But after a couple of dozen lightning bolts from the trident. I managed to persuade the Kraken it was time to leave. Then I reassembled the broken pieces from the breach and fused them back into place, sealing the North Cavern again." Then looking around, I asked, "Where's Nestor?"

Ajax replied now, saying, "The Senior Physician is treating the wounded after we tangled with the Kraken, your majesty."

And I nodded to Ajax as Captain Theron exclaimed now, "Wow! We have lost thirty good men trying do what you just did single-handed with trident, your majesty, Congratulations!" And pausing to nod his head again, Theron added, "I was at the helm when those enormous Kraken came out of the breach and grabbed onto the Neptune. And I saw my whole life flash before my eyes, sure my time was up now, your majesty!" Ajax and I both chuckled at Captain Theron's confession.

And putting my hand on the Theron's shoulder, I admitted, "I was a little nervous myself Captain Theron when those two enormous Kraken grabbed onto my shield and started pulling me down as they fought over which one was going to eat me!" Ajax and Theron chuckled at my confession now. Then looking at Theron again, I said, "Let's head for home, captain. The sooner I get back to the palace, the sooner their majesties will stop worrying!"

Slapping his hand to his chest now, Theron replied, "Right away, your majesty!"

Returning Theron's salute, I reached for the cloth to wrap Atlas's trident back up again. And Ajax and Theron both lent a hand now in getting the trident wrapped back up again. Then turning, Theron led us back to the second deck. And as we climbed, I told Ajax, "I think we should wait a day before beginning pumping out the North Cavern." And reaching the second deck, we followed Theron down the passageway to the dining area now, as I added, "In case the Kraken attempt to return to the cavern tonight or tomorrow morning."

Nodding in agreement behind me, Ajax replied, "I agree, your majesty. One day won't make any difference now that the breach has been repaired. No sense risking our men or glide-subs, your majesty." And as we neared the dining room, Ajax added, "I will inform Captain Theron that it is your wish that they wait until tomorrow night before beginning pumping operations, your majesty."

And I nodded to Ajax as we entered the mess hall now and found Nestor and the Neptune's medic hard at work bandaging up a half dozen of Theron's injured crewmen now. Raising my hand to them to remain seated now, I said, "No need to rise or salute!" And Ajax immediately translating my orders, and Nestor smiled as he calmly put his hands on two of the crewmen holding them down now as they attempted to rise anyway.

Moving to the empty table in the corner, I leaned the trident up in the corner, before sitting down and saying, "Some tsia, and breakfast or lunch would be good now?" Which Ajax quickly translated to the cook standing head bowed in the doorway of the galley. The cook stepped forward whispering into Ajax's ear briefly before nodding his head to Ajax and disappeared back into the galley.

Moving to the table now, Ajax nodded his head and took the seat across from me before saying quietly in English, "The cook apologizes for the wait your majesty. But it will a few minutes as our little encounter with the Kraken has made a shambles of his galley, your majesty." Grinning, I nodded my head to Ajax, knowing it would take six hours to get back to the Glide-sub base, so I wasn't in a hurry anyway.

Breakfast was Attean porridge, toasted bread, honey, and tsia, which I liked. After breakfast, Nestor finished treating the wounded, and after receiving their grateful thanks, sat down with Ajax and me for some tsia. Ten minutes later, Captain Theron joined us again. And informed us that the Neptune was back in order, and enroute to the east airlock now.

And the cook showed up with a fresh pot of tsia and another cup for Captain Theron. And exchanging nods with the cook, he set both down on the table now before returning to the galley. And I asked Theron now, "How are Captain Orius and the Poseidon doing?"

Smiling, Theron replied, "They're fine, your majesty. Orius is a good man and a good captain, which is why I recommended him. And the Poseidon is following behind us now, your majesty."

And speaking up, Nestor asked Theron, "Is there anyone on the Poseidon in need of medical attention, captain?"

Shaking his head negatively, Theron grinned at Nestor now for his dedication to duty before nodding his head to the Senior Physician and replying, "No, but since you were onboard, I did ask Captain Orius. And he said they have a few bumps and bruises, but nothing requiring a physician. But thank you for asking, Nestor." Grinning at Theron, Nestor raised his cup before returning the captain's nod now.

We sat in the dining area for the next six hours discussing the draining of the North Cavern over tsia and lunch. And Captain Theron agreed that we should wait a day before starting pumping. Then we discussed the construction of the airlock in the Caves of Mephisto, the Wild Ones' promises, and the saltwater damage to the soil in the North Cavern, which he agreed must be extensive. After which, I told him of my plan to ask the Elders for their blessing to keep Atlas's trident for another two weeks to repair the soil inside the North Cavern before returning the trident to Atlas's tomb. And Theron stating that the Elders would have to be fools not to agree. After I had driven the Kraken out of the North Cavern and repaired the breach. Which Nestor, Ajax, and I all agreed was a valid point.

Reaching the glide-sub base again, I was surprised to find both the Neptune's and Poseidon's crews waiting for me in formation on the Neptunes dock when we disembarked. The two glide-subs chiefs stepped forward now as their crews saluted and nodded their heads. Then two chiefs nodded their heads now, before the older chiefs said in Attean, "The men would like to thank his majesty now for repairing the breach. As it means, their fellow sailors who lost their lives trying to repair the breach have been avenged and can now rest in peace. And no more lives will be lost trying to reclaim the North Cavern."

Returning their salutes and nods, I said, "Thank you. Her majesty Amy and I were told our first day here in Attea of the lives lost attempting to repair the North Cavern. Which is why, when King Atlas's trident suddenly became available, my first thought was to use it to defeat the Kraken and to repair the breach in the North Cavern. As you men know having rescued her majesty Amy and me from the outlands. We were not raised as royals. And your lives our no less important than mine or anyone else's here in the kingdom." And nodding my head to them again, I added, "And I thank you men now, for your sacrifices, and for your service to the kingdom of Attea." And after Ajax had finished translating my words, the crew of the two glide-subs stomped their feet three times loudly on the dock, saluting and nodding their heads to me in unison again.

I returned their salutes and nods, then Captain Theron held his arm out indicating for us to move up ramp into the base now. And as I turned to climb the ramp, I saw Orius and our five guards standing by the railing now, saluting with heads bowed. Ajax, Theron, and I each returned their salutes and nods as we cleared the ramp and stepped out onto the cobblestone road again. Then the squad leader stepped forward saluting Ajax before leaning in and whispering something into his ear. After which, Ajax stepped back and returned the squad leaders salute.

Then turning to Nestor and me, Ajax saluted and said, "We are ready to go whenever you are, your majesty."

Frowning and nodding his head, Nestor said, "Their majesties have probably begun to worry already now, your majesty."

Returning Ajax's salute, I turned to Captain Theron now and said, "I am afraid Nestor is right, Captain Theron. We need to go now."

Saluting me again, Captain Theron nodded his head and replied, "Captain Orius and I will escort you to the other side of the airlocks, your majesty." And Theron held his arm out towards the tunnel now. Returning Theron's salute, I latched onto Nestor's arm now and led the way into the tunnel. Ajax casually chatted with Captain Theron and Orius as they walked along behind us now followed by our five guards. Ajax complementing them both now and stating how impressed he was with the Neptune and the Poseidon. And asking a couple of engineering questions as we walked towards the airlock. Reaching the airlock, Captain Theron stepped forward now operating the airlocks for us.

And once we were on the other side of the airlocks, we exchanged salutes and nods, before I handed King Atlas's trident to the surprised Nestor. And stepping forward now, exchanged the two-handed clasp of friendship with Captain Theron. Then I stepped over to Captain Orius, and exchanged the two-handed clasp with Orius too, before thanking them both again for their help.

Turning to Nestor, I smiled at Nestor and held my hand out now. And Nestor gladly returned the trident to me, and taking hold of my father-in-law's arm again, we began descending down the long tunnel to the exit. Our guards saluting Captain Theron and Orius now before following Nestor and me. And Ajax stayed behind for a minute to exchange handshakes and farewells with Theron and Orius, before quickly descending the stairs catching up with Nestor and me again.

And reaching the great hall below, we stopped just long enough to exchange salutes, and for Ajax to tell Hektor and his men now of the defeat of the Kraken and the repair the North Cavern. And of the Kraken's attack on the Neptune and Poseidon, and my rescue of the two glide-subs. And Hektor congratulated us, stating he was glad no more men would be lost trying to reclaim the North Cavern.

Then parting ways by the portcullis at the entrance. Nestor and I waited as Ajax and Hektor exchanged the two-handed clasp of friendship again and Ajax bid his old mentor farewell now. Turning around, Ajax ordered our guards out into flanking positions again. As we followed the wagon trail back around the cavern to north side and the same spot we came down through the vineyards yesterday. Once we climbed back up into the olive grove again and reached that foot trail leading back to the palace. Ajax found an olive tree where we could all sit in the shade together and called a stop.

The cooks at the Glide-sub base had refilled the guards' bota bags and filled a couple of sacks with sandwiches and fruit for our return trip. Sitting under the olive tree we all took a short break. And after eating a sandwich and drinking from the bota bags. We got up again and headed for the palace, which was plainly visible ahead now.

Reaching the east wall of the palace, Ajax ordered the guards to fan out and watch the hillside again while he searched the wall for the chipped stone. After a minute Ajax found it, and quickly checked the hillside and our guards again, before pushing the fourth stone down. The secret passage audibly unlocked now before the section of wall popped out an inch. And grabbing the section of wall now, Ajax pulled it free from the other stones, before grabbing the back of the door and swinging it open. Then stepping up into the passageway, Ajax opened the inner door now letting the light from the garden flood into the secret passageway.

Then stepping back outside, Ajax indicated for Nestor and me to enter first. And once we were up in the passageway, Ajax ordered the guard to follow us in now. When all five guards were in, Ajax grabbed the handle on the outer door and pulled it shut with an audible click. And stepping back into the garden, Ajax ordered the guards to "attention," again, then "about face" as he closed the inner door now in the garden. And I watched as the fourth stone down moved slightly as Ajax closed and locked the inner door to the passageway again.

Then grinning at Nestor and me now, Ajax turned around and ordered our guards to reform before starting across the garden for the East Atrium. And climbing the stairs up to the royal chambers, we found four royal guards outside the royal chamber doors now. Pylos having doubled the guard in my absence. Ajax and our guards saluting me now as Nestor nodded outside my chambers. And handing Nestor the trident again, I exchanged the two-handed clasp of friendship with Ajax now, and he congratulated me again on successfully reclaiming the North Cavern. And relieving Nestor of the trident, we exchanged our farewells. And Nestor excused himself now, eager to go report to the Elders that I had driven the Kraken out and repaired the North Cavern with the trident, even though it was late. That, and having done it now without losing a single Attean life this time.

Chapter - 24

Opening the inner doors to the royal chambers, I was greeted by the nods of Agis and the stewards who were lined up on the left by my chamber door. And I returned their nods, the door to the Lady's chamber on the right opened as Amy, Sandra, and Petra walked into the room followed by the handmaids. Ignoring everyone in the room, Amy and Sandra ran forward nearly tackling me as they grabbed me and hugged me now with tears glistening in their eyes. Smiling at them, I returned their hugs and kisses. Then, with my free hand, I wiped the tears from Amy's face before kissing her sweetly on the lips. And turning to Sandra, I wiped the tears from Sandra's smiling face now before kissing her on the lips too. Agis, Petra, and the servants' all grinning now as they calmly looking the other way.

Then stepping back, Amy put her hands on her hips and Sandra mimicked her pose now as Amy frowned and asked, "Well, since you're standing here, husband. Should we assume that you successfully repaired in the North Cavern now?"

Putting my arm across my stomach, I bowed to my two beautiful wives now, replying, "Yes, my loves. It was a complete success!" Dropping their hands, Amy and Sandra both smiled as they moved forward hugging me again and congratulating me. Chuckling, I kissed the top of their heads now as they clung to me.

Then Agis nodded and cleared his throat, before saying, "You still has enough time for a bath and a change of clothes before dinner, if you wish your majesty?"

Amy and Sandra leaned now giving me a quick sniff before nodding to Agis and answering, "He does!"

Grinning, I nodded to Agis and said, "You heard their majesties, Agis. Lead on!" And parting company with my lovely wives now, I followed Agis and the stewards into my dressing room where they removed my armor, then Agis led me across the hall for my bath. And after a minute the three young ladies entered and nodded, then they sat their trays down and removed my bathrobe. After my bath, Agis led me back into my dressing room. Where the stewards quickly dressed me in a sky blue tunic with a gold seahorse on the front and a matching blue sash. Then nodding again, Agis led me back into the main chamber just as the cooks arrived outside with our dinner.

And after seating Amy and Sandra at the table, I proceeded to down two full glasses of wine before starting on dinner. And seeing this, Amy and Sandra asked me now if I was planning on getting plastered tonight to celebrate my success in the North Cavern.

So, as we ate our dinner now, I related to my wives all the events from when I left yesterday up to the dry hot walk back from the airlock this afternoon. Amy and Sandra were both stunned and surprised when I told them the actual size of the Kraken in the North Cavern, and of my battle with the giant Kraken. Both of which were angry at me now for risking my life, but glad it was over. And there wasn't anything left to do other than remove the salt from the inside of the North Cavern. Though it meant I would have to leave them for a week to travel to the Caves of Mephisto and back again to accomplish it. But we had still twenty days before the glide-subs finished pumping out of North Cavern and the workers finished the new airlock.

The next day over tsia with Nestor and Ajax. Nestor informed me that after my success against the Kraken and the repair of the North Cavern. The Elders decided that I was more than welcome to keep Atlas's trident for as long as I deemed it necessary to fix the North Cavern. Or anything else, that I thought needed fixing in the Kingdom. Ajax and I both chuckled upon hearing this, and Nestor joined us.

Then I asked Ajax to have Captain Hyllus raise the white flags out at the canopy now. So, we could meet with Lycus to discuss the terms of the Wild one's pardons, and Lycus's duties as the Mayor of the North Cavern. And I asked Nestor to have Lycus's appointment as Mayor of the North Cavern drawn up now and ready to sign by the end of the day. And since the recovery of the North Cavern was drawing near. Nestor informed me that the city in the North Cavern was called Cadiz, and the fortress at the north end named Hermes.

The next few days seemed to drag on now as we waited for the work on the North Cavern to be completed. My only distraction and pleasure being my beautiful wives, who were both glowing now. But on the third day, Pylos appeared during our morning tsia to inform me that Lycus and the Wild one chiefs were out in the canopy drinking our wine now.

After Agis and the steward dressed in my armor. Pylos escorted me down to the palace courtyard where Ajax, Nestor, and a full squad of the royal guards waited for us. And marching down to the city, our guards formed their phalanx around us now as we entered the city. This time though, we were greeted by throngs of cheering Atteans in the streets and blue and gold banners waving down at us from above.

Apparently the news of the Krakens' defeat and the repair of the North Cavern had spread through the kingdom. Reaching the city gates, Captain Hyllus's and two full squads of Spearmen greeted our phalanx with three loud smacks of their spears, followed a loud growl from the Archers above as we stopped in front of the main gates. And after our phalanx came to a stop, our royal guards smacked their spears on the ground three times loudly in response to warm welcome from the city guards now.

As our phalanx parted to let Captain Hyllus and his lieutenant in, I smiled at Hyllus and his lieutenant as we exchanged salutes. And chuckling at Hyllus now, I said, "I am about to go promote your cousin above you, my friend. Any last words, Captain Hyllus?"

Smiling back now, Hyllus nodded his head and replied, "No, your majesty. But after to think it over, I decided that I would rather salute my cousin than shove a xiphos in his guts, your majesty."

Nodding my head to Hyllus now, I replied, "A wise decision, my friend." Pylos and Ajax both nodded their heads now agreeing with Hyllus's decision. And since everyone knew about the trident, I untied the cords and handed both the cloth and cords to Pylos now. Who accepted them, though Ajax and Pylos both gave me a puzzled look now. And turning to Nestor now, I asked, "You feel up to a little walk, my friend?"

Surprised now, Nestor nodded his head and replied, "Certainly, your majesty." And Nestor held up the scroll with Lycus's appointment as the new Mayor of the North Cavern now.

Then turning to Pylos now, I said, "No offense cousin, but I need my Chief Advisor's for the meeting today." Ajax and Pylos both saluted now, knowing we were perfectly safe as long as I had King Atlas's trident in my hand.

Returning my cousin's nods, I smiled at Nestor now and held my arm out towards the gate saying, "Shall we?" Nodding again, Nestor and I started for the front gate as all the soldiers saluted and the Atteans bowed now. Quickly returning their salutes and bows, Nestor and I walked out the gates now.

It was a good twenty minute walk out to the canopy. And I was expecting Nestor to be a little apprehensive, but he seemed calm considering the situation. Maybe after having seen the power of the trident, Nestor realized that we were perfectly safe now, and it was the Wild Ones who should be afraid.

As we neared the canopy, to our surprise Lycus and his chieftains rose and bowed to us now. And Lycus put his hand on his chest and remained bowed as he said, "Welcome, your majesty."

Nodding my head in return, I indicated the chairs before saying, "Please sit, Lycus." And waiting until Nestor and I had sat down, Lycus nodded again and slid into the chair across from us now.

Then Lycus said, "Our spies informed us that your majesty has defeated the Kraken and repaired the breach in North Cavern now. As you said you would, your majesty?"

Speaking up now, Nestor replied, "Your spies are well informed?"

Shaking his head now, Lycus replied, "Not really, one need only sit in any local Kapeleia for an hour to overhear the news which has spread throughout all of Attea now."

Grinning at Lycus, I asked, "So, are the Wild Ones ready to obey the laws of Attea and live in peace from now on, in exchange for their pardons and the North Cavern to call home?"

Holding up his finger, Lycus quickly translated my words to his three chieftains, who nodded their heads now to Lycus, and who in turn nodded his head to me now. And turning to Nestor, I said, "Okay Nestor. Please read Lycus's his appointment as the new Mayor of the North Cavern now."

Reaching into his medical pouch at his waist, Nestor retrieved the scroll now. And breaking the wax seal on the now, Nestor opened it and began to read it now, saying, "From this day fourth, Lycus, leader of the Wild Ones is fully pardoned of all crimes he may have committed in the past. And is hereby appointed Mayor of the city of Cadiz, and entire North Cavern of Attea. With the understanding that Mayor Lycus will be held accountable for keeping the peace and any acts of violence committed by the Wild Ones from this day forth. Signed, His royal majesty Andrew Tallfer, King of Attea and all the people within." After which, Nestor passed the scroll to Lycus now, so he could read it for himself and see my signature and seal below.

When Lycus had finished reading the scroll, Nestor held out his hand out. And Lycus nodded his head as he handed the scroll back to Nestor again. Then pointing my finger at the gold crown on my head now, as I asked Lycus, "Are you ready to swear allegiance to this crown Lycus, and accept the responsibilities that goes with your appointment as the new Mayor of the North Cavern?"

Rising from his chair, Lycus dropped to one knee and bowed his head now, replying, "I am, your majesty."

And rising from my chair now, I said, "Do you Lycus, leader of the Wild Ones, swear from this day forward, to follow the Laws of Attea, be loyal to king and crown, and ensure to the best of your ability as Mayor of the Cadiz and the North Cavern that the Wild Ones live in peace from this day forth?"

Looking up at me, Lycus nodded his head, and said, "Ποιῶ!" I do.

Smiling at Lycus now, I said, "Well, stand up Mayor Lycus." And taking the scroll from Nestor's hand now, handed it to Lycus. Who nodded his head as he accepted his appointment from my hand now. Then moving left to the end of the table as Lycus moved right, we met on the end. And switching the trident to my left hand now, I extended my right out to Lycus, and we shook on it.

As we shook hands, Lycus's bio-suit suddenly started to change color. The white stripes on his head and chest fading away as the top half of his bio-suit from his waist up changed from dark grey to a sandy-gold color now, and Lycus's lower half changed to a chocolate brown color. And Nestor and I stood there frozen, while Lycus's chieftains stepped back gasping in surprise now.

Nodding his head, Lycus held up the scroll as he looked down at his changed bio-suit now, and said, "Thank you, your majesty. I swear I shall not fail you, my king."

Grinning at Lycus, I returned his nod replying, "I know, Mayor Lycus. Nestor has told us of Lady Amara and your son."

Smiling brightly, Lyus said, "It's true, your majesty. Lady Amara and I are very much in love, and we have a fine son whom I hope you will meet one day, your majesty." And changing the subject now, Lycus continued adding, "I did not kill Amara's husband Laios, as generally believed. Nor do I know who did. But Laios, being from a wealthy family, grew up with Prince Helios and was one of Helios's companions. And Laios drank too much and talked too much. Often bragging about his friendship with Prince Helios. I suspect now that Helios either killed Laios himself or had him killed, knowing that I would get blamed for it, your majesty."

Nodding in agreement with Lycus, I replied, "That has the ring of truth to it and makes sense, Mayor Lycus." And looking at Nestor, he nodded his head now agreeing that it sounded true to him too.

Looking at Lycus again, I said, "Twelve days from now, we expect the North Cavern to be drained, and the airlock completed. Then I will go into the North Cavern and use Atlas's trident to try and remove all the salt from the soil inside the cavern. So, things will grow again inside the cavern." And pausing to take a breath and let that sink in, I continued now adding, "Can you have all the Wild Ones assembled in the Crossroads that afternoon? Once we open the cavern, and I remove the salt. I will accept the Wild one's oaths and hand out their pardons."

And quickly speaking with his chieftains. Lycus asked them if they agreed to assemble all their people at the Crossroads in twelve days, and give their oaths of peace to me in exchange for their pardons? The chieftains reluctantly agreed, though they expressed concern that this could be some sort of trap that we were setting for them now. And unrolling his appointment scroll now Lycus handed it to them first. Then Lycus angrily shouted at them now. That I, the King, promised them I would defeat the Kraken, repair the North Cavern, and appoint Lycus as its new Mayor. And having kept my word and proven myself, they should trust their king now. And recoiling from Lycus's sudden outburst, they all quickly nodded in agreement.

Then turning back to me, Lycus put his on his chest again and bowed before, saying, "It will be done, your majesty."

Returning Lycus's bow now, I replied, "Thank you, Mayor Lycus. And your free to come into Attea and see Lady Amara and your son anytime you wish?"

Nodding his head again, Lycus replied, "As much as I want to see my beloved Amara and son, your majesty. I must see to my new duties as Mayor first. And go with the chieftains now to convince the Wild Ones in my restored bio-suit, that I am still their leader. And make sure that every Wild One in the kingdom is at the crossroads in twelve days. Ready to give their oaths, and receive their pardons, your majesty."

Returning Lycus's nod, I said, "Understood, Mayor Lycus. And I will see you in twelve days, my friend." Then turning to Nestor I said, "Shall we head back now, Nestor?" And Nestor nodded his head in agreement as the three chieftains bowed to us now. And returning their bows, as Nestor and I turned now and started back to the city.

Once we got out of earshot of the Lycus and the Wild Ones, Nestor said, "You were right your majesty, Lycus is impressive, and I think he will make a great Mayor, your majesty." Chuckling now, Nestor asked, "Did you see the fear on those chieftains faces when Lycus reprimanded them for suggesting that this might be a trap, and not trusting you, your majesty?"

Smiling as we walked along, I replied, "Yes, and I tried my best not to grin at them." Nodding his head again, Nestor and I walked along enjoying fresh air and the scenery now. With the crops covered fields on our right, and orchards and vineyards covering the hills to our left, and the city of Attea looming up in front of us now.

And no surprise, Ajax, Pylos, and Captain Hyllus were all standing outside the gates now waiting on our return. And after exchanging salutes, Ajax asked, "How did it go, your majesty?"

And as we walked back in through the gates now, I replied, "Good, Mayor Lycus has agreed to have all the Wild Ones assembled at the Crossroads in twelve days. Ready to give their oaths and promises of peace in exchange for their pardons."

Grinning and shaking his head now, Captain Hyllus repeated my words, muttered, "Mayor Lycus?"

And we all turned to look at Hyllus, as I said, "Yes, and don't forget to salute your cousin if he should drop in to visit Lady Amara and his son, or his parents, Captain Hyllus?" And as the four of us chuckling now, I added, "Mayor Lycus has sworn his oath to me already, and has been officially appointed the new Mayor of the North Cavern now. Oh, and Lycus's bio-suit changed to a sandy-gold and brown color as we shook hands."

Speaking up quickly, Hyllus said, "Yes, that was the color of Lycus's bio-suit before he fled the city, your majesty." Nestor and I both nodded our heads acknowledging Hyllus's statement.

Turning to Pylos now, I said, "Okay cousin, take us back to the palace, please?" And after exchanging salutes with Hyllus and his lieutenant again, we moved back into our little pocket inside the phalanx. Then raising a hand in farewell, Pylos ordered our phalanx to reform. And nodding to Pylos, he gave the order to move out now for the palace. And we were greeted by thousands of bowing Atteans on the streets again or leaning out from the windows above. Cheering and waving blue and gold banners down at us as we passed through the center of Attea again. Once we rounded the first corner of switchbacks up to the palace. Pylos barked out the order for our formation to open up again as we climbed the hill back up to the palace gates. And I leaned over to Nestor now, asking, "Are the people going to greet their majesties and me like that from now on?"

And leaning in, Nestor replied, "Yes, your majesty. The people know you are a great King. Having rid them of the Prince Helios and securing the throne now. Plus, defeating the Kraken and repairing the North Cavern to give it to the Wild Ones. Ending decades of killings and raiding of their merchant wagons. We are all grateful now, your majesty."

Grinning now, I told Nestor, "Well, I am happy to be of service to Attea and its people finally. And earn the respect that you all have shown their majesties and me, my friend."

Shaking his head, Nestor grinned and said, "Sometimes you amaze me, your majesty. And it makes me happy to know that her majesty Sandra is married to a man like you, your majesty."

And I replied, "In case you weren't sure before, I am very much in love with Sandra now, and I couldn't imagine my life without her."

Nodding again, Nestor said, "That wonderful news, and it makes me proud and grateful, your majesty." Returning Nestor's nod now, I patted him on the arm as we passed through the gates into the palace again. And reaching the center of the cobblestone courtyard, Pylos ordered a halt, then he ordered the front of the formation to split now clearing a path for us to the keep's entrance. And turning to Pylos, Ajax winked at him before informing Pylos he would see me back to my chambers. And Pylos saluted now acknowledging Ajax orders.

Then turning to Nestor and me now, Ajax saluted us before saying, "If you and the Senior Physician are ready, your majesty?" And Ajax extended his arm out towards the keep in front of us now.

Getting a nod from Nestor, I returned Ajax's salute now replying, "We are cousin, lead the way." And nodding again, Ajax barked out order for the first row of royal guards to form up for escort duty now. And the first four guards from either side of the formation came running forward now, four moving to the front, and four stepping to the rear. And a few seconds later, Ajax gave the order to moveout, as I heard Pylos behind us now bark out, "Reform, attention, and dismissed."

Reaching the royal chambers, we exchanged salutes, before Ajax left with the escort. Pausing there for a moment, I asked Nestor if he and Lady Sophia could join us for dinner tonight. And Nestor graciously accepted again, saying it would be their pleasure.

And bidding Nestor farewell, I entered the royal chambers to find Agis and the stewards standing ready now. Returning their nods, I followed them into the dressing room now. And after leaning Atlas's trident back up against my display of swords on the wall, I stepped up onto the podium to let the steward remove my armor and slip my bathrobe over my shoulders. Then I followed Agis across the hall into the bathing room. And once I was clean, the stewards dressed me in a dark blue tunic with medium blue sash, before Agis led me back out into the sitting area again. Where I found a fresh pot of tsia and cup sitting on the coffee table waiting for me. Returning his nod, I thanked Agis and let him know Nestor and Lady Sophia would be joining us for dinner tonight. Smiling and nodding his head now, Agis turned and left the room again. And after a cup of tsia, I stretched out on the couch to catch a quick nap before dinner.

Dinner was good, and I let Nestor tell Amy and Sandra what happened out at the canopy today with Lycus and the three Wild one chieftains. After which, Amy and Sandra asked Sophia if she would speak to Lady Amara and offer them the use of the palace garden now to get married in. As they figured that would happen quickly, now that Lycus had been pardoned and appointed Mayor of the Cadiz and the North Cavern. As Amy and Sandra both wished to attend Mayor Lycus's and Lady Amara's wedding now. Nestor and I sat back quietly now enjoying a couple of carafes of wine while the women talked for an hour about Amara's and Lycus's romance, and their expected wedding.

After which, I asked my two wives if they had heard anything lately about Lady Kassandra and Brigadier Ajax? And to my surprise it was Lady Sophia who answered now. Saying that Lady Ismene had informed her that Ajax had been over to dinner once and taken Kassandra out for dinner twice. Also, they have gone out for walks three or four times now. And though Ajax is shy around other people, apparently he isn't shy when they're alone. And judging from what Kassandra has told Ismene, Kassandra is in love with Ajax now, and was just waiting for Ajax to ask her, to accept his proposal.

Grinning wickedly at Nestor, he grinned back at me now nodding his head. And I volunteered to give Ajax a little nudge in the right direction now with the proposal. Which put a smile on the women's faces now, as they all envisioned Ajax on his knee proposing to Kassandra. And Sandra offered to invite Kassandra and Cressida for dinner tomorrow night, while Amy agreed to invite Ajax and Pylos. Though Nestor and Sophia declined to join us, saying that dinner was for our generation. Sophia content to wait until the following day to get all the juicy details from their majesties.

The next morning after my usual breakfast with my wives, my bath, and a change of clothes. I met with Nestor and Ajax over tsia again, as they updated me on the progress out at the North Cavern. After receiving their reports that everything was proceeding on schedule, and that the North Cavern should be ready in eleven days. I surprised Ajax now by changing the subject and asking, "So how is Lady Kassandra doing these days, cousin?" Nestor and Ajax both nearly blowing tsia out of our noses and Ajax face turning brown under his green bio-suit now as he blushed. Nestor and I both covered our faces now as we tried to conceal our laughter.

Regaining his composure, Ajax calmly replied, "Splendid, your majesty,"

Leaning in, I gave Ajax a serious look now before saying, "That's good, cousin. Because last night at dinner their majesties asked which you would rather face. A thousand charging Wild Ones, or having to make an honest woman out of Kassandra now and propose to her?"

This time Nestor did snort his tsia out his nose, quickly covering his face as he tried to hide his laughter. Ajax, on the other hand, was stunned speechless, unable or unsure how to respond now to a direct question about Kassandra's and his love life.

While Ajax was frozen, trying to figure out how to respond to my question. I didn't show him any mercy, and taking a quick sip of tsia now, I asked him, "What should I tell their majesties, Ajax. Or would you rather wait and answer them yourself tonight?"

Finally recovering, Ajax replied, "I am very fond of Kassandra, and that thought has been on my mind of late, your majesty."

Nodding to Ajax, I said, "Good. After you propose to Kassandra, and she says yes. Let me know, and I will have Nestor pick out a selection of the royal jewels for you to choose Kassandra's wedding present from now."

Returning my nod, Ajax replied, "That is very generous of you, your majesty. I hadn't gotten that far in mind yet, but thank you, your majesty!"

Grinning at Ajax, I said, "Your family Ajax and welcome!"

Later at lunch with Amy and Sandra, I told them about my meeting with Ajax and Nestor. And the little nudge I gave Ajax today at the meeting. Amy and Sandra both took Ajax's side now. Amy saying that I was shameless, while Sandra said I was cruel to tease Ajax that way. Though both were excited now to see what happens tonight when Kassandra learns what I had asked Ajax this morning.

After lunch, my wives retreated to their private chambers with Petra again. While I stretched out on the couch to catch a nap before dinner. And I lay there with my hands behind my head, thinking about the long walk out to the caves of Mephisto now. Which would take the six days, there and back again. Plus, however long it took inside the North Cavern, and receiving the Wild Ones' oaths afterwards. Which was six days more than I cared to spend away from my lovely wives. Thinking too bad there wasn't a faster mode of travel here in Attea.

Finally nodding off, I dreamed of my fight with Prince Helios in Atlas's tomb again. And as the dream unfolded, at one point as Prince Helios and I exchanged blows, Helios was outlined by the large yellow platter on the wall behind him. And when the dream ended, the image of that large yellow platter on the wall of the tomb stuck in my mind. Seeming to trigger some memory in the back of my mind, like I had seen it before, but I just couldn't remember where now?

Sitting up, I poured myself another cup of lukewarm tsia as I tried remembering where I had seen the five-foot wide yellow platter before. Then suddenly it dawned on me, it was in the slideshow of Atlas's life. And rising from the couch now, I entered my private chambers and paused at the open door on the left. As Agis and the three stewards all rose and nodded their heads. And I held my hand out for them to sit again as I returned their nods and said, "Remain seated please, I just need to check something with the trident now. Relax and enjoy your tsia." And nodding again, they sat back down, as I smiled and moved down the hall to my dressing room.

Crossing the room, I picked up Atlas's trident from off the sword display now. And turning to face the door again, I raised my left hand and brought up the slideshow of King Atlas's life again. Waiting until the slideshow reached the end. I used my left hand now as I began swiping the images to the left, working my way back through Atlas's life looking for the enormous yellow platter. And finding it, I was surprised to see King Atlas and two of his advisors riding through the air on the platter like a magic carpet inside their blue shield. After watching this for a few moments, I started swiping left again back through Atlas life until I reached the image where Atlas's advisors presented the King with the large yellow platter. Which was made of the same material as the tiles covering the palace's roof, which they called "orichalcum." And I watched now as Atlas's advisors instructed the King on how to make the platter rise and fly. Like everything else, it was just a matter of envisioning it in your mind, then using your hand to control the platter's movements.

And waving my left hand outwards now, I made the slideshow disappear again. Then setting the trident back down, I turned and walked back down to the hall to the steward's breakroom.

And rising from their chairs again, they quickly nodded as Agis asked, "How may we be of service, your majesty."

Returning their nods, I said, "I need my armor on, and for you to send for Brigadier Ajax and my escort now please, Agis. I need to go out to King Atlas's tomb now."

Nodding his head, Agis replied, "Understood, your majesty." And Agis and the stewards went to work. Stepping forward, Agis pulled the purple ribbon on the wall before holding his arm out, indicating for me to step back into my dressing room so they could get me into armor again. And while the stewards fitted me into my armor, one of the royal guard appeared in the doorway, and spoke briefly with Agis before saluting Agis and disappearing again.

Dressed in my armor now, I returned the stewards nods and thanked them. Then taking the trident, I followed Agis back out into the main chamber to await Ajax and my personal bodyguard arrival.

Ten minutes later, Agis walked back into the chamber and stopped to nod as he announced Brigadier Ajax was outside. And rising from the couch, I returned Agis's nod, then picking up the trident, and replied, "Thank you Agis, I can get the door now."

Nodding again, Agis turned and went back into my private chambers closing the door behind him. Crossing to the inner doors now, I opened the righthand door to find Ajax standing inside the entryway. And snapping me a salute now, Ajax said, "Your majesty?"

Grinning at my cousin, I returned his salute saying, "I learned something new about the trident today. And I need to go to Atlas's tomb and to test it out now."

Nodding again, Ajax replied, "At your service, your majesty."

And smiling at Ajax, I replied, "Thank you, cousin." And Ajax turned and opened the outer door, leading the way out into the hallway now where my personal bodyguards stood waiting heads bowed. Then Ajax led the way down the stairs and across the atrium. The two guards by the doors stepping forward to open doors for us and nodding their heads as we went out the doors. Crossing the terrace, we went down the steps and into the garden now. Ajax made a beeline now for Atlas's tomb. And he didn't stop until we reached the steps at the tomb. Where he turned around to face us again.

Stepping up to Ajax now, I said, "I need the guards to go down into the tomb and remove the giant yellow platter hanging on the south wall and bring it out into the garden now." Snapping me a salute now, Ajax turned and repeated my instructions to the guards. And all five men snapping Ajax a salute now acknowledging his orders. And after Ajax returned their salutes, the guards turned and disappeared down into the tomb.

A couple of minutes later, the guards returned carrying enormous yellow platter between the four of them, their squad leader following behind carrying their spears now. Coming out of the tomb, the four guards carried the platter down the steps and out into the garden. And I noticed fours short, curled feet on the bottom of the platter as the guards set it down in the grass to the left of the walkway. Then facing Ajax and me on steps, the five guards saluted. After which, the squad leader quickly handed them back their spears. Ajax and I returned their salutes, then I led the way over to the platter in the grass now.

Reaching the platter, I turned to Ajax and said, "The trident showed me that I can fly with this platter, cousin. But since the guards have never seen me use the trident before. You might want to warn them that I'm going to attempt to fly now using this platter? So, they don't panic."

Nodding his head, Ajax chuckled now replying, "Sound advice, your majesty. Though we might have gotten a good laugh out of the look of panic and terror on their faces, your majesty."

Grinning at Ajax, I shook my head now and replied, "Tempting, cousin. But as King now, I am obliged not to terrorize my subjects, especially those who are loyal to me."

Nodding his head again, Ajax replied, "True, your majesty." Then turning to the guards, Ajax told them I was going to attempt to fly now using Atlas's trident and the platter they had just brought up from the tomb. So, Ajax told them to hold their ground now and not to be too surprised when his majesty flies.

Snapping Ajax another salute now, Ajax returned their salutes as I stepped up onto the platter now and said, "You might want to back up a few steps, cousin?" Nodding, Ajax barked out the order for the guards to back up and spread out. And the guards didn't need any encouragement following Ajax's orders now.

Once Ajax and the men were back a good ten feet, I closed my eyes and envisioned my blue defensive shield around me. And as my shield appeared, the guards involuntarily took a couple more steps back. Then using my left hand, I shrunk the shield down around me now, so that it just covered the platter and me. And glancing down at my feet, I noticed a large pair of winged sandals engraved into the top of the platter now, which made sense to me, and I nodded my head. Next, I envisioned the platter rising up off the ground, and it did to my relief, hovering several feet off the ground now. All five of the guards gasping in surprise as they involuntarily took a couple more steps back.

And raising my left hand slowly, the platter began to rise now, until I was a good hundred feet off the ground. Then holding my left hand out in front of me now, I was afraid the rest of the Attea would have the same reaction as my guards below. So, I moved my hand to the left slightly, turning the platter east. Then extending my arm out I started flying east. And experimenting a little now, I shoved my arm out further and pulled it back, as my speed increased and decreased again. It was intoxicating, and I thoroughly enjoyed flying on the platter towards the east end of the cavern. And I decided to take a quick lap around the east end of the cavern now before returning to the garden where my guards waited nervously. And I chuckled now as I accelerated and swung around the east end of the cavern before swinging back to the north again to avoid the city, and approaching the garden from the south now, so I wouldn't freak out the guards patrolling the walls.

And I slowly brought the platter back down in the same spot I had taken off from. As my five guards, getting over their initial surprise, looked a little more relaxed now as I set the platter back down on the grass of the garden again.

Stepping off the platter now, I smiled at Ajax and said, "That is so much fun it should be a crime, cousin! You should really try this Ajax while we still have the trident." And giving me a look of dismay, Ajax shook his head "no" now. And I chuckling at Ajax, as I added, "Too bad, we can fly to the Crossroads in an hour with this platter, Ajax."

Saluting me again now, Ajax replied, "I'll take your word for it, your majesty. But I prefer to keep my feet on the ground!"

And grinning at Ajax, I said, "Have the guards put the platter on top of the stairs, then we can head back in. So, you have time to prepare for dinner tonight with Kassandra and their majesties."

Ignoring my jab, Ajax turned and ordered the five amazed guards to put the flying platter back up on top of stairs now and leave it there. And exchanging salutes with Ajax, the five guards nervously approached the flying platter. Poking it with the butt of their spears first a couple of times to make sure it wouldn't move now. Then bending down, the guards picked up the platter again and carried it back to the top of the stairs before setting it down on the right. After the guards came back down, Ajax ordered them to form up and we headed back to the royal chambers. I felt good about the successful test of the flying platter. Too bad we had to return Altas's trident to the tomb, though I knew it was the right thing to do.

Chapter - 25

Ajax and the guards delivered me back to my royal chambers. And parting at the doors, I told Ajax I would see him later at dinner. Then stepping back into the royal chambers, Agis was standing by my chamber door head bowed. Returning Agis's nod, he held out his arm out indicating the stewards were waiting to remove my armor now. Then nodding again, Agis turned and led the way down the hallway to the dressing room. Though the stewards wouldn't come anywhere near me as long as I was holding the trident. Crossing the room now, I leaned Atlas's trident back up against the wall before stepping onto the podium. And while the stewards removed my armor. I told them now of using Atlas's orichalcum platter to fly around the whole east end of the cavern to their shock and amazement.

Then Agis led me back out into the sitting area again. And knowing my habits well, Agis asked me if I preferred tsia or wine before dinner. And I told Agis wine now since I was celebrating my successful flight with the trident. Shaking his head slightly, I could tell Agis was still trying to get over the thought of me flying. Then nodding again, Agis said he would be back shortly with my wine.

I was on my second cup of wine when my lovely wives stepped out of their private chambers with Petra, pausing by the door to smile and nod at me on the couch. Rising, I returned their nods and held my arm out now inviting them to join me. Eager to tell them of my successful flight today while we waited for dinner guests to arrive.

And I told them of my dream this afternoon, and of making the connection with the large yellow platter in Atlas's tomb. Then I told them of my successful flight around the east end of the cavern. Of course, Amy was eager to try it. Though concerned how safe it was considering the precious cargo she was carrying now. Sandra on the other hand was terrified at the thought of flying. But willing to give it a try now, if Amy was going to fly.

I was still describing my flight to my wives when Agis stepped into the room to inform us that Pylos and Cressida were waiting outside. Helping Amy and Sandra up off the couches, we all rose to greet our cousins. And returning Agis's nod, I asked him to show our cousins in. Pylos and Cressida smiling as they entered the room, and we quickly exchanged salutes and bows. Then Amy and Sandra stepped forward greeting Cressida, as I stepped forward exchanging the two-handed clasp of friendship with Pylos. And as Pylos and I stepped back, the woman suddenly got loud now and began hugging each other again before touching Cressida's stomach. And turning to look at Pylos, I asked, "Judging from their majesties reactions, I'm assuming congratulations are in order now, cousin?"

Grinning and nodding his head, Pylos replied, "Yes, your majesty. Cressida just learned today that she is expecting now."

And thumping my fist on Pylos shoulder three times now, I smiled at Pylos and said, "That's wonderful news, Pylos. I'm happy for you and Cressida!" And as Pylos nodded his head in thanks now, I asked, "How did your father-in-law, the General, react when you informed him he was going to be a grandfather?"

Smiling now, Pylos leaned in and whispering, "After we shook hands, Aetolus stepped forward and gave me a hug, your majesty!"

And looking at Pylos in surprise now, I replied, "Wow! That is a surprise. And high praise from your father-in-law, Pylos!" And nodded his head again now, Pylos grinned back at me.

Stepping into the room now, Agis nodded before saying "Brigadier Ajax and the Lady Kassandra are outside now, your majesties."

Smiling at Agis, I returned his nod and replied, "Thank you Agis, would you show them in please?" And nodding again, Agis moved to the front doors opening them for Ajax and Kassandra. And we were all pleasantly surprised to see Kassandra's hand on Ajax's arm now, and Kassandra smiling as Ajax led her into the room. Then stopping, Kassandra bowed now as Ajax saluted. Amy and Sandra quickly returned Kassandra's bow, while Pylos and I returned Ajax's salute. And the stewards stepped into the room from the left now and nodded their heads while we were exchanging greeting in the center of the room. Then Petra and the handmaids entered from the right, and all stopped to nod, so I knew that dinner was outside now.

Nodding to the left and the right, I turned to the ladies and my cousins now, and held out my arm towards the table saying, "Dinner is here, shall we move to the table?" Amy, Sandra, and Cressida pausing their conversation with Kassandra to look up. And seeing the servants waiting, Amy and Sandra returned their nods now before moving to the table. As Ajax, Pylos, and I followed along behind them now to get their chairs. Then Agis opened the front doors, and the servants went to work setting the table. After the table was set and the servants had lined up by the doors again. Amy, Sandra, and I all returned their nods now and thanked them.

And when the ladies finished congratulating Cressida and Pylos on their pregnancy. I asked Ajax to tell everyone what he thought about me flying around the cavern today. Which took some time and fascinated Kassandra, but terrified Cressida and Pylos. Though apparently, Kassandra already knew this, since Ajax had taken Kassandra out to Atlas's tomb before dinner to show her the flying platter. Which we all thought was a little odd, especially since Kassandra blushed after Ajax told us. And curious now, I asked Ajax, "So, do you have answer for their majesties question yet, cousin?"

And looking embarrassed now, Ajax shook his head negatively replying "No your majesty, I couldn't decide. So, I asked Kassandra to come out into the garden on the pretext of showing her Altas's flying platter. And when we were alone, I asked Kassandra to marry me, your majesty."

And we all turned to look at Kassandra now, eager to know what her answer had been. And nodding shyly, Kassandra smiled across at Ajax and said, "I love Ajax, so my answer was yes of course!" And a cheer rose up from the table as the ladies all rose and moved to Kassandra's side now, hugging her and welcoming her to the family. While Pylos and I both moved to Ajax's side now. Exchanging the two-handed clasp of friendship with our cousin and congratulating him now on his engagement to the beautiful Kassandra. Before teasing Ajax that he didn't deserve her.

Once the congratulations had died down and the woman finished welcoming Kassandra to the family. We all sat down again, and holding my wine cup up to them both now, I said, "Congratulations Ajax and Kassandra, we wish you a lifetime of happiness! And here's to Kassandra, who I gladly welcome to the family and hereby promote you to the honorary rank of General now. And here's to cousin Ajax, whom I wish the blessing of many children! So, he can outrank someone in his own home!" And we all chuckled as we drank the toast to Kassandra's and Ajax's happiness now.

The next morning over tsia, Nestor congratulated Ajax on his engagement to Kassandra. Stating in his opinion, that Ajax was engaged to the finest woman in all Attea now, next to their majesties of course.

And though we still had ten days before we were scheduled to go to the Cave of Mephisto, I informed Nestor and Ajax now that I needed them both in attendance. Ajax to help keep the peace, and Nestor to help me with the Wild one's oaths and handing out the pardons. And I told them both they were welcome to fly with me on Atlas's platter that morning. Or spend six days walking there and back, their choice now. Ajax immediately stated that he definitely preferred to walk and would be bringing the other half of the Spearmen and Archers squads with him, so we would have two full squads at the Crossroads. And though he was scared, Nestor hesitantly agreed to fly with me. After which, Nestor asked Ajax how many Wild ones we should expect at the crossroads, so Nestor and the scribes could start drawing up the pardons. Unfortunately, no one really knew for sure, but after his victory at the Caves of Mephisto, Ajax guessed there were somewhere between 100 to 150 Wild Ones left now. Agreeing on the higher number, it was decided that the Nestor and scribes would draw up 150 blank pardons for me to sign now. And over the next five days, I signed thirty pardons a day until all 150 pardons were signed and stamped with the royal seal.

During which time, I took Amy, Sandra, and Nestor for a lap around the East Cavern on the flying platter. Starting with Amy first, I didn't make her walk out to the tomb but levitated the platter and brought it over to the stairs by the atrium terrace. And guiding Amy up onto the platter, I was curious as Amy wrapped her arms around my waist what side effects if any the trident might have on the baby and her now. And after asking everyone to step back, I raised the blue shield around us first before asking Amy how she was feeling, or if she felt anything now?

Shaking her head negatively, Amy said she wasn't feeling anything unusual. But stared at me now before saying, "Your eyes do turn completely blue when you use the trident, my love." And slowly raising the platter up to two hundred feet, I proceeded to take Amy on a lap around the east half of the cavern now. Which Amy enjoyed, and we watched the farmers out in the fields stop working and stare up at us now in awe and amazement. Realizing that she was perfectly safe on the flying platter now, Amy took one arm off my waist and began waving down at the farmers below. Who unconsciously waved back now, though I doubted they had any idea who they were actually waving to overhead.

Returning to the garden ten minutes later, Amy gave me a big kiss on the cheek thanking me for the ride. Which, judging by the smile on Amy's face now, she thoroughly enjoyed. Then taking Sandra's hand, Amy guided her sister up onto the platter now, telling her that it is perfectly safe and so much fun. And trusting Amy, Sandra grabbed me around the waist and smiled. As Amy climbed the steps back up onto the terrace beside Nestor and turned to wave at us.

And raising the shield up around us now, Sandra immediately said, "I can see what you have on your mind now, husband. And thank you Andrew, I'm flattered that even putting my arms around you now makes you want to do a little research!"

And Amy asked, "What was that, Sandra?"

Smiling at Amy, Sandra replied, "I can see everything on our husband's mind now. And he is thinking about doing a little more research tonight!" And covering her mouth now, Amy giggled and nodded now at Sandra's reply.

Luckly, Nestor had no idea what Sandra and Amy were giggling or talking about now. And I smiled at Sandra, saying, "Well, we know one thing for sure now, my love. You are a direct descendant of Atlas, otherwise, you won't be affected by the power of the trident."

Lifting the platter off the ground, Sandra clutched my waist a little tighter now. Which made me think about later tonight and made Sandra smile as she looked back at Amy and Nestor on the terrace. And Sandra quickly overcame her fear of flying as we flew toward the east wall of the cavern. Maybe because she could see into my mind now and see what I was going to do next. And I took Sandra around the valley slowly at first. Until she lifted her head up off my back and started looking around us as we circled the east end of the cavern and started west now. Once Sandra had smile returned, I accelerated and took her along the south side of the cavern before turning north and heading back to the garden.

Once we touched back down in the garden again, Sandra leaned in and kissed me on the cheek and smiled at me before walking up the steps to hug her Amy on the terrace. Then they both turned to look at Nestor now.

Who, after seeing both their majesty fly with me and return safely, was ready to give it a try now. Walking down the steps, Nestor paused to exchange nods with me before stepping up onto the platter beside me. And I was relieved now as Nestor took hold of my arm and I raised the blue shield, we found out that Sandra's relationship to King Atlas came from Sophia's side and not Nestor's. As that would have been slightly embarrassing had Nestor been able to read my mind and found out what "research" really meant now.

Taking the platter up again, I slowly moved eastward, and Nestor finally began to relax and look around enjoying the ride through the eastern half of the cavern. And when we landed back in the garden again, Nestor stepped off the platform and smiled as he said, "Thank you, your majesty. I really enjoyed that and found it invigorating."

Returning Nestor nod now, I replied, "Good! So, when we fly out to the Crossroads in three days, you can relax and enjoy the scenery, my friend." And stepping off the platter now, I quickly lifted it up again and sent it back to Atlas's tomb. Then walking up onto the terrace, I held my left arm out to Amy now, while Nestor nodded and held his arm out to his daughter and we escorted their majesties back up into the royal chambers followed dutifully by our royal escort.

As the next three days dragged on as I waited for the big day at the North Cavern. The only break in our daily routine now was helping Sandra lotion Amy's bulging stomach twice a day. With a lotion which Sandra told us was made from the oil of hazelnuts, grape seeds, and olives. Which the three of us did together, providing us with a daily source of humor and bad jokes as we carefully greased Amy's growing stomach up now.

Finally, the appointed day came, and after breakfast with Amy and Sandra. I kissed them both now before following Agis into my dressing room. And once the stewards dressed me in my armor, I returned their nods and thanked them. Then picking up Atlas's trident, I followed Agis back out to the main chamber where a pot of tsia and cup awaited me. I was halfway through my second cup of tsia, when Agis stepped back into the room and informed me that Nestor and Captain Pylos were outside waiting for me now. Quickly downing the rest of the tsia, I rose from the couch returning Agis's nod. Then picking up the trident, I told Agis I would get the door. And nodding again, Agis turned and went back into my private chambers.

Reaching the doors, I found Nestor and cousin Pylos waiting inside. Nestor had his white medical pouch at his waist as usual, and another larger dark canvas bag over his other shoulder now too. Which I assumed contained the 150 pardons. Quickly exchanging salutes and nods with them, I held my hand out to Pylos indicating for him to lead the way out the doors. And reaching the terrace outside the East Atrium, I quietly told Pylos to remain on the terrace with my personal guard while Nestor and I continued down into the garden.

Closing my eyes, I envisioned the flying platter at Atlas's tomb in my mind and brought it floating over to where Nestor and I stood in the garden now and set it down on the grass in front of us. Then stepping up onto the platter, I turned to face Pylos and my personal guard on the terrace again. And they all snapped me a salute now. Returning their salutes, I held my hand out to Nestor now to help him up on the flying platter.

Once Nestor was on the platter, I closed my eyes and raised the blue defensive shield around us before envisioning the platter rising off the ground. And raising my left hand now, we slowly began to rise above the palace. Nestor grabbing my left arm firmly now as we began to rise. Opening my eyes again, I kept my left hand up until we were a good three hundred feet above the palace. And not wanting to scare the folks in the city, I swung north around the palace, following over the north slope towards the Caves of Mephisto. Not wanting to waste time, I informed Nestor I was going to go faster. And Nestor took a firmer grip on my arm as I accelerated up to 100 mph, and we shot west now toward the entrance of the caves. The shield blocking the wind and Nestor and I only felt a light breeze on our faces now as we flew towards the Caves of Mephisto.

Seeing the dark entrance approaching fast, I pulled my arm back decelerating as we approached the entrance. Then turning my hand over, I closed it slightly, shrinking our defensive shield down now to fit inside the tunnel's entrance. And travelling at about 20 mph, we entered the east tunnel now. The blue light from our shield illuminating the tunnel ahead now as we moved forward. And slowly extending my hand out, I gradually increased our speed until I found a balance between our speed and my vision ahead. And we ended up traveling at about 25 mph west though the tunnel now.

The trident showed me the tunnel ahead, and I could see a caravan of five merchant wagons between us and Ajax and the soldiers now. Who were nearing the opening of the Crossroads now. Dropping down to one knee now, I pulled Nestor down next to me and he turned to look at me as I shrunk our blue shield down even tighter around us. Then I said, "Merchant wagons ahead." Relaxing now, Nestor nodded his head. Though I suspect the drivers and guards on the wagons needed a change of shorts after we blew past them inside the tunnel. Looking back, Nestor let a chuckle slip out now as he watched the mayhem we caused behind us with the merchant drivers and their frightened teams of donkeys.

Nestor looked at me now, wondering why I hadn't stood back up yet. And I answered his question before he could ask, saying, "Ajax and his troops are just ahead near the entrance to the Crossroads."

To which Nestor replied, "ah," now. And we saw the reflections off the rear guards' faces now as they turned to look at the bright blue light rapidly closing on the rear of their formation. The guards in the rear had just enough time to raise their horns and sound the alarm before we shot past them overhead.

Then slowing to a stop, I hovered inside the tunnel before turning around to face Ajax and his squad of men stopped in phalanx formation now after the alarm had been sounded. Then Ajax stepped out of the phalanx and saluted us. And standing back up with Nestor again, I returned Ajax's salute now. As Ajax barked out to the order to resume their travel formation and move out again.

Turning to face the Crossroads again, I closed my eyes for a moment as the trident showed me the Wild Ones gathered in the center of the cavern. With Lycus and his three chieftains standing on the north side now, between the Wild Ones and Captain Peleus's men. Who were spread out in a defensive rectangle now around the two dozen construction workers and their wagons. The airlock completed, the workers were sitting on the ground having a bite to eat now as they nervously watched the group of Wild Ones gathered in the center of the Crossroads. Beyond the workers, I could see the airlock doors, the engineer and construction boss busy giving the airlock one final test now in anticipation of our arrival.

Ajax and his squad were closing on us from behind now. So, I extended my hand out again, and we slowly began creeping forward now. The bright blue glow from our defensive shield drawing everyone's attention and frightened stares from all the Wild Ones as we reached the east entrance and moved into the Crossroads now.

Clear of the opening, the Wild Ones all gasped and dropped to their knees, while Lycus and his chieftains turned and bowed now. The construction workers quickly rising from the ground now to face us and bow. And Peleus called his men to attention now before turning to salute us and nod his head.

Slowly floating across the north half of the cavern, I returned the Wild one's nods first, loudly saying, "Εγείρεσθαι" or "rise" in Attean. Then turning facing Captain Peleus and the construction workers, I returned their salutes and nods before repeating, "Εγείρεσθαι," rise in Attean again. And turning to Nestor, I said, "Could you tell Captain Peleus good morning, and let him know Brigadier Ajax and his squad of men will be here in a few minutes, Nestor?" Nodding his head, Nestor turned and quickly translated my words to Captain Peleus.

And Peleus saluted again, replying, "Good morning, your majesty. We had learned of your majesty's flying platter from the merchants.

And when I heard the alarm horn sound in the tunnel, I figured you were passing brigadier Ajax and his men, your majesty?"

Returning his nod now, I chuckled as I confirmed that and replied, "Yes, but they weren't as startled as the caravan of merchant wagons we passed first." And Peleus and Nestor both chuckling now as Nestor translated my reply. And moving my hand left and down, I brought the flying platter to rest in the space between Peleus's men and the Wild Ones now. Then I envisioned our defensive shield gone again and it disappeared. After our shield disappeared it was pretty dark in the Crossroads. So, closing my eyes I envisioned a ball of light above my head and a bright white ball of light about two feet in diameter suddenly appeared above my head blinding everyone in the Crossroads now. And closing my left fist now, I quickly shrank the ball of light down to a quarter of its size, making the light bearable before raising my hand and lifting the ball of light up twenty feet, so everyone in the Crossroads could see again.

Then walking over to Lycus and his chieftains, I returned their bows as they all bowed again. And speaking to Lycus now, I said, "Good morning, Mayor Lycus. Are all the Wild Ones in the kingdom here now?" As Nestor translated my words for the chieftains.

All four men nodding as Lycus replied, "Good morning, your majesty. Yes, this is all 158 remaining Wild Ones, your majesty."

Returning their nods, I said, "Good, and thank you all for coming." Then turning to Nestor, I said, "This more than we counted on. But the trident is showing me there is ten children and babies amongst the Wild Ones now who are too young to have committed a crime." And sensing Ajax and his men were about to enter the crossroads, I turned to Lycus now, and said, "Brigadier Ajax, whom I think you are familiar with, is about to enter the Crossroads now with more soldiers. They're here solely because I am the King. It's not a trap, or breach in my promise to you and your people, Mayor Lycus. So, you may want to have your chiefs reassure them now." Nodding his head, Lycus turned and translating my words to his chieftains who nodded now and went among their people spreading the news that more soldiers were arriving and not to be alarmed. And to help reinforce this, I put my hand on Lycus shoulder now, saying, "Walk with me to the airlock Lycus and show your people our new friendship and peace."

Nodding his head, Lycs replied, "Gladly, your majesty." Then turning to Nestor, I added, "Come along Nestor, let's go see if the airlock is ready?" And nodding his head, Nestor began following us at the same time as Ajax and his men entered Crossroads from the east tunnel. And I heard the nervous mumbling of the Wild Ones behind us now. But I also heard the chieftains as they moved amongst their people calmly speaking to the more nervous of the Wild Ones. Nestor knew the Engineer and construction boss now, having met them when Ajax had hired the men to build the airlock. And moving past Lycus and me now, Nestor approached the two men smiling and shaking hands with them as they turned to greet us. Then both men bowed as Nestor said, "The airlock is finished and tested now, your majesty."

Returning their bows, I told Nestor, "Tell them they have my thanks, and the thanks of the entire kingdom now for completing the airlock so quickly, Nestor." And Nestor translated my words to the two men. Who bowed again and backed up as the engineer held his arm out now indicating the airlock was ready for me. Nodding again, we continued towards the airlock, my left arm still resting on Lycus's shoulder now in a show of trust for the Wild Ones behind us. Ajax having wisely chosen to turn north after entering the Crossroads. Staying clear of the Wild Ones in the center as he moved to join Captain Peleus and his men now.

Reaching the outer airlock door, I let go of Lycus shoulder and stepped up to the control panel on the wall next to the doors. And seeing two small lights lit on the top of the panel and the three seahorses below, I turned the first seahorse 90 degrees. And we heard the seals on the enormous doors break as they slowly separating in the center and swung inwards now into the airlock. Turning to look at Nestor and Lycus now, I said, "Wait here my friends, this could take quite a while." And all four men nodded again as I turned and walked into the airlock headed for the control panels on the right wall.

Reaching the control panels on the right. I turned the second seahorse on the righthand panel now closing the outer doors. And when the lights at the top of the panels lit up again, I turned the first seahorse on the left panel opening the inner doors into the short section of cave now. Just long enough to allow the doors to open fully without hitting tunnel wall ahead. And walking into the short section of the tunnel, I had to go around the right door now to reach the control panel on the wall before turning the second seahorse and closing the inner doors again, sealing me inside the short tunnel now.

And once the inner doors closed and the small lights on top of the control panel lit again. I turned to face the sealed off tunnel into the North Cavern and closed my eyes. The trident showing me there was about three hundred feet of rock, dirt, and sand between me and the opening of the North Cavern now. And raising my shield up again, I quickly reduced its size as it appeared, as it was nearly touching the airlock door now.

Looking at the walls around me now, I got an idea of the tunnel's original size. Then closing my eyes now, I envisioned the half-circle of the tunnel here extending straight out into the North Cavern. And with my eyes closed, I shot fire out of Atlas's trident burning through the rocks, dirt, and sand now into the North Cavern. In the same shape and size as the semi-circle I was standing in now. And once the fire had burned all the way through into the North Cavern, I held the semi-circle of stone aloft until it cooled. Then I let enormous block of stone and dirt drop to the floor, shaking the ground under my feet.

Then envisioning the enormous semi-circle of stone in my mind, I lifted it up off the floor again and pushed the entire three hundred foot long piece of stone out of the tunnel now. Sliding it out into the North Cavern, I set it down on the ground again. And I could sense that the tunnel into the North Cavern was clear now. But the trident illuminated several spots now on the roof of the tunnel, where the rocks were loose and ready to fall. Closing my eyes again, I sent fire out to each of the locations now. And one by one, I melted the rocks together at the locations making the tunnel safe. Opening my eyes again, I walked the three hundred feet to the opening of the tunnel on the other end and stepped out into the North Cavern now.

The damp ground beneath my feet steaming and sizzling as my defensive shield dried the ground beneath my feet now. The light from the glowing ball above my head now seemed tiny and insignificant now in the enormous expanse of the North Cavern. Envisioning the ball of light above my head, I opened my left hand tripling its size now before lifting it up a hundred feet and letting it hover there.

After which, I could just make out the outline of enormous ruins of the city of Cadiz in the center of the cavern. And there was a large depression at the base of the west slope where Ajax's armored hose protruded now. And seeing a rock outcropping next to it, I closed my eyes and sent fire out of the trident again. Melting the outcropping down into a pool of molten rock now. Then lifting the pool of molten rock of the ground now, I sent it up the groove with the armored hose for about a hundred yards. The molten rock melting the Ajax's armored hose now as it rose. Finally, I let the molten rock cool and fuse to the surrounding rock now, permanently sealing it the groove. And with the Noth Cavern secure now, I turned my attention to the inside of the cavern itself. The trident illuminating the pools and pockets of saltwater now laying in the low spots and depressions of the cavern. And sending fire out to each of these locations now, I vaporized the remaining saltwater, creating a haze at the top of the cavern now, not unlike the one in the other caverns.

Pausing for a moment, the trident illuminated the salt in everything around me and I was at a loss as to what to do with it now. And having a small epiphany now, I closed my eyes and sent out fire from the trident again, cutting two fifty-foot pieces off ends of the three hundred foot long section of rock I had removed from the tunnel. After which, I envisioned a large excavating bucket in my mind and dug out the depression where the armored hose had been, making it deeper and larger now. Then lifting the first fifty foot piece of stone up off the ground, I moved it to the far side of the hole now and set it down there. Then lifting large center piece off the ground, I moved it over and set it down across the front of the hole. And lifting the last fifty foot piece of stone now, I moved it over and set it down on this end of the hole, forming a large tank now to store all salt in.

And closing my eyes again, I went around the cavern removing the salt from the soil and rocks and funneling it into the tank now. This required time and concentration on my part, as there was a massive amount of salt here inside the North Cavern, and it rapidly filled the tank. Stopping the collection process, I turned my attention to the salt tank now. And raising the salt up on all four sides, I formed a three-foot thick wall of salt all the way around the inside of the tank. Then sending out fire of the trident, I heated the stones around the tank until the salt started to melt forming a twenty-foot high crystal box inside the tank. And once that cooled, I went back to work removing the salt from inside the cavern. After forty-five minutes of this, I had most of the salt removed from the cavern and funneled into the enormous salt box.

But it was still dark inside the cavern. I had hoped that once the salt water had been removed, the Staff of Attea would start to shine again. But no such luck.

Chapter - 26

Spotting a large flat rock a half dozen feet away, I walked over and stepped onto the center of it. Hoping I could use it now like the flying platter to go up the top of the cavern and try to figure out how to restart the Staff of Attea.

Closing my eyes, I pictured the stone in my mind and tried to raise it, and to my relief it lifted just like the flying platter now. And rising off the ground, I moved forward as the trident showed me the location of the staff ahead. And stopping a dozen feet below the Staff of Attea, I hovered there as I tried to envision the staff in my head. But to my dismay, the staff defied all attempts to picture it in my mind now.

Opening my eyes again, I was surprised to be face to face now with the shadowy blue-eyed outline of the staff's owner. It was one of King Atlas's advisors, who I remember now was named Pheidon. Smiling at me, Pheidon put his hand on his chest now and bowed to me. So, smiling back at Pheidon, I placed my hand on my heart and returned Pheidon's bow now. Then smiling again, the shadowy figure of Pheidon nodded his head now before turning and disappearing back into the Staff of Attea again.

Suddenly the staff began to blaze brightly again. So bright that I was blinded now. Turning away, I quickly lowered the rock down a couple of hundred feet passing through the layer of haze at the top of the cavern now. And once I could see again, I found I was directly over the large walled city of Cadiz. And at the north end of the cavern, I could make out Fort Hermes sitting on the hillside now. The ruined buildings and streets of the Cadiz below me were covered in seaweed now and littered with bleached out bones. Probably from the south end of a northbound Kraken.

Feeling drained now after spending so much time and energy getting the salt out of the cavern. I decided to leave the seaweed and bones for Lycus and the Wild Ones to deal with. And guiding the rock back to the tunnel entrance, I set it down in the same spot I found it. Then I shrunk my ball of light back down to a comfortable brightness, and I brought it down above my head before turning and walking back into the tunnel now headed for the airlock doors.

As I neared the airlock, I could see Nestor, Ajax, and Lycus on the other side pacing back and forth. Impatiently waiting on my return and taking turns stopping to peer through the doors. Reaching the controls panel on the left, I turned the first seahorse and waited for the inner doors to part and open. Then walking around the door, I moved over to the control panels in the center of the airlock. And turning the second seahorse on the left panel, I closed the inner doors again and waited for the small lights above the panels to light up again signaling that the inner doors had sealed. Then turning the first seahorse on the right panel, I opened the outer doors of the airlock now.

And as soon as the outer doors parted, Ajax, Nestor, and Lycus all came rushing in to greet me now and find out how it had gone inside the North Cavern. Ajax snapping me a salute, while Nestor and Lycus bowed their heads, and Nestor excitedly asking now, "You were gone for a long time, your majesty. Were you able to remove the salt from the inside the North Cavern, your majesty?"

Nodding my head and returning Ajax's salute, I looked at them now and replied, "Yes, I removed the salt and stored on the west side of the of the cavern for now." And pausing for a moment, I added, "It was a lot of work, and I am tired. I need to rest for a couple of minutes and something to drink now before I'm ready to start receiving the oaths and passing out pardons." Ajax didn't speak, he just nodded and strode back out of the airlock now disappearing. Only to return a few moments later carrying a bota bag, and nodding first, Ajax held the bota bag out to me now.

Leaning the trident up against the wall, the ball of light above my head suddenly disappeared as I let go of the trident to accept the bota bag from Ajax's hands. And pulling the cork out of the end now, I tipped the bota bag up and took a good long drink. Then handing the bota bag back to Ajax, I smiled at him and said, "Thank you Ajax, that's what I needed."

Then picking the trident up again, I envisioned the little ball of light above my head again to light our way back now, before saying,

"Why don't all three of you go inside the North Cavern and have a look now while I rest, hmm?"

Curiosity getting the better of them now, having never imagined they would see the inside North Cavern, let alone the City of Cadiz and Fort Hermes in their lifetimes. They all nodded their heads eagerly, and Ajax handed the bota bag back to me now, which I gladly accepted as I returned their nods. Then all the three of them turned and quickly moved into the airlock now. And a few seconds later the outer doors swing shut and close again.

And finding a flat rock here between the workers and the airlock, I sat down on it with the trident and the bota bag now. Captain Peleus only thirty feet from me, but his back to me, and his attention focused on the Wild Ones in the center of the Crossroads. And not even the ball of light floating above my head now breaking his concentration as he stood there watching the Wild Ones.

Taking a couple more drinks from the bota bag, it was a good twenty minutes before I heard the seals on the airlock doors break again. And the doors slowly opened now as Ajax, Nestor, and Lycus came walking out of the airlock smiling and excitedly chatting back and forth. Seeing me resting on the rock, they changed direction now moving to my side. And stopping to salute and nod, Nestor spoke first again, saying, "The North Cavern is amazing! I never thought I'd see the City of Cadiz, or the North Cavern in my lifetime, your majesty." Then nodding again, Nestor added, "And what you did with all that salt is impressive, your majesty."

Returning their nods, I replied, "Thank you, but it was a lot of work, and that's why it took me so long."

Nodding now, Lycus said, "I shall forever be in your debt, your majesty. For my promotion, my pardon, and giving the North Cavern to the Wild Ones now as a home of our own, your majesty."

Returning Lycus's nod, I replied, "Nothings free, Lycus. It's going to take a lot of work restoring the North Cavern. And I am counting on you to control the Wild Ones and keep the peace, Mayor Lycus. And I am serious about keeping peace. So, don't be afraid to ask for Brigadier Ajax's or my help if you need it, okay?"

Nodding again, Lycus replied, "I will not fail you, your majesty."

Grinning at them now, I said, "The Wild Ones have waited long enough. Let's not keep them waiting any longer, my friends." And the three of them nodded now, I rose from the rock and handed Ajax the bota bag back before walking towards Captain Peleus and the men.

And speaking to Peleus, Ajax ordered him to have his men part for the king now. Peleus turned and saluted Ajax acknowledging the order before barking out orders for the soldiers on the left to take four steps to the left, and the soldiers on the right, to take four steps to the right now, creating an opening in the center. And pausing as we came abreast of Captain Peleus, I returned his salute before walking between the soldiers and over to the crowd of Wild Ones gathered in the center of the Crossroads. The Wild Ones quickly rose and turned to face us now as they saw us approaching.

And seeing a large flat rock about a foot high ahead, I stepped up on top of it now and planted the trident beside me facing the Wild Ones as they moved forward to hear what I had to say. And looking right, I motioned for Lycus and Nestor to join me on the rock now.

Then raising my left hand up to the Wild Ones, I asked Nestor to translate for me now, and Nestor nodded his head as I said, "All those wishing to be pardoned and to live in peace from now on, kneel and place their hand over their heart." And I watched as Nestor translated my words, as I tried to make eye contact with each every Wild One now as they all kneeled down to the last man, woman, and child.

Then I said, "From this day forth, do you solemnly swear to live in peace and obey the laws of Attea? And promise never to raise your hand against a fellow Attean again, unless in self-defense?"

And I listened as Nestor took his time now slowly, and clearly translating the oath to the Wild Ones. At the end of which, all but the children bowed their heads and unanimously replied, "Ποιῶ!" I do.

And returning their nods now, I said, "Ἐγείρεσθαι," rise. And the Wild Ones rose from their knees and stared at each other now in surprise as the stripes on their bio-suits began to fade. And their bio-suits began changing back to whatever color they had been before they committed the crime and fled. Nestor, Lycus, and I all stood there transfixed as we watched the Wild One's bio-suits changing.

And turning look at Ajax, I could see him smiling as he watched in fascination now as the Wild Ones bio-suits all changed. And I asked him, "Ajax, the North Cavern is safe now. Is there a way to lock the doors open? And could you ask the engineer if we could borrow his drafting table and chair for a little while, please? So, Nestor can fill out the names on the pardons by the airlock. That way, once the Wild Ones receive their pardons, they can walk straight into his new home."

Snapping me a salute now, Ajax nodded his head accepting my requests and replied, "Immediately, your majesty." Then turning, Ajax strode back to the wagons to speak with the engineer, who was one of Ajax's classmates and Ajax knew fairly well.

Then looking at Nestor and Lycus now, I asked, "Does that sound like a plan?"

Nodding his head, Nestor replied, "Yes, your majesty. And with your permission now, I shall meet you by the airlock with pardons?"

Returning my father-in-law's nod, I turned to Lycus now as Nestor left, and said, "Mayor Lycus, could you have your chieftains line the people up single file now. Then can you stand by Nestor and pass me their pardons as Nestor fills in the names? And I will present the pardons to our new citizens. How does that sound, my friend?"

And putting his hand on his chest, Lycus nodded his head now replying, "Yes, your majesty. And speaking for myself, my family, and all the Wild Ones now, we sincerely thank you, your majesty."

Returning Lycus's nod, he grinned at me as he turned and stepped down of the rock to speak with the chieftains. Turning towards the airlock and the entrance to the North Cavern again, I started walking back towards gap in the Peleus's men. Who, as soon as I turned all saluted and nodded their heads. And pausing a couple of feet short of the gap in the soldiers now, I returned their salutes and nods before passing between them and back into their defensive rectangle again with Captain Peleus. Who saluted and nodded his head now. And quickly returning Captain Peleus's salute, we both turned to face Ajax as he came walking back from the airlock now casually chatting with the engineer as they walked. And reaching Peleus and me, Ajax saluted me again while the engineer put his hand on his chest and nodded his head. And when we had returned Ajax's salute and the engineer's nod, then the Engineer handed Ajax a four sided metal key on a silver chain. And the two men shook hands with each other before the Engineer nodded to me again and said in Attean, "It's my great honor to be of service to your majesty."

I returned the Engineer's nod now. And turning the engineer strode over to the wagons before telling the men they were done, and to load the wagons now as it was time to head back to Attea.

Holding up the key now, Ajax nodded and said, "The doors are locked open, and the table and chair have been set up for the Nestor now, your majesty."

Returning Ajax's nod, I replied, "Thank you, cousin. Can you have Peleus his men back now so the Wild Ones can approach?"

Saluting acknowledging my request now, Ajax turned to Peleus and said in Attean. Have the men reform on the east side of the cavern now so the Wild Ones can come forward and receive their pardons.

And facing Ajax, Captain Peleus saluted and nodded as he accepted Ajax's order replying, "Right away, Brigadier Ajax!" And after Ajax returned Peleus's salute, Peleus turned and strode back to his men stopping now barking out, left face, standard formation east side of the wagons now, move your asses! Followed by some colorful remarks from Peleus that it shouldn't take this long to reform. Ajax casually covering his mouth now to conceal his grin.

Tilting my head towards Nestor, I indicated for Ajax to follow me over to Nestor at the engineer's table by the airlock. The brown bag containing the pardons sitting out on the table now, as Nestor tried to flatten and straighten out the large stack of pardons in front of him. And seeing the guards moving to the east side of the wagons, Lycus led the Wild Ones forward to the airlock now.

Pausing by Nestor, Lycus nodded again, and when I returned his nod, Lycus pointed to the man behind him saying, "This is one of our chieftains, Eudorus, his wife Melite, and their son Kimon, your majesty." And Nestor quickly wrote Eudorus's name on the first pardon and paused to blow the ink dry before handing it to Lycus and writing Melite's name on the second pardon. Lycus nodded again as he handed the pardon to me, and I turned to face Eudorus now as he dropped to one knee, putting his hand over his heart, and nodded his head. And handing the pardon to Eudorus now, he accepted it from my hand, and said, "Thank you, your majesty."

And returning his nod, I said, "Ἐγείρεσθαι," rise.

Then Eudorus stepped to the left as his wife Melite dropped to one knee and put her hand over her heart, nodding her head. Accepting the next pardon from the Lycus's hand, I extended it out to Melite now. Who seemed relieved as she gently accepted it from my hand and said, "Thank you so much, your majesty!"

And returning her nod now, I said, "Ἐγείρεσθαι," rise. And getting up again, Melite moved next to Eudorus, as they both eagerly watched their son Kimon drop to one knee and put his right hand over his heart now bowing his head. Accepting the third pardon from Lycus, I held it out to Kimon, who accepted it and said, "Thank you, your majesty."

Returning Kimon's nod, I said, "Ἐγείρεσθαι," rise again.

As Kimon rose joining his parents, then Lycus said in Attean, "Go into the cavern and check out our new home, Eudorus. I'll join you as soon as were finished here." Nodding to Lycus, Eudorus turned and led his wife and son into the airlock now.

This went on for two hours before I got all one hundred and forty-eight pardons handed out. And as we stood there now watching the last of the Wild Ones disappear into the tunnel. At the end of which, Nestor rose and stretched before nodding to me and saying, "There are two pardons left, your majesty."

Returning Nestors nod, I held out my hand to Nestor saying, "Hand them to me please, Nestor" Nodding his head, Nestor rolled the two remaining pardons up and handed them to me. And turning to Lycus now, I extended the pardons out to him, saying, "I am entrusting these to you, Mayor Lycus. In case any more Wild Ones appear. And I will let you go now, as you need to get in there and take charge. But I will arrange to have food sent out to you and the Wild Ones on my return, Mayor Lycus."

Nodding as he accepted the pardons from my hand now, Lycus replied, "Thank you, your majesty. You have kept your word and earned my loyalty, allegiance, and respect now, your majesty."

Returning Lycus's nod, I added, "Thank you, Mayor Lycus." And putting his hand over his heart, Lycus backed up a half dozen steps before turning and walking into the airlock now to start his new life.

Turning left, Nestor and I silently walked over to where Ajax and Peleus were standing now arms folded. Just as the construction workers' wagons disappeared into the entrance of the east tunnel. And reaching their side, they both saluted and nodded again. And grinning now, as Ajax said, "I think the men are going to get fat and lazy now that you have removed our only adversary, your majesty."

Returning their salutes, I grinned at Ajax now, replying, "You may be right, cousin. But not to worry, nine hundred years ago, the outlander kings created 'tournaments,' where the best soldiers from their kingdoms came together to compete for honor and prizes. And I think we can do the same here in Attea too, can't we?"

Turning to Peleus, Ajax quickly translated my words to Peleus. And the two men smiled at each other for a second before nodding their heads agreeing it was a promising idea. And looking at Ajax again, I asked, "You sure you don't want to ride back to the palace with me and Nestor now, cousin?"

Shaking his head adamantly now, Ajax nodded before replying, "No thank you, your majesty. I prefer to keep my feet on the ground, and I am content to walk back to the palace with Captain Peleus and the men now, your majesty." And handing Atlas's trident to Nestor for a minute, I stepped forward to exchange the two-handed clasp of friendship with both Ajax and Peleus now. Then smiling and nodding to them both. I took the trident back from Nestor, who was happy to hand it back to me. And turning now, Nestor and I walked back over the Atlas's flying platter.

Stepping up onto the platter again, Nestor didn't hesitate this time in joining me on the platter. And closing my eyes, I raised our defensive shield up around us again before raising the platter up off the ground. And opening my eyes, I shrunk our shield down around us again before guiding the platter across the Crossroads and back into the entrance of the east tunnel. The trident showing me the four contractor wagons ahead in the tunnel now approaching fast. And kneeling again, I pulled Nestor down next to me as we passed over the top of the construction worker's wagons startling their donkeys. And with the tunnel ahead being clear, I slid my hand forward now increasing our speed, and a few moments later shot out of the tunnel into the open of the East Cavern again. Free of the tunnel now, I raised the platter up a hundred yards and took a northerly route back to the palace now extending my hand out and quadrupling our speed as we flew over the north slope back to the palace at over 100 mph now. Nestor had gotten used to flying, but at the slower speeds, and suddenly grabbed my arm and ducked his head as I hurried back to the palace and the garden now.

Slowing down as we neared the palace, I brought the platter to rest smoothly in the grass in front of the east terrace. And opening his eyes again, Nestor realized the we had landed already. And letting go of my arm, Nestor nodded again now out of embarrassment or relief, I don't know which.

Dropping our shield, we stepped off the platter onto the stone path in the center of the garden. And closing my eyes, I raised the flying platter up and sent it back across the garden to Atlas's tomb. Then turning to Nestor at the base of the stairs, I said, "It's almost dinner time. I'm sure their majesties will want to hear your version of the flight out to Crossroads and the events at the North Cavern today. Could you and the Lady Sophia join us for dinner tonight, Nestor?"

Nodding his head now, Nestor replied, "I will check with Sophia first, but I am certain she will accept your invitation, your majesty." And the guards stepped forward now opening the doors for us and bowing their heads as we entered the East Atrium. Nestor and I exchanged nods again in the East Atrium, as Nestor excused himself now to go make his report to the Consul of Elders. And after he was gone, I climbed the south stairs back up to the royal chambers.

Entering the royal chambers again, I found Agis standing ready. And exchanging nods with Agis now, he informed me that I still had time for a bath and change of clothes before dinner now if we got a move on it. And holding my arm out, I indicated for Agis to lead the way, and informing Agis that the Senior Physician and Lady Sophia would be joining us for dinner again tonight. When I was clean and dressed again, Agis led me back out to the main chamber where I found my two lovely wives calmly chatting on the couch together. Entering the room, Agis and I bowed to their majesties on the couch, before Agis nodded to me and stepped back out of the room now. And moving forward, I joined my two lovely wives on the couch.

With Agis gone and the door closed, Amy and Sandra moved to the outside of the couch making room in the center now wanting me to sit between them. And pausing in front of the couch, I bent down and kissed the top of Amy's head now before kissing the top of Sandra's head then sat down between them. Acting like today was just another day, and I hadn't gone out to the North Cavern. After a moment, Amy asked, "So how was your day, husband?"

Chuckling at Amy, I replied, "Not bad." And I just left that hanging there now, not expanding on it, and waiting to see how long my two lovely wives could stand it. After a minute, they started glaring at me, and I added, "Oh, I invited Nestor and Sophia for dinner tonight." Finally losing their patients, they giggled as they attacked me from both sides now, tickling me mercilessly to get me to give up the details of my trip out to the North Cavern today. Laughing, I nodded my head in defeat as I pulled them to me now and kissed them both. As I tried to stop them from tickling me long enough to tell them about the events in the North Cavern.

So, I told them everything that happened now. Starting with our flight out of the Crossroads, to watching the Wild Ones disappear into the North Cavern. Also, mentioning the "Staff of Attea" not working. And exchanging bows with the ghost of King Atlas's advisor Pheidon, to get the staff working again.

But before Amy and Sandra could ask any questions, Agis, Petra, and the servants entered the room to let us know that Nestor and Sophia were waiting outside now, along with our dinner. Rising, we greeted Nestor and Sophia now before moving to the table. And after the servants had set the table and left again. We loaded our plates as my wives took turns asking Nestor questions now. Getting Nestor to tell them all over again the events at the Crossroads today. Nestor especially enjoyed the part where I had Ajax, Lycus, and him go into the North Cavern and see it themselves, while I took a break. That, and watching all the Wild Ones bio-suits change right in front of our eyes after they had taken their oaths.

Dinner ran later than usual. As Amy, Sandra, and Lady Sophia all asked Nestor questions now about the North Cavern and the city of Cadiz. Plus, the reactions of the Wild Ones, as they swore their oaths and received their pardons before entering their new home.

After Nestor and Sophia had bid us goodnight. The servants returned to cleared table. Then we returned their nods and thanked them before they filed out of the room. And knowing that I was tired tonight, my wives graciously gave me the night off now. That, and their permission to climb into bed and pass out. Amy and Sandra snuggling up together on the right side of the bed now as they continued to discuss the day's events. How long they talked I couldn't say, as I only heard the first two minutes before nodding off.

The next morning over tsia, Nestor informed me that he had met with the Elders and reported everything. After which, the Elders wanted Nestor to express their gratitude to me again for accomplishing what they never dreamed possible. And Nestor informed me that the Stonecutters had finished the new cover for Atlas's sarcophagus, and if I was ready? The Senior Stonecutter would like to meet us in Atlas's tomb tomorrow, to return Atlas's trident to his sarcophagus and seal it again. And with no serious issues remaining in the Kingdom now, I agreed. Then rising, Nestor excused himself now to go arrange for the five wagon loads of foods that I requested last night be sent out to Mayor Lycus and the Wild Ones in the North Cavern every week until further notice.

The next morning after breakfast, the stewards dressed me in my armor again for the trip out to Atlas's tomb. And I had a cup of tsia while I waited for Nestor and Pylos to arrive with my personal bodyguard. Then picking up the trident, we proceeded out to Atlas's tomb to meet the Senior Stonecutter and return Atlas's trident to its rightfully resting place. During which, Nestor seemed unusually cheerful considering we were losing the power of Atlas's trident.

Leaving the guards at the entrance, Nestor, Pylos, and I descended down into Atlas's tomb to meet the Senior Stonecutter Keteus now. And reaching the floor of the tomb, I was surprised to see the four

Elders standing beside the Senior Stonecutter now at King Atlas sarcophagus. Since Nestor hadn't mentioned that the Elders being present to witness the return of Atlas's trident to his sarcophagus.

And crossing the tomb to Atlas sarcophagus, we exchanged nods with the Elders and Senior Stonecutter. The new cover suspended now about three feet above the Atlas's sarcophagus. How, or by what means, I couldn't see now?

Nodding his head, Tydeus spoke first, saying, "Good morning your majesty. After learning that the trident was genetically coded for King Atlas's descendants. And your majesty's successful use of the trident to defeat the Kraken and repair the North Cavern. The Elders and I unanimously decided to contact Keteus and have King Atlas's sarcophagus modified so that your majesty would have access to King Atlas's trident, should the need arise again." And the other three Elders nodded now agreeing with Tydeus's words.

Returning their nods, I replied, "Thank you, Tydeus. And thank the Elders for their faith in me. And I agree, having access to King Atlas's trident if the need should arise, is a good safety precaution."

And nodding again, Tydeus said, "If your majesty would place the trident back into the sarcophagus with King Atlas, we can set up your secure access here on the rear of the sarcophagus, your majesty?"

Returning Tydeus's nod, I turned and bowed to King Atlas, and everyone in the room joined me now in bowing. Then stepping forward, I carefully set the trident back inside the sarcophagus beside King Atlas now. Then taking two steps back, I bowed to King Atlas again before turning and moving to the back of the sarcophagus now with Keteus and the Elders.

And with Tydeus translating now, Keteus nodded and said, "If your majesty would place his right hand on the panel here for a moment. please?"

Returning Keteus's nod, I reached forward now and put my right hand on the white outline in the center of the console's screen. And Keteus pushed a button on the right side of the console and waited until a small green light appeared in the upper left corner. Then reaching down, Keteus turned a large key on a gold chain sticking out on the right side now before removing the key from the console. And nodding to me again, Tydeus translated Keteus's words now, as he said, "King Atlas sarcophagus will now open for you alone, your majesty." Then Keteus pushed the second of three seahorses on the top of the panel, and the sarcophagus cover slowly began to descend now until it closed with a solid thump.

And turning to Tydeus now, Keteus's nodded and handed him the key, saying, "With this key, you can change who has access to King Atlas's sarcophagus and the trident. But his majesty must first open the sarcophagus before the key can be used."

Then Tydeus and I both returned Keteus's nod now, as Tydeus replied, "Thank you, Keteus. That's perfect."

Finished now, Nestor, Pylos, and I exchanged nods with the four Elders and Keteus again before turning and proceeded back out of the tomb to my personal bodyguard waiting outside. And reaching my chambers again, I said goodbye to Pylos and Nestor at the doors now before going inside to get changed out of my armor. And hopefully, I still had time now for a short nap before my wives returned for lunch.

The next month and half passed by peacefully. And I made sure that five wagon loads of food were sent out to Lycus and the Wild Ones in the North Cavern every week. And Lycus begun sending me weekly reports on the Wild one's progress in the North Cavern.

Amy's size having reached the point now where it was affecting her daily routine. And Sandra's stomach having grown now too and really showed her off glorious condition. As we eagerly awaited Ajax's and Lady Kassandra's wedding. Kassandra happily agreed to hold the wedding in the palace garden so that their majesties could both attend.

And Nestor took both Sophia and Lady Ismene with him when he went to the royal treasury to pick out the perfect wedding gift Kassandra. And I was with Ajax when he chose a thumb sized diamond surrounded by emeralds on a finely wrought gold chain as Kassandra's wedding gift. Nestor and I both agreed with his choice now. And Nestor informing us that the Lady Ismene and Sophia had both admired that particular necklace.

And we all got a surprise now, after Ajax and Kassandra exchanged their vows and Kassandra received her gift. As the moment Tydeus pronounced them husband and wife, Kassandra leapt straight up into Ajax's arms, kissing passionately and raising her feet behind her. Which made Ajax blush, not Kassandra! And we laughed until our sides hurt, certain there would be a little Ajax on the way before the Staff of Attea went dark tomorrow. I said as much to Amy and Sandra now, which made them laugh even harder as they nodded their heads in agreement.

The End

A month later I was having tsia with Ajax and Nestor. And Ajax reported things were going well in the North Cavern, as Lycus was keeping a tight rein on the Wild Ones. That, and there hadn't been a single attack reported since the Wild Ones gave their oaths. And Nestor reported that the merchants delivering the food out to the North Cavern each week were having to take a sixth wagon with them just to drop off all fruit trees and pots of grapes starters that were being donated now by the people in all three caverns.

Three months later, Amy gave birth to a beautiful baby girl. Who was the spitting image of her beautiful mother, with bright red hair and crystal blue eyes. Followed by a month later by Sandra giving birth to a baby boy with light brown hair and Sandra's green eyes.

We named our daughter "Irene," after Amy's mother who she missed dearly, and which meant "peace" in Attean. And Sandra named our son "Andreas" after me, which meant "strength and wisdom" in Attean. Once Nestor pronounced both mothers' and babies in perfect health, we waited seven months before holding the celebration in the palace courtyard to show off Prince Andreas and Princess Irene to the people of Attea.

And later that night, after we climbed into bed together again, I was surprised when my beautiful wives suddenly confronted me now. And Amy informed me she was jealous of Andreas and wanted a son of her own. And Sandra informed me that she was jealous of Irene and wanted a daughter now. Then they both giggled now as they informed me not to expect a night off until I had successfully completed my husbandly obligations and they were both pregnant. Outnumbered and out voted now, there wasn't anything I could do but frown and nod my head to my beautiful wives.

Made in United States
Troutdale, OR
09/02/2025

34174358R00216